Percy Bysshe Shelley, William J. Alexander

Select Poems of Shelley

Percy Bysshe Shelley, William J. Alexander

Select Poems of Shelley

ISBN/EAN: 9783337391072

Printed in Europe, USA, Canada, Australia, Japan

Cover: Foto ©Andreas Hilbeck / pixelio.de

More available books at **www.hansebooks.com**

Athenæum Press Series

SELECT POEMS

OF

SHELLEY

EDITED WITH INTRODUCTION AND NOTES

BY

W. J. ALEXANDER

PROFESSOR OF ENGLISH IN UNIVERSITY COLLEGE, TORONTO

BOSTON, U.S.A., AND LONDON
GINN & COMPANY, PUBLISHERS
The Athenæum Press
1898

PREFACE.

In accordance with the general plan of the *Athenæum Press Series*, the aim of the present volume is to afford a suitable selection of Shelley's Poems for the student and the general reader, and to give some help towards the understanding and appreciation of a writer whose spirit and whose power are confessedly not always apparent on a merely casual perusal.

The text of the poems is, with a few variations, that of Mr. Forman's latest edition of Shelley's poetical works in the *Aldine Series*. The arrangement of the selections is as nearly as may be chronological. It has been deemed advisable to limit the choice to complete poems; fragmentary pieces and extracts have been excluded, with the exception of three passages from *Hellas*, which lose little by separation from their context.

In a volume of this nature the editor is at every step under great obligations to his predecessors, — obligations which often cannot be traced and acknowledged. Apart from particular cases of indebtedness indicated throughout the volume, the editor is conscious of having received great assistance from the editions of Mr. Forman and of Professor Woodberry, from Professor Dowden's *Life* of the poet, from the various contributions to Shelley literature of Mr. W. M. Rossetti, from the Essays of Mr. Stopford Brooke, Mr. Bagehot, and Mr. R. H. Hutton, from Professor Hale's annotations to the *Adonais*, and from the suggestions of Professor Winchester, one of the general editors of the *Athenæum Press Series*.

TORONTO, Sept. 12, 1897.

CONTENTS.

———•·•———

INTRODUCTION.

THE impress of Shelley's character is stamped everywhere upon his work. In his case, to an even greater degree than usual, some knowledge of the man is necessary for the understanding of his writings. To furnish this knowledge, in as far as our narrow limits will permit, is the aim of the following sketch. It seems superfluous, therefore, to occupy space in giving the present writer's opinion on those many points in Shelley's conduct which have been the subject of controversy, and upon which such divergent judgments have been pronounced. There were passages in Shelley's life from boyhood onward which, had he not been a man of genius, would incur the unhesitating censure of the world in general. He set parental and scholastic authority at defiance; he was guilty of indoctrinating the immature minds of youth with religious opinions which their natural guardians held in abhorrence; he tried to convince a younger sister, just entering womanhood, that legal marriage was a needless form; he deserted his wife without, as far as is known, any grounds which would ordinarily be regarded as adequate, and eloped with a girl not yet seventeen years old, — the daughter of an intimate friend. Yet Shelley has inspired many of his admirers with an enthusiasm which leads them to write in terms of unbroken eulogy, not merely of the poet, but of the man; to treat with injustice persons who came into collision with him during his lifetime; and sometimes to play fast and loose with the dictates of good sense and sound morals. On the other hand, unqualified condemnation, such as one readily pronounces on a man guilty of actions like those specified above, is shown by a thorough examination of Shelley's life and character to be as unjustifiable as indiscriminate approval.

Shelley was, in truth, a man of quite abnormal type. With certain qualities he was endowed to an extraordinary degree; others, which belong to the average man, were almost totally lacking in him. Owing to his extreme sensitiveness to certain aspects of life and his comparative blindness to others, he was not actuated by the same motives as other men — or, rather, motives did not have the same relative weight with him as with others. He was, further, to an unusual degree the creature of impulse; yet he was not, like most creatures of impulse, dominated by ignoble and transitory aims. His actions, though the outcome of an unchecked will, were not sensual or consciously selfish, but directed, as far as his insight went, towards the benefiting of his fellows. Though justice, kindness, and forbearance were the objects of his passionate admiration and pursuit, yet, owing to his incapacity for understanding other people and his subjection to the impulse of the moment, he continually, both by his judgments and his actions, wronged those with whom he came in contact. It is difficult to characterize him without overstating or overlooking essential qualities; hence the complex impression of his personality is best rendered directly from a record of his life. Such a record should be written rather from the point of view of Shelley himself than from that of a moralizing critic. A sketch as brief as the following can give only a small selection from the biographical material available. The selection is determined, not by the absolute importance of the facts chosen, but by their effectiveness in producing an impression of Shelley's character, and especially of those sides of it which most influenced his poetic work.

I.

PERCY BYSSHE SHELLEY was born August 4, 1792, at Field Place, near Horsham, in Sussex. He came of gentle lineage; the Shelley family had belonged to the squirearchy of Sussex for centuries. His father, Timothy Shelley, was a county magnate and Whig member of parliament, — a puzzle-headed, irritable, not unkindly, man of a commonplace and narrow type. Shelley's mother was a woman of beauty, possessed of greater sense and ability than her husband, but commonplace, also, without breadth of knowledge or sympathy. Sir Bysshe Shelley, the poet's grandfather, had revived the fortunes of this branch of the family. In early years he had been possessed of great personal attractions and of much adroitness and push. He had begun life as an adventurer, and laid the foundations of his wealth by his two marriages — on each occasion eloping with an heiress. As Percy knew him, he was an eccentric, avaricious old man living in a cottage in the village of Horsham. The desire to accumulate wealth, to found a family, to win social standing — such were the ruling motives of Sir Bysshe and his son Timothy.

In Field Place, among the surroundings which belong to an English country gentleman, Percy Shelley, the eldest child and heir, grew from infancy to boyhood. At the age of ten he was sent to a private boarding-school near Brentford. He was not an ordinary boy, was of a gentle and dreamy temperament, and, doubtless, seemed girlish to his companions. "He passed among his school fellows," writes his cousin and fellow pupil, Thomas Medwin, "as a strange and unsocial being ; for when a holiday relieved us from our tasks, and the other boys were engaged in such sports as the narrow limits of our prison court allowed, Shelley, who entered into none of them, would pace backwards and for-

wards — I think I see him now — along the southern wall,
indulging in various vague and undefined ideas, the chaotic
elements, if I may say so, of what afterwards produced so
beautiful a world." His life among other boys could scarcely
have been very happy, but at school he found at least one
kindred spirit. Shelley's description of this friend, though
written in later life, reveals something of the boyish Percy
himself.

There was a delicacy and a simplicity in his manners inexpres-
sibly attractive. . . . The tones of his voice were so soft and
winning that every word pierced into my heart, and their pathos
was so deep that in listening to him the tears have involuntarily
gushed from my eyes. . . . I remember in my simplicity writing
to my mother a long account of his admirable qualities and my own
devoted attachment. I suppose she thought me out of my wits,
for she returned no answer to my letter. I remember we used to
walk the whole play hours up and down by some moss-covered
palings, pouring out our hearts in youthful talk. We used to
speak of the ladies with whom we were in love, and I remember
our usual practice was to confirm each other in the everlasting
fidelity in which we had bound ourselves towards them and
towards each other. I recollect thinking my friend exquisitely
beautiful. Every night when we parted to go to bed we kissed
each other like children, as we still were.

In 1804 Shelley went to Eton, where he was even less in
harmony with his environment than at Brentford. His gentleness and oddity exposed him to teasing and bullying. " I
have seen him," writes a school fellow, "surrounded, hooted,
baited like a maddened bull, and at this distance of time I
seem to hear ringing in my ears the cry which Shelley was
wont to utter in the paroxysms of revengeful anger." " His
name," says Dowden, " would suddenly be sounded through
the cloisters, in an instant to be taken up by another and
another voice, until hundreds joined in the clamor, and the

roof would echo and reëcho with ' Shelley! Shelley! Shelley! '
Then a space would be opened in which, as in a ring or
alley, the victim must stand and exhibit his torture ; or some
urchin would dart in behind and by one dexterous push
scatter at Shelley's feet the books which he held under his
arm ; or mischievous hands would pluck at his garments ; or
a hundred fingers would point at him from every side, while
still the outcry ' Shelley! Shelley! ' rang against the walls.
An access of passion — the desired result — would follow,
which, declares a witness of these persecutions, ' made his
eyes flash like a tiger's, his cheeks grow pale as death, his
limbs quiver.' " He was a rebel against the fagging system,
and thus, doubtless, deprived himself of the protection of
elder and better disposed boys.   Yet he, too, had pleasures
and friends at Eton ; he was fond of rambling with a chosen
companion among the beautiful scenes of the neighborhood,
such as the churchyard of Stoke Pogis, which is said to
have inspired Gray's *Elegy*.   In his studies he was not unsuccessful, though he never distinguished himself as an accurate scholar.   His intellectual precocity was manifested in
his reading of classical authors outside his school work and
of Godwin and Franklin among English writers.   It may have
been through his studies of Godwin and Lucretius that he
acquired the name of " Atheist," by which he was known
among his contemporaries at school.   He was certainly a
propagandist of revolutionary ideas at Eton, and, at least
during the earlier years of his residence there, was on no
very good terms either with teachers or taught.   In scientific
studies, which, of course, were not included in the school
curriculum of those days, he was also interested; he made
chemical experiments, and possessed an electric battery.
But from his general character, as well as from references
to these pursuits in his writings, we gather that he was not
inspired by a genuinely scientific spirit, but was attracted by

the stimulus which such pursuits afforded to his imagination, by his love of mystery, and by the vague possibilities of some tremendous discovery. His scientific interests led to the forming of a friendship with a certain Doctor Lind, of Windsor, whose idealized portrait appears in the Hermit of *The Revolt of Islam* and in Zonaras of *Prince Athanase.* There is a story told by Shelley that once during the holidays he had an attack of fever, and during convalescence heard remarks of the servants which showed that his father designed to send him to a private madhouse; in great terror the boy despatched a messenger to Doctor Lind, who responded to the appeal, saw Mr. Timothy Shelley, and induced him to abandon the design. Whatever the basis for this story, the idea of malevolent plot against himself must have arisen from that tendency to illusions and that deep-rooted suspicion of his father which haunted the poet throughout his life.

The isolation and persecutions of Shelley's boyhood were the prelude of similar trials in mature life; and, if we are to take literally some of his later poetic utterances, he had already embraced those lofty principles of justice, kindness, and forbearance which he proclaimed and sought to practice in later days:

Thoughts of great deeds were mine, dear Friend, when first
The clouds which wrap this world from youth did pass.
I do remember well the hour which burst
My spirit's sleep: a fresh May-dawn it was,
When I walked forth upon the glittering grass,
And wept, I know not why; until there rose
From the near schoolroom voices that, alas!
Were but one echo from a world of woes —
The harsh and grating strife of tyrants and of foes.

And then I clasped my hands and looked around —
But none was near to mock my streaming eyes,

Which poured their warm drops on the sunny ground —
So, without shame, I spake : " I will be wise,
And just, and free, and mild, if in me lies
Such power, for I grow weary to behold
The selfish and the strong still tyrannize
Without reproach or check." I then controlled
My tears, my heart grew calm, and I was meek and bold.[1]

Very early in life Shelley cherished literary ambitions, and before leaving school he was an author. Already, in May, 1809, the greater part of a romance entitled *Zastrozzi* had been written. It was published in the following year. *Zastrozzi* exhibits in full measure the lack of originality, truth, and power which we expect in the writings of a boy. It is a slavish imitation of the absurdly mysterious and romantic fiction which enjoyed a temporary popularity about the beginning of the century. About the same time, probably in the winter 1809-10, Shelley and his cousin Medwin composed a poem on the Wandering Jew, under the influence of a translation of a German work on the same theme. It failed to find a publisher. In the autumn of 1810 Shelley and an unknown collaborateur issued a volume of *Original Poetry by Victor and Cazire*. The publisher discovered that it contained a piece plagiarized from the works of M. G. Lewis, and it was in consequence withdrawn from circulation almost as soon as published. It is quite likely that the plagiarist was Shelley's collaborateur, but it is extraordinary that a poem by Lewis should have escaped Shelley's notice. When his attention was drawn to the matter he expressed great indignation at the fraud.

In the autumn of 1810 Shelley went into residence at Oxford. The most important factor in his brief sojourn there was the friendship he formed with Thomas Jefferson Hogg, his future biographer. In many respects Hogg was

---

[1] Dedication to *The Revolt of Islam.*

the antithesis of Shelley. He was gifted with much shrewd-ness and worldly wisdom, measured things by utilitarian and matter-of-fact standards, and had a tendency to cynicism. But he was intellectual and witty, and shared Shelley's love of reading and discussion. With a certain contempt for his friend's idealism, enthusiasm, and neglect of ordinary aims, there was mingled in Hogg a genuine admiration for his intellectual power, fine spirit, and unselfish practice. Hogg's biography can only be accepted with some qualifications; the author's desire to be lively, to make a good story, is often prejudicial to accuracy. His lack of sympathy may some-what distort his portrait. But, when allowance is made for these things, the most vivid and, taken all together, the most accurate impression of the young Shelley is to be found in his pages.

Their acquaintance, accidentally made in the dining-hall at University College, of which they were both members, swiftly ripened into close intimacy. Hogg thus describes Shelley's personal appearance at the time : " It was a sum of many contradictions. His figure was slight and fragile, and yet his bones and joints were large and strong. He was tall, but he stooped so much that he seemed of low stature. His clothes were expensive and made according to the most approved mode of the day; but they were tumbled, rumpled, unbrushed. His gestures were abrupt and sometimes violent, occasionally even awkward, yet more frequently gentle and graceful. His complexion was delicate and almost feminine, of the purest red and white; yet he was tanned and freckled by exposure to the sun, having passed the autumn, as he said, in shooting. His features, his whole face, and particularly his head were, in fact, unusually small; yet the last *appeared* of a remarkable bulk, for his hair was long and bushy, and in fits of absence and in the agonies (if I may use the word) of anxious thought he often rubbed it fiercely with his hands or passed his fingers quickly through his locks unconsciously, so that it was singularly wild and rough. . . . His features were not symmetrical (the mouth, perhaps, excepted), yet was the effect of the whole extremely powerful. They breathed an animation, a fire, an enthusiasm, a vivid and preternatural intelligence that I never met with in any other countenance. Nor was the moral expression less beautiful than the intellectual; for there was a softness, a delicacy, a gentleness, and especially (though this will surprise many) that air of profound religious veneration that characterises the best works and chiefly the frescoes (and into these they infused their whole souls) of the great masters of Florence and Rome."

The appearance of his room was not less striking. "Books, boots, papers, shoes, philosophical instruments, clothes, pistols, linen, crockery, ammunition, and phials innumerable, with money, stockings, prints, crucibles, bags, and boxes were scattered on the floor and in every place; as if the young chemist, in order to analyse the mystery of creation, had endeavored first to reconstruct the primeval chaos. The tables, and especially the carpet, were already stained with large spots of various hues, which frequently proclaimed the agency of fire. An electrical machine, an air-pump, the galvanic trough, a solar microscope, and large glass jars and receivers were conspicuous amidst the mass of matter. Upon the table by his side were some books lying open, several letters, a bundle of new pens, and a bottle of Japan ink that served as an inkstand; a piece of deal, lately part of the lid of a box, with many chips, and a handsome razor that had been used as a knife. There were bottles of soda-water, sugar, pieces of lemon, and the traces of an effervescent beverage. Two piles of books supported the tongs, and these upheld a small glass retort above an argand lamp. I had not been seated many minutes before the liquor in the vessel boiled over, adding fresh stains to the table and rising in fumes with a disagreeable odor. Shelley snatched the glass quickly, and, dashing it in pieces among the ashes of the grate, increased the unpleasant and penetrating effluvium."

The two friends had interminable talks about all sorts of subjects over the fire or during the long walks which they were accustomed to take every afternoon. The intellectual stimulus of Oxford in those days was not great; the university as a whole was sunk in indolence and pleasure-seeking. In the regular studies of the place Shelley took but little interest; but, as at Eton, he carried on his own development by reading those authors who commended themselves to his taste and by the discussion of those questions which he deemed most important. "The examination," says Hogg, "of a chapter of Locke's *Essay Concerning the Human Understanding* would induce him at any moment to quit every other pursuit. We read together Hume's *Essays* and some productions of Scotch metaphysicians of inferior ability. . . . We read also certain popular French works that treat of man, for the most part in a mixed method, metaphysically, morally, and politically. Hume's *Essays* were a favorite book with Shelley, and he was always ready to put forward in argument the doctrines they uphold." He was never weary of reading Plato (in translation in these earlier days), especially the *Phaedo.* "I never beheld eyes," continues Hogg, "that devoured the pages more voraciously than his; I am convinced that two-thirds of the period of day and night were often employed in reading. It is no exaggeration to affirm that out of the twenty-four hours he frequently read sixteen. At Oxford his diligence in this respect was exemplary, but it greatly increased afterwards." As to the impression which Shelley's moral character made upon Hogg, a few extracts will suffice. "As his love of intellectual pursuits was vehement and the vigor of his genius almost celestial, so were the purity and sanctity of his life most conspicuous." " His speculations were as wild as the experience of twenty-one years has shown them to be ; but the zealous earnestness for the augmentation of knowledge and the glowing philanthropy and boundless benevolence that marked them and beamed forth in the whole deportment of that extraordinary boy are not less astonishing than they would have been if the whole of his glorious anticipations had been prophetic ; for these high qualities, at least, I have never found a parallel." " I have had the happiness to associate with some of the best specimens of gentlemen ; but, with all due deference for those admirable persons (may my candor and my preference be pardoned), I can affirm that Shelley was almost the only example I have yet found that was never wanting, even in the most minute particular, of the infinite and various observances of pure, entire, and perfect gentility." "Shelley was actually offended, and indeed more indignant than would appear to be consistent with the singular mildness of his nature, at a coarse and awkward jest, especially if it were immodest or uncleanly ; in the latter case his anger was unbounded and his uneasiness preëminent." " I never could discern in him more than two fixed principles. The first was a strong, irrepressible love of liberty, — of liberty in the abstract, and somewhat after the manner of ancient republics, without reference to the English constitution, respecting which he knew little and cared nothing, heeding it not at all. The second was an equally ardent love of toleration of all opinions, but more especially of religious opinions ; of toleration complete, entire, universal, unlimited ; and, as a deduction and corollary from which latter principle, he felt an intense abhorrence of persecution of every kind, public or private."

At Oxford Shelley's literary activity was continued. In November, 1810, a volume of poems by Shelley, *The Post-humous Fragments of Margaret Nicholson, Edited by John Fitzvictor*, was published. These poems were written originally in a serious vein, but, on Hogg's suggestion, a burlesque atmosphere was thrown about them by their ascription to the above-mentioned female, — a mad washerwoman who had attempted to stab the king. Early in the following year appeared a second romance of the same general character as *Zastrozzi*, written probably at Eton, and entitled *St. Irvyne.*

About the date of the publication of *St. Irvyne*, when Shelley was at home spending his Christmas vacation, he became involved in various troubles. The latitude of his religious opinions came to the notice of his father, who suspected Hogg of corrupting Percy. In consequence Mr. Shelley, who was in London at the time, addressed a letter to his son which made the latter imagine himself, with boyish exaggeration, a victim of intolerance and a martyr for the truth. He writes to Hogg:

My father wrote to me, and I am now surrounded, environed by dangers to which compared the devils who besieged St. Anthony were all inefficient. They attack me for my detestable principles. I am reckoned an outcast ; yet I defy them and laugh at their ineffectual efforts. . . . My father wished to withdraw me from college ; I would not consent to it. There lowers a terrific tempest ; but I stand, as it were, on a pharos, and smile exultingly at the beating of the billows below.

In a subsequent letter he tells how he attempted to enlighten his father, who admitted his son's principles, but when they were applied, silenced the young reasoner " with an equine argument, in effect with these words : ' I believe because I believe.' " " My mother imagines me to be in the highroad to Pandemonium ; she fancies I want to make

a deistical coterie of all my little sisters.   How laughable!"
His cousin, Harriet Grove, to whom he had been engaged,
also turned against him.   Happiness, it seemed to the young
enthusiast, had vanished forever — and all from the hateful
spirit of intolerance.

> Here I swear [he writes to Hogg on January 2], and as I
> break my oaths may Infinity, Eternity blast me, here I swear that
> I never will forgive intolerance.   It is the only point on which I
> allow myself to encourage revenge ; every moment shall be
> devoted to my object which I can spare ; and let me hope that
> it will not be a blow which spends itself, and leaves the wretch at
> rest — but lasting, long revenge!   I am convinced, too, that it is
> of great disservice to society — that it encourages prejudices
> which strike at the root of the dearest, the tenderest of its ties.
> Oh! how I wish I were the avenger! that it were mine to crush
> the demon, to hurl him to his native hell, never to rise again, and
> thus to establish forever perfect and universal toleration.   I expect
> to gratify some of this insatiable feeling in poetry.   You shall
> see, you shall hear, how it has injured me.   She is no longer
> mine!   She abhors me as a skeptic, as what *she* was before.   Oh,
> bigotry!   When I pardon this last, this severest of thy persecu-
> tions, may heaven (if there be wrath in heaven) blast me!

Shelley's zeal for toleration showed itself also in matters
beyond his own personal concerns.   After his return to college, he gave practical testimony to his sympathy with the
cause of free speech.   He was one of the first subscribers
to a fund in behalf of an Irish journalist whose attacks on
the government had led to imprisonment.   In connection
with this matter he addressed a letter to Leigh Hunt, editor
of *The Examiner*, the mouthpiece of English radicalism,
suggesting the formation of an organization of the friends
of liberty.

But Shelley's disposition towards revolutionary views had
its most important immediate outcome in a matter which

concerned himself. He had written a little pamphlet to show that there were no proofs of the existence of a deity. This he entitled *The Necessity of Atheism ;* he added a preface, claiming that the desire for truth was the author's only motive for publishing, and expressing the hope that any reader who might be able to meet the arguments, would do so. The pamphlet was advertised for sale, and copies were sent to university dignitaries and other prominent personages. It was anonymous, but rumor ascribed the authorship to Shelley. He was summoned before the college authorities, refused either to acknowledge or deny the authorship, and was expelled. Hogg, of his own accord, went before the authorities to protest against Shelley's condemnation, and involved himself in the same penalty.

On the morning of March the twenty-sixth, 1811, the two friends quitted Oxford. They proceeded to London, took lodgings together, and for a short time continued their walking, talking, and reading, much as before their expulsion. This, however, could not last long ; both were dependent on their parents, who, it need scarcely be said, did not regard their conduct with approval. Shelley's father commanded him to break off all communications with Hogg, to return home, and place himself under the care and instruction of such a person as his father might select. Shelley refused to comply. In a few weeks Hogg had to leave for York, where he was to study law, and his companion was left in comparative loneliness. Two of Shelley's sisters were at school in the suburbs, at Clapham ; there Shelley frequently visited them, and, young though they were, attempted to indoctrinate them with some of his peculiar views. Among their schoolmates was a certain Harriet Westbrook, not yet sixteen, and endowed with marked personal attractions. She had regular features, an exquisite complexion, symmetrical form, and graceful movements.

Her father was a retired coffee-house keeper, well-to-do in the world. Her mother seems to have been an incapable sort of person; and an elder sister, Eliza, almost twice Harriet's age, exercised over her the care and influence which naturally belong to a mother. Shelley had already, earlier in the year, become acquainted with the younger sister, and now the acquaintance ripened into intimacy. Harriet did not share in the horror with which the other girls at Mrs. Fenning's school looked upon the atheist, and she was, in consequence, exposed to some petty persecutions. Her elder sister, also, showed sympathy with Shelley and interest in his doctrines, and he became a not infrequent visitor at their home in London. It is not improbable that matrimonial views in regard to Harriet lay at the bottom of Eliza's encouragement of Shelley. "Her father," too, as Shelley notices, "is civil to me, very strangely." But as far as can be judged, ideas of love and marriage were not consciously present in Shelley's mind. Harriet was to him an interesting disciple, — a young soul to be brought into that illumination which he himself enjoyed.

Meanwhile, through the intervention of a maternal uncle and the good offices of the Duke of Norfolk, who was a sort of patron and friend to Timothy Shelley, an accommodation was effected between father and son. The latter was to receive an allowance of £200 a year, and was left to do as he pleased with respect to place of abode. He returned to Field Place, but found the surroundings uncongenial. "I am a perfect hermit," he says in a letter, "not a being to speak with! I sometimes exchange a word with my mother on the subject of the weather, upon which she is irresistibly eloquent; otherwise all is deep silence! I wander about this place, walking all over the grounds, with no particular object in view." Again : " It is most true that the mass of mankind are Christians only in name ; their religion has no

reality. . . . Certain members of my family are no more
Christians than Epicurus himself was; the discanonisation
of this saint of theirs is impossible until something more
worthy of devotion is pointed out; but where eyes are shut,
nothing can be seen. They would ask, Are we wrong to
regard the opinion of the world? what would compensate us
for the loss of it? Good heavens, what a question! Is it
not to be answered by a word? So I have little of their
confidence." His eldest sister Elizabeth, whom he had
hoped to win over to his peculiar views, and, in his day-
dreams, had designed for Hogg, cared more for amusements
and worldly advantage than for truth and philosophy. She
received with contempt or aversion her brother's teachings
as to the evils of legal marriage and the folly of substitut-
ing any merely external tie for the true love that binds
kindred hearts together.

As a partial substitute for companionship with a sympathetic spirit, Shelley maintained a close correspondence, not
merely with Hogg, but also with a Miss Hitchener, a school-
mistress whom he had lately met. Miss Hitchener was some
thirty years old, angular and swarthy, but of advanced views
and deeply interested in those questions, philosophical and
political, for which the young enthusiast most cared. She
seemed to Shelley an ideal spirit, with that complete understanding of his point of view and that perfect sympathy for
which his heart yearned. Their correspondence treated of
the widest and profoundest questions, — the existence of
God, immortality, political and social equality. To Miss
Eliza Westbrook, also, and her sister he from time to time
addressed letters, though not finding the former wholly to
his mind.

About the beginning of July, Shelley went to Wales to pass
some weeks with a cousin. One motive for this journey may
have been the wish to meet the Westbrooks, who intended

to spend a part of the summer in the same neighborhood. But Shelley's strongest desire was for the companionship of Hogg; and, as their intercourse was interdicted by his father, he hoped to find, during this absence from home, an opportunity for a clandestine visit. Neither the meeting with the Westbrooks nor that with Hogg took place. The former had already returned to London, and thence came letters from Harriet in quick succession: she was persecuted at home; she must return to school where she was wretched; she had no one to love and was useless in the world; she asked if it would be wrong to put an end to her miserable life. At length came a letter in which she threw herself on Shelley's protection and proposed to fly with him. Shelley hastened to London, and, after the delay of a week or two, eloped with Harriet to Scotland. In Edinburgh, on August 28, 1811, they were married.

It is evident that this connection with Harriet Westbrook was, on Shelley's part, unpremeditated, — the result of circumstances, rather than of design. There was certainly no strong passion on his side; he was moved more by the feeling that he was helping a victim of oppression and by the romance of the situation than by the ordinary motives of a love-match. In the letters which passed between him and Hogg during the weeks which immediately preceded the elopement, the question whether legal marriage was or was not permissible to the "illuminated," was discussed. Shelley was in theory opposed to marriage as one of the pernicious forms of oppression imposed and consecrated by society; Hogg argued, on practical grounds, in favor of the legal tie. To Hogg's arguments Shelley yielded; although, he writes, he does not anticipate being "directly called upon to evince his attachment to either theory." "The ties of love and honor," he says in a letter to his friend, dated August 15, "are doubtless of sufficient strength to bind congenial souls. . . . Yet the argument of impracticability, and, what is even worse, the disproportionate sacrifice which the female is called upon to make, — these arguments, which you have urged in a manner immediately irresistible, I cannot withstand." The following extract from a letter to Miss Hitchener, written some two months after the marriage, gives a compendious statement of the facts from Shelley's point of view, and is in every respect most characteristic of the writer.

I will explain, however, the circumstances which caused my marriage; these must certainly have caused much conjecture in your mind. Some time ago, when my sister was at Mrs. Fenning's school, she contracted an intimacy with Harriet. At that period I attentively watched over my sister, designing, if possible, to add her to the list of the good, the disinterested, the free. I desired, therefore, to investigate Harriet's character; for which purpose I called upon her, requested to correspond with her, designing that *her* advancement should keep pace with, and possibly accelerate, that of my sister. Her ready and frank acceptance of my proposal pleased me; and, though with ideas the remotest to those which have led to this conclusion of our intimacy, I continued to correspond with her for some time. The frequency of her letters became greater during my stay in Wales. I answered them; they became interesting. They contained complaints of the irrational conduct of her relatives, and the misery of living where she could *love* no one. Suicide was with her a favorite theme, and her total uselessness was urged in its defence. This I admitted, supposing she could prove her inutility, and that she was powerless. Her letters became more and more gloomy. At length one assumed a tone of such despair as induced me to quit Wales precipitately. I arrived in London. I was shocked at observing the alteration of her looks. Little did I divine its cause. She had become violently attached to me, and feared that I should not return her attachment. Prejudice made the confession painful. It was impossible to avoid being much affected; I promised to unite my fate with hers. I stayed in London several days, during which she recovered her spirits. I had promised, at her bidding, to come again to London. They endeavored to compel her to return to school where malice and pride embittered every hour. She wrote to me. I came to London. I proposed marriage, for the reasons which I have given you, and she complied. Blame me if thou wilt, dearest friend, for *still* thou art dearest to me ; yet pity even this error if thou blamest me. If Harriet be not, at sixteen, all that you are at a more advanced age, assist me to mould a really noble soul into all that can make its nobleness useful and lovely. Lovely it is now, or I am the weakest slave to error.

On hearing of his son's marriage, Mr. Timothy Shelley stopped his allowance, and Mr. Westbrook also refused supplies. Hence great pecuniary embarrassments for the young couple ; but, apart from these, the weeks in Edinburgh passed pleasantly enough. Hogg took advantage of a holiday to join them, and the pleasant intercourse of the two friends was renewed. Harriet, with the pliancy of youth, adapted herself to her surroundings ; read much, especially aloud ; adopted her husband's language, and, so far as she understood them, his ideas, also ; and talked much of virtue and perfectibility. When, of necessity, Hogg's visit terminated, the Shelleys accompanied him to York, and were there presently joined by Eliza Westbrook. Eliza, who had naturally great influence over her younger sister, and who did not altogether approve of the ways of the household, took the reins into her own hands, and effected a revolution in the habits of the little circle. An event even more revolutionary was a sudden rupture with Hogg. During a brief absence of her husband and before the arrival of her sister, Hogg, as we gather from Shelley's letters, was guilty of gross misconduct towards Harriet. Shelley writes to Miss Hitchener in reference to Hogg: "We walked to the fields beyond York. I desired to know fully the account of this affair. I heard it *from him*, and I believe he was sincere. All that I can recollect of that terrible day was that I pardoned him, — fully, freely pardoned him ; that I would still be a friend to him, and hoped soon to convince him how lovely virtue was ; that his crime, not himself, was the object of my detestation ;

that I value a human being, not for what it has been, but
for what it is; that I hoped the time would come when he
would regard this horrible error with as much disgust as I
did. He said little ; he was pale, terror-struck, remorseful."
It is extraordinary that twelve months after an offence of so
signal a character as that indicated in this letter, Shelley re-
sumed his friendly relations with Hogg; that the latter was
received, apparently on the old footing, not merely by
Shelley, but by Harriet and Eliza; and that he was set down
for a legacy of £2000 in Shelley's will.

His companionship with Hogg thus suddenly interrupted,
his relations to Harriet being rather those of a protector and
teacher than of an intellectual equal, Shelley turned with
renewed enthusiasm to Miss Hitchener, in whom he seemed
to find the possibilities of friendship of the truest and
highest character. He writes to her: "I could have borne
to die, to die eternally with my once-loved friend [Hogg].
I could coolly have reasoned to the conclusions of reason ; I
could have unhesitatingly submitted. Earth seemed to be
enough for our intercourse; on earth its bounds appeared to
be stated, as the event hath dreadfully proved. But with
you — your friendship seems to have generated a passion to
which fifty such fleeting, inadequate existences as these appear to be but a drop in the bucket, too trivial for account.
With you, I cannot submit to perish with the flower of the
field ; I cannot consent that the same shroud which shall
moulder around these perishing frames shall enwrap the
vital spirit which hath produced, sanctified — may I say
eternized? — a friendship such as ours." Again: "I look
upon you as a mighty mind. I anticipate the era of reform
with more eagerness as I picture to myself *you* the barrier
between violence and renovation." He is eager that she
should become a member of his household. "How Harriet
and her sister long to see you! and how *I* long to see you,

never to part with you again." "The union of our minds will
be more efficacious than a state of separate endeavor. I
shall excite you to action, you will excite me to just specula-
tion. . . . I should possibly gain the advantage in the
exchange of qualities ; but my powers are such as would
augment yours. I perceive in you the embryon of a mighty
intellect which may one day enlighten thousands. How de-
sirous ought I not to be, if I conceive that the one spark
which glimmers through mine should kindle a blaze by
which nations may rejoice ! . . . Come, come, and share
with us the noblest success or the most glorious martyrdom."

The breach with Hogg was speedily followed by removal
from York to Keswick. Thither Shelley was attracted by the
presence of Southey, whose poetry he admired. But Southey
was, at this date, as conservative as Shelley was radical, and
between the two there was little community of sentiment.
At first, when they met, Shelley, whilst strenuously protesting
against Southey's views and considering him "far from
being a man of great reasoning powers," yet regarded him
with sincere admiration : "He is a man of virtue. He will
never belie what he thinks ; his professions are in compati-
bility with his practice." But in a month or two Shelley
writes : "He is a man who *may* be amiable in his private
character, stained and false as is his public one. He *may*
be amiable, but, if he is, my feelings are liars."

Money affairs continued to harass the poet. His grandfather, Sir Bysshe Shelley, was anxious to entail his large
accumulated property ; but to effect this, it was needful that
his grandson should consent. Through his uncle, Captain
Pilfold, Shelley heard that an income of £2000 a year would
be settled on him, provided he would consent to the entail.
The spirit in which this suggestion was received — a suggestion to do something which society regarded as eminently
proper — is very characteristic. " I have since heard from

Captain P. His letter contains the account of a meditated proposal, on the part of my father and grandfather, to make my income immediately larger than the former's, in case I will consent to entail the estate on my eldest son, and in default of issue on my brother. Silly dotards! that I will forswear my principles in consideration of £2000 a year? that the good will I could thus purchase or the ill will I could thus overbear, would recompense me for the loss of self-esteem, of conscious rectitude? And with what face can they make me a proposal so insultingly hateful? Dare one of them propose such a condition to my face — to the face of any virtuous man — and not sink into nothing at his disdain? That I should entail £120,000 of command over labour, of power to remit this, to employ it for beneficent purposes, on one whom I know not, — who might, instead of being the benefactor of mankind, be its bane, or use this for the worst purposes, which the real delegates of my chance-given property might convert into a most useful instrument of benevolence! No! this you will not suspect me of." After many delays and much worry, Mr. Westbrook agreed to give the young people an allowance of £200, and Timothy Shelley bestowed the same sum, taking, in his usual fashion, all graciousness from the gift by telling his son that it was given to prevent him from cheating strangers.

In the beginning of the year 1812 Shelley introduced himself by letter to the philosopher Godwin, whose writings exercised a profound influence on the poet's thought, and whose daughter he was one day to marry. In answer to Godwin's request for specific details, Shelley, in a second letter, sent the following account of himself :

I am the son of a man of fortune in Sussex. The habits of thinking of my father and myself never coincided. Passive obedience was inculcated and enforced in my childhood. I was required to love because it was *my duty* to love ; it is scarcely necessary to remark that coercion obviated its own intention. I was haunted with a passion for the wildest and most extravagant romances. Ancient books of chemistry and magic were perused with an enthusiasm of wonder almost amounting to belief. My sentiments were unrestrained by anything within me; external impediments were numerous and strongly applied ; their effect was merely temporary.

From a reader, I became a writer of romances ; before the age of seventeen I had published two, *St. Irvyne* and *Zastrozzi*, each of which, though quite uncharacteristic of me as I am now, yet serves to mark the state of my mind at the period of their composition. I shall desire them to be sent to you ; do not, however, consider this as any obligation to yourself to misapply your valuable time.

It is now a period of more than two years since first I saw your inestimable book of *Political Justice;* it opened to my mind fresh and more extensive views ; it materially influenced my character, and I rose from its perusal a wiser and a better man. I was no longer the votary of romance ; till then I had existed in an ideal world — now I found that in this universe of ours was enough to excite the interest of the heart, enough to employ the discussions of reason; I beheld, in short, that I had duties to perform. Conceive the effect which the *Political Justice* would have upon a mind before zealous of its independence and participating somewhat singularly in a peculiar susceptibility.

My age is now *nineteen;* at the period to which I allude I was at Eton. No sooner had I formed the principles which I now profess than I was anxious to disseminate their benefits. This was done without the slightest caution. I was twice expelled, but recalled by the interference of my father. I went to Oxford. Oxonian society was insipid to me, uncongenial to my habits of thinking. I could not descend to common life ; the sublime interests of poetry, lofty and exalted achievements, the proselytism of the world, the equalization of its inhabitants were to me the soul of my soul. You can probably form an idea of the contrast exhibited to my character by those with whom I was surrounded. Classical reading and poetical writing employed me during my residence at Oxford.

In the meantime I became, in the popular sense of the word "God," an atheist. I printed a pamphlet, avowing my opinion and its occasion. I distributed this anonymously to men of thought and learning, wishing that reason should decide on the case at issue ; it was never my intention to deny it. Mr. Coplestone, at Oxford, among others, had the pamphlet ; he showed it to the Master and the Fellows of University College, and *I* was sent for. I was informed that in case I denied the publication no more would be said. I refused and was expelled.

It will be necessary, in order to elucidate this part of my history, to inform you that I am heir by entail to an estate of £6000 per annum. My principles have induced me to regard the law of primogeniture an evil of primary magnitude. My father's notions of family honour are incoincident with my knowledge of public good. I will never sacrifice the latter to any consideration. My father has ever regarded me as a blot, a defilement of his honour. He wished to induce me by poverty to accept of some commission in a distant regiment, and in the interim of my absence to prosecute the pamphlet, that a process of outlawry might make the estate, on his death, devolve on my younger brother. These are the leading points in the history of the man before you. Others exist, but I have thought proper to make some selection ; not that it is my design to conceal or extenuate any part, but that I should by their enumeration quite outstep the bounds of modesty. Now it is for you to judge whether, by permitting me to cultivate your friendship, you are exhibiting yourself more really useful than by the pursuance of those avocations of which the time spent in allowing this cultivation would deprive you. I am now earnestly pursuing studious habits. I am writing "An Enquiry into the causes of the failure of the French Revolution to benefit mankind." My plan is that of resolving to lose no opportunity to disseminate truth and happiness.

I am married to a woman whose views are similar to my own. To you, as the regulator and former of my mind, I must ever look with real respect and veneration.

Commenting on this in his *Life of Shelley*, Hogg says: " Shelley's letters to William Godwin must be received with caution; the young poet saw events through the spectacles of his pregnant and prurient fancy, and not as they really were. He was altogether incapable of rendering an account of any transaction whatsoever according to the strict and precise truth, and the bare, naked realities of actual life; not through an addiction to falsehood, which he cordially detested, but because he was the creature, the unsuspecting and unresisting victim, of his irresistible imagination." Hogg proceeds to point out examples of this tendency in the letter quoted. Regarding the statement: "I was informed that in case I denied the publication no more would be said," Hogg says, "No such offer was made . . . but, musing on the affair, as he was wont, he dreamed that the proposal had been declined by him, and thus he had the gratification of believing that he was more a martyr than he really was." Hogg notes other misstatements: "He never published anything controversial at Eton; he was never expelled. . . . No offer of a commission in the army was ever made to Bysshe; it is only in a dream that the prosecution, outlawry, and devolution of the estate could find a place." The same tendency to the imaginative amplification of facts is illustrated in the account which Shelley gave to Peacock of his expulsion. According to this account, "his expulsion was a matter of great form and solemnity; there was a sort of public assembly, before which he pleaded his own cause, in a long oration, in the course of which he called on the illustrious spirits who had shed glory on those walls to look down on their degenerate successors."

Various literary plans engaged Shelley's attention during the months which followed his marriage — most of them not, at this time, realized. He was eager to contribute some practical help towards the improvement of humanity. The agitation in Ireland on behalf of "Catholic emancipation" seemed to afford an opportunity, and he prepared an address to the Catholics of Ireland. The address, he says to Godwin,

consists of the benevolent and tolerant deductions of philosophy reduced into the simplest language, and such as those who by their uneducated poverty are most susceptible of evil impressions from Catholicism may clearly comprehend. I know it can do no harm; it cannot excite rebellion, as its main principle is to trust the success of a cause to the energy of its truth. It cannot "widen the breach between the kingdoms," as it attempts to convey to the vulgar mind sentiments of universal philanthropy; and, whatever impressions it may produce, they can be no others but those of peace and harmony; it owns no religion but benevolence, no cause but virtue, no party but the world. I shall devote myself with unremitting zeal, as far as the uncertain state of health will permit, towards forwarding the great ends of virtue and happiness in Ireland, regarding, as I do, the present state of that country's affairs as an opportunity which if I, being thus disengaged, permit to pass unoccupied, I am unworthy the character which I have assumed.

In the desire, then, to take some active part in forwarding the progress of humanity, Shelley, accompanied by his wife and Miss Westbrook, left Keswick for Dublin, where he arrived on February 12, 1812. Whilst sympathizing with the movement for Catholic emancipation and the repeal of the union, he regarded these as intrinsically matters of small moment, except in so far as they were initial steps towards a far wider movement which should include not Ireland merely, but the world, and should culminate in the abolition of all government and of all class distinctions. In harmony with this view, his *Address* is not really political; it does not consider what are the immediate measures especially adapted to the situation of Ireland; it is an exhortation to tolerance, sobriety, wisdom, and kindliness. In its writer's opinion, political reform was to be attained through the reform of individuals. What Shelley urged was that each Irishman should set about reforming himself. In the *Address*, the main object of touching upon emancipation and repeal appears to be that the author may thereby gain the ear of the reader for higher and broader themes.

The pamphlet was printed in the cheapest style; the price was five pence; it was also distributed gratis by the author. "For two days," he writes to Miss Hitchener, "I have omitted writing to you, but each day has been filled up with the employment of disseminating the doctrines of philanthropy and freedom. I have already sent four hundred of my little pamphlets into the world, and they have excited a sensation of wonder in Dublin; eleven hundred yet remain for distribution. Copies have been sent to sixty public houses. No prosecution is yet attempted. I do not see how it can be. Congratulate me, my friend, for everything proceeds well. I could not expect more rapid success." Again: "I send a man out every day to distribute copies, with instructions how and where to give them. . . . I stand on the balcony of our window and watch till I see a man *who looks likely;* I throw a book to him." The tone of Shelley's letter may be compared with that of Harriet, who also writes to Miss Hitchener: "I am sure you would laugh were you to see us give the pamphlets. We throw them out of the window and give them to men we pass in the streets. For myself, I am ready to die of laughter when it is done, and Percy looks so grave. Yesterday he put one into a woman's hood of a cloak; she knew nothing of it, and we passed her. I could hardly get on, my muscles were so irritated."

A second pamphlet was printed, proposing the formation of an association whose immediate object should be Catholic emancipation, but whose ultimate aim was to be the destruction of all grievances, political and moral. Shelley also xxxviiiINTRODUCTION.

spoke at a great public meeting in which O'Connell and
other leaders took a prominent part. But his visionary
expectations of reforming the Irish or of solving the Irish
question were, of course, destined to disappointment. In
not even the slightest degree did he produce the effects
which he had anticipated; and he abandoned his attempt
even more speedily than he had undertaken it. He writes:
"The association proceeds slowly, and I fear will not be
established. Prejudices are so violent in contradiction to
my principles, that more hate me as a freethinker than love
me as a votary of freedom." He was further discouraged
by Godwin's disapproval of his premature interference in
practical politics; and after a seven weeks' stay in Ireland
set sail for England on April 4th.

The twelve months which followed formed a period of
wanderings hither and thither. Political questions continued
to occupy a large part of his attention, and the outspoken
radicalism of some of his printed pamphlets, especially of
A Declaration of Rights, which he purposed to distribute
among the peasantry, led to his being put under surveil-
lance by the authorities. In the village of Lynmouth, on
the coast of Devon, he was accustomed, in company with
Miss Hitchener (who had now joined the household) to
launch upon the sea boxes fitted with masts and sails containing copies of his pamphlets. Bottles were used for the
same purpose, and even fire-balloons were sent skyward to
spread his ideas for the amelioration of the world. He
employed a servant, Dan Healy, to post up copies of the
Declaration of Rights in the neighboring town of Barnstaple.
Healy was arrested, in consequence, and imprisoned for six
months, Shelley doing all in his power to alleviate the hap-
less victim's fate. Later, Shelley took up his abode in the
little Welsh town of Tremadoc, where he became deeply
interested in a work which was being carried on by a gentle-

man of the neighborhood, — the reclaiming of a large tract of land from the sea. This appealed to Shelley as a noble and beneficent undertaking; it was suffering from lack of funds; he subscribed £100, and threw himself with ardor into the work of interesting others. In pursuance of this object he went to London in October, 1812, accompanied by the other members of the family. This visit was notable because the poet, for the first time, met Godwin; henceforward there was frequent intercourse between them. Mary Godwin, now a girl of fifteen, was absent during the greater part of Shelley's stay in London, and he may not have seen her. Friendly relations were renewed with Hogg, who was now studying law in London. Here, too, Miss Hitchener received her *congé*. This lady, whom he had idealized as the pattern of all that is highest in woman, had been resident with the Shelleys since July. At first all had gone well; but it was inevitable that misunderstandings should grow up between a person so situated and one or all of the group, Shelley, Harriet, and Eliza. By and by, we find them speaking of her as an unendurable incubus. To be rid of her, Shelley, in consideration of the fact that she had been induced to give up her school in order to join their circle, promised her an annuity of £100; we do not know for how long. He writes to Hogg in December of this year: "I pay it with a heavy heart and an unwilling hand; but it must be so. She was deprived by our misjudging haste of a situation where she was going on smoothly; and now she says that her reputation is gone, her health ruined, her peace of mind destroyed by my barbarity; a complete victim to all the woes, mental and bodily, that heroine ever suffered! This is not all fact; but certainly she is embarrassed and poor, and we being in some degree the cause, we ought to obviate it." It is characteristic that, from idealizing the lady and ascribing to her all imaginable graces and powers, he passes to the other extreme, and writes : " She is a woman of desperate views and dreadful passions, but of cool and undeviating revenge."

About the middle of November Shelley returned to Trema- doc, and there exhausted himself in efforts on behalf of the embankment. He was saddened by the condition of the neighboring poor. It was a winter of much distress among the working people, and Shelley was indefatigable in his efforts on their behalf, — visiting them and spending his income re- lieving their wants. He was busy, as always, with writing and reading. He studied with avidity French philosophy, espe- cially Holbach's *Système de la Nature;* he read history, to which he had an innate aversion, because Godwin urged it. Among his own writings the most important was a long nar- rative and philosophical poem, *Queen Mab,* which was not, however, printed until the spring of 1813, and then privately.

The residence of the Shelleys at Tremadoc was brought to an end by an extraordinary occurrence, which is described in the following extract from one of Mrs. Shelley's letters.

On Friday night, the 26th of February, we retired to bed between ten and eleven o'clock. We had been in bed about half an hour when Mr. S. heard a noise proceeding from one of the parlours. He immediately went downstairs with two pistols, which he had loaded that night, expecting to have occasion for them. He went into the billiard room, when he heard footsteps retreating ; he followed into another little room, which was called an office. He there saw a man in the act of quitting the room through a glass window which opens into the shrubbery. The man fired at Mr. S., which he avoided. Bysshe then fired, but it flashed in the pan. The man then knocked Bysshe down, and they struggled on the ground. Bysshe then fired his second pistol, which he thought wounded him in the shoulder, as he uttered a shriek and got up, when he said these words : " By God, I will be revenged ! I will murder your wife ; I will ravish your sister ! By God, I will be revenged !" He then fled — as we hoped for

the night. Our servants were not gone to bed, but were just
going, when the horrible affair happened. This was about eleven
o'clock. We all assembled in the parlour, where we remained for
two hours. Mr. S. then advised us to retire, thinking it impossible
that he should make a second attack. We left Bysshe and our
manservant, who had only arrived that day, and who knew nothing
of the house, to sit up. I had been in bed three hours when I
heard a pistol go off. I immediately ran downstairs, when I perceived that Bysshe's flannel gown had been shot through, and the
window-curtain. Bysshe had sent Daniel to see what hour it was,
when he heard a noise at the window. He went there, and a man
thrust his arm through the glass and fired at him. Thank Heaven!
the ball went through his gown and he remained unhurt. Mr. S.
happened to stand sideways ; had he stood fronting, the ball must
have killed him. Bysshe fired his pistol, but it would not go off ;
he then aimed a blow at him with an old sword which we found
in the house. The assassin attempted to get the sword from him,
and just as he was pulling it away, Dan rushed into the room,
when he made his escape.

This was at four in the morning. It had been a most dreadful
night ; the wind was as loud as thunder, and the rain descended
in torrents. Nothing has been heard of him ; and we have every
reason to believe it was no stranger, as there is a man of the name
of Leeson, who the next morning that it happened went and told
the shopkeepers of Tremadoc that it was a tale of Mr. Shelley's
to impose upon them, that he might leave the country without
paying his bills. This they believed, and none of them attempted
to do anything towards his discovery.

On the day after this Shelley addressed the following letter
to his friend Hookham, the publisher :

My Dear Sir,

I have just escaped an atrocious assassination. Oh ! send me
the £20 if you have it.[1] You will perhaps hear of me no more.

friend,   Percy Shelley.

---

[1] Referring to £20 which he had sent, a little before, as a subscription for the benefit of Leigh Hunt.

Mr. Shelley is so dreadfully nervous to-day from having been up all night that I am afraid what he has written will alarm you very much. We intend to leave this place as soon as possible, as our lives are not safe so long as we remain. It is no common robber we dread, but a person who is actuated by revenge, and who threatens my life and my sister's as well. If you can send us the money, it will greatly add to our comfort.

Sir, I remain your sincere friend,

H. SHELLEY.

A person who was a neighbor of the Shelleys at this time, writing in 1860, states that Shelley further asserted that he saw a ghost or devil when he looked from the window on this occasion, and that Shelley set fire to the wood to destroy the apparition. Hogg states that "persons acquainted with the localities and with the circumstances, and who carefully investigated the matter, were unanimously of opinion that no such attack was ever made." On the other hand, there are sufficient indications that there was no intentional fraud on Shelley's part. It should be remembered that, in addition to possessing a peculiar temperament, Shelley was at times in the habit of taking laudanum to excess. Many of the details mentioned in Harriet's letter must have had their origin in the poet's excited imagination; but it is just possible that there was some substratum of fact. Peacock, who knew Shelley well, considers that this was one of the cases of semi-delusion to which, in his opinion, his friend was subject. In his *Memoirs of Shelley*, he illustrates this tendency by the following narrative : " In the early summer of 1816 the spirit of restlessness again came over him, and resulted in a second visit to the Continent. The change of scene was preceded, as more than once before, by a mysterious communication from a person seen only by himself, warning him of immediate personal perils to be incurred by him if he did not instantly depart. I was alone at Bishops-gate with him and Mrs. Shelley when the visitation alluded to occurred." Peacock was sceptical as to the visit ; where-upon Shelley said, "You know Williams of Tremadoc? It was he who was here to-day. He came to tell me of a plot laid by my father and uncle to entrap me and lock me up. He was in great haste and could not stop a minute, and I walked with him to Egham." Peacock remained unconvinced, and adduced some facts which showed that it was highly im-probable that Shelley had walked to Egham. To this the latter replied, "It is very hard on a man who has devoted his life to the pursuit of truth, who has made great sacrifices and incurred great sufferings for it, to be treated as a visionary. If I do not know that I saw Williams, how do I know that I see you?" Finally, Shelley stated that Williams was stay-ing at the Turk's Head Coffee-house in London; and if Peacock would walk thither on the following day he would find that things were as Shelley asserted. They started out the next morning ; but before going far Shelley, suddenly turning round, exclaimed, "I do not think we shall find Williams at the Turk's Head;" and proposed a walk in another direction. Peacock heard nothing more of the mysterious visit for some days, when Shelley said to him, "I have some news from Williams, a letter and an enclosure; I cannot show you the letter ; I will show you the enclo-sure. It is a diamond necklace." Peacock objected that the necklace would prove nothing as to Williams's alleged visit. "Then," answered Shelley, "if you will not believe me, I must submit to your incredulity." "I had," continues Peacock, "on one or two previous occasions, argued with him against similar semi-delusions, and I believe if they had always been received with similar scepticism they would not have been so often repeated. . . . I call them semi-delusions because, for the most part, they had their basis in his firm belief that his father and uncle had designs upon his liberty. On this basis his imagination built a fabric of romance, and when he presented it as substantive fact, and it was found to contain more or less of inconsistency, he felt his self-esteem interested in maintaining it by accumulated circumstances, which severally vanished under the touch of investigation, like Williams's location at the Turk's Head Coffee-house. I must add that in the expression of these differences there was not a shadow of anger. They were discussed with freedom and calmness, with the good temper and good feeling which never forsook him in conversations with his friends. There was an evident anxiety for acquiescence, but a quiet and gentle toleration of dissent. A personal discussion, however interesting to himself, was carried on with the same calmness as if it related to the most abstract question in metaphysics."

In April, 1813, Shelley took lodgings in London. There he had now several intimate friends: Hogg, the Godwins, Peacock the poet and novelist, whose acquaintance he had recently made, Leigh ·Hunt, and others. Hogg again affords a series of lively pictures of the Shelleys and their method of living. Harriet was bright, blooming, and placid as ever, and still addicted to reading aloud. Owing to the multitude of books, their sitting-room presented a scene of confusion which recalled Shelley's bachelor apartments in Oxford. Meals came at irregular hours. Throughout life the poet was very simple in his diet and neglectful of regular meals. "When he felt hungry," writes Hogg of Shelley in 1813, " he would dash into the first baker's shop, buy a loaf, and rush out again, bearing it under his arm ; and he strode onwards in his rapid course, breaking off pieces of bread and rapidly swallowing them." He eschewed spirituous liquors and drank tea or water ; both he and Harriet were vegetarians at this time. But Shelley was not fanatical in this respect ; when away from home he ate what came in his way, and did not refuse the weaker sorts of wine.   Peacock ascribes Shelley's ill-health largely to vegetarianism and irregularity in eating.   In his sleeping he was not less eccentric, inclined to be drowsy in the evenings, and never so wakeful as when the rest of the world is in the habit of taking repose.   As to dress, Hogg says that he never remembers to have seen Shelley in a greatcoat, even in the coldest weather.   He wore his waistcoat much, or entirely, open ; his throat was bare, the collar of his shirt unbuttoned; he wore a hat reluctantly in town, but in fields or gardens had no other covering for his head than his long, wild locks. " He took strange caprices, unfounded frights and dislikes, vain apprehensions and panic terrors, and therefore he absented himself from formal and sacred engagements.   He was unconscious and oblivious of times, places, persons, and seasons ; and, falling into some poetic vision, some day-dream, he quickly and completely forgot all that he had repeatedly and solemnly promised or ran away after some object of imaginary urgency and importance which suddenly came into his head, setting off in vain pursuit of it, he knew not whither."

In June, 1813, a daughter, Ianthe, was born.   This event, which should have bound husband and wife more closely together, marks the beginnings of estrangement.   We have seen the quixotic fashion in which Shelley married.   The marriage turned out, at first, more happily than could have been expected.   Harriet had beauty and amiability ; she adopted, though in a somewhat childish fashion no doubt, the views of her husband ; she employed his phraseology. Shelley's love for his young wife grew ; his letters and poems written while in Devonshire and Wales witness to the happiness of their union.   But the poet's eccentricities were such as to put a strain on the most appreciative affection; and Harriet was not specially adapted, in character and intellect, to comprehend him. On the other side, the time was sure to come when Shelley would feel with exaggerated sensitiveness the difference between the real person and the ideal which he had conceived. Harriet was essentially commonplace, without extraordinary spiritual or mental endowments. As she grew to full maturity, as the pliancy and docility of girlhood passed away, she doubtless developed tastes and opinions little in harmony with her husband's unconventional views. Her patience must have been tried by his unpractical aims and by his neglect of those things which society about her deemed important. In 1813 Shelley made a purchase of plate and set up a carriage — certainly not of his own impulse. To intensify any divergencies of thought and feeling between husband and wife, there were the continued presence and influence of Eliza Westbrook. However she may have dissembled in the early days of their acquaintance, she had no natural interest or sympathy for Shelley's peculiar ways and opinions. She was not at all literary or intellectual in her tastes; her aims were commonplace; her character, mature and strong; her influence over her sister, great. Shelley now cordially detested his sister-in-law, and his dislike was intensified when he saw her in chief charge of the little Ianthe. Peacock says: "I have often thought that if Harriet had nursed her own child [contrary to the father's wishes, a wet-nurse was employed], and if this sister had not lived with them, the link of their married love would not have been so readily broken."

The sense of disparity between himself and his wife may have been quickened by the congenial female society which he now enjoyed among some new friends, — the Newtons and Boinvilles. The circle into which he was thus introduced was composed of persons of an enthusiastic and

somewhat eccentric type. Mr. Newton was a strong vege-
tarian; to animal food and the drinking of undistilled water
he ascribed most of the ills of humanity; he saw, too, profound meanings in the signs of the zodiac. His wife and
Mrs. Boinville were sisters. To the latter Shelley was
especially drawn. Recalling in 1819 the time of which we
are now speaking, he wrote : "I could not help considering
Mrs. Boinville, when I knew her, as the most admirable
specimen of a human being I had ever seen. Nothing
earthly ever appeared to me more perfect than her character
and manners." She was an enthusiast for liberty, full of
sensibility and intensity, of gracious and refined manners.
Under her teaching and that of her married daughter,
Cornelia Turner, Shelley began the study of Italian poetry.
To the cynical and common-sense Hogg and Peacock, the
absurdities of this circle were more apparent than its
charms. "The greater part of her [Mrs. Boinville's]
associates," says Hogg, "were odious. I generally found
there two or three sentimental young butchers, an eminently
philosophical tinker, and several very unsophisticated medical practitioners, or medical students, all of low origin and
vulgar and offensive manners. They sighed, turned up their
eyes, retailed philosophy, such as it was, and swore by William Godwin and *Political Justice.*" During the summer
of 1813 Shelley was much in the society of these people,
having rented a cottage at Bracknell, where the Boinvilles
were spending the summer months.

From Bracknell, Shelley, on the invitation of his mother,
paid a clandestine visit to Field Place while his father was
absent. There he met a young officer, Captain Kennedy,
whose impressions of the poet are interesting : "His eyes
were most expressive, his complexion beautifully fair, his
features exquisitely fine; his hair was dark, and no particular attention to its arrangement was manifest. In per-

son he was slender and gentlemanlike, but inclined to stoop; his gait was decidedly not military. The general appearance indicated great delicacy of constitution. One would pronounce of him that he was different from other men. There was an earnestness in his manner and such perfect gentleness of breeding and freedom from everything artificial as charmed every one. I never met a man who so immediately won upon me. . . . He reasoned and spoke like a perfect gentleman, and treated my arguments, boy as I was (I had lately completed my sixteenth year), with as much consideration and respect as if I had been his equal in ability and attainment." Shelley told Captain Kennedy that he owed everything to Godwin, "from whose book, *Political Justice*, he had derived all that was valuable in knowledge and virtue."

In the autumn of the same year, Shelley, in company with Harriet, Eliza, and Peacock, made a tour through the Lake country to Scotland. Under Peacock's influence he plunged deep into classical literature. The chief literary product of the year was a dialogue entitled *A Refutation of Deism*, which exhibits a great advance both in style and thought upon his earlier prose writings.

The year 1814 brought matters between Shelley and his Harriet to a crisis. The divergence in views and practice between husband and wife had probably been gradually widening. From Peacock's account, we gather that the latter had begun to laugh at Shelley's enthusiasms and at some of his friends. Hogg says that after the birth of her child she relinquished reading aloud. "Neither did she read much to herself; her studies, which had been so constant and exemplary, dwindled away to nothing, and Bysshe had ceased to express any interest in them or to urge her, as of old, to devote herself to the cultivation of her mind. When I called upon her she proposed a walk, if the weather was fine, instead of the vigorous and continuous readings of previous years. The walk commonly conducted us to some fashionable bonnet shop." And then there was Miss Westbrook. Shelley writes to Hogg, under date of March 16, 1814: "Eliza is still with us — not here ! — but will be with me when the infinite malice of destiny forces me to depart [from the Boinville's, where he had been staying]. I am now little inclined to contest this point. I certainly hate her with all my heart and soul. It is a sight which awakens an inexpressible sensation of disgust and horror to see her caress my poor little Ianthe, in whom I may hereafter find the consolation of sympathy. I sometimes feel faint with the fatigue of checking the overflowings of my unbounded abhorrence for this miserable wretch." Whatever may have been the state of his feelings, he certainly appears, in the spring of 1814, to have had no idea of the step which he was to take in two or three months, — that of abandoning his marital relations with Harriet. This may be inferred, for example, from the fact that towards the end of March he, a second time, went through the ceremony of marriage with her. Professor Dowden suggests that the cause of this act may have been some doubts cast upon the validity of the Scotch rite in the course of negotiations with money-lenders in which he was at this time engaged. During the early part of the following summer Harriet was for a somewhat long period absent from her husband. The latter was, meanwhile, engaged in helping Godwin out of money difficulties, in which that sage was continually involved; and was in consequence repeatedly at Godwin's house. It was now that Mary Godwin first attracted his attention. She was in her seventeenth year, " with shapely golden head, a face very pale and pure, great forehead, earnest hazel eyes, and an expression at once of sensibility and firmness about her delicately curved lips." Her father

describes her at fifteen as " singularly bold, somewhat imperi-
ous, and active in mind ; her desire of knowledge is great
and her perseverance in everything she undertakes almost
invincible." Between Shelley and her, a friendship sprang
up, which quickly developed into mutual passion. Early in
June, Shelley and Hogg called at Godwin's house. Godwin
did not appear; but presently, Hogg narrates, "the door was
partially and softly opened. A thrilling voice called
'Shelley !' A thrilling voice answered 'Mary !' And he
darted out of the room like an arrow from the bow of the
far-shooting king. A very young female, fair and fair-
haired, pale indeed, and with a piercing look, wearing a
frock of tartan, an unusual dress in London at that time,
had called him out of the room. He was absent a very
short time, — a minute or two, — and then returned. . . . 'Who
was that, pray?' I asked ; 'a daughter?' 'Yes.' 'A
daughter of William Godwin ?' 'The daughter of William
and Mary.'[1] This was the first time that I beheld a very
distinguished lady, of whom I have much to say hereafter."
A month later, Harriet, who was still absent, became alarmed
at the cessation, during four days, of Shelley's letters. She
wrote to Hookham, the publisher, a friend of Shelley; he in
turn communicated with Shelley and Godwin, and the sus-
picions of the latter seem to have been aroused. In response
to a letter from Shelley, Harriet returned to London, July
14th. Shelley proposed a separation, and Harriet had a fit
of illness in consequence. About this time occurred an
interview between Shelley and Peacock, of which the latter

---

[1] That is, Mary Wollstonecraft, the writer, the vindicator of the
rights of women, and Godwin's first wife. The Godwin household
was curiously complicated; besides Mary, there were an elder daughter
of Mary Wollstonecraft, by an American named Imlay, commonly known
as Fanny Godwin; Jane Clairmont (usually called Claire) and her
brother Charles, children of the second Mrs. Godwin by a former marriage; as well as children of Godwin and his second wife.

gives the following account : " Nothing that I ever read in tale or history could present a more striking image of sudden, irresistible, uncontrollable passion than that under which I found him laboring when, at his request, I went up from the country to call upon him in London. Between his old feelings towards Harriet, from whom he was not then separated, and his new passion for Mary, he showed in his looks, in his gestures, in his speech, the state of mind 'suffering, like a little kingdom, the nature of an insurrection.' His eyes were bloodshot, his hair and dress disordered. He caught up a bottle of laudanum and said : 'I never part from this.' He added, 'I am always repeating to myself your lines from Sophocles :

> Man's happiest lot is not to be,
> And when we tread life's thorny steep,
> Most blest are they who, earliest free,
> Descend to death's eternal sleep.'

Again he said more calmly : ' Every one who knows me must know that the partner of my life should be one who can feel poetry and understand philosophy. Harriet is a noble animal, but she can do neither.' I said : ' It always appeared to me that you were very fond of Harriet.' Without affirming or denying this, he answered : ' But you did not know how I hated her sister.' " [1]

[1] Shelley subsequently believed that, before the separation, Harriet had been guilty of such heinous misconduct as would amply justify his abandonment of her, even in the judgment of those who hold most strongly the inviolability of the marriage bond. (See Dowden's *Life*, I, pp. 425-428.) Professor Dowden further maintains that Shelley believed this *at the time of his elopement*, and that it was a factor in his conduct towards his wife. Existing evidence on the point is not absolutely conclusive ; but, in the present writer's opinion, the evidence unmistakably points to the fact that no such idea with regard to Harriet was present in his mind when he deserted her. It was developed after the catastrophe, and was almost certainly not warranted by facts.

On July 28, unknown to Godwin and his wife, Shelley and Mary, accompanied by Jane Clairmont, set out for the Continent. According to Shelley's conviction, the obligations of marriage were no longer binding when love had ceased. Similar views he may have pointed out to Mary in the writings both of her father and of her mother. That Mary was, both by intellect and character, better suited to be Shelley's wife than was Harriet, cannot be doubted. Their union seems to have been very happy in its earlier years; and to the end genuine affection and esteem bound them together. But in course of time insufficiencies in Mary disclosed themselves to Shelley. Constancy in love, as his writings abundantly show, was no virtue in his eyes; from time to time, he thought he had discovered in the women he met incarnations of the feminine ideal; and Mary was not unnaturally jealous. *Epipsychidion* and other later poems, as well as Trelawny's *Records*, testify that he suffered under the sense of her imperfect sympathy. She was a woman of force and very considerable mental endowments, and had opinions of her own which did not always coincide with those of her husband. Among other things, she regarded the judgment of the world with more reverence than became the wife of the poet, and was anxious to mingle with it. "Poor Mary," said Shelley to Trelawny, "hers is a sad fate. She can't bear solitude, nor I society — the quick coupled with the dead."

After some stay in Paris the three travellers began, on foot, a tour through France to Switzerland. An account of it is given in *The History of a Six Weeks Tour*, published by Shelley in 1817. Before leaving England, he had made provision for the payment of an allowance to Harriet. The following letter, written by him soon after the beginning of the tour, reveals his extraordinary way of viewing the situation and his utter incapacity for comprehending the very different feelings of another in regard to the same facts:

Troyes, 120 miles from Paris, on the way to Switzerland,

August 13, 1814.

My DEAREST HARRIET,

I write to you from this detestable town. I write to show that I do not forget you ; I write to urge you to come to Switzerland, where you will at least find one firm and constant friend, to whom your interests will be always dear — by whom your feelings will never wilfully be injured. From none can you expect this but me — all else are either unfeeling or selfish, or have beloved friends of their own, as Mrs. Boinville, to whom their attention and affection is confined. . . . [Here follows a matter-of-fact account of the journey.] You shall know our adventures more detailed if I do not hear at Neufchatel that I am soon to have the pleasure of communicating with you in person, and of welcoming you to some sweet retreat I will procure for you among the mountains. I have written to Peacock to superintend your money affairs ; he is expensive, inconsiderate, and cold, but surely not utterly perfidious and unfriendly and unmindful of our kindness to him ; besides, interest will secure his attention to these things. I wish you to bring with you the two deeds which Tahourdin has to prepare for you, as also a copy of the settlement. Do not part with any of your money. But what shall be done about the books? You can consult on the spot. With love to my sweet little Ianthe,

Ever affectionately yours,

S.

The travellers did not remain in Switzerland, but sailed down the Rhine, and arrived in England on September 13th.

The remainder of the year 1814 was filled with embarrassments connected with money matters. Shelley had not only his own debts upon his shoulders, but also those of Godwin ; the latter, while refusing to pardon or have any direct intercourse with Shelley and Mary, condescended to receive pecuniary aid through lawyers. Shelley was in continual hiding from the bailiffs and separated from Mary ; hence much unhappiness and the pouring out of fervent love in multitudinous notes. He continued to maintain communications with

Harriet, who evidently hoped that the alienation was only temporary. In December she gave birth to a son. The death of Sir Bysshe Shelley in the beginning of 1815 made a great change for the better in the poet's pecuniary condition. It was Sir Bysshe's desire that the property should be entailed; but only £80,000 of the whole fortune of £200,000 was thus settled, and even this entail did not extend beyond Percy's life. Accordingly, at his father's death, Shelley would be complete master of this £80,000. To prevent this result, Sir Bysshe in his will made provision that Percy, should he consent to prolong this entail and also agree to the entail of the unsettled estates, was, upon the death of his father, to enjoy all the rentals and also the income from the large amount of personal property; on the other hand, should Percy not consent, then he was to receive nothing except that of which his grandfather could not deprive him, the reversion of the entailed estates. The poet was, in principle, opposed to entailing property, and had no desire for great wealth; what he did wish for, was an immediate competence which would leave him perfectly free. His father, Sir Timothy, was anxious that Percy's younger brother John should be the heir, and was willing to buy his elder son's interest in the reversion. The grandfather's will, however, put legal difficulties in the way of such an arrangement, and the negotiations dragged on interminably. It is sufficient to say that in June, 1815, Sir Timothy advanced money to pay his son's debts; and during the remainder of his life Percy received an income of £1,000 a year. He immediately sent Harriet £200 to discharge her debts, and gave directions that she should henceforth be paid £200 per annum. Mr. Westbrook allowed her a similar sum.

The excitement and anxiety of the year told unfavorably upon Shelley's health; in the spring an eminent physician pronounced him to be rapidly dying of consumption. The summer was spent in wanderings to and fro. In autumn Shelley and Mary took a furnished house at Bishopsgate, on the borders of Windsor Forest. It was here that Shelley wrote *Alastor*. Hitherto, though poetry had always engaged his attention, his main interests and work had rather been philosophical than poetical. Henceforward this relation is reversed, and he produces a continuous series of poems of a far higher character than anything he had previously written.

There was a disturbing factor in the even tenor of his life at Bishopsgate, — Godwin and Godwin's debts. One thousand pounds which Shelley had given him in the previous spring were already exhausted, and creditors still harassed the philosopher for money. Godwin, in turn, harassed Shelley, whilst denouncing him in bitter terms. The combination of meanness, arrogance, and self-righteousness which Godwin exhibits in his correspondence even now arouses the gall of the reader. Shelley's letters, on the other hand, are in the highest degree creditable to both head and heart. Their clearness and business-like character are utterly at variance with the usual conception of the poet; and they exhibit a self-contained patience and persistent effort to do the best for Godwin, combined with dignity and, at times, with pathos. On March 16 he writes :

In my judgment, neither I nor your daughter nor her offspring ought to receive the treatment which we encounter on every side. It has perpetually appeared to me to be your especial duty to see that, so far as mankind value your good opinion, we were justly dealt by, and that a young family, innocent and benevolent and united, should not be confounded with prostitutes and seducers. My astonishment, and, I will confess, when I have been treated with most harshness and cruelty by you, my indignation has been extreme, that, knowing as you do my nature, any consideration

should have prevailed on you to be thus harsh and cruel. I
lamented also over my ruined hopes of all that your genius once
taught me to expect from your virtue, when I found that for yourself, your family, and your creditors, you would submit to that
communication with me which you once rejected and abhorred,
and which no pity for my poverty and sufferings, assumed will-
ingly for you, could avail to extort. Do not talk of *forgiveness*
again to me, for my blood boils in my veins, and my gall rises
against all that bears the human form when I think of what I,
their benefactor and ardent lover, have endured of enmity and
contempt from you and from all mankind.

To this Godwin answered in his lofty and unrelenting vein,
and Shelley rejoined :

The hopes which I had conceived of receiving from you the
treatment and consideration which I esteem to be justly due to
me were destroyed by your letter dated the 5th. The feelings
occasioned by this discovery were so bitter and so excruciating
that I am resolved for the future to stifle all those expectations
which my sanguine temper too readily erects on the slightest re-
laxation of the contempt and the neglect in the midst of which I live.
I must appear the reverse of what I really am, haughty and hard,
if I am not to see myself and all that I love trampled upon and
outraged. Pardon me, I do entreat you, if, pursued by the conviction that where my true character is most entirely known I
there meet with the most systematic injustice, I have expressed
myself with violence. Overlook a fault caused by your own
equivocal politeness, and I will offend no more. We will confine
our communications to business.

In May, 1816, Shelley, accompanied by Mary and Miss
Clairmont, made a second journey to Switzerland, and
rented a cottage on the shore of the Lake of Geneva. In
the neighboring villa lived Byron, and the two households
were much together. Shelley had a profound admiration
for Byron's genius ; of his morals and principles he did not

approve. Together, he and Byron circumnavigated the lake.
In no amusement did Shelley take more delight than in
boating; water had a special fascination for him; in his
poetry he loves to follow the course of a river, and dwells
with peculiar fondness on scenery reflected in the water.
There was a kindred but more childish pursuit in which he
delighted to indulge. "He had a passion," says Peacock,
"for sailing paper boats. . . . The best spot he had ever
found for it was a large pool of transparent water on a
heath above Bracknell, with determined borders free from
weeds, which admitted launching the miniature craft on the
windward and running round to receive it on the leeward
side.   On the Serpentine he would sometimes launch a
boat constructed with more than usual care and freighted
with half-pence. He delighted to do this in presence of
boys, who would run round to meet it, and when it landed
in safety, and the boys scrambled for the prize, he had difficulty in restraining himself from shouting as loudly as they
did."

Enjoyable though Shelley's visit to Switzerland was, he
soon yearned for his native land.   "My present intention,"
he writes, "is to return to England and to make that most
excellent of nations my perpetual resting place." Accordingly, at the end of September, the Shelleys returned, and whilst
seeking for a suitable house took temporary lodgings at Bath.
It would appear that when they reached England, Harriet
was no longer at her father's house, and Shelley's efforts to
discover her were futile.   In the middle of December, he
suddenly learned that her body had been found in the
Serpentine.   There she had drowned herself a month
before. Whatever may have been the immediate causes of
this deed, it cannot be doubted that Shelley's desertion of
her was a remote antecedent.   And, though through life he
continued to believe that his action towards her was justi-

fiable, her suicide was at the time a terrible shock and continued to haunt him with horror.

Shelley's two children, Ianthe and Charles, were in the hands of their maternal grandfather and aunt, who refused to surrender them. The consequence was a suit in Chancery, which dragged itself out for many months, and caused Shelley wearing anxieties during its continuance, and bitter pain by its result. On the grounds that Shelley had published immoral views with regard to marriage in *Queen Mab*, and had to some extent carried them out in practice, the Lord Chancellor, Eldon, decided that the latter was not a proper person to have the control of his children. Accordingly, it was decreed that they should be educated under the supervision of the court and by persons of whom the court approved. Shelley was permitted to nominate these persons, subject to the Chancellor's approval; but was not allowed to see his children more than twelve times a year, and then only in presence of their guardians. He was, therefore, virtually to have no influence in their upbringing, and they were to be instructed in those orthodox views in religious and social matters of which he utterly disapproved. His indignation found vent in his poem *To the Lord Chancellor:*

> I curse thee by a parent's outraged love,
>   By hopes long cherished and too lately lost,
> By gentle feelings thou couldst never prove,
>   By griefs which thy stern nature never crossed;
>
>   .   .   .
>
> By those unpracticed accents of young speech,
>   Which he who is a father sought to frame
> To gentlest lore, such as the wisest teach —
>   *Thou* strike the lyre of mind! O grief and shame;
>
>   .   .   .   .   .   .

By the false cant which on their innocent lips
Must hang like poison on an opening bloom,
By the dark creeds which cover with eclipse
Their pathway from the cradle to the tomb.

Another result of Harriet's death was the marriage of Shelley and Mary, and, in consequence, reconciliation with Godwin.

During the early months of 1817 Shelley was detained in London by business connected with the suit; in March he took a house in Marlow on the Thames, some thirty miles from London, where he lived for a year. During this time he was visited by many of his friends, among them Leigh Hunt, who gives a description of his manner of life: "He was said to be keeping a seraglio at Marlow, and his friends partook of the scandal. This keeper of a seraglio, who, in fact, was extremely difficult to please in such matters, and who had no idea of love unconnected with sentiment, passed his days like a hermit. He rose early in the morning, walked and read before breakfast, took that meal sparingly, wrote and studied the greater part of the morning, walked and read again, dined on vegetables (for he took neither meat nor wine), conversed with his friends (to whom his house was ever open), again walked out, and usually furnished reading to his wife till ten o'clock, when he went to bed. This was his daily existence. His book was generally Plato or Homer or one of the Greek tragedies or the Bible, in which last he took a great, though peculiar, and often admiring, interest."

He was vexed as usual by the importunities of creditors; it was not mainly his own expenses that involved him with these. He was, indeed, a bad manager of money; his needs, however, were few; but he continually incurred obligations on behalf of his friends. His generosity brought endless claims upon him. Of his liberality to Godwin, we have already spoken; Hunt, too, was lavishly helped by Shelley,

and on Peacock, the poet conferred an annuity of £100 a
year.   Among the poor of Marlow he had numerous pen-
sioners, and he gave freely to chance applicants.   He
caught ophthalmia visiting the cottagers, and on one occasion came home barefoot, having given his boots to some
unfortunate.   His charity extended to the brute creation;
he is reported to have bought crayfish from peddlers that
he might return them to their native haunts.   He spent
much time boating on the Thames and walking in the fields
and woods.   "I have often met him," wrote a lady, "going
or coming from his island retreat near Medmenham
Abbey. . . .   He was the most interesting figure I ever
saw; his eyes were like a deer's, bright, but rather wild.
His white throat unfettered, his slender, but to me almost
faultless, shape, his brown long coat with curling lamb's wool
collar and cuffs — in fact, his whole appearance — are as fresh
in my recollection as an occurrence of yesterday. . . .   On
his return his steps were often hurried, and sometimes he
was rather fantastically arrayed: . . . on his head would be
a wreath of what in Marlow we call 'old man's beard' and
wild flowers intermixed; at these times he seemed quite
absorbed, and he dashed along regardless of all he met or
passed."

The time Shelley spent at Marlow was a period of great
literary activity.   His health was ailing, and he thought that
this was his last opportunity of instilling his peculiar views.
These views he embodied in the longest poem he ever wrote,
Laon and Cythna.   This work, completed in the autumn of
1817, failed to find a publisher, but several booksellers
undertook to sell it at Shelley's risk.   Only a few copies
had been issued when one of these booksellers, Ollier, noted
some passages certain to excite the abhorrence of most
readers, and likely to bring down legal penalties on those
engaged in circulating the book.   The issue was stopped;

Shelley, though most reluctantly, at length consented to certain alterations, which, in his opinion, spoiled the poem. These changes having been made, it appeared under a new title, *The Revolt of Islam*. " It is," says the author, " a tale illustrative of such a revolution as might be supposed to take place in a European nation acted upon by the opinions of what has been called (erroneously, as I think) the modern philosophy, and contending with ancient notions and the supposed advantage derived from them to those who support them." " This poem," he says in a letter to Godwin, " was produced by a series of thoughts which filled my mind with unbounded and sustained enthusiasm. I felt the precariousness of my life, and I resolved in this book to leave some records of myself. Much of what the volume contains was written with the same feeling — as real, though not so prophetic — as the communications of a dying man. I never presumed, indeed, to consider it anything approaching to faultless, but when I considered contemporary productions of the same apparent pretensions, I will own that I was filled with confidence. I felt that it was in many respects a genuine picture of my own mind. I felt that the sentiments were true, not assumed. And in this I have long believed that my power consists — in sympathy, and that part of the imagination which relates to sympathy and contemplation. I am formed, if for anything not in common with the herd of mankind, to apprehend minute and remote distinctions of feeling, whether relative to external nature or the living beings which surround us, and to communicate the conceptions which result from considering either the moral or material universe as a whole."

Two prose pamphlets referring to the state of the nation were produced during the year 1817. The earlier of the two proposed that the sense of the nation in regard to Parliamentary Reform (of which Shelley was an advocate) should

be ascertained by a plebiscite under the care of a voluntary association. Towards the expenses of such a plan
Shelley offered a subscription of £100. The moderation
and good sense of the pamphlets are remarkable when we
consider the ardor of Shelley's feelings. "Nothing," he
says, "can less consist with reason or afford smaller hopes
of any beneficial issue than the plan which should abolish
the regal or aristocratical branches of our constitution before
the public mind, through many gradations of improvement,
shall have arrived at the maturity which can disregard
these symbols of its childhood." Again : " Political institu-
tion is undoubtedly susceptible of such improvement as no
rational person can consider possible as long as the present
degraded condition to which the vital imperfections in the
existing system of government has reduced the vast multitude of men shall subsist. The securest method of arriving
at such beneficial innovations is to proceed gradually and
with caution."

For various reasons, Shelley had for some time been contemplating a visit to Italy ; thither he set out on March 11,
1818, accompanied by his family. There the remaining
years of his short life, the years of his best poetic work,
were spent. In Italy, as in England, he continually changed
his place of abode. At first, the Shelleys were drawn to
Leghorn by the presence of a Mrs. Gisborne. This lady
had been the friend both of Mary's father and of her mother.
She attracted Shelley by various qualities. " Mrs. Gisborne,"
he writes in 1819, "is a sufficiently amiable and very accomplished woman; she is δημοκρατικη and αθεη — how far she
may be φιλανθρωπη I don't know, for she is the antipodes
of enthusiasm. Her husband, a man with little thin lips,
receding forehead, and a prodigious nose, is an excessive
bore. His nose is something quite Slawkenbergian — it
weighs on the imagination to look at it. . . . It is a nose

once seen never to be forgotten, and which requires the utmost strength of Christian charity to forgive. I, you know, have a little turn-up nose ; Hogg has a large hook one ; but add them both together, square them, cube them, you will have but a faint idea of the nose to which I refer." The son of Mrs. Gisborne by a former marriage, Henry Reveley, was an engineer and inventor. Shelley became interested in the construction of a steamboat which Reveley was engaged in working out, and furnished some of the needful money.

In August he visited Byron at Venice. Byron offered him the use of his villa at Este. Shelley accepted, and was joined by Mary and her two children. But no sooner had the latter arrived in Venice than the infant daughter died ; hence sadness hung over them during their stay at Este, a sadness which is apparent in *Lines Written among the Euganean Hills.* The poet's creative activity, which had been dormant during the first months in Italy, revived. He wrote *Julian and Maddalo*, which contains idealized portraits of Byron and himself, a veiled account of some of his personal experiences, and reminiscences of Venetian scenes. Here, also, he began the *Prometheus Unbound*, and completed the first act.

Winter and spring were spent in southern Italy, in Naples, and in Rome. In the former city he suffered much from depression of spirits, partly the result of ill health and isolation ; partly, perhaps, arising from a connection with a certain mysterious lady which is vaguely hinted at but cannot now be elucidated.[1] In March he took up his residence in Rome. He read classical writers and diligently visited the galleries and antiquities. "You know not," he writes to Peacock, "how delicate the imagination becomes by dieting with antiquity day after day." Most of all he delighted in

[1] See note on *Stanzas Written in Dejection.*

those massive ruins where, in his day, art and nature were inextricably blended, — the Palatine, the Colosseum, and the Baths of Caracalla. In a letter to Peacock, he gives a description of the last mentioned, which is interesting as exhibiting points of resemblance with the imaginary scenery of some of his own poetry.

The next most considerable relic of antiquity, considered as a ruin, is the Thermæ of Caracalla. These consist of six enormous chambers above two hundred feet in height, and each enclosing a vast space like that of a field. There are, in addition, a number of towers and labyrinthine recesses, hidden and woven over by the wild growth of weeds and ivy. Never was any desolation more sublime and lovely. The perpendicular wall of ruin is cloven into steep ravines filled up with flowering shrubs, whose thick, twisted roots are knotted in the rifts of the stones. At every step the aerial pinnacles of shattered stone group into new combinations of effect, and tower above the lofty yet level walls as the distant mountains change their aspect to one travelling rapidly along the plain. . . . These walls surround green and level spaces of lawn, on which some elms have grown, and which are interspersed towards their skirts by masses of the fallen ruin overtwined with the broad leaves of the creeping weeds. The blue sky canopies it, and is as the everlasting roof of these enormous halls. But the most interesting effect remains. In one of the buttresses that supports an immense and lofty arch which " bridges the very winds of heaven " are the crumbling remains of an antique winding staircase, whose sides are open in many places to the precipice. This you ascend and arrive on the summit of these piles. There grow on every side thick entangled wildernesses of myrtle, and the myrletus, and bay, and the flowering laurustinus, whose white blossoms are just developed, the wild fig, and a thousand nameless plants sown by the wandering winds. These woods are intersected on every side by paths, like sheep tracks through the copse wood of steep mountains, which wind to every part of this immense labyrinth. From the midst rise those pinnacles and masses, themselves like immense mountains, which have been seen

from below. . . . Come to Rome. It is a scene by which expression is overpowered, which words cannot convey. Still farther,
winding up one-half of the shattered pyramids by the path through
the blooming copse-wood, you come to a little mossy lawn surrounded by wild shrubs; it is overgrown with anemones, wall-
flowers, and violets, whose stalks pierce the starry moss, and with
radiant blue flowers whose names I know not, and which scatter
through the air the divinest odour, which, as you recline under the
shade of the ruin, produces sensations of voluptuous faintness like
the combinations of sweet music. The paths still wind on, thread-
ing the perplexed windings, other lawns, and deep dells of wood
and lofty rocks and terrific chasms. When I tell you that these
ruins cover several acres, and that the paths above penetrate at
least half their extent, your imagination will fill up all that I am
unable to express of this astonishing scene.

Amidst such scenes the poet wandered while he composed
the second and third acts of the *Prometheus.* Nature and
art, however, were not enough. He felt keenly the contempt of the world for him as a man, its neglect of him as a
poet. " I am regarded by all who know or hear me, except,
I think, on the whole, five individuals, as a prodigy of crime
and pollution whose look even might infect. . . . Such is
the spirit of the English abroad as well as at home." In
June another sorrow befell Shelley and his wife, — their
remaining child died. Shelley wrote to Peacock : " Yesterday, after an illness of only a few days, my little William
died. There was no hope from the moment of the attack.
You will be kind enough to tell all my friends, so that I need
not write to them. It is a great exertion to me to write this,
and it seems to me as if, hunted by calamity as I have been,
that I should never recover my cheerfulness again."

The summer of 1819 was spent in Leghorn and its neighborhood. Its chief literary outcome was *The Cenci.* The
inspiration had come from the story and picture of Beatrice,
with both of which he had become acquainted at Rome. A

visit to Florence gave him an opportunity of enjoying the
splendid works of art gathered there. " All worldly thoughts
and cares," he wrote, "seem to vanish from before the sublime emotions such spectacles create ; and I am deeply
impressed with the great difference of happiness enjoyed by
those who live at a distance from these incarnations of all
that the finest minds have conceived of beauty, and those
who can resort to their company at pleasure. What should
we think if we were forbidden to read the great writers who
have left us their works ? And yet to be forbidden to live
at Florence or Rome is an evil of the same kind and hardly
of less magnitude." But his sympathies were not lacking
for more mundane matters ; he considered poetry, he said
about this time, very subordinate to moral and political
science. It was this summer that a great Reform meeting
at Manchester had been dispersed by military force at the
expense of several lives. The event led Shelley to write a
series of political poems, *The Masque of Anarchy*, *Song to
the Men of England*, etc. Whatever the bitterness of these
poems, their author was always opposed to violence. " The
true patriot," he writes, " will endeavor to enlighten and to
unite the nation and animate it with enthusiasm and confidence. . . . Lastly, if circumstances had collected a considerable number, as at Manchester on the memorable 16th
of August, if the tyrants send their troops to fire upon them
or cut them down unless they disperse, he will exhort them
peaceably to defy the danger, and to expect without resistance
the onset of the cavalry, and wait with folded arms the event
of the fire of the artillery, and receive with unshrinking
bosoms the bayonets of charging battalions. . . . And
this not because active resistance is not justifiable, but
because in this instance temperance and courage would produce greater advantages than the most decisive victory."

Shelley's works were almost unread in his own lifetime.

In so far as he was known to the public, he was known through second-hand reports of the immorality of *Queen Mab* and through the notoriety of the chancery suit. In this year, however, he was reviewed in two leading periodicals. The *Quarterly* attacked *The Revolt of Islam* and the personal character of its author. On the other hand, his work received the most appreciative notice which it ever received during the life of the poet, in three articles in *Blackwood* written by Professor Wilson ("Christopher North"). Another joyful event of the same year was the birth of a son, Percy.

During the last two years of Shelley's life (1820–1822) a circle of friends gathered about him. One of these was the Greek leader, Prince Mavrocordato, through whom the poet came into close relations with the revolutionary movement which was passing over Europe. To him was dedicated the lyrical drama *Hellas* (1821), based on the contemporary events of the Greek uprising, and framed after the model of the *Persæ* of Æschylus. Another person to join the circle was Medwin, Shelley's former schoolfellow and subsequent biographer. There were, besides, several Italians of whom he saw a good deal. Towards the close of 1821 he became acquainted with Emilia Viviani, a young Italian lady, whose unhappiness, beauty, and sensibility elevated her, for a short time, in the poet's estimation into an incarnation of womanly perfection. This experience he embodied in *Epipsychidion*. A friendship not less important for his poetic work, and more important in his personal life, was that formed with Mr. and Mrs. Edward Williams. The former was a year or two younger than Shelley, of a simple and bright disposition, with literary interests, gentle, generous, and fearless. He shared in Shelley's fondness for boating, and the two friends made many expeditions on the water together. Mrs. Williams, the Jane so often addressed in Shelley's later lyrics, was possessed of great grace and sweetness. She seemed to Shelley to realize the idea he had formed of the lady in *The Sensitive Plant.* She also played and sang charmingly. In the happiness of this wedded pair and their mutual sympathy, Shelley saw the realization of a paradise such as he had dreamed might be his own, but which he had never yet found.

In 1821 a bitter attack was made upon Shelley in *The London Literary Gazette,* on the occasion of the publication (notwithstanding Shelley's efforts to suppress it) of a pirated edition of *Queen Mab.* Shocking accusations, too, were circulated among personal friends in Italy by former household servants. Under all this Shelley suffered. A visit to Byron at Ravenna seemed to intensify this feeling of depression; for Shelley regarded Byron's genius as greatly superior to his own, and intercourse with Byron made him dissatisfied with his own work. Weighed down by these various influences, he writes from Ravenna to Mary: "My greatest content would be utterly to desert all human society. I would retire with you and our child to a solitary island in the sea and build a boat, and shut upon my retreat the flood-gates of the world. I would read no reviews and talk with no authors. If I dared trust my imagination, it would tell me that there are one or two chosen companions besides yourself whom I should desire. But to this I would not listen — where two or three are gathered together the devil is among them. And good, far more than evil impulses, love, far more than hatred, has been to me, except as you have been its object, the source of all sorts of mischief. So on this plan I would be *alone,* and would devote either to oblivion or to future generations the overflowings of a mind which, timely withdrawn from contagion, should be kept fit for no baser object."

The sadness of Shelley's last years is mirrored in his later poems, and his power of giving it expression is the unique distinction of his work. It was not merely that there was little of joy and much of positive evil in the life of the homeless wanderer; a nature so visionary, so ardent, so blind to practical considerations was inevitably doomed to disappointment. Even *his* hopeful and unpractical spirit must have often become conscious that the millennium whose speedy approach he had in his early days anticipated was far remote; sometimes the chilling thought may have come home to him that it could never be realized. In the narrower sphere of his own personal concerns his faith in human nature had received many a shock; the anticipations of youthful love and friendship had been repeatedly disappointed. Miss Hitchener, Harriet, Mary, Emilia, Hogg, Southey, Godwin, had all fallen short of the poet's ideal. His own life and work must have seemed a failure. Not merely had he been wholly unsuccessful in reforming the world — he had not even caught the public ear. His poetic gifts were almost unrecognized. He was a mark for scorn, and was avoided as a social leper. And so his sensitive nature gave utterance to that wonderful lyric note of loneliness, sadness, and yearning which pervades his work, and even to that strange cry for annihilation, for the dissolution of the finite in the infinite, which closes the *Adonais* and the last chorus of *Hellas*.

In the autumn of 1821 Byron moved to Pisa, where Shelley was residing. The two poets determined to establish a periodical for the dissemination of advanced views, to be named *The Liberal*, and to be edited by Leigh Hunt. The desire of assisting Hunt was Shelley's chief motive for embarking in the enterprise. The circle at Pisa was increased in the beginning of 1822 by the addition of Edward John Trelawny, whose *Records* give by far the most vivid and satisfying impression of Shelley in his last days. Trelawny became acquainted with the poet through the Williamses, and thus narrates his first meeting: "The Williamses received me in their earnest, cordial manner; we had a great deal to communicate to each other, and were in loud and animated conversation, when I was rather put out by observing in the passage near the open door, opposite to where I sat, a pair of glittering eyes steadily fixed on mine; it was too dark to make out whom they belonged to. With the acuteness of a woman, Mrs. Williams's eyes followed the direction of mine, and, going to the doorway, she laughingly said, 'Come in, Shelley; it's only our friend Tre just arrived.' Swiftly gliding in, blushing like a girl, a tall, thin stripling held out his hands; and, although I could hardly believe as I looked at his flushed, feminine, and artless face that it could be the Poet, I returned his warm pressure. After the ordinary greetings and courtesies he sat down and listened. I was silent from astonishment. Was it possible this mild-looking, beardless boy could be the veritable monster at war with all the world, excommunicated by the Fathers of the Church, deprived of his civil rights by the fiat of a grim Lord Chancellor, discarded by every member of his family, and denounced by the rival sages of our literature as the founder of a Satanic school? I could not believe it; it must be a hoax. . . . He was habited like a boy, in a black jacket and trousers which he seemed to have outgrown, or his tailor, as is the custom, had most shamefully stinted him in his 'sizings.' Mrs. Williams saw my embarrassment, and to relieve me asked Shelley what book he had in his hand. His face brightened and he answered briskly, 'Calderon's *Magico Prodigioso;* I am translating some passages in it.' 'Oh, read it to us!' Shoved off from the shore of commonplace incidents that could not interest him, and fairly launched on a theme that did, he instantly became oblivious of everything but the book in his hand. The masterly manner in which he analyzed the genius of the author, his lucid interpretation of the story, and the ease with which he translated into our language the most subtle and imaginative passages of the Spanish poet were marvellous, as was his command of the two languages. After this touch of his quality I no longer doubted his identity. A dead silence ensued. Looking up, I asked, 'Where is he?' Mrs. Williams said, 'Who? Shelley? oh, he comes and goes like a spirit, no one knows when or where.'"

Another anecdote of Trelawny's may be quoted: "I called on him one morning at ten; he was in his study with a German folio open, resting on the broad marble mantelpiece over an old-fashioned fireplace, and with a dictionary in his hand. He always read standing if possible. He had promised over night to go with me, but now begged me to let him off. I then rode to Leghorn, eleven or twelve miles distant, and passed the day there; on returning at six in the evening to dine with Mrs. Shelley and the Williamses as I had engaged to do, I went into the Poet's room and found him exactly in the position in which I had left him in the morning, but looking pale and exhausted. 'Well,' I said, 'have you found it?' Shutting the book and going to the window, he replied, 'No, I have lost it,' with a deep sigh: 'I have lost a day.' 'Cheer up, my lad, and come to dinner.' Putting his long fingers through his masses of wild, tangled hair, he answered faintly, 'You go; I have dined — late eating don't do for me.' 'What is this?' I asked as I was going out of the room, pointing to one of his bookshelves with a plate containing bread and cold meat upon it. 'That?' colouring, 'why, that must be my dinner. It's very foolish; I thought I had eaten it.'"

Again Trelawny writes: "Shelley's mental activity was infectious; he kept your brain in constant action. Its effect on his comrade was very striking. Williams gave up all his accustomed sports for books and the bettering of his mind."

"His mental faculties," Trelawny says in another place,
"completely mastered his material nature, and hence he
unhesitatingly acted up to his own theories if they only
demanded sacrifices on his part; it was where they implicated others that he forbore."

For the summer of 1822, the Shelleys and Williamses took
a house in common, close to the sea, in a cove of the Bay of
Spezzia.   Here the chief amusement was sailing, and the
two friends had a boat built, twenty-eight feet long and eight
feet broad, which they managed themselves with the assistance of a young lad.   The incessant boating improved
Shelley's health ; he was unusually well and happy.   Yet
on June 18 he wrote to Trelawny to procure him some
prussic acid.   "I need not tell you," he adds, "that I have
no intention of suicide at present ; but I confess it would be
a comfort to me to hold in my possession that golden key to
the chamber of perpetual rest."   On June 29 he wrote: "I
still inhabit this divine bay, reading Spanish dramas and
sailing and listening to the most enchanting music [Mrs. Williams's singing and playing].   If the past and future could
be obliterated, the present would content me so well that I
could say with Faust to the passing moment, 'Remain thou,
thou art so beautiful.'"

In order to welcome Leigh Hunt on his arrival in Italy to
take charge of *The Liberal,* Shelley and Williams sailed on
their own boat as far as Pisa.   Having seen Hunt, Byron,
and other friends, they left Pisa, July 8, on their return
voyage.   The weather was threatening.   Trelawny had intended to accompany them some distance in another boat ;
he was, however, detained, and watched them from his
anchorage ; but they were soon hidden by a rising mist ;
presently the storm burst.   Neither Shelley, Williams, nor
the sailor boy was ever seen alive again.   The bodies were
subsequently found.   On account of the quarantine laws

Shelley's body was burned on the shore, the ashes conveyed to Rome and buried in the beautiful Protestant cemetery described by himself in the closing stanzas of the *Adonais*.

II.

The sphere of poetry is wide; the particular province which any writer occupies is determined by his personal character, the circumstances of his life, and the tendencies of his time. Of the character of Shelley the foregoing pages are intended to give some impression. It was not a character of the normal type; Shelley did not act like other people, and he had a very inadequate idea of the relative strength of the various forces which influence the ordinary individual and have shaped the history of the race. Add to these peculiarities a nature of unusual intensity, swayed and mastered by its own emotion, and we can easily understand, not merely that his views were eccentric, but also that he was incapacitated for attaining to the point of view of others, for understanding persons unlike himself, and for seeing things as they really are. In actual life he constantly misrepresented and distorted what he saw; he was often incapable of discriminating between the facts and his emotional and imaginative additions to them; he condemned and eulogized extravagantly; and with regard to one and the same object would pass from one extreme to the other under the influence of feeling. From such a man we cannot expect poetry which will successfully represent the world as it is, which will bring before us the varied types of men and women so that they shall seem real to us, and so that we may involuntarily enter into their feelings. The real external world is feebly outlined, or becomes disproportioned, grotesque, gigantic in its passage through Shelley's mind. This is illustrated by his view of history as reflected,

for example, in *Queen Mab*. "He conceived it in a series of
visions — visions which were thrown before him, as it were,
by the phantasmagoria of his own imagination. Empires
rose and fell as if by the power of earthquakes, and anarchs
stalked huge across the scene, and priests were banded in
dark conclaves, and patriot martyrs endured the agony; and
then the series was exhausted and the same pictures were
shown over again."[1] In *The Revolt of Islam*, the poet passes
without notice and without sense of incongruity from the
world of reality to the world of pure fancy; and incidents
which are supposed to happen in nineteenth-century Europe
seem as incredible and remote as those out of which he constructed his boyish romances, *Zastrozzi* and *St. Irvyne*. *Rosalind and Helen*, professedly a story of contemporary domestic
life, though free from the extravagant incidents of *The Revolt
of Islam*, has as little power of holding the reader's interest,
because of the feebleness and ineffectiveness of plot and char-
acterization. The only apparent exception to Shelley's limitations as a portrayer of incident and character is *The Cenci*,—
unquestionably one of the most powerful dramatic works
produced in English since the close of the seventeenth
century. It is significant, however, that, although he here
treats a tradition concerning real men and women, it is a
story of unnatural and almost incredible horror, representing
human nature in abnormal conditions and events which
would not be out of place in the most extravagant romance.
The structure of the play is defective, close imitations of
Shakespeare are frequent, and the minor characters are
mere reproductions of regular dramatic types. The greatness of the play lies in its two leading personages, and these
are of a simplicity that approximates them to abstractions —
Cenci is the incarnation of evil, Beatrice of suffering innocence. We have, indeed, in *The Cenci*, a treatment of

[1] Dowden's *Life of Shelley*, I, p. 335.

Shelley's oft-repeated theme, — goodness, weak and persecuted, struggling with evil, strengthened by authority and
consecrated by custom. Beatrice is an impersonation of the
spirit of good as it has hitherto been imperfectly realized
among men — imperfectly, because it has not learned the
lesson taught in the *Prometheus*, that good, if it is to triumph,
must abjure hatred and violence. Beatrice's neglect of this
truth brings about the tragic catastrophe.

From the sphere, then, of the great objective poets like
Shakespeare — from the successful embodiment in his works
of the world outside of us, Shelley was excluded. It was
not in external but in internal experiences, — that life of his
own soul which he so intensely lived, — that Shelley found
the material for his best work. Notwithstanding his isolation, this inner life was not self-centered, as was, for example,
the inner life of Keats. The world as it affected him per-
sonally, his own joys and sorrows, did not make up the sum
of his existence. On the contrary, his keenest interest was
concerned with the well-being of society at large. "The
predominant impulse in Shelley," it has been said, "was a
passion for reforming mankind." A great part of his inner
life was made up of thoughts and feelings about his fellow-
men, — their past history, their present condition, their future
destiny. The constant friction between Shelley and his environment, his extreme sensitiveness, his peculiarly keen perception of the difference between desire and attainment, the
misfortunes of his own life, — all these led him to emphasize
the ills of the present state of things; whilst his inexperience and his ardent temperament made it natural that he
should anticipate the speedy realization of a millennium
whence evil and misery would be banished. This revolution would be accomplished if only men would lay to heart
and put in practice certain truths. Of these truths Shelley
considered himself to be in possession, and attempted to

disseminate them by his writings. Accordingly, one part of
Shelley's inner life and one part of his poetic work is concerned with the world at large — with social, political, and
religious matters, and with views as to the constitution of
the universe which are naturally connected with these.
Another part of his poetic work reflects the thoughts and
feelings which pertained to his own individual life.

To the first division belong some of Shelley's longest and
most ambitious efforts: *Queen Mab, The Revolt of Islam,
Prometheus Unbound.* In so far as these poems embody
the poet's ideas in concrete pictures of actual human life, we
have already characterized them as comparatively unsuccessful. But Shelley had a strong innate tendency to turn from
the concrete to the abstract, from men and things to man in
the abstract and generalizations about the universe. He
had, in short, as is shown by his favorite studies, the philosophic bent. He is early interested in Godwin, Locke,
Hume, Condorcet, Plato, and other theoretical writers. His
fondness for discussing abstract questions is emphasized by
Hogg, and is manifest in his correspondence. To history,
on the other hand, which deals with individual facts and
actual life, he entertained a strong repugnance. When he
attacked the Irish question he knew little of and cared little
for the special circumstances of the case. His argument
deals in broad generalities, and had no special cogency for
the Irish and the crisis then existing. This preference for
the general and abstract is unusual among poets; for poetry
is essentially concrete, as science is abstract and general.
It is a circumstance of capital import that Shelley was at
once a poet and a student of philosophical generalizations
rather than substantial facts, who thought much about man
in general, and understood but little of men as individuals.
So when Shelley takes the larger life of humanity as his
theme, he tends to turn from the direct picturing of that life

to the unfolding of theories and generalizations concerning it. Other poets have done the same thing, but philosophical poetry has been cold. It is Shelley's unique distinction that he is able to infuse intense emotion into such themes, and to clothe them with all that passion and beauty which usually gather about more tangible objects. The philosophical poet, in his anxiety to give a complete exposition of his views, becomes purely intellectual and prosaic. Whereas Shelley's emotional nature so far predominates, that he subordinates exposition to the expression of feeling ; and his poetry becomes a series of lyrical outbursts about abstract ideas which he only vaguely indicates. By far the best illustration of his philosophical poetry is the *Prometheus Unbound.* It is the most complete single embodiment of Shelley's views as to the constitution of the universe, the past history of mankind, the principles which should at present guide the wise and good, the future of the world if these principles are followed. The poem does not take the form of an exposition — a form so fatal to the poetic spirit ; nor, though a drama, does it attempt the delineation of human life, — an attempt which must, in the face of Shelley's limitations, have been unsatisfactory. The stage is occupied with personifications, and the great movements of human development presented through symbolic situations. These personifications win something of reality and life from Shelley's earnestness; and, in monologue and song, give utterance to the varying moods which agitate the poet's soul as he contemplates the condition and prospects of the race. If their significance is somewhat vague and the plot incoherent, this is the natural outcome of lack of clearness and connectedness in the poet's thinking.

The particular philosophic ideas imbedded in Shelley's poetry bear markedly the impress of his time. He grew to maturity while society about him was under the influence of a revulsion of feeling produced by the excesses of the French

Revolution and whilst the national energies were concen-
trated in resisting the aggressions of Napoleon. The intense
conservatism and the political narrowness of this era, the
repressive measures, the encroachments on individual liberty,
the wrongs perpetrated in political prosecutions under the
name of justice aroused, in turn, a desire for change and the
spirit of resistance in a growing minority. With this minority
Shelley was led to sympathize by the predominating characteristics of his intellect and temperament. He had a disposition to quarrel with authority, sufficiently evident in his
private life, a sensitiveness to evil which made him overlook
the good in existing institutions, a youthful inexperience and
impetuosity which undervalued slow developments, a tendency to depend upon abstract reasoning and individual
thinking rather than on the gradually evolved results of the
experience of the race. Every one of these peculiarities
made congenial to him the radical and doctrinaire philosophy which is associated with the French Revolution.
He became the disciple of Godwin and Condorcet; and,
although, in time, the imaginative and mystic elements in his
nature induced him to add to the teachings of such men,
doctrines borrowed from philosophers as unlike them as
Berkeley and Plato, certain fundamental principles of the
French school were retained by him throughout life and
continue to color his writings. These were especially such
as bore upon the political and social conditions of men, —
the belief in the natural goodness of human nature; the idea
that evil is the result of defective social, national, and
religious institutions; the dislike of accepted doctrines and
of established organizations; the love of liberty for its
own sake; unlimited confidence in democracy. For a more
minute statement of Shelley's views on these matters the
reader is referred to the *Prometheus* and to the notes on
that poem in this volume.

In his religious views and in his theories as to the ultimate nature of the universe, he was not, in his riper years at least, in such complete sympathy with eighteenth-century scepticism. It is true that at first — in the notes to *Queen Mab*, for instance — he adopted the tone and principles of this school, and regarded all religions, Christianity among them, as hateful systems of imposture. That Christianity had prescription of its side, and that, as practically realized in the community in which he lived, it was full of defects, — these were sufficient grounds to prejudice Shelley against it. Subsequently, however, Shelley abandoned the purely hostile attitude, and came to acknowledge the charm of the personality of Jesus as revealed in the gospels. In *Prometheus* and in *Hellas* he regards the founder of Christianity as a great ethical teacher and a martyr in the cause of good. In the more systematic treatment of the *Essay on Christianity* he contrasts what he conceives to have been the teachings and practice of Jesus himself with those of the Christian churches — much to the disadvantage of the latter. But the supernatural in Christianity he consistently rejected, and continued to regard religion, like government, as an evil influence among men. Shelley was, indeed, naturally nonreligious. The two fundamental religious emotions, the feeling of awe and reverence and the feeling of sin, he almost entirely lacked. There was no holy ground for him; the sacred and the awful served merely to titillate his inquisitive intellect, to excite it to the work of investigation and analysis. And so, too, acting, as he so uniformly did, on impulse, he knew little of the conflict between the natural man and the higher law, which begets in spirits such as Paul or Bunyan, the sense of personal unworthiness, the need of dependence on some higher power. Hence, Shelley easily adopted atheism in his college days; and later, when his nature mellowed, he never felt the need, in the emotional sphere, of an infinite being to love and reverence ; any more than in the intellectual sphere he perceived any necessity for some central, personal force to account for the phenomena of the universe.

The sense of personality was extraordinarily weak in Shelley. Mr. Bagehot says: "It is a received opinion in metaphysics that the idea of personality is identical with the idea of will. . . . If this theory be true — and doubtless it is an approximation to the truth — it is evident that a mind ordinarily moved by simple impulse will have little distinct consciousness of personality. While thrust forward by such impulse it is a mere instrument; outward things set it in motion; it goes where they bid ; it exerts no will upon them ; it is, to speak expressively, a mere conducting thing. When such a mind is free from such impulse there is even less will ; thoughts, feelings, ideas, emotions pass before it in a sort of dream ; for the time it is a mere perceiving thing. In neither case is there any trace of voluntary character." Accordingly, personality and will, and even mind, were rejected in Shelley's earlier philosophy, enunciated in the text and notes of *Queen Mab.* There he appears as a believer in crude materialism ; the world is the result of a fortuitous concourse of atoms. As he grew maturer this most unpoetical of philosophical systems was abandoned ; from a materialist he became a kind of idealist. He denied, following Hume, any essential difference between thoughts and things, and reduced them both to sensations. "Nothing exists but as it is perceived." He now admitted the existence of mind ; not, however, of individual minds, but of mind in general, of universal mind — whatever that may mean. The very vagueness and impalpableness of this philosophy commended it to his perception. In his *Essay on Life*, conjecturally dated 1815, he writes: "Let us recollect our sensations as children. . . . We less habitually distinguished all that we saw and felt, from ourselves. They seemed, as it were, to constitute one mass. There are some persons who, in this respect, are always children. Those who are subject to the state called reverie feel as if their nature were dissolved into the surrounding universe, or as if the surrounding universe were absorbed into their being. They are conscious of no distinction. And these are states which precede or accompany or follow an unusually intense and vivid apprehension of life. . . . The view of life presented by the most refined deductions of intellectual philosphy, is that of unity. Nothing exists but as it is perceived. The difference is merely nominal between those two classes of thought, which are vulgarly distinguished by the names of ideas and of external objects. Pursuing the same thread of reasoning, the existence of individual minds, similar to that which is employed in now questioning its own nature, is likewise found to be a delusion. The words *I, you, they* are not signs of any actual difference subsisting between the assemblage of thoughts thus indicated, but are merely marks employed to denote the different modifications of the one mind. Let it not be supposed that this doctrine conducts to the monstrous presumption that I, the person who now write and think, am that one mind. I am but a portion of it. The words *I, you,* and *they* are grammatical devices invented simply for arrangement, and totally devoid of the intense and exclusive sense usually attached to them. It is difficult to find terms adequate to express so subtle a conception as that to which the Intellectual Philosophy has conducted us. We are on that verge where words abandon us, and what wonder if we grow dizzy to look down the dark abyss of how little we know."[1]

"This doctrine was," says Mr. Bagehot, "a better description of his universe than of most people's; his mind was

[1] *Prose Works* (Forman's ed.), Vol. II, pp. 261, 262.

filled with a swarm of ideas, fancies, thoughts, streaming on
without his volition, without plan or order; he might be
pardoned for fancying that they were all; he could not see
the outward world for them, their giddy passage occupied
him till he forgot himself."

This doctrine he derived from the writings of Berkeley
and Hume, though he differs from each of these philosophers : from Berkeley in denying the existence of individual
minds, from Hume in admitting the existence of something
besides sensations, — universal mind.   Yet this mind is
neither personal, nor the ultimate cause of things.   It is not
a cause at all, for " it cannot create : it can only perceive."
And he adds, " It is extremely improbable that the cause of
mind, that is, of existence, is similar to mind." [1]

These ideas are mainly negative; but to them Shelley
added a positive conception derived from Plato, *viz. :* that
these sensations, with which alone we are acquainted in this
world, are imperfect shadows of a higher world into which,
perhaps, we may pass at death, where exist in perfection the
archetypes of all we dimly perceive here.[2]   He did not bring
this conception into logical connection with his other theories.   Logic had nothing to do with his acceptance of it.
He was brought to it by his persistent discontent with the
actual and by his yearning for ideals that would completely
satisfy the cravings of his nature.   " I seek in what I see,"
he said, " the manifestation of something beyond the present and tangible object."

One of these archetypes plays a very important rôle in
Shelley's poetry, — the archetype of beauty.   About this
conception some of those feelings cluster which, in the case
of the majority of men, connect themselves with the idea of
a personal god.   Upon this conception of an all-sufficing

---

[1] *On Life,* in *Prose Works,* Vol. II, p. 263.
[2] See the concluding stanzas of the *Adonais,* and notes thereon.

beauty which but faintly manifests itself in the various forms of beauty known in this world, the poet dwells with extraordinary fondness and enthusiasm in the *Hymn to Intellectual Beauty*, the *Prometheus*, and elsewhere ; and the intense passion which permeates the lines in which he speaks of it, is one of the most extraordinary of Shelley's peculiarities. Sometimes, in his impatient yearning for that perfect rapture which should gratify at once every complex need of his nature, he hoped to find, even in this world, the incarnation of this ideal in female form. The consequent experience, the inevitable disappointment is enshrined in *Alastor* and *Epipsychidion.* As the desire for the ideal, — in other words, beauty, — was his strongest motive, he sometimes conceives this beauty as the moving force of the universe, — the ultimate spirit which works toward good in the mind of man and in the external world. This is Shelley's nearest approach to the conception of the divine, and it receives its most adequate poetic expression in the *Adonais.* But, though there spoken of as a 'spirit,' it is a spirit without personal attributes, — a blind power which impels all that is highest and best in the world, something as vague and impersonal as the modern conception of *force*, one and indestructible, though manifesting itself in various forms and in countless phenomena.

Poetry whose substance consists of philosophical and abstract ideas labors under a twofold disadvantage. In the first place, such themes lack interest for ordinary readers and lend themselves but little to emotional treatment. In the second place, there is less of permanence in the results attained by the abstract reason than in the direct results of observation. The pictures of human life by a Homer or a Shakespeare are always fresh ; the theories of one generation of philosophic thinkers become inadequate and childish to another. Shelley was not even a profound philosophic thinker; his theories were at no time systematically wrought out; their inadequacy is unfavorable to the popularity and permanence of the writings in which they are embodied. To our generation, the absence of the conception of development is a prime defect. On the other hand, Shelley's work is interesting historically as the most adequate and beautiful expression, in English poetry, of certain tendencies in thought and feeling associated with the beginnings of the modern democratic period. And some of these tendencies are still potent forces, and seem likely to remain so. The enthusiasm for humanity, the feeling of the brotherhood of man, the sense of the responsibility of society at large and of each individual in it for the condition of its members, the belief in the capacity of woman for a wider and more public sphere of action,— these and kindred feelings find their first, and, as yet, their most beautiful poetic expression in the writings of Shelley.

Let us now turn to the second division of Shelley's poetry, — to that portion which reflects his more purely individual life and feelings. The matter is personal; the form usually, though not always, lyric. It is in his lyrics that Shelley is most successful, and among them are to be found the only poems which are in any degree popular. As a lyric poet, he is unsurpassed in a certain peculiar and limited sphere,—a sphere, too, somewhat outside of the experiences and understanding of the ordinary man.

In the beginnings of literary development, lyric poetry gives expression to universal and obvious emotions. The joys of victory, of love, of feasting, the sorrows of death and parting, — these are things which all men have felt, and which all can understand. But, in process of ages, as life grows more complex, and men more observant and self-conscious, less obvious shades of these joys and sorrows, subtle interminglings of them, new and unusual emotions

connected with higher intellectual experiences, are repro-
duced by the lyric poet. For the singing of many of the
substantial joys and sorrows of humanity, Shelley was not
specially qualified either by temperament or by experience.
His abnormal physical and mental constitution made him
much less fit for such a task than many of his predecessors.
On the other hand, the peculiarities and intensity of his
nature did furnish him with the experience which fitted him
to be the exponent of more subtle and impalpable states of
mind. More particularly, his feeble hold on reality, his discontent with existing things, the disposition to take refuge
from them in the realm of his own thoughts and fancies,
enabled him to write of the feelings connected with the ideal,
the remote, the impalpable. In the substantial present Shelley did not much delight; but the future, with its possibilities
and its promise of perfections not yet realized, and the past,
with that halo of imaginative beauty which does not belong
to it when in our grasp, but which it wins as it recedes, —
these were themes that suited his genius. We see this illustrated when he writes of love. "No one," says Mr. Stopford Brooke, "has expressed so well the hopes and fears
and fancies and dreams which the heart creates for its own
pleasure and sorrow when it plays with love which it realizes
within itself, but which it never means to realize without.
. . . But still more perfect, and perhaps more beautiful
than any other work of his, are the poems written in the
realm of ideal Regret. Whenever he came close to earthly
love, touched it, and then of his own will passed it by, it
became, as he looked back upon it, ideal, and a part of that
indefinite world he loved. The ineffable regret of having
lost that which one did not choose to take is most marvellously, most passionately expressed by Shelley." Here, as
elsewhere, he does not sing the joys of satisfaction, for he
was never satisfied, but the yearnings of desire. Again,

there are emotional sequences which are scarcely connected
with anything actual, or, at least, with anything definitely
realized,—such emotions as are expressed and aroused by
music. These are too vague to be called thought or to be
uttered as such, but Shelley is skilled in suggesting them in
an indirect way, through analogies, imagery, and the music
of verse. Again and again this power is illustrated in the
Prometheus. Even when the feelings which he voices are
based upon substantial experiences, Shelley is so wrapped
up in the emotion that he neglects altogether, or vaguely
indicates, the concrete causes. Hence such obscurity as we
find in *Julian and Maddalo*, where the facts which would
enable us to grasp the situation of the poor lunatic are
withheld. "Facts," says Shelley, "are not what we want
to know in poetry, in history, in the lives of individual men,
in satire, or in panegyric. They are the mere divisions, the
arbitrary points on which we hang, and to which we refer
those delicate and evanescent hues of mind which language
delights and instructs us in proportion as it expresses."
All this gives a vagueness to Shelley's poetry which almost
forbids analysis or reduction to a kernel of solid fact. The
hard-headed man who may be able to appreciate the good
sense and accurate observation enshrined in the plays of
Shakespeare, but who has little experience of or care for the
subtle feelings and vague aspirations belonging to imaginative and emotional natures, and on whom the purely technical
graces of verse have but little effect, turns aside from the
poetry of Shelley as meaningless rhetoric.

Shelley's love for the ideal and the vague influences his
treatment of material nature. Here, with a tendency analogous to that exhibited in his treatment of human life, he
turns from scenery of an ordinary character to the unusual,
gigantic, and mysterious,—huge cliffs, vast mountains, dark
woods and caves. Indeed, much of the scenery of his

poems is not, strictly speaking, *natural* scenery. It is scenery whose elements are, of course, taken from nature; but these are magnified and brought together in novel combinations, with the purpose, not so much of reproducing or suggesting nature as of reflecting or symbolizing the poet's feelings, or of forming a suitable background for them. Not that Shelley always does this; he can also bring before us vivid pictures of actual nature, — a gift which belonged to all the great poets of his time. But here he has his own special sphere. The aspects of nature which he excels in rendering are those, as Mr. Stopford Brooke has pointed out, of a vast, indefinite, or changeful character, — the scenery of the sky, of storm and cloud, of sunset and sunrise, or of wide landscapes like that "which the poet in *Alastor* looks upon from the edge of a mountain precipice." He delighted in scenery reflected in the water; the softened, impalpable, and suggestive character of the image, as compared with the scene of which it is the reflection, is analogous to the difference between the ideal and the actual.

In another and very different way, Shelley introduces nature in his poetry. There is a stage in the development of the race in which men commonly conceive all active things in the world as beings with a conscious life of their own. This is the mythopœic tendency which plays so important a part in early religion and fable. As men advance, the faculty for so conceiving things falls into abeyance. More profound and philosophic theories as to the forces which we see about us, displace this simple method of accounting for the universe. But in children the old tendency remains; we see it strikingly illustrated in the story of a poet's childhood, which Browning tells in *Sordello*. Shelley, who was childlike in so many respects, — in his impetuosity, simplicity, and ignorance of the world, — and who had no sense of the immanence of a personal force manifesting itself

in all the phenomena of the universe, possessed this mythopœic faculty to a degree unparalleled among later poets. Instead of using nature as a basis for meditation on human life
or as a medium to reflect his own moods, instead of seeing
in its phenomena, as does Wordsworth, the workings of one
divine being, Shelley is frequently content, for the nonce,
to look upon various objects in nature as independent
beings, each leading its own conscious life. He sympathizes with such an entity, and describes its imaginary experiences, as another poet might enter into and describe the
life of a fellow-man. He does this in *The Cloud*, in *Arethusa*, and repeatedly in the *Prometheus*, in the case of such
characters as "The Earth" and "The Moon." Perhaps
the most extreme case of the exercise of this faculty is that
afforded by *The Witch of Atlas*, where he describes, not the
personification of an abstract quality or of a natural object,
but a purely fanciful being. In this poem he finds pleasure
in his own creations without desire to bring them to bear
upon human life, or to give them anything which ordinary
men would call a meaning.

As the peculiarities of Shelley's mind and temperament
leave their impress upon the general character of the substance of his writings, so they determine the peculiarities of
his form and style. His defective grasp of the concrete and
real is unfavorable to the structure of his poems. His
stories lack narrative force ; his thought, consecutive development. This is one of the reasons why he is less successful in his longer and more ambitious works. Further,
the abstract ideas which he conveys in most of these longer
poems do not lend themselves to the concrete expression
which poetry demands. Accordingly, he almost necessarily
resorts to allegory and symbolism, as is illustrated by *Alastor*
and *Prometheus ;* and allegory and symbolism chill the normal
reader. In the men and women of *Romeo and Juliet* or of

Hamlet we are naturally interested ; they are creatures like ourselves. But it is only by an effort that we can over-come our initial distaste for the personified abstractions of the *Prometheus.*

` As to his expression in a narrower sense, — add to what we have already noted in Shelley's mental constitution, an extraordinarily lavish endowment of specifically poetic gifts, — skill in language, imagery, and versification, — we have the main factors in his style. We do not expect in him the qualities which arise from untiring self-criticism, from respect to the accepted canons of poetic art, such as we find in a workman like Tennyson. Shelley writes under the influence of the poetic afflatus. He is content if he gives expression to his feelings and ideas, without being careful to note occa-sional defects in logical structure, in grammatical concord, in congruity of images, in the regularity of his prosody. Here, as in more practical matters, he sometimes lacks self-restraint. He does not sufficiently condense; he is carried on by the flow of language and imagery until thought is obscured or lost in musical words. But amends are made for occasional faults of this character by a spontaneous felicity, an unsought and unconventional grace to which a more conscious and less ardent artist could not have attained. This happiness is perhaps most easily noted in versification. As the unimaginative spirit will fail to appreciate Shelley's poetry in general, so will the pedantic student of metre who depends upon his fingers and his rules, fail to appreciate the subtle and varied music of Shelley's lines.

As to this and other matters in regard to his style, we cannot do better than quote the words of Professor Baynes:[1] "This uncritical negligence, the want of minute accuracy in the details of his verse, seems to us intimately connected

---

[1] *Edinburgh Review,* April, 1871; quoted in Mr. Forman's Preface to his edition of Shelley.

with the whole character of Shelley's mind, and especially
with the lyrical sweep and intensity of his poetical genius.
He had an intellect of the rarest delicacy and analytical
strength, that intuitively perceived the most remote analogies and discriminated with spontaneous precision the finest
shades of sensibility, the subtilest differences of perception
and emotion. He possessed a swift, soaring, and prolific
imagination, that clothed every thought and feeling with imagery in the moment of its birth and instinctively read the spiritual meanings of material symbols. His fineness of sense was
so exquisite that eye and ear and touch became, as it were,
organs and inlets, not merely of sensitive apprehension, but
of intellectual beauty and ideal truth. Every nerve in his
slight but vigorous frame seemed to vibrate in unison with
the deeper life of nature in the world around him, and, like
the wandering harp, he was swept to music by every breath
of material beauty, every gust of poetic emotion. Above
all, he had a strength of intellectual passion and a depth of
ideal sympathy that in moments of excitement fused all the
powers of his mind into a continuous stream of creative
energy, and gave the stamp of something like inspiration to
all the higher productions of his muse. His very method
of composition reflects these characteristics of his mind.
He seems to have been urged by a sort of irresistible
impulse to write, and displayed a vehement and passionate
absorption in the work that recalls the old traditions of poetical frenzy and divine possession. His conceptions crowded
so thickly upon him, were embodied in such exquisite verbal
forms, and so enriched by illustrations flashed from remote
and multiplied centres of association that while the fever
lasted his whole nature was carried impetuously forward on
a full tide of mingled music and imagery. From this exuber-
ance of poetical power some of his critics have reproached
him with accumulating image upon image, without pausing

to select, discriminate, or contrast them. And it is no doubt true that there are passages in which metaphors and similes are heaped upon each other in almost dazzling profusion. But even in his most opulent and ornate descriptions there is hardly a trace of conscious labor or deliberate effort. . . . His finest passages have a witchery of aerial music, an exquisiteness of ideal beauty, and a white intensity of spiritual passion. . . . But the very qualities of mind and heart out of which these perfections spring carry with them the conditions of relative imperfections in the minor details of his work. The lyrical depth and impetuosity of feeling which carries Shelley on and gives such freedom and grace to the poetical movements of his kindled thought is unfavorable to perfect smoothness and accuracy in the mechanical details of his verse. He was often, in fact, too completely absorbed in the glorious substance of his poetry to give any minute attention to subordinate points of form. Thus, although from native fineness of ear his lines are never unrhythmical, the rhyme is often defective, and sometimes the metre as well. And, while his thought, even in its most subtle requirements, is always lucid, the expression, from haste or extreme condensation, is sometimes far from being clear."

SELECTED POEMS.

ALASTOR ;

OR,

THE SPIRIT OF SOLITUDE.

PREFACE.

THE poem entitled "ALASTOR" may be considered as allegorical of one of the most interesting situations of the human mind. It represents a youth of uncorrupted feelings and adventurous genius led forth by an imagination inflamed and purified through familiarity with all that is excellent and 5 majestic, to the contemplation of the universe. He drinks deep of the fountains of knowledge, and is still insatiate. The magnificence and beauty of the external world sinks profoundly into the frame of his conceptions, and affords to their modifications a variety not to be exhausted. So long 10 as it is possible for his desires to point towards objects thus infinite and unmeasured, he is joyous, and tranquil, and self-possessed. But the period arrives when these objects cease to suffice. His mind is at length suddenly awakened and thirsts for intercourse with an intelligence similar to itself. He images 15 to himself the Being whom he loves. Conversant with specu-lations of the sublimest and most perfect natures, the vision in which he embodies his own imaginations unites all of wonder-ful, or wise, or beautiful, which the poet, the philosopher, or the lover could depicture. The intellectual faculties, the 20

imagination, the functions of sense, have their respective
requisitions on the sympathy of corresponding powers in other
human beings. The Poet is represented as uniting these
requisitions, and attaching them to a single image. He seeks
5 in vain for a prototype of his conception. Blasted by his
disappointment, he descends to an untimely grave.

The picture is not barren of instruction to actual men.
The Poet's self-centred seclusion was avenged by the furies of
an irresistible passion pursuing him to speedy ruin. But that
10 Power which strikes the luminaries of the world with sudden
darkness and extinction, by awakening them to too exquisite a
perception of its influences, dooms to a slow and poisonous
decay those meaner spirits that dare to abjure its dominion.
Their destiny is more abject and inglorious as their delinquency
15 is more contemptible and pernicious. They who, deluded by
no generous error, instigated by no sacred thirst of doubtful
knowledge, duped by no illustrious superstition, loving nothing
on this earth, and cherishing no hopes beyond, yet keep aloof
from sympathies with their kind, rejoicing neither in human joy
20 nor mourning with human grief; these, and such as they, have
their apportioned curse. They languish, because none feel with
them their common nature. They are morally dead. They
are neither friends, nor lovers, nor fathers, nor citizens of the
world, nor benefactors of their country. Among those who
25 attempt to exist without human sympathy, the pure and tender-
hearted perish through the intensity and passion of their search
after its communities, when the vacancy of their spirit suddenly
makes itself felt. All else, selfish, blind, and torpid, are those
unforeseeing multitudes who constitute, together with their own,
30 the lasting misery and loneliness of the world. Those who love
not their fellow-beings, live unfruitful lives, and prepare for
their old age a miserable grave.

The good die first,
And those whose hearts are dry as summer dust,
35   Burn to the socket!

December 14, 1815.

ALASTOR;

OR,

THE SPIRIT OF SOLITUDE.

Nondum amabam, et amare amabam, quærebam quid amarem,
amans amare. — *Confess. St. August.*

EARTH, ocean, air, belovèd brotherhood!
If our great Mother has imbued my soul
With aught of natural piety to feel
Your love, and recompense the boon with mine;
If dewy morn, and odorous noon, and even,   5
With sunset and its gorgeous ministers,
And solemn midnight's tingling silentness;
If autumn's hollow sighs in the sere wood,
And winter robing with pure snow and crowns
Of starry ice the gray grass and bare boughs;   10
If spring's voluptuous pantings when she breathes
Her first sweet kisses, have been dear to me;
If no bright bird, insect, or gentle beast
I consciously have injured, but still loved
And cherished these my kindred; then forgive   15
This boast, belovèd brethren, and withdraw
No portion of your wonted favour now!

Mother of this unfathomable world!
Favour my solemn song, for I have loved
Thee ever, and thee only; I have watched   20
Thy shadow, and the darkness of thy steps,
And my heart ever gazes on the depth
Of thy deep mysteries. I have made my bed
In charnels and on coffins, where black death
Keeps record of the trophies won from thee,   25

Hoping to still these obstinate questionings
Of thee and thine, by forcing some lone ghost,
Thy messenger, to render up the tale
Of what we are.   In lone and silent hours,
When night makes a weird sound of its own stillness,   30
Like an inspired and desperate alchymist
Staking his very life on some dark hope,
Have I mixed awful talk and asking looks
With my most innocent love, until strange tears
Uniting with those breathless kisses, made   35
Such magic as compels the charmèd night
To render up thy charge: . . . and, though ne'er yet
Thou hast unveiled thy inmost sanctuary,
Enough from incommunicable dream,
And twilight phantasms, and deep noonday thought,   40
Has shone within me, that serenely now
And moveless, as a long-forgotten lyre
Suspended in the solitary dome
Of some mysterious and deserted fane,
I wait thy breath, Great Parent, that my strain   45
May modulate with murmurs of the air,
And motions of the forests and the sea,
And voice of living beings, and woven hymns
Of night and day, and the deep heart of man.

There was a Poet whose untimely tomb   50
No human hands with pious reverence reared,
But the charmed eddies of autumnal winds
Built o'er his mouldering bones a pyramid
Of mouldering leaves in the waste wilderness: —
A lovely youth, — no mourning maiden decked   55
With weeping flowers, or votive cypress wreath,
The lone couch of his everlasting sleep: —
Gentle, and brave, and generous, — no lorn bard

Breathed o'er his dark fate one melodious sigh:
He lived, he died, he sung, in solitude.   60
Strangers have wept to hear his passionate notes,
And virgins, as unknown he passed, have pined
And wasted for fond love of his wild eyes.
The fire of those soft orbs has ceased to burn,
And Silence, too enamoured of that voice,   65
Locks its mute music in her rugged cell.

   By solemn vision, and bright silver dream,
His infancy was nurtured.   Every sight
And sound from the vast earth and ambient air,
Sent to his heart its choicest impulses.   70
The fountains of divine philosophy
Fled not his thirsting lips, and all of great,
Or good, or lovely, which the sacred past
In truth or fable consecrates, he felt
And knew.   When early youth had passed, he left   75
His cold fireside and alienated home
To seek strange truths in undiscovered lands.
Many a wide waste and tangled wilderness
Has lured his fearless steps; and he has bought
With his sweet voice and eyes, from savage men,   80
His rest and food.   Nature's most secret steps
He like her shadow has pursued, where'er
The red volcano overcanopies
Its fields of snow and pinnacles of ice
With burning smoke, or where bitumen lakes   85
On black bare pointed islets ever beat
With sluggish surge, or where the secret caves
Rugged and dark, winding among the springs
Of fire and poison, inaccessible
To avarice or pride, their starry domes   90
Of diamond and of gold expand above

Numberless and immeasurable halls,
Frequent with crystal column, and clear shrines
Of pearl, and thrones radiant with chrysolite.
Nor had that scene of ampler majesty   95
Than gems or gold, the varying roof of heaven
And the green earth, lost in his heart its claims
To love and wonder; he would linger long
In lonesome vales, making the wild his home,
Until the doves and squirrels would partake   100
From his innocuous hand his bloodless food,
Lured by the gentle meaning of his looks,
And the wild antelope, that starts whene'er
The dry leaf rustles in the brake, suspend
Her timid steps to gaze upon a form   105
More graceful than her own.
                    His wandering step,
Obedient to high thoughts, has visited
The awful ruins of the days of old :
Athens, and Tyre, and Balbec, and the waste
Where stood Jerusalem, the fallen towers   110
Of Babylon, the eternal pyramids,
Memphis and Thebes, and whatsoe'er of strange
Sculptured on alabaster obelisk,
Or jasper tomb, or mutilated sphynx,
Dark Æthiopia in her desert hills   115
Conceals.   Among the ruined temples there,
Stupendous columns, and wild images
Of more than man, where marble dæmons watch
The Zodiac's brazen mystery, and dead men
Hang their mute thoughts on the mute walls around,   120
He lingered, poring on memorials
Of the world's youth, through the long burning day
Gazed on those speechless shapes, nor, when the moon
Filled the mysterious halls with floating shades,

Suspended he that task, but ever gazed   125
And gazed, till meaning on his vacant mind
Flashed like strong inspiration, and he saw
The thrilling secrets of the birth of time.

Meanwhile an Arab maiden brought his food,
Her daily portion, from her father's tent,   130
And spread her matting for his couch, and stole
From duties and repose to tend his steps: —
Enamoured, yet not daring for deep awe
To speak her love: — and watched his nightly sleep,
Sleepless herself, to gaze upon his lips   135
Parted in slumber, whence the regular breath
Of innocent dreams arose: then, when red morn
Made paler the pale moon, to her cold home
Wildered, and wan, and panting, she returned.

The Poet wandering on, through Arabie   140
And Persia, and the wild Carmanian waste,
And o'er the aërial mountains which pour down
Indus and Oxus from their icy caves,
In joy and exultation held his way;
Till in the vale of Cashmire, far within   145
Its loneliest dell, where odorous plants entwine
Beneath the hollow rocks a natural bower,
Beside a sparkling rivulet he stretched
His languid limbs. A vision on his sleep
There came, a dream of hopes that never yet   150
Had flushed his cheek. He dreamed a veilèd maid
Sate near him, talking in low solemn tones.
Her voice was like the voice of his own soul
Heard in the calm of thought; its music long,
Like woven sounds of streams and breezes, held   155
His inmost sense suspended in its web
Of many-coloured woof and shifting hues.

Knowledge and truth and virtue were her theme,
And lofty hopes of divine liberty,
Thoughts the most dear to him, and poesy,   160
Herself a poet.   Soon the solemn mood
Of her pure mind kindled through all her frame
A permeating fire : wild numbers then
She raised, with voice stifled in tremulous sobs
Subdued by its own pathos : her fair hands   165
Were bare alone, sweeping from some strange harp
Strange symphony, and in their branching veins
The eloquent blood told an ineffable tale.
The beating of her heart was heard to fill
The pauses of her music, and her breath   170
Tumultuously accorded with those fits
Of intermitted song.   Sudden she rose,
As if her heart impatiently endured
Its bursting burthen : at the sound he turned,
And saw by the warm light of their own life   175
Her glowing limbs beneath the sinuous veil
Of woven wind, her outspread arms now bare,
Her dark locks floating in the breath of night,
Her beamy bending eyes, her parted lips
Outstretched, and pale, and quivering eagerly.   180
His strong heart sunk and sickened with excess
Of love.   He reared his shuddering limbs and quelled
His gasping breath, and spread his arms to meet
Her panting bosom : . . . she drew back a while,
Then, yielding to the irresistible joy,   185
With frantic gesture and short breathless cry
Folded his frame in her dissolving arms.
Now blackness veiled his dizzy eyes, and night
Involved and swallowed up the vision ; sleep,
Like a dark flood suspended in its course,   190
Rolled back its impulse on his vacant brain.

Roused by the shock he started from his trance —
The cold white light of morning, the blue moon
Low in the west, the clear and garish hills,
The distinct valley and the vacant woods, 195
Spread round him where he stood. Whither have fled
The hues of heaven that canopied his bower
Of yesternight? The sounds that soothed his sleep,
The mystery and the majesty of Earth,
The joy, the exultation? His wan eyes 200
Gaze on the empty scene as vacantly
As ocean's moon looks on the moon in heaven.
The spirit of sweet human love has sent
A vision to the sleep of him who spurned
Her choicest gifts. He eagerly pursues 205
Beyond the realms of dream that fleeting shade ;
He overleaps the bounds. Alas! alas!
Were limbs, and breath, and being intertwined
Thus treacherously? Lost, lost, for ever lost,
In the wide pathless desert of dim sleep, 210
That beautiful shape! Does the dark gate of death
Conduct to thy mysterious paradise,
O Sleep? Does the bright arch of rainbow clouds,
And pendent mountains seen in the calm lake,
Lead only to a black and watery depth, 215
While death's blue vault, with loathliest vapours hung,
Where every shade which the foul grave exhales
Hides its dead eye from the detested day,
Conduct, O Sleep, to thy delightful realms?
This doubt with sudden tide flowed on his heart, 220
The insatiate hope which it awakened stung
His brain even like despair.
                  While day-light held
The sky, the Poet kept mute conference
With his still soul. At night the passion came,

Like the fierce fiend of a distempered dream,   225
And shook him from his rest, and led him forth
Into the darkness. — As an eagle grasped
In folds of the green serpent, feels her breast
Burn with the poison, and precipitates
Through night and day, tempest, and calm, and cloud,   230
Frantic with dizzying anguish, her blind flight
O'er the wide aëry wilderness: thus driven
By the bright shadow of that lovely dream,
Beneath the cold glare of the desolate night,
Through tangled swamps and deep precipitous dells,   235
Startling with careless step the moon-light snake,
He fled.   Red morning dawned upon his flight,
Shedding the mockery of its vital hues
Upon his cheek of death.   He wandered on
Till vast Aornos seen from Petra's steep   240
Hung o'er the low horizon like a cloud;
Through Balk, and where the desolated tombs
Of Parthian kings scatter to every wind
Their wasting dust, wildly he wandered on,
Day after day, a weary waste of hours,   245
Bearing within his life the brooding care
That ever fed on its decaying flame.
And now his limbs were lean; his scattered hair
Sered by the autumn of strange suffering
Sung dirges in the wind; his listless hand   250
Hung like dead bone within its withered skin;
Life, and the lustre that consumed it, shone
As in a furnace burning secretly
From his dark eyes alone.   The cottagers,
Who ministered with human charity   255
His human wants, beheld with wondering awe
Their fleeting visitant.   The mountaineer,
Encountering on some dizzy precipice

That spectral form, deemed that the Spirit of wind
With lightning eyes, and eager breath, and feet   260
Disturbing not the drifted snow, had paused
In its career: the infant would conceal
His troubled visage in his mother's robe
In terror at the glare of those wild eyes,
To remember their strange light in many a dream   265
Of after-times; but youthful maidens, taught
By nature, would interpret half the woe
That wasted him, would call him with false names
Brother, and friend, would press his pallid hand
At parting, and watch, dim through tears, the path   270
Of his departure from their father's door.

    At length upon the lone Chorasmian shore
He paused, a wide and melancholy waste
Of putrid marshes. A strong impulse urged
His steps to the sea-shore. A swan was there,   275
Beside a sluggish stream among the reeds.
It rose as he approached, and with strong wings
Scaling the upward sky, bent its bright course
High over the immeasurable main.
His eyes pursued its flight. — "Thou hast a home,   280
Beautiful bird; thou voyagest to thine home,
Where thy sweet mate will twine her downy neck
With thine, and welcome thy return with eyes
Bright in the lustre of their own fond joy.
And what am I that I should linger here,   285
With voice far sweeter than thy dying notes,
Spirit more vast than thine, frame more attuned
To beauty, wasting these surpassing powers
In the deaf air, to the blind earth, and heaven
That echoes not my thoughts?" A gloomy smile   290
Of desperate hope wrinkled his quivering lips.

For sleep, he knew, kept most relentlessly
Its precious charge, and silent death exposed,
Faithless perhaps as sleep, a shadowy lure,
With doubtful smile mocking its own strange charms.   295

    Startled by his own thoughts he looked around.
There was no fair fiend near him, not a sight
Or sound of awe but in his own deep mind.
A little shallop floating near the shore
Caught the impatient wandering of his gaze.   300
It had been long abandoned, for its sides
Gaped wide with many a rift, and its frail joints
Swayed with the undulations of the tide.
A restless impulse urged him to embark
And meet lone Death on the drear ocean's waste;   305
For well he knew that mighty Shadow loves
The slimy caverns of the populous deep.

    The day was fair and sunny, sea and sky
Drank its inspiring radiance, and the wind
Swept strongly from the shore, blackening the waves.   310
Following his eager soul, the wanderer
Leaped in the boat, he spread his cloak aloft
On the bare mast, and took his lonely seat,
And felt the boat speed o'er the tranquil sea
Like a torn cloud before the hurricane.   315

    As one that in a silver vision floats
Obedient to the sweep of odorous winds
Upon resplendent clouds, so rapidly
Along the dark and ruffled waters fled
The straining boat. — A whirlwind swept it on,   320
With fierce gusts and precipitating force,
Through the white ridges of the chafèd sea.
The waves arose.   Higher and higher still

Their fierce necks writhed beneath the tempest's scourge
Like serpents struggling in a vulture's grasp.   325
Calm and rejoicing in the fearful war
Of wave ruining on wave, and blast on blast
Descending, and black flood on whirlpool driven
With dark obliterating course, he sate:
As if their genii were the ministers   330
Appointed to conduct him to the light
Of those belovèd eyes, the Poet sate
Holding the steady helm.   Evening came on,
The beams of sunset hung their rainbow hues
High 'mid the shifting domes of sheeted spray   335
That canopied his path o'er the waste deep;
Twilight, ascending slowly from the east,
Entwined in duskier wreaths her braided locks
O'er the fair front and radiant eyes of day;
Night followed, clad with stars.   On every side   340
More horribly the multitudinous streams
Of ocean's mountainous waste to mutual war
Rushed in dark tumult thundering, as to mock
The calm and spangled sky.   The little boat
Still fled before the storm; still fled, like foam   345
Down the steep cataract of a wintry river;
Now pausing on the edge of the riven wave;
Now leaving far behind the bursting mass
That fell, convulsing ocean.   Safely fled —
As if that frail and wasted human form,   350
Had been an elemental god.
                          At midnight
The moon arose: and lo! the ætherial cliffs
Of Caucasus, whose icy summits shone
Among the stars like sunlight, and around
Whose caverned base the whirlpools and the waves   355
Bursting and eddying irresistibly

Rage and resound for ever.— Who shall save?—
The boat fled on, — the boiling torrent drove,—
The crags closed round with black and jaggèd arms,
The shattered mountain overhung the sea,   360
And faster still, beyond all human speed,
Suspended on the sweep of the smooth wave,
The little boat was driven. A cavern there
Yawned, and amid its slant and winding depths
Ingulphed the rushing sea. The boat fled on   365
With unrelaxing speed.—"Vision and Love!"
The Poet cried aloud, "I have beheld
The path of thy departure. Sleep and death
Shall not divide us long!"
                 The boat pursued
The windings of the cavern. Day-light shone   370
At length upon that gloomy river's flow;
Now, where the fiercest war among the waves
Is calm, on the unfathomable stream
The boat moved slowly. Where the mountain, riven,
Exposed those black depths to the azure sky,   375
Ere yet the flood's enormous volume fell
Even to the base of Caucasus, with sound
That shook the everlasting rocks, the mass
Filled with one whirlpool all that ample chasm;
Stair above stair the eddying waters rose   380
Circling immeasurably fast, and laved
With alternating dash the knarlèd roots
Of mighty trees, that stretched their giant arms
In darkness over it. I' the midst was left,
Reflecting, yet distorting every cloud,   385
A pool of treacherous and tremendous calm.
Seized by the sway of the ascending stream,
With dizzy swiftness, round, and round, and round,
Ridge after ridge the straining boat arose,

Till on the verge of the extremest curve,   390
Where through an opening of the rocky bank,
The waters overflow, and a smooth spot
Of glassy quiet 'mid those battling tides
Is left, the boat paused shuddering. — Shall it sink
Down the abyss? Shall the reverting stress   395
Of that resistless gulph embosom it?
Now shall it fall? — A wandering stream of wind,
Breathed from the west, has caught the expanded sail
And, lo! with gentle motion, between banks
Of mossy slope, and on a placid stream,   400
Beneath a woven grove it sails, and, hark!
The ghastly torrent mingles its far roar,
With the breeze murmuring in the musical woods.
Where the embowering trees recede, and leave
A little space of green expanse, the cove   405
Is closed by meeting banks, whose yellow flowers
For ever gaze on their own drooping eyes,
Reflected in the crystal calm. The wave
Of the boat's motion marred their pensive task,
Which nought but vagrant bird, or wanton wind,   410
Or falling spear-grass, or their own decay
Had e'er disturbed before. The Poet longed
To deck with their bright hues his withered hair,
But on his heart its solitude returned,
And he forbore. Not the strong impulse hid   415
In those flushed cheeks, bent eyes, and shadowy frame
Had yet performed its ministry: it hung
Upon his life, as lightning in a cloud
Gleams, hovering ere it vanish, ere the floods
Of night close over it.
                        The noonday sun   420
Now shone upon the forest, one vast mass
Of mingling shade, whose brown magnificence

A narrow vale embosoms.   There, huge caves,
Scooped in the dark base of their aëry rocks
Mocking its moans, respond and roar for ever.   425
The meeting boughs and implicated leaves
Wove twilight o'er the Poet's path, as led
By love, or dream, or god, or mightier Death,
He sought in Nature's dearest haunt, some bank,
Her cradle, and his sepulchre.   More dark   430
And dark the shades accumulate.   The oak,   .
Expanding its immense and knotty arms,
Embraces the light beech.   The pyramids
Of the tall cedar overarching, frame
Most solemn domes within, and far below,   435
Like clouds suspended in an emerald sky,
The ash and the acacia floating hang
Tremulous and pale.   Like restless serpents, clothed
In rainbow and in fire, the parasites,
Starred with ten thousand blossoms, flow around   440
The gray trunks, and, as gamesome infants' eyes,
With gentle meanings, and most innocent wiles,
Fold their beams round the hearts of those that love,
These twine their tendrils with the wedded boughs
Uniting their close union; the woven leaves   445
Make net-work of the dark blue light of day,
And the night's noontide clearness, mutable
As shapes in the weird clouds.   Soft mossy lawns
Beneath these canopies extend their swells,
Fragrant with perfumed herbs, and eyed with blooms   450
Minute yet beautiful.   One darkest glen
Sends from its woods of musk-rose, twined with jasmine,
A soul-dissolving odour, to invite
To some more lovely mystery.   Through the dell,
Silence and Twilight here, twin-sisters, keep   455
Their noonday watch, and sail among the shades,

Like vaporous shapes half seen; beyond, a well,
Dark, gleaming, and of most translucent wave,
Images all the woven boughs above,
And each depending leaf, and every speck   460
Of azure sky, darting between their chasms;
Nor aught else in the liquid mirror laves
Its portraiture, but some inconstant star
Between one foliaged lattice twinkling fair,
Or, painted bird, sleeping beneath the moon,   465
Or gorgeous insect floating motionless,
Unconscious of the day, ere yet his wings,
Have spread their glories to the gaze of noon.

   Hither the Poet came.   His eyes beheld
Their own wan light through the reflected lines   470
Of his thin hair, distinct in the dark depth
Of that still fountain ; as the human heart,
Gazing in dreams over the gloomy grave,
Sees its own treacherous likeness there.   He heard
The motion of the leaves, the grass that sprung   475
Startled and glanced and trembled even to feel
An unaccustomed presence, and the sound
Of the sweet brook that from the secret springs
Of that dark fountain rose.   A Spirit seemed
To stand beside him — clothed in no bright robes   480
Of shadowy silver or enshrining light,
Borrowed from aught the visible world affords
Of grace, or majesty, or mystery; —
But, undulating woods, and silent well,
And leaping rivulet, and evening gloom   485
Now deepening the dark shades, for speech assuming,
Held commune with him, as if he and it
Were all that was, — only . . . when his regard
Was raised by intense pensiveness, . . . two eyes,

Two starry eyes, hung in the gloom of thought,   490
And seemed with their serene and azure smiles
To beckon him.
              Obedient to the light
That shone within his soul, he went, pursuing
The windings of the dell. — The rivulet
Wanton and wild, through many a green ravine   495
Beneath the forest flowed.   Sometimes it fell
Among the moss with hollow harmony
Dark and profound.   Now on the polished stones
It danced; like childhood laughing as it went:
Then, through the plain in tranquil wanderings crept,   500
Reflecting every herb and drooping bud
That overhung its quietness. — "O stream!
Whose source is inaccessibly profound,
Whither do thy mysterious waters tend?
Thou imagest my life.   Thy darksome stillness,   505
Thy dazzling waves, thy loud and hollow gulphs,
Thy searchless fountain, and invisible course
Have each their type in me: and the wide sky,
And measureless ocean may declare as soon
What oozy cavern or what wandering cloud   510
Contains thy waters, as the universe
Tell where these living thoughts reside, when stretched
Upon thy flowers my bloodless limbs shall waste
I' the passing wind!"
              Beside the grassy shore
Of the small stream he went; he did impress   515
On the green moss his tremulous step, that caught
Strong shuddering from his burning limbs.   As one
Roused by some joyous madness from the couch
Of fever, he did move; yet, not like him,
Forgetful of the grave, where, when the flame   520
Of his frail exultation shall be spent,

He must descend. With rapid steps he went
Beneath the shade of trees, beside the flow
Of the wild babbling rivulet; and now
The forest's solemn canopies were changed   525
For the uniform and lightsome evening sky.
Gray rocks did peep from the spare moss, and stemmed
The struggling brook: tall spires of windlestrae
Threw their thin shadows down the rugged slope,
And naught but knarled roots of ancient pines,   530
Branchless and blasted, clenched with grasping roots
The unwilling soil. A gradual change was here,
Yet ghastly. For, as fast years flow away,
The smooth brow gathers, and the hair grows thin
And white, and where irradiate dewy eyes   535
Had shone, gleam stony orbs: — so from his steps
Bright flowers departed, and the beautiful shade
Of the green groves, with all their odorous winds
And musical motions. Calm, he still pursued
The stream, that with a larger volume now   540
Rolled through the labyrinthine dell; and there
Fretted a path through its descending curves
With its wintry speed. On every side now rose
Rocks, which, in unimaginable forms,
Lifted their black and barren pinnacles   545
In the light of evening, and its precipice
Obscuring the ravine, disclosed above,
'Mid toppling stones, black gulphs and yawning caves,
Whose windings gave ten thousand various tongues
To the loud stream. Lo! where the pass expands   550
Its stony jaws, the abrupt mountain breaks,
And seems, with its accumulated crags,
To overhang the world: for wide expand
Beneath the wan stars and descending moon
Islanded seas, blue mountains, mighty streams,   555

Dim tracts and vast, robed in the lustrous gloom
Of leaden-coloured even, and fiery hills
Mingling their flames with twilight, on the verge
Of the remote horizon.   The near scene,
In naked and severe simplicity,   560
Made contrast with the universe.   A pine,
Rock-rooted, stretched athwart the vacancy
Its swinging boughs, to each inconstant blast
Yielding one only response, at each pause
In most familiar cadence, with the howl,   565
The thunder and the hiss of homeless streams
Mingling its solemn song, whilst the broad river,
Foaming and hurrying o'er its rugged path,
Fell into that immeasurable void
Scattering its waters to the passing winds.   570

　　Yet the gray precipice and solemn pine,
And torrent, were not all; — one silent nook
Was there.   Even on the edge of that vast mountain,
Upheld by knotty roots and fallen rocks,
It overlooked in its serenity   575
The dark earth, and the bending vault of stars.
It was a tranquil spot, that seemed to smile
Even in the lap of horror.   Ivy clasped
The fissured stones with its entwining arms,
And did embower with leaves for ever green,   580
And berries dark, the smooth and even space
Of its inviolated floor, and here　.
The children of the autumnal whirlwind bore,
In wanton sport, those bright leaves, whose decay,
Red, yellow, or ætherially pale,   585
Rivals the pride of summer.   'T is the haunt
Of every gentle wind, whose breath can teach
The wilds to love tranquillity.   One step,

One human step alone, has ever broken
The stillness of its solitude : — one voice   590
Alone inspired its echoes ; — even that voice
Which hither came, floating among the winds,
And led the loveliest among human forms
To make their wild haunts the depository
Of all the grace and beauty that endued   595
Its motions, render up its majesty,
Scatter its music on the unfeeling storm,   .
And to the damp leaves and blue cavern mould,
Nurses of rainbow flowers and branching moss,
Commit the colours of that varying cheek,   600
That snowy breast, those dark and drooping eyes.

   The dim and hornèd moon hung low, and poured
A sea of lustre on the horizon's verge
That overflowed its mountains. Yellow mist
Filled the unbounded atmosphere, and drank   605
Wan moonlight even to fulness: not a star
Shone, not a sound was heard; the very winds,
Danger's grim playmates, on that precipice
Slept, clasped in his embrace. — O, storm of death!
Whose sightless speed divides this sullen night: 610
And thou, colossal Skeleton, that, still
Guiding its irresistible career
In thy devastating omnipotence,
Art king of this frail world, from the red field
Of slaughter, from the recking hospital,   615
The patriot's sacred couch, the snowy bed
Of innocence, the scaffold and the throne,
A mighty voice invokes thee.   Ruin calls
His brother Death.   A rare and regal prey
He hath prepared, prowling around the world;   620
Glutted with which thou mayst repose, and men

Go to their graves like flowers or creeping worms,
Nor ever more offer at thy dark shrine
The unheeded tribute of a broken heart.

When on the threshold of the green recess   625
The wanderer's footsteps fell, he knew that death
Was on him.   Yet a little, ere it fled,
Did he resign his high and holy soul
To images of the majestic past,
That paused within his passive being now,   630
Like winds that bear sweet music, when they breathe
Through some dim latticed chamber.   He did place
His pale lean hand upon the rugged trunk
Of the old pine.   Upon an ivied stone
Reclined his languid head, his limbs did rest,   635
Diffused and motionless, on the smooth brink
Of that obscurest chasm; — and thus he lay,
Surrendering to their final impulses
The hovering powers of life.   Hope and despair,
The torturers, slept; no mortal pain or fear   640
Marred his repose, the influxes of sense,
And his own being unalloyed by pain,
Yet feebler and more feeble, calmly fed
The stream of thought, till he lay breathing there
At peace, and faintly smiling: — his last sight   645
Was the great moon, which o'er the western line
Of the wide world her mighty horn suspended,
With whose dun beams inwoven darkness seemed
To mingle.   Now upon the jaggèd hills
It rests, and still as the divided frame   650
Of the vast meteor sunk, the Poet's blood,
That ever beat in mystic sympathy
With nature's ebb and flow, grew feebler still:
And when two lessening points of light alone

Gleamed through the darkness, the alternate gasp   655
Of his faint respiration scarce did stir
The stagnate night: — till the minutest ray
Was quenched, the pulse yet lingered in his heart.
It paused — it fluttered.   But when heaven remained
Utterly black, the murky shades involved   660
An image, silent, cold, and motionless,
As their own voiceless earth and vacant air.
Even as a vapour fed with golden beams
That ministered on sunlight, ere the west
Eclipses it, was now that wondrous frame —   665
No sense, no motion, no divinity —
A fragile lute, on whose harmonious strings
The breath of heaven did wander — a bright stream
Once fed with many-voicèd waves — a dream
Of youth, which night and time have quenched for ever, 670
Still, dark, and dry, and unremembered now.

O, for Medea's wondrous alchemy,
Which wheresoe'er it fell made the earth gleam
With bright flowers, and the wintry boughs exhale
From vernal blooms fresh fragrance! O, that God,   675
Profuse of poisons, would concede the chalice
Which but one living man has drained, who now,
Vessel of deathless wrath, a slave that feels
No proud exemption in the blighting curse
He bears, over the world wanders for ever,   .   680
Lone as incarnate death! O, that the dream
Of dark magician in his visioned cave,
Raking the cinders of a crucible
For life and power, even when his feeble hand
Shakes in its last decay, were the true law   685
Of this so lovely world! But thou art fled
Like some frail exhalation ; which the dawn

Robes in its golden beams, — ah! thou hast fled!
The brave, the gentle, and the beautiful,
The child of grace and genius.   Heartless things   690
Are done and said i' the world, and many worms
And beasts and men live on, and mighty Earth
From sea and mountain, city and wilderness,
In vesper low or joyous orison,
Lifts still its solemn voice: — but thou art fled —   695
Thou canst no longer know or love the shapes
Of this phantasmal scene, who have to thee
Been purest ministers, who are, alas!
Now thou art not.   Upon those pallid lips
So sweet even in their silence, on those eyes   700
That image sleep in death, upon that form
Yet safe from the worm's outrage, let no tear
Be shed — not even in thought.   Nor, when those hues
Are gone, and those divinest lineaments,
Worn by the senseless wind, shall live alone   705
In the frail pauses of this simple strain,
Let not high verse, mourning the memory
Of that which is no more, or painting's woe
Or sculpture, speak in feeble imagery
Their own cold powers.   Art and eloquence,   710
And all the shows o' the world are frail and vain
To weep a loss that turns their lights to shade.
It is a woe too 'deep for tears,' when all
Is reft at once, when some surpassing Spirit,
Whose light adorned the world around it, leaves   715
Those who remain behind, not sobs or groans,
The passionate tumult of a clinging hope;
But pale despair and cold tranquillity,
Nature's vast frame, the web of human things,
Birth and the grave, that are not as they were.   720

Autumn, 1815.

A SUMMER-EVENING CHURCH-YARD,

LECHLADE, GLOUCESTERSHIRE.

THE wind has swept from the wide atmosphere
  Each vapour that obscured the sunset's ray;
And pallid evening twines its beaming hair
  In duskier braids around the languid eyes of day :
Silence and twilight, unbeloved of men,   5
Creep hand in hand from yon obscurest glen.

They breathe their spells towards the departing day,
  Encompassing the earth, air, stars, and sea ;
Light, sound, and motion own the potent sway,
  Responding to the charm with its own mystery.   10
The winds are still, or the dry church-tower grass
Knows not their gentle motions as they pass.

Thou too, aërial Pile! whose pinnacles
  Point from one shrine like pyramids of fire,
Obeyest in silence their sweet solemn spells,   15
  Clothing in hues of heaven thy dim and distant spire,
Around whose lessening and invisible height
Gather among the stars the clouds of night.

The dead are sleeping in their sepulchres :
  And, mouldering as they sleep, a thrilling sound   20
Half sense, half thought, among the darkness stirs,
  Breathed from their wormy beds all living things around,
And mingling with the still night and mute sky
Its awful hush is felt inaudibly.

Thus solemnized and softened, death is mild   25
  And terrorless as this serenest night :
Here could I hope, like some enquiring child

Sporting on graves, that death did hide from human sight
Sweet secrets, or beside its breathless sleep
That loveliest dreams perpetual watch did keep.   30

September, 1815.

LINES.

I.

THE cold earth slept below,
    Above the cold sky shone;
And all around, with a chilling sound,
    From caves of ice and fields of snow,
    The breath of night like death did flow   5
    Beneath the sinking moon.

II.

The wintry hedge was black,
    The green grass was not seen,
The birds did rest on the bare thorn's breast,
    Whose roots, beside the pathway track,   10
    Had bound their folds o'er many a crack,
    Which the frost had made between.

III.

Thine eyes glowed in the glare
    Of the moon's dying light;
As a fenfire's beam on a sluggish stream   15
    Gleams dimly, so the moon shone there,
    And it yellowed the strings of thy raven hair,
    That shook in the wind of night.

IV.

The moon made thy lips pale, beloved —
    The wind made thy bosom chill —   20

The night did shed on thy dear head
  Its frozen dew, and thou didst lie
Where the bitter breath of the naked sky
  Might visit thee at will.

November, 1815.

TO WORDSWORTH.

POET of Nature, thou hast wept to know
  That things depart which never may return :
Childhood and youth, friendship and love's first glow,
  Have fled like sweet dreams, leaving thee to mourn.
These common woes I feel.   One loss is mine   5
  Which thou too feel'st, yet I alone deplore.
Thou wert as a lone star, whose light did shine
  On some frail bark in winter's midnight roar :
Thou hast like to a rock-built refuge stood
Above the blind and battling multitude :   10
In honoured poverty thy voice did weave
  Songs consecrate to truth and liberty, —
Deserting these, thou leavest me to grieve,
  Thus having been, that thou shouldst cease to be.

1816.

HYMN TO INTELLECTUAL BEAUTY.

I.

THE awful shadow of some unseen Power
  Floats though unseen amongst us, — visiting
  This various world with as inconstant wing
As summer winds that creep from flower to flower, —

Like moonbeams that behind some piny mountain shower,   5
    It visits with inconstant glance
    Each human heart and countenance ;
Like hues and harmonies of evening, —
    Like clouds in starlight widely spread, —
    Like memory of music fled, —   10
    Like aught that for its grace may be
Dear, and yet dearer for its mystery.

II.

Spirit of BEAUTY, that dost consecrate
    With thine own hues all thou dost shine upon
    Of human thought or form, — where art thou gone ?   15
Why dost thou pass away and leave our state,
This dim vast vale of tears, vacant and desolate ?
    Ask why the sunlight not for ever
    Weaves rainbows o'er yon mountain river,
Why aught should fail and fade that once is shown,   20
    Why fear and dream and death and birth
    Cast on the daylight of this earth
    Such gloom, — why man has such a scope
For love and hate, despondency and hope ?

III.

No voice from some sublimer world hath ever   25
    To sage or poet these responses given —
    Therefore the names of Dæmon, Ghost, and Heaven,
Remain the records of their vain endeavour,
Frail spells—whose uttered charm might not avail to sever,
    From all we hear and all we see,   30
    Doubt, chance, and mutability.
Thy light alone — like mist o'er mountains driven,
    Or music by the night wind sent,
    Through strings of some still instrument,

Or moonlight on a midnight stream,   35
Gives grace and truth to life's unquiet dream.

IV.

Love, Hope, and Self-esteem, like clouds depart
  And come, for some uncertain moments lent,
  Man were immortal, and omnipotent,
Didst thou, unknown and awful as thou art,   40
Keep with thy glorious train firm state within his heart.
    Thou messenger of sympathies,
    That wax and wane in lovers' eyes —
Thou — that to human thought art nourishment,
    Like darkness to a dying flame !   45
    Depart not as thy shadow came,
    Depart not — lest the grave should be,
Like life and fear, a dark reality.

V.

While yet a boy I sought for ghosts, and sped
  Through many a listening chamber, cave and ruin,   50
  And starlight wood, with fearful steps pursuing
Hopes of high talk with the departed dead.
I called on poisonous names with which our youth is fed,
    I was not heard — I saw them not —
    When musing deeply on the lot   55
Of life, at the sweet time when winds are wooing
    All vital things that wake to bring
    News of birds and blossoming, —
    Sudden, thy shadow fell on me ;
I shrieked, and clasped my hands in ecstasy !   60

VI.

I vowed that I would dedicate my powers
  To thee and thine — have I not kept the vow ?
With beating heart and streaming eyes, even now

I call the phantoms of a thousand hours
Each from his voiceless grave: they have in visioned bowers 65
    Of studious zeal or love's delight
    Outwatched with me the envious night —
They know that never joy illumed my brow
    Unlinked with hope that thou wouldst free
    This world from its dark slavery,   70
    That thou — O awful LOVELINESS,
Wouldst give whate'er these words cannot express.

VII.

The day becomes more solemn and serene
    When noon is past — there is a harmony
    In autumn, and a lustre in its sky,   75
Which through the summer is not heard or seen,
As if it could not be, as if it had not been !
    Thus let thy power, which like the truth
    Of nature on my passive youth
Descended, to my onward life supply   80
    Its calm — to one who worships thee,
    And every form containing thee,
    Whom, SPIRIT fair, thy spells did bind
To fear himself, and love all human kind.
    Summer, 1816.

ON FANNY GODWIN.

    HER voice did quiver as we parted,
        Yet knew I not that heart was broken
    From which it came, and I departed
        Heeding not the words then spoken.
        Misery — O Misery,   5
        This world is all too wide for thee.
                1817.

LINES.

I.

THAT time is dead for ever, child,
Drowned, frozen, dead for ever !
    We look on the past
    And stare aghast
At the spectres wailing, pale and ghast,   5
Of hopes which thou and I beguiled
    To death on life's dark river.

II.

The stream we gazed on then, rolled by;
Its waves are unreturning;
    But we yet stand   10
    In a lone land,
Like tombs to mark the memory
Of hopes and fears, which fade and flee
    In the light of life's dim morning.

November 5, 1817.

SONNET.

OZYMANDIAS.

I MET a traveller from an antique land
Who said : Two vast and trunkless legs of stone
Stand in the desert.   Near them, on the sand,
Half sunk, a shattered visage lies, whose frown,
And wrinkled lip, and sneer of cold command,   5
Tell that its sculptor well those passions read
Which yet survive, (stamped on these lifeless things,)
The hand that mocked them and the heart that fed :

And on the pedestal these words appear :
" My name is Ozymandias, king of kings :   10
Look on my works, ye Mighty, and despair ! "
Nothing beside remains. Round the decay
Of that colossal wreck, boundless and bare
The lone and level sands stretch far away.

1817.

PASSAGE OF THE APENNINES.

LISTEN, listen, Mary mine,
To the whisper of the Apennine ;
It bursts on the roof like the thunder's roar,
Or like the sea on a northern shore,
Heard in its raging ebb and flow   5
By the captives pent in the cave below.
The Apennine in the light of day
Is a mighty mountain dim and gray,
Which between the earth and sky doth lay ;
But when night comes, a chaos dread   10
On the dim starlight then is spread,
And the Apennine walks abroad with the storm.

May 4, 1818.

THE PAST.

I.

WILT thou forget the happy hours
Which we buried in Love's sweet bowers,
Heaping over their corpses cold
Blossoms and leaves instead of mould ?

Blossoms which were the joys that fell,   5
    And leaves, the hopes that yet remain.

II.

Forget the dead, the past? O yet
There are ghosts that may take revenge for it,
Memories that make the heart a tomb,
Regrets which glide through the spirit's gloom,   10
    And with ghastly whispers tell
        That joy, once lost, is pain.

1818.

LINES WRITTEN AMONG THE EUGANEAN HILLS.

OCTOBER, 1818.

MANY a green isle needs must be
In the deep wide sea of misery,
Or the mariner, worn and wan,
Never thus could voyage on
Day and night, and night and day,   5
Drifting on his dreary way,
With the solid darkness black
Closing round his vessel's track ;
Whilst above the sunless sky,
Big with clouds, hangs heavily,   10
And behind the tempest fleet
Hurries on with lightning feet,
Riving sail, and cord, and plank,
Till the ship has almost drank
Death from the o'er-brimming deep ;   15
And sinks down, down, like that sleep
When the dreamer seems to be
Weltering through eternity ;

And the dim low line before
Of a dark and distant shore   20
Still recedes, as ever still
Longing with divided will,
But no power to seek or shun,
He is ever drifted on
O'er the unreposing wave   25
To the haven of the grave.
What if there no friends will greet ;
What if there no heart will meet
His with love's impatient beat ;
Wander wheresoe'er he may,   30
Can he dream before that day
To find refuge from distress
In friendship's smile, in love's caress?
Then 't will wreak him little woe
Whether such there be or no :   35
Senseless is the breast, and cold,
Which relenting love would fold ;
Bloodless are the veins and chill
Which the pulse of pain did fill ;
Every little living nerve   .   40
That from bitter words did swerve
Round the tortured lips and brow,
Are like sapless leaflets now
Frozen upon December's bough.
On the beach of a northern sea   45
Which tempests shake eternally,
As once the wretch there lay to sleep,
Lies a solitary heap,
One white skull and seven dry bones,
On the margin of the stones,   50
Where a few gray rushes stand,
Boundaries of the sea and land :

Nor is heard one voice of wail
But the sea-mews', as they sail
O'er the billows of the gale ;   55
Or the whirlwind up and down
Howling, like a slaughtered town,
When a king in glory rides
Through the pomp of fratricides :
Those unburied bones around   60
There is many a mournful sound ;
There is no lament for him,
Like a sunless vapour, dim,
Who once clothed with life and thought
What now moves nor murmurs not.   65

Aye, many flowering islands lie
In the waters of wide Agony :
To such a one this morn was led,
My bark by soft winds piloted :
'Mid the mountains Euganean   70
I stood listening to the pæan,
With which the legioned rooks did hail
The sun's uprise majestical ;
Gathering round with wings all hoar,
Through the dewy mist they soar   75
Like gray shades, till the eastern heaven
Bursts, and then, as clouds of even,
Flecked with fire and azure, lie
In the unfathomable sky,
So their plumes of purple grain,   80
Starred with drops of golden rain,
Gleam above the sunlight woods,
As in silent multitudes
On the morning's fitful gale
Through the broken mist they sail,   85

And the vapours cloven and gleaming
Follow down the dark steep streaming,
Till all is bright, and clear, and still,
Round the solitary hill.

Beneath is spread like a green sea   90
The waveless plain of Lombardy,
Bounded by the vaporous air,
Islanded by cities fair;
Underneath day's azure eyes,
Ocean's nursling, Venice lies,   95
A peopled labyrinth of walls,
Amphitrite's destined halls,
Which her hoary sire now paves
With his blue and beaming waves.
Lo! the sun upsprings behind,   100
Broad, red, radiant, half reclined
On the level quivering line
Of the waters crystalline;
And before that chasm of light,
As within a furnace bright,   105
Column, tower, and dome, and spire,
Shine like obelisks of fire,
Pointing with inconstant motion
From the altar of dark ocean
To the sapphire-tinted skies;   110
As the flames of sacrifice
From the marble shrines did rise,
As to pierce the dome of gold
Where Apollo spoke of old.

Sun-girt City, thou hast been   115
Ocean's child, and then his queen;
Now is come a darker day,

And thou soon must be his prey,
If the power that raised thee here
Hallow so thy watery bier.   120
A less drear ruin then than now,
With thy conquest-branded brow
Stooping to the slave of slaves
From thy throne, among the waves
Wilt thou be, when the sea-mew   125
Flies, as once before it flew,
O'er thine isles depopulate,
And all is in its ancient state,
Save where many a palace gate
With green sea-flowers overgrown   130
Like a rock of ocean's own,
Topples o'er the abandoned sea
As the tides change sullenly.
The fisher on his watery way,
Wandering at the close of day,   135
Will spread his sail and seize his oar
Till he pass the gloomy shore,
Lest thy dead should, from their sleep
Bursting o'er the starlight deep,
Lead a rapid mask of death   140
O'er the waters of his path.

Those who alone thy towers behold
Quivering through aërial gold,
As I now behold them here,
Would imagine not they were   145
Sepulchres, where human forms,
Like pollution-nourished worms
To the corpse of greatness cling,.
Murdered, and now mouldering :
But if Freedom should awake   150

In her omnipotence, and shake
From the Celtic Anarch's hold
All the keys of dungeons cold,
Where a hundred cities lie
Chained like thee, ingloriously,   155
Thou and all thy sister band
Might adorn this sunny land,
Twining memories of old time
With new virtues more sublime ;
If not, perish thou and they,   160
Clouds which stain truth's rising day
By her sun consumed away,
Earth can spare ye: while like flowers,
In the waste of years and hours,
From your dust new nations spring   165
With more kindly blossoming.
Perish — let there only be
Floating o'er thy heartless sea
As the garment of thy sky
Clothes the world immortally,   170
One remembrance, more sublime
Than the tattered pall of time,
Which scarce hides thy visage wan ; —
That a tempest-cleaving Swan
Of the songs of Albion,   175
Driven from his ancestral streams
By the might of evil dreams,
Found a nest in thee ; and Ocean
Welcomed him with such emotion
That its joy grew his, and sprung   180
From his lips like music flung
O'er a mighty thunder-fit
Chastening terror : — what though yet
Poesy's unfailing River,

Which through Albion winds for ever   185
Lashing with melodious wave
Many a sacred Poet's grave,
Mourn its latest nursling fled?
What though thou with all thy dead
Scarce can for this fame repay   190
Aught thine own? oh, rather say
Though thy sins and slaveries foul
Overcloud a sunlike soul?
As the ghost of Homer clings
Round Scamander's wasting springs;   195
As divinest Shakespeare's might
Fills Avon and the world with light
Like omniscient power which he .
Imaged 'mid mortality ;
As the love from Petrarch's urn,   200
Yet amid yon hills doth burn,
A quenchless lamp by which the heart
Sees things unearthly ; — so thou art,
Mighty spirit — so shall be
The City that did refuge thee.   205

Lo, the sun floats up the sky
Like thought-wingèd Liberty,
Till the universal light
Seems to level plain and height ;
From the sea a mist has spread,   210
And the beams of morn lie dead
On the towers of Venice now,
Like its glory long ago.
By the skirts of that gray cloud
Many-domèd Padua proud   215
Stands, a peopled solitude,
'Mid the harvest-shining plain,

Where the peasant heaps his grain
In the garner of his foe,
And the milk-white oxen slow   220
With the purple vintage strain,
Heaped upon the creaking wain,
That the brutal Celt may swill
Drunken sleep with savage will;
And the sickle to the sword   225
Lies unchanged, though many a lord,
Like a weed whose shade is poison,
Overgrows this region's foison,
Sheaves of whom are ripe to come
To destruction's harvest home :   230
Men must reap the things they sow,
Force from force must ever flow,
Or worse; but 't is a bitter woe
That love or reason cannot change
The despot's rage, the slave's revenge.   235

Padua, thou within whose walls
Those mute guests at festivals,
Son and Mother, Death and Sin,
Played at dice for Ezzelin,
Till Death cried, " I win, I win ! "   240
And Sin cursed to lose the wager,
But Death promised, to assuage her,
That he would petition for
Her to be made Vice-Emperor,
When the destined years were o'er   245
Over all between the Po
And the eastern Alpine snow,
Under the mighty Austrian.
Sin smiled so as Sin only can,
And since that time, aye, long before,   250

Both have ruled from shore to shore,
That incestuous pair, who follow
Tyrants as the sun the swallow,
As Repentance follows Crime,
And as changes follow Time.   255

In thine halls the lamp of learning,
Padua, now no more is burning;
Like a meteor, whose wild way
Is lost over the grave of day,
It gleams betrayed and to betray: 260
Once remotest nations came
To adore that sacred flame,
When it lit not many a hearth
On this cold and gloomy earth:
Now new fires from antique light   265
Spring beneath the wide world's might;
But their spark lies dead in thee,
Trampled out by tyranny.
As the Norway woodman quells,
In the depth of piny dells,   270
One light flame among the brakes,
While the boundless forest shakes,
And its mighty trunks are torn
By the fire thus lowly born :
The spark beneath his feet is dead,   275
He starts to see the flames it fed
Howling through the darkened sky
With a myriad tongues victoriously,
And sinks down in fear : so thou,
O Tyranny, beholdest now   280
Light around thee, and thou hearest
The loud flames ascend, and fearest :
Grovel on the earth : aye, hide
In the dust thy purple pride !

Noon descends around me now :   285
'T is the noon of autumn's glow,
When a soft and purple mist
Like a vaporous amethyst,
Or an air-dissolvèd star
Mingling light and fragrance, far   290
From the curved horizon's bound
To the point of heaven's profound,
Fills the overflowing sky ;
And the plains that silent lie
Underneath, the leaves unsodden   295
Where the infant frost has trodden
With his morning-wingèd feet,
Whose bright print is gleaming yet ;
And the red and golden vines,
Piercing with their trellised lines   300
The rough, dark-skirted wilderness ;
The dun and bladed grass no less,
Pointing from this hoary tower
In the windless air ; the flower
Glimmering at my feet ; the line   305
Of the olive-sandalled Apennine
In the south dimly islanded ;
And the Alps, whose snows are spread
High between the clouds and sun ;
And of living things each one ;   310
And my spirit which so long
Darkened this swift stream of song,
Interpenetrated lie
By the glory of the sky :
Be it love, light, harmony,   315
Odour, or the soul of all
Which from heaven like dew doth fall,
Or the mind which feeds this verse
Peopling the lone universe.

Noon descends, and after noon   320
Autumn's evening meets me soon,
Leading the infantine moon,
And that one star, which to her
Almost seems to minister
Half the crimson light she brings   325
From the sunset's radiant springs :
And the soft dreams of the morn,
(Which like wingèd winds had borne
To that silent isle, which lies
'Mid remembered agonies,   330
The frail bark of this lone being,)
Pass, to other sufferers fleeing,
And its ancient pilot, Pain,
Sits beside the helm again.

Other flowering isles must be   335
In the sea of life and agony :
Other spirits float and flee
O'er that gulph : even now, perhaps,
On some rock the wild wave wraps,
With folded wings they waiting sit   340
For my bark, to pilot it
To some calm and blooming cove,
Where for me, and those I love,
May a windless bower be built,
Far from passion, pain, and guilt,   345
In a dell 'mid lawny hills,
Which the wild sea-murmur fills,
And soft sunshine, and the sound
Of old forests echoing round,
And the light and smell divine   350
Of all flowers that breathe and shine :
We may live so happy there,

That the spirits of the air,
Envying us, may even entice
To our healing paradise   355
The polluting multitude;
But their rage would be subdued
By that clime divine and calm,
And the winds whose wings rain balm
On the uplifted soul, and leaves   360
Under which the bright sea heaves;
While each breathless interval
In their whisperings musical
The inspired soul supplies
With its own deep melodies,   365
And the love which heals all strife
Circling, like the breath of life,
All things in that sweet abode
With its own mild brotherhood:
They, not it, would change; and soon   370
Every sprite beneath the moon
Would repent its envy vain,
And the earth grow young again.

SONNET.

Lift not the painted veil which those who live
Call Life: though unreal shapes be pictured there,
And it but mimic all we would believe
With colours idly spread, — behind, lurk Fear
And Hope, twin destinies; who ever weave   5
Their shadows, o'er the chasm, sightless and drear.
I knew one who had lifted it — he sought,
For his lost heart was tender, things to love,

But found them not, alas! nor was there aught
The world contains, the which he could approve.　10
Through the unheeding many he did move,
A splendour among shadows, a bright blot
Upon this gloomy scene, a Spirit that strove
For truth, and like the Preacher found it not.

1818.

SONG, ON A FADED VIOLET.

I.

THE odour from the flower is gone
　　Which like thy kisses breathed on me ;
The colour from the flower is flown
　　Which glowed of thee and only thee !

II.

A shrivelled, lifeless, vacant form,　　　　5
　　It lies on my abandoned breast,
And mocks the heart which yet is warm,
　　With cold and silent rest.

III.

I weep, — my tears revive it not !
　　I sigh, — it breathes no more on me ;　　10
Its mute and uncomplaining lot
　　Is such as mine should be.

1818.

STANZAS,

WRITTEN IN DEJECTION NEAR NAPLES.

I.

THE sun is warm, the sky is clear,
　　The waves are dancing fast and bright,
Blue isles and snowy mountains wear
　　　The purple noon's transparent might,
　　　The breath of the moist earth is light,　　　5
Around its unexpanded buds;
　　　Like many a voice of one delight,
The winds, the birds, the ocean floods,
The City's voice itself is soft like Solitude's.

II.

I see the Deep's untrampled floor　　　10
　　　With green and purple seaweeds strown;
I see the waves upon the shore,
　　　Like light dissolved in star-showers, thrown:
　　　I sit upon the sands alone,
The lightning of the noon-tide ocean　　　15
　　　Is flashing round me, and a tone
Arises from its measured motion,
How sweet! did any heart now share in my emotion.

III.

Alas! I have nor hope nor health,
　　　Nor peace within nor calm around,　　　20
Nor that content surpassing wealth
　　　The sage in meditation found,
　　　And walked with inward glory crowned —
Nor fame, nor power, nor love, nor leisure.
　　　Others I see whom these surround —　　　25

Smiling they live, and call life pleasure ; —
To me that cup has been dealt in another measure.

IV.

Yet now despair itself is mild,
    Even as the winds and waters are;
I could lie down like a tired child,   30
    And weep away the life of care
    Which I have borne and yet must bear,
Till death like sleep might steal on me,
    And I might feel in the warm air
My cheek grow cold, and hear the sea   35
Breathe o'er my dying brain its last monotony.

V.

Some might lament that I were cold,
    As I, when this sweet day is gone,
Which my lost heart, too soon grown old,
    Insults with this untimely moan ;   40
    They might lament — for I am one
Whom men love not, — and yet regret,
    Unlike this day, which, when the sun
Shall on its stainless glory set,
Will linger, though enjoyed, like joy in memory yet.   45

December, 1818.

PROMETHEUS UNBOUND:

A LYRICAL DRAMA IN FOUR ACTS.

PREFACE.

THE Greek tragic writers, in selecting as their subject any portion of their national history or mythology, employed in their treatment of it a certain arbitrary discretion. They by no means conceived themselves bound to adhere to the common interpretation or to imitate in story as in title their rivals 5 and predecessors. Such a system would have amounted to a resignation of those claims to preference over their competitors which incited the composition. The Agamemnonian story was exhibited on the Athenian theatre with as many variations as dramas. 10

I have presumed to employ a similar licence. The *Prometheus Unbound* of Æschylus supposed the reconciliation of Jupiter with his victim as the price of the disclosure of the danger threatened to his empire by the consummation of his marriage with Thetis. Thetis, according to this view of the 15 subject, was given in marriage to Peleus, and Prometheus, by the permission of Jupiter, delivered from his captivity by Hercules. Had I framed my story on this model, I should have done no more than have attempted to restore the lost drama of Æschylus; an ambition which, if my preference to this mode 20 of treating the subject had incited me to cherish, the recollection of the high comparison such an attempt would challenge might well abate. But, in truth, I was averse from a catastrophe so feeble as that of reconciling the Champion with the Oppressor of mankind. The moral interest of the fable, which 25 is so powerfully sustained by the sufferings and endurance of

Prometheus, would be annihilated if we could conceive of him
as unsaying his high language and quailing before his successful and perfidious adversary. The only imaginary being resembling in any degree Prometheus, is Satan; and Prometheus is,
5 in my judgment, a more poetical character than Satan, because,
in addition to courage, and majesty, and firm and patient opposition to omnipotent force, he is susceptible of being described
as exempt from the taints of ambition, envy, revenge, and a
desire for personal aggrandizement, which, in the Hero of
10 *Paradise Lost,* interfere with the interest. The character of
Satan engenders in the mind a pernicious casuistry which
leads us to weigh his faults with his wrongs, and to excuse
the former because the latter exceed all measure. In the
minds of those who consider that magnificent fiction with a
15 religious feeling it engenders something worse. But Prometheus is, as it were, the type of the highest perfection of moral
and intellectual nature, impelled by the purest and the truest
motives to the best and noblest ends.

This Poem was chiefly written upon the mountainous ruins
20 of the Baths of Caracalla, among the flowery glades, and
thickets of odoriferous blossoming trees, which are extended in
ever winding labyrinths upon its immense platforms and dizzy
arches suspended in the air. The bright blue sky of Rome,
and the effect of the vigorous awakening spring in that divin-
25 est climate, and the new life with which it drenches the spirits
even to intoxication, were the inspiration of this drama.

The imagery which I have employed will be found, in many
instances, to have been drawn from the operations of the
human mind, or from those external actions by which they are
30 expressed. This is unusual in modern poetry, although Dante
and Shakespeare are full of instances of the same kind: Dante
indeed more than any other poet, and with greater success. But
the Greek poets, as writers to whom no resource of awakening
the sympathy of their contemporaries was unknown, were in the
35 habitual use of this power; and it is the study of their works,
(since a higher merit would probably be denied me,) to which
I am willing that my readers should impute this singularity.

One word is due in candour to the degree in which the study of contemporary writings may have tinged my composition, for such has been a topic of censure with regard to poems far more popular, and indeed more deservedly popular, than mine. It is impossible that any one who inhabits the same age with 5 such writers as those who stand in the foremost ranks of our own, can conscientiously assure himself that his language and tone of thought may not have been modified by the study of the productions of those extraordinary intellects. It is true that, not the spirit of their genius, but the forms in which it 10 has manifested itself, are due less to the peculiarities of their own minds than to the peculiarity of the moral and intellectual condition of the minds among which they have been produced. Thus a number of writers possess the form, whilst they want the spirit of those whom, it is alleged, they imitate; because the 15 former is the endowment of the age in which they live, and the latter must be the uncommunicated lightning of their own mind.

The peculiar style of intense and comprehensive imagery which distinguishes the modern literature of England, has not 20 been, as a general power, the product of the imitation of any particular writer. The mass of capabilities remains at every period materially the same; the circumstances which awaken it to action perpetually change. If England were divided into forty republics, each equal in population and extent to Athens, 25 there is no reason to suppose but that, under institutions not more perfect than those of Athens, each would produce philosophers and poets equal to those who (if we except Shakespeare) have never been surpassed. We owe the great writers of the golden age of our literature to that fervid awakening 30 of the public mind which shook to dust the oldest and most oppressive form of the Christian religion. We owe Milton to the progress and development of the same spirit: the sacred Milton was, let it ever be remembered, a republican, and a bold enquirer into morals and religion. The great writers of 35 our own age are, we have reason to suppose, the companions and forerunners of some unimagined change in our social condition or the opinions which cement it. The cloud of mind is discharging its collected lightning, and the equilibrium between institutions and opinions is now restoring, or is about to be restored.

5   As to imitation, poetry is a mimetic art. It creates, but it creates by combination and representation. Poetical abstractions are beautiful and new, not because the portions of which they are composed had no previous existence in the mind of man or in nature, but because the whole produced by their
10 combination has some intelligible and beautiful analogy with those sources of emotion and thought, and with the contemporary condition of them: one great poet is a masterpiece of nature which another not only ought to study but must study. He might as wisely and as easily determine that his mind
15 should no longer be the mirror of all that is lovely in the visible universe, as exclude from his contemplation the beautiful which exists in the writings of a great contemporary. The pretence of doing it would be a presumption in any but the greatest; the effect, even in him, would be strained, unnatural,
20 and ineffectual. A poet is the combined product of such internal powers as modify the nature of others, and of such external influences as excite and sustain these powers; he is not one, but both. Every man's mind is, in this respect, modified by all the objects of nature and art; by every word and
25 every suggestion which he ever admitted to act upon his consciousness; it is the mirror upon which all forms are reflected, and in which they compose one form. Poets, not otherwise than philosophers, painters, sculptors, and musicians, are, in one sense, the creators, and, in another, the creations, of their
30 age. From this subjection the loftiest do not escape. There is a similarity between Homer and Hesiod, between Æschylus and Euripides, between Virgil and Horace, between Dante and Petrarch, between Shakespeare and Fletcher, between Dryden and Pope; each has a generic resemblance under
35 which their specific distinctions are arranged. If this similarity be the result of imitation, I am willing to confess that I have imitated.

Let this opportunity be conceded to me of acknowledging that I have, what a Scotch philosopher characteristically terms, "a passion for reforming the world": what passion incited him to write and publish his book, he omits to explain. For my part I had rather be damned with Plato and Lord Bacon, than go to Heaven with Paley and Malthus. But it is a mistake to suppose that I dedicate my poetical compositions solely to the direct enforcement of reform, or that I consider them in any degree as containing a reasoned system on the theory of human life. Didactic poetry is my abhorrence; nothing can be equally well expressed in prose that is not tedious and supererogatory in verse. My purpose has hitherto been simply to familiarize the highly refined imagination of the more select classes of poetical readers with beautiful idealisms of moral excellence; aware that until the mind can love, and admire, and trust, and hope, and endure, reasoned principles of moral conduct are seeds cast upon the highway of life which the unconscious passenger tramples into dust, although they would bear the harvest of his happiness. Should I live to accomplish what I purpose, that is, produce a systematical history of what appear to me to be the genuine elements of human society, let not the advocates of injustice and superstition flatter themselves that I should take Æschylus rather than Plato as my model.

The having spoken of myself with unaffected freedom will need little apology with the candid; and let the uncandid consider that they injure me less than their own hearts and minds by misrepresentation. Whatever talents a person may possess to amuse and instruct others, be they ever so inconsiderable, he is yet bound to exert them: if his attempt be ineffectual, let the punishment of an unaccomplished purpose have been sufficient; let none trouble themselves to heap the dust of oblivion upon his efforts; the pile they raise will betray his grave which might otherwise have been unknown.

PROMETHEUS UNBOUND.

ACT I.

Scene, *A Ravine of Icy Rocks in the Indian Caucasus.* Prometheus *is discovered bound to the Precipice.* Panthea *and* Ione
are seated at his feet. Time, *Night.* *During the Scene, Morning slowly breaks.*

Prometheus.

Monarch of Gods and Dæmons, and all Spirits
But One, who throng those bright and rolling worlds
Which Thou and I alone of living things
Behold with sleepless eyes! regard this Earth
Made multitudinous with thy slaves, whom thou　　　5
Requitest for knee-worship, prayer, and praise,
And toil, and hecatombs of broken hearts,
With fear and self-contempt and barren hope.
Whilst me, who am thy foe, eyeless in hate,
Hast thou made reign and triumph, to thy scorn,　　　10
O'er mine own misery and thy vain revenge.
Three thousand years of sleep-unsheltered hours,
And moments aye divided by keen pangs
Till they seemed years, torture and solitude,
Scorn and despair, — these are mine empire.　　　15
More glorious far than that which thou surveyest
From thine unenvied throne, O, Mighty God!
Almighty, had I deigned to share the shame
Of thine ill tyranny, and hung not here
Nailed to this wall of eagle-baffling mountain,　　　20

Black, wintry, dead, unmeasured ; without herb,
Insect, or beast, or shape or sound of life.
Ah me ! alas, pain, pain ever, for ever !

No change, no pause, no hope !   Yet I endure.
I ask the Earth, have not the mountains felt?   25
I ask yon Heaven, the all-beholding Sun,
Has it not seen ?   The Sea, in storm or calm,
Heaven's ever-changing Shadow, spread below,
Have its deaf waves not heard my agony?
Ah me ! alas, pain, pain ever, for ever !   30

The crawling glaciers pierce me with the spears
Of their moon-freezing crystals, the bright chains
Eat with their burning cold into my bones.
Heaven's wingèd hound, polluting from thy lips
His beak in poison not his own, tears up   35
My heart ; and shapeless sights come wandering by,
The ghastly people of the realm of dream,
Mocking me : and the Earthquake-fiends are charged
To wrench the rivets from my quivering wounds
When the rocks split and close again behind :   40
While from their loud abysses howling throng
The genii of the storm, urging the rage
Of whirlwind, and afflict me with keen hail.
And yet to me welcome is day and night,
Whether one breaks the hoar-frost of the morn,   45
Or starry, dim, and slow, the other climbs
The leaden-coloured east ; for then they lead
The wingless, crawling hours, one among whom
— As some dark Priest hales the reluctant victim —
Shall drag thee, cruel King, to kiss the blood   50
From these pale feet, which then might trample thee
If they disdained not such a prostrate slave.

Disdain ! Ah no ! I pity thee. What ruin
Will hunt thee undefended through the wide Heaven !
How will thy soul, cloven to its depth with terror, 55
Gape like a hell within ! I speak in grief,
Not exultation, for I hate no more,
As then ere misery made me wise. The curse
Once breathed on thee I would recall. Ye Mountains,
Whose many-voicèd Echoes, through the mist 60
Of cataracts, flung the thunder of that spell !
Ye icy Springs, stagnant with wrinkling frost,
Which vibrated to hear me, and then crept
Shuddering through India ! Thou serenest Air,
Through which the Sun walks burning without beams ! 65
And ye swift Whirlwinds, who on poisèd wings
Hung mute and moveless o'er yon hushed abyss,
As thunder, louder than your own, made rock
The orbèd world ! If then my words had power,
Though I am changed so that aught evil wish 70
Is dead within ; although no memory be
Of what is hate, let them not lose it now !
What was that curse ? for ye all heard me speak.

FIRST VOICE : *from the Mountains.*

Thrice three hundred thousand years
   O'er the Earthquake's couch we stood : 75
Oft, as men convulsed with fears,
   We trembled in our multitude.

SECOND VOICE : *from the Springs.*

Thunder-bolts had parched our water,
   We had been stained with bitter blood,
And had run mute, 'mid shrieks of slaughter, 80
   Through a city and a solitude.

THIRD VOICE: *from the Air.*

I had clothed, since Earth uprose,
  Its wastes in colours not their own,
And oft had my serene repose
  Been cloven by many a rending groan.   85

FOURTH VOICE: *from the Whirlwinds.*

We had soared beneath these mountains
  Unresting ages ; nor had thunder,
Nor yon volcano's flaming fountains,
  Nor any power above or under
  Ever made us mute with wonder.   90

FIRST VOICE.

But never bowed our snowy crest
As at the voice of thine unrest.

SECOND VOICE.

Never such a sound before
To the Indian waves we bore.
A pilot asleep on the howling sea   95
Leaped up from the deck in agony,
And heard, and cried, "Ah, woe is me!"
And died as mad as the wild waves be.

THIRD VOICE.

By such dread words from Earth to Heaven
My still realm was never riven: 100
When its wound was closed, there stood
Darkness o'er the day like blood.

Fourth Voice.

And we shrank back : for dreams of ruin
To frozen caves our flight pursuing
Made us keep silence — thus — and thus —   105
Though silence is a hell to us.

The Earth.

The tongueless Caverns of the craggy hills
Cried, " Misery ! " then ; the hollow Heaven replied,
" Misery ! "   And the Ocean's purple waves,
Climbing the land, howled to the lashing winds,   110
And the pale nations heard it, " Misery ! "

Prometheus.

I hear a sound of voices : not the voice
Which I gave forth.   Mother, thy sons and thou
Scorn him, without whose all-enduring will
Beneath the fierce omnipotence of Jove,   115
Both they and thou had vanished, like thin mist
Unrolled on the morning wind.   Know ye not me,
The Titan ?   He who made his agony
The barrier to your else all-conquering foe ?
Oh, rock-embosomed lawns, and snow-fed streams,   120
Now seen athwart frore vapours, deep below,
Through whose o'ershadowing woods I wandered once
With Asia, drinking life from her loved eyes ;
Why scorns the spirit which informs ye, now
To commune with me ? me alone, who checked,   125
As one who checks a fiend-drawn charioteer,
The falsehood and the force of him who reigns
Supreme, and with the groans of pining slaves
Fills your dim glens and liquid wildernesses :
Why answer ye not, still ?   Brethren !

THE EARTH.

They dare not! 130

PROMETHEUS.

Who dares? for I would hear that curse again.
Ha, what an awful whisper rises up!
'T is scarce like sound: it tingles through the frame
As lightning tingles, hovering ere it strike.
Speak, Spirit! from thine inorganic voice   135
I only know that thou art moving near
And love.   How cursed I him?

THE EARTH.

How canst thou hear
Who knowest not the language of the dead?

PROMETHEUS.

Thou art a living spirit: speak as they.

THE EARTH.

I dare not speak like life, lest Heaven's fell King   140
Should hear, and link me to some wheel of pain
More torturing than the one whereon I roll.
Subtle thou art and good, and though the Gods
Hear not this voice, yet thou art more than God
Being wise and kind: earnestly hearken now.   145

PROMETHEUS.

Obscurely through my brain, like shadows dim,
Sweep awful thoughts, rapid and thick.   I feel
Faint, like one mingled in entwining love;
Yet 't is not pleasure.

The Earth.

No, thou canst not hear:
Thou art immortal, and this tongue is known   150
Only to those who die.

Prometheus.

And what art thou,
O, melancholy Voice?

The Earth.

I am the Earth,
Thy mother; she within whose stony veins,
To the last fibre of the loftiest tree
Whose thin leaves trembled in the frozen air,   155
Joy ran, as blood within a living frame,
When thou didst from her bosom, like a cloud
Of glory, arise, a spirit of keen joy!
And at thy voice her pining sons uplifted
Their prostrate brows from the polluting dust,   160
And our almighty Tyrant with fierce dread
Grew pale, until his thunder chained thee here.
Then, see those million worlds which burn and roll
Around us: their inhabitants beheld
My spherèd light wane in wide Heaven; the sea   165
Was lifted by strange tempest, and new fire
From earthquake-rifted mountains of bright snow
Shook its portentous hair beneath Heaven's frown;
Lightning and Inundation vexed the plains;
Blue thistles bloomed in cities; foodless toads   170
Within voluptuous chambers panting crawled:
When Plague had fallen on man, and beast, and worm,
And Famine; and black blight on herb and tree;

And in the corn, and vines, and meadow-grass,
Teemed ineradicable poisonous weeds   175
Draining their growth, for my wan breast was dry
With grief; and the thin air, my breath, was stained
With the contagion of a mother's hate
Breathed on her child's destroyer; aye, I heard
Thy curse, the which, if thou rememberest not,   180
Yet my innumerable seas and streams,
Mountains, and caves, and winds, and yon wide air,
And the inarticulate people of the dead,
Preserve, a treasured spell. We meditate
In secret joy and hope those dreadful words   185
But dare not speak them.

PROMETHEUS.

                    Venerable mother!
All else who live and suffer take from thee
Some comfort; flowers, and fruits, and happy sounds,
And love, though fleeting; these may not be mine.
But mine own words, I pray, deny me not.   190

THE EARTH.

They shall be told. Ere Babylon was dust,
The Magus Zoroaster, my dead child,
Met his own image walking in the garden.
That apparition, sole of men, he saw.
For know there are two worlds of life and death :   195
One that which thou beholdest; but the other
Is underneath the grave, where do inhabit
The shadows of all forms that think and live
Till death unite them and they part no more;
Dreams and the light imaginings of men,   200

And all that faith creates or love desires,
Terrible, strange, sublime and beauteous shapes.
There thou art, and dost hang, a writhing shade,
'Mid whirlwind-peopled mountains ; all the gods
Are there, and all the powers of nameless worlds,   205
Vast, sceptred phantoms; heroes, men, and beasts;
And Demogorgon, a tremendous gloom ;
And he, the supreme Tyrant, on his throne
Of burning gold.   Son, one of these shall utter
The curse which all remember.   Call at will   210
Thine own ghost, or the ghost of Jupiter,
Hades or Typhon, or what mightier Gods
From all-prolific Evil, since thy ruin,
Have sprung, and trampled on my prostrate sons.
Ask, and they must reply : so the revenge   215
Of the Supreme may sweep through vacant shades,
As rainy wind through the abandoned gate
Of a fallen palace.

PROMETHEUS.

            Mother, let not aught
Of that which may be evil, pass again
My lips, or those of aught resembling me.   220
Phantasm of Jupiter, arise, appear !

IONE.

My wings are folded o'er mine ears :
    My wings are crossèd o'er mine eyes :
Yet through their silver shade appears,
    And through their lulling plumes arise,   225
A Shape, a throng of sounds ;
    May it be no ill to thee
O thou of many wounds !

Near whom, for our sweet sister's sake,
Ever thus we watch and wake.   230

PANTHEA.

The sound is of whirlwind underground,
   Earthquake, and fire, and mountains cloven ;
The shape is awful like the sound,
   Clothed in dark purple, star-inwoven.
A sceptre of pale gold   235
   To stay steps proud, o'er the slow cloud
His veinèd hand doth hold.
Cruel he looks, but calm and strong,
Like one who does, not suffers wrong.

PHANTASM OF JUPITER.

Why have the secret powers of this strange world   240
Driven me, a frail and empty phantom, hither
On direst storms?   What unaccustomed sounds
Are hovering on my lips, unlike the voice
With which our pallid race hold ghastly talk
In darkness?   And, proud sufferer, who art thou?   245

PROMETHEUS.

Tremendous Image, as thou art must be
He whom thou shadowest forth.   I am his foe,
The Titan.   Speak the words which I would hear,
Although no thought inform thine empty voice.

THE EARTH.

Listen ! And though your echoes must be mute,   250
Gray mountains, and old woods, and haunted springs,
Prophetic caves, and isle-surrounding streams,
Rejoice to hear what yet ye cannot speak.

PHANTASM.

A spirit seizes me and speaks within :
It tears me as fire tears a thunder-cloud. 255

PANTHEA.

See, how he lifts his mighty looks, the Heaven
Darkens above.

IONE.

He speaks!   O shelter me !

PROMETHEUS.

I see the curse on gestures proud and cold,
And looks of firm defiance, and calm hate,
And such despair as mocks itself with smiles, 260
Written as on a scroll : yet speak : Oh, speak !

PHANTASM.

Fiend, I defy thee ! with a calm, fixed mind,
    All that thou canst inflict I bid thee do ;
Foul Tyrant both of Gods and Human-kind,
    One only being shalt thou not subdue. 265
Rain then thy plagues upon me here,
Ghastly disease, and frenzying fear ;
    And let alternate frost and fire
    Eat into me, and be thine ire
Lightning, and cutting hail, and legioned forms 270
Of furies, driving by upon the wounding storms.

    Aye, do thy worst.   Thou art omnipotent.
        O'er all things but thyself I gave thee power,
    And my own will.   Be thy swift mischiefs sent
        To blast mankind, from yon ætherial tower. 275

Let thy malignant spirit move
In darkness over those I love :
On me and mine I imprecate
The utmost torture of thy hate ;
And thus devote to sleepless agony,   280
This undeclining head while thou must reign on high.

But thou, who art the God and Lord : O, thou,
  Who fillest with thy soul this world of woe,
To whom all things of Earth and Heaven do bow
  In fear and worship : all-prevailing foe !   285
I curse thee ! let a sufferer's curse
Clasp thee, his torturer, like remorse ;
Till thine Infinity shall be
A robe of envenomed agony ;
And thine Omnipotence a crown of pain,   290
To cling like burning gold round thy dissolving brain.

Heap on thy soul, by virtue of this Curse,
  Ill deeds, then be thou damned, beholding good ;
Both infinite as is the universe,
  And thou, and thy self-torturing solitude.   295
An awful image of calm power
Though now thou sittest, let the hour
Come, when thou must appear to be
That which thou art internally.
And after many a false and fruitless crime   300
Scorn track thy lagging fall through boundless space and
      time.

PROMETHEUS.

Were these my words, O, Parent ?

THE EARTH.
                    They were thine.

PROMETHEUS.

It doth repent me : words are quick and vain ;
Grief for awhile is blind, and so was mine.
I wish no living thing to suffer pain. 305

THE EARTH.

Misery, Oh misery to me,
That Jove at length should vanquish thee.
Wail, howl aloud, Land and Sea,
The Earth's rent heart shall answer ye.
Howl, Spirits of the living and the dead, 310
Your refuge, your defence lies fallen and vanquishèd.

FIRST ECHO.

Lies fallen and vanquishèd !

SECOND ECHO.

Fallen and vanquishèd !

IONE.

Fear not : 't is but some passing spasm;
The Titan is unvanquished still. 315
But see, where through the azure chasm
Of yon forked and snowy hill
Trampling the slant winds on high
With golden-sandalled feet, that glow
Under plumes of purple dye, 320
Like rose-ensanguined ivory,
A Shape comes now,
Stretching on high from his right hand
A serpent-cinctured wand.

PANTHEA.

'T is Jove's world-wandering herald, Mercury.   325

IONE.

And who are those with hydra tresses
  And iron wings that climb the wind,
Whom the frowning God represses
  Like vapours steaming up behind,
  Clanging loud, an endless crowd —   330

PANTHEA.

These are Jove's tempest-walking hounds,
  Whom he gluts with groans and blood,
When charioted on sulphurous cloud
  He bursts Heaven's bounds.

IONE.

Are they now led, from the thin dead   335
On new pangs to be fed?

PANTHEA.

The Titan looks as ever, firm, not proud.

FIRST FURY.

Ha! I scent life!

SECOND FURY.

Let me but look into his eyes!

THIRD FURY.

The hope of torturing him smells like a heap
Of corpses, to a death-bird after battle.   340

First Fury.

Darest thou delay, O Herald! take cheer, Hounds
Of Hell: what if the Son of Maia soon
Should make us food and sport — who can please long
The Omnipotent?

Mercury.

     Back to your towers of iron,
And gnash, beside the streams of fire and wail,   345
Your foodless teeth. Geryon, arise! and Gorgon,
Chimæra, and thou Sphinx, subtlest of fiends
Who ministered to Thebes Heaven's poisoned wine,
Unnatural love, and more unnatural hate:
These shall perform your task.

First Fury.

       Oh, mercy! mercy!   350
We die with our desire: drive us not back!

Mercury.

Crouch then in silence.
      Awful Sufferer
To thee unwilling, most unwillingly
I come, by the great Father's will driven down,
To execute a doom of new revenge.   355
Alas! I pity thee, and hate myself
That I can do no more: aye from thy sight
Returning, for a season, Heaven seems Hell.
So thy worn form pursues me night and day,
Smiling reproach. Wise art thou, firm and good,   360
But vainly wouldst stand forth alone in strife
Against the Omnipotent; as yon clear lamps

That measure and divide the weary years
From which there is no refuge, long have taught
And long must teach.   Even now thy Torturer arms   365
With the strange might of unimagined pains
The powers who scheme slow agonies in Hell,
And my commission is to lead them here,
Or what more subtle, foul, or savage fiends
People the abyss, and leave them to their task.   370
Be it not so! there is a secret known
To thee, and to none else of living things,
Which may transfer the sceptre of wide Heaven,
The fear of which perplexes the Supreme :
Clothe it in words, and bid it clasp his throne   375
In intercession; bend thy soul in prayer,
And like a suppliant in some gorgeous fane,
Let the will kneel within thy haughty heart :
For benefits and meek submission tame
The fiercest and the mightiest.

PROMETHEUS.

                       Evil minds   380
Change good to their own nature.   I gave all
He has; and in return he chains me here
Years, ages, night and day : whether the Sun
Split my parched skin, or in the moony night
The crystal-wingèd snow cling round my hair :   385
Whilst my belovèd race is trampled down
By his thought-executing ministers.
Such is the tyrant's recompense : 't is just :
He who is evil can receive no good ;
And for a world bestowed, or a friend lost,   390
He can feel hate, fear, shame ; not gratitude :
He but requites me for his own misdeed.
Kindness to such is keen reproach, which breaks

With bitter stings the light sleep of Revenge.
Submission, thou dost know I cannot try: 395
For what submission but that fatal word,
The death-seal of mankind's captivity,
Like the Sicilian's hair-suspended sword,
Which trembles o'er his crown, would he accept,
Or could I yield?   Which yet I will not yield.   400
Let others flatter Crime, where it sits throned
In brief Omnipotence: secure are they:
For Justice, when triumphant, will weep down
Pity, not punishment, on her own wrongs,
Too much avenged by those who err.   I wait,   405
Enduring thus, the retributive hour
Which since we spake is even nearer now.
But hark, the hell-hounds clamour: fear delay:
Behold!   Heaven lowers under thy Father's frown.

MERCURY.

Oh, that we might be spared, — I to inflict   410
And thou to suffer!   Once more answer me:
Thou knowest not the period of Jove's power?

PROMETHEUS.

I know but this, that it must come.

MERCURY.

                                        Alas!
Thou canst not count thy years to come of pain?

PROMETHEUS.

They last while Jove must reign: nor more, nor less   415
Do I desire or fear.

MERCURY.

Yet pause, and plunge
Into Eternity, where recorded time,
Even all that we imagine, age on age,
Seems but a point, and the reluctant mind
Flags wearily in its unending flight,   420
Till it sink, dizzy, blind, lost, shelterless;
Perchance it has not numbered the slow years
Which thou must spend in torture, unreprieved?

PROMETHEUS.

Perchance no thought can count them, yet they pass.

MERCURY.

If thou might'st dwell among the gods the while   425
Lapped in voluptuous joy?

PROMETHEUS.

I would not quit
This bleak ravine, these unrepentant pains.

MERCURY.

Alas! I wonder at, yet pity thee.

PROMETHEUS.

Pity the self-despising slaves of Heaven,
Not me, within whose mind sits peace serene,   430
As light in the sun, throned: how vain is talk!
Call up the fiends.

IONE.

O sister, look! White fire
Has cloven to the roots yon huge snow-loaded cedar:
How fearfully God's thunder howls behind!

MERCURY.

I must obey his words and thine: alas!   435
Most heavily remorse hangs at my heart!

PANTHEA.

See where the child of Heaven, with wingèd feet,
Runs down the slanted sunlight of the dawn.

IONE.

Dear sister, close thy plumes over thine eyes
Lest thou behold and die: they come: they come   440
Blackening the birth of day with countless wings,
And hollow underneath, like death.

FIRST FURY.

Prometheus!

SECOND FURY.

Immortal Titan!

THIRD FURY.

Champion of Heaven's slaves!

PROMETHEUS.

He whom some dreadful voice invokes is here,
Prometheus, the chained Titan. Horrible forms,   445
What and who are ye? Never yet there came

Phantasms so foul through monster-teeming Hell
From the all-miscreative brain of Jove ;
Whilst I behold such execrable shapes,
Methinks I grow like what I contemplate,   450
And laugh and stare in loathsome sympathy.

FIRST FURY.

We are the ministers of pain, and fear,
And disappointment, and mistrust, and hate,
And clinging crime ; and as lean dogs pursue
Through wood and lake some struck and sobbing fawn,   455
We track all things that weep, and bleed, and live,
When the great King betrays them to our will.

PROMETHEUS.

Oh ! many fearful natures in one name,
I know ye ; and these lakes and echoes know
The darkness and the clangour of your wings.   460
But why more hideous than your loathèd selves
Gather ye up in legions from the deep ?

SECOND FURY.

We knew not that : Sisters, rejoice, rejoice !

PROMETHEUS.

Can aught exult in its deformity ?

SECOND FURY.

The beauty of delight makes lovers glad,   465
Gazing on one another : so are we.
As from the rose which the pale priestess kneels
To gather for her festal crown of flowers

The aërial crimson falls, flushing her cheek,
So from our victim's destined agony 470
The shade which is our form invests us round;
Else we are shapeless as our mother Night.

PROMETHEUS.

I laugh your power, and his who sent you here,
To lowest scorn.   Pour forth the cup of pain.

FIRST FURY.

Thou thinkest we will rend thee bone from bone, 475
And nerve from nerve, working like fire within?

PROMETHEUS.

Pain is my element, as hate is thine;
Ye rend me now: I care not.

SECOND FURY.

                Dost imagine
We will but laugh into thy lidless eyes?

PROMETHEUS.

I weigh not what ye do, but what ye suffer, 480
Being evil.   Cruel was the power which called
You, or aught else so wretched, into light.

THIRD FURY.

Thou think'st we will live through thee, one by one,
Like animal life, and though we can obscure not
The soul which burns within, that we will dwell 485
Beside it, like a vain loud multitude
Vexing the self-content of wisest men:

That we will be dread thought beneath thy brain,
And foul desire round thine astonished heart,
And blood within thy labyrinthine veins   490
Crawling like agony.

PROMETHEUS.

Why, ye are thus now;
Yet am I king over myself, and rule
The torturing and conflicting throngs within,
As Jove rules you when Hell grows mutinous.

CHORUS OF FURIES.

From the ends of the earth, from the ends of the earth, 495
Where the night has its grave and the morning its birth,
Come, come, come!
Oh, ye who shake hills with the scream of your mirth,
When cities sink howling in ruin ; and ye
Who with wingless footsteps trample the sea,   500
And close upon Shipwreck and Famine's track,
Sit chattering with joy on the foodless wreck ;
Come, come, come!
Leave the bed, low, cold, and red,
Strewed beneath a nation dead ;   505
Leave the hatred, as in ashes
Fire is left for future burning :
It will burst in bloodier flashes
When ye stir it, soon returning :
Leave the self-contempt implanted   510
In young spirits, sense-enchanted,
Misery's yet unkindled fuel :
Leave Hell's secrets half unchanted
To the maniac dreamer ; cruel

More than ye can be with hate 515
Is he with fear.
Come, come, come!
We are steaming up from Hell's wide gate
And we burthen the blast of the atmosphere,
But vainly we toil till ye come here. 520

IONE.

Sister, I hear the thunder of new wings.

PANTHEA.

These solid mountains quiver with the sound
Even as the tremulous air: their shadows make
The space within my plumes more black than night.

FIRST FURY.

Your call was as a wingèd car 525
Driven on whirlwinds fast and far;
It rapt us from red gulphs of war.

SECOND FURY.

From wide cities, famine-wasted;

THIRD FURY.

Groans half heard, and blood untasted;

FOURTH FURY.

Kingly conclaves stern and cold, 530
Where blood with gold is bought and sold;

FIFTH FURY.

From the furnace, white and hot,
In which —

A FURY.

Speak not : whisper not:
I know all that ye would tell,
But to speak might break the spell   535
Which must bend the Invincible,
    The stern of thought ;
He yet defies the deepest power of Hell.

FURY.

Tear the veil !

ANOTHER FURY.

It is torn.

CHORUS.

    The pale stars of the morn
Shine on a misery, dire to be borne.   540
Dost thou faint, mighty Titan? We laugh thee to scorn.
Dost thou boast the clear knowledge thou wakenedst for
        man?
Then was kindled within him a thirst which outran
Those perishing waters; a thirst of fierce fever,
Hope, love, doubt, desire, which consume him for ever. 545
    One came forth of gentle worth
    Smiling on the sanguine earth ;
    His words outlived him, like swift poison
        Withering up truth, peace, and pity.
    Look! where round the wide horizon   550
        Many a million-peopled city
    Vomits smoke in the bright air.
    Mark that outcry of despair !
    'T is his mild and gentle ghost
        Wailing for the faith he kindled :   555
    Look again, the flames almost

To a glow-worm's lamp have dwindled:
The survivors round the embers
    Gather in dread.
        Joy, joy, joy!   560
Past ages crowd on thee, but each one remembers,
And the future is dark, and the present is spread
Like a pillow of thorns for thy slumberless head.

SEMICHORUS I.

Drops of bloody agony flow
From his white and quivering brow.   565
Grant a little respite now:
See a disenchanted nation
Springs like day from desolation;
To Truth its state is dedicate,
And Freedom leads it forth, her mate;   570
A legioned band of linkèd brothers
Whom Love calls children —

SEMICHORUS II.

                    'T is another's:
See how kindred murder kin:
'T is the vintage-time for death and sin:
Blood, like new wine, bubbles within: 575
    Till Despair smothers
The struggling world, which slaves and tyrants win.
                [All the FURIES *vanish, except one.*

IONE.

Hark, sister! what a low yet dreadful groan
Quite unsuppressed is tearing up the heart
Of the good Titan, as storms tear the deep,   580
And beasts hear the sea moan in inland caves.
Darest thou observe how the fiends torture him?

PANTHEA.

Alas! I looked forth twice, but will no more.

IONE.

What didst thou see?

PANTHEA.

A woful sight: a youth
With patient looks nailed to a crucifix.   585

IONE.

What next?

PANTHEA.

The heaven around, the earth below
Was peopled with thick shapes of human death,
All horrible, and wrought by human hands,
And some appeared the work of human hearts,
For men were slowly killed by frowns and smiles: 590
And other sights too foul to speak and live
Were wandering by.   Let us not tempt worse fear
By looking forth: those groans are grief enough.

FURY.

Behold an emblem: those who do endure
Deep wrongs for man, and scorn, and chains, but heap 595
Thousandfold torment on themselves and him.

PROMETHEUS.

Remit the anguish of that lighted stare;
Close those wan lips; let that thorn-wounded brow
Stream not with blood; it mingles with thy tears!
Fix, fix those tortured orbs in peace and death,   600
So thy sick throes shake not that crucifix,

So those pale fingers play not with thy gore.
O, horrible! Thy name I will not speak,
It hath become a curse.   I see, I see
The wise, the mild, the lofty, and the just,   605
Whom thy slaves hate for being like to thee,
Some hunted by foul lies from their heart's home,
An early-chosen, late-lamented home ;
As hooded ounces cling to the driven hind ;
Some linked to corpses in unwholesome cells :   610
Some — Hear I not the multitude laugh loud?
Impaled in lingering fire : and mighty realms
Float by my feet, like sea-uprooted isles,
Whose sons are kneaded down in common blood
By the red light of their own burning homes.   615

FURY.

Blood thou canst see, and fire ; and canst hear groans ;
Worse things, unheard, unseen, remain behind.

PROMETHEUS.

Worse ?

FURY.

In each human heart terror survives
The ruin it has gorged : the loftiest fear
All that they would disdain to think were true :   620
Hypocrisy and custom make their minds
The fanes of many a worship, now outworn.
They dare not devise good for man's estate,
And yet they know not that they do not dare.
The good want power, but to weep barren tears.   625
The powerful goodness want : worse need for them.
The wise want love ; and those who love want wisdom ;
And all best things are thus confused to ill.

Many are strong and rich, and would be just,
But live among their suffering fellow-men 630
As if none felt: they know not what they do.

PROMETHEUS.

Thy words are like a cloud of wingèd snakes;
And yet I pity those they torture not.

FURY.

Thou pitiest them? I speak no more! [*Vanishes.*

PROMETHEUS.

Ah woe!
Ah woe! Alas! pain, pain ever, for ever! 635
I close my tearless eyes, but see more clear
Thy works within my woe-illumèd mind,
Thou subtle tyrant! Peace is in the grave.
The grave hides all things beautiful and good:
I am a God and cannot find it there, 640
Nor would I seek it: for, though dread revenge,
This is defeat, fierce king, not victory.
The sights with which thou torturest gird my soul
With new endurance, till the hour arrives
When they shall be no types of things which are. 645

PANTHEA.

Alas! what sawest thou?

PROMETHEUS.

There are two woes;
To speak, and to behold; thou spare me one.
Names are there, Nature's sacred watch-words, they
Were borne aloft in bright emblazonry;

The nations thronged around, and cried aloud,   650
As with one voice, Truth, liberty, and love!
Suddenly fierce confusion fell from heaven
Among them: there was strife, deceit, and fear:
Tyrants rushed in, and did divide the spoil.
This was the shadow of the truth I saw.   655

THE EARTH.

I felt thy torture, son, with such mixed joy
As pain and virtue give.   To cheer thy state
I bid ascend those subtle and fair spirits,
Whose homes are the dim caves of human thought,
And who inhabit, as birds wing the wind,   660
Its world-surrounding æther: they behold
Beyond that twilight realm, as in a glass,
The future: may they speak comfort to thee!

PANTHEA.

Look, sister, where a troop of spirits gather,
Like flocks of clouds in spring's delightful weather,   665
Thronging in the blue air!

IONE.

                And see! more come,
Like fountain-vapours when the winds are dumb,
That climb up the ravine in scattered lines.
And, hark! is it the music of the pines?
Is it the lake?   Is it the waterfall?   670

PANTHEA.

'T is something sadder, sweeter far than all.

Chorus of Spirits.

From unremembered ages we
Gentle guides and guardians be
Of heaven-oppressed mortality;
And we breathe, and sicken not,   675
The atmosphere of human thought:
Be it dim, and dank, and gray,
Like a storm-extinguished day,
Travelled o'er by dying gleams;
   Be it bright as all between   680
Cloudless skies and windless streams,
   Silent, liquid, and serene;
As the birds within the wind,
   As the fish within the wave,
As the thoughts of man's own mind   685
   Float through all above the grave;
We make there our liquid lair,
Voyaging cloudlike and unpent
Through the boundless element:
Thence we bear the prophecy   690
Which begins and ends in thee!

Ione.

More yet come, one by one: the air around them
Looks radiant as the air around a star.

First Spirit.

On a battle-trumpet's blast
I fled hither, fast, fast, fast,   695
'Mid the darkness upward cast.
From the dust of creeds outworn,
From the tyrant's banner torn,
Gathering round me, onward borne,

There was mingled many a cry —   700
Freedom! Hope! Death! Victory!
Till they faded through the sky;
And one sound, above, around,
One sound beneath, around, above,
Was moving; 't was the soul of love;   705
'T was the hope, the prophecy
Which begins and ends in thee.

SECOND SPIRIT.

A rainbow's arch stood on the sea,
Which rocked beneath immovably;
And the triumphant storm did flee,   710
Like a conqueror, swift and proud,
Between, with many a captive cloud,
A shapeless, dark and rapid crowd,
Each by lightning riven in half:
I heard the thunder hoarsely laugh: 715
Mighty fleets were strewn like chaff
And spread beneath a hell of death
O'er the white waters. I alit
On a great ship lightning-split,
And speeded hither on the sigh   720
Of one who gave an enemy
His plank, then plunged aside to die.

THIRD SPIRIT.

I sate beside a sage's bed,
And the lamp was burning red
Near the book where he had fed,   725
When a Dream with plumes of flame,
To his pillow hovering came,
And I knew it was the same

Which had kindled long ago
Pity, eloquence, and woe;   730
And the world awhile below
Wore the shade, its lustre made.
It has borne me here as fleet
As Desire's lightning feet:
I must ride it back ere morrow,   735
Or the sage will wake in sorrow.

FOURTH SPIRIT.

On a poet's lips I slept
Dreaming like a love-adept
In the sound his breathing kept;
Nor seeks nor finds he mortal blisses,   740
But feeds on the aërial kisses
Of shapes that haunt thought's wildernesses.
He will watch from dawn to gloom
The lake-reflected sun illume
The yellow bees in the ivy-bloom,   745
Nor heed nor see, what things they be;
But from these create he can
Forms more real than living man,
Nurslings of immortality!
One of these awakened me,   750
And I sped to succour thee.

IONE.

Behold'st thou not two shapes from the east and west
Come, as two doves to one belovèd nest,
Twin nurslings of the all-sustaining air
On swift still wings glide down the atmosphere?   755
And, hark! their sweet, sad voices! 't is despair
Mingled with love and then dissolved in sound.

PANTHEA.

Canst thou speak, sister? all my words are drowned.

IONE.

Their beauty gives me voice. See how they float
On their sustaining wings of skiey grain,   760
Orange and azure deepening into gold:
Their soft smiles light the air like a star's fire.

CHORUS OF SPIRITS.

Hast thou beheld the form of Love?

FIFTH SPIRIT.

                          As over wide dominions
I sped, like some swift cloud that wings the wide air's
    wildernesses,
That planet-crested shape swept by on lightning-braided
    pinions,   765
Scattering the liquid joy of life from his ambrosial tresses:
His footsteps paved the world with light; but as I passed
    't was fading,
And hollow Ruin yawned behind: great sages bound in
    madness,
And headless patriots, and pale youths who perished,
    unupbraiding,
Gleamed in the night. I wandered o'er, till thou, O King
    of sadness,   770
Turned by thy smile the worst I saw to recollected glad-
    ness.

SIXTH SPIRIT.

Ah, sister! Desolation is a delicate thing:
It walks not on the earth, it floats not on the air,

But treads with killing footstep, and fans with silent wing
The tender hopes which in their hearts the best and
  gentlest bear; 775
Who, soothed to false repose by the fanning plumes above
And the music-stirring motion of its soft and busy feet,
Dream visions of aërial joy, and call the monster, Love,
And wake, and find the shadow Pain, as he whom now
  we greet.

CHORUS.

Though Ruin now Love's shadow be, 780
Following him, destroyingly,
 On Death's white and wingèd steed,
Which the fleetest cannot flee,
 Trampling down both flower and weed,
Man and beast, and foul and fair, 785
Like a tempest through the air;
Thou shalt quell this horseman grim,
Woundless though in heart or limb.

PROMETHEUS.

Spirits! how know ye this shall be?

CHORUS.

In the atmosphere we breathe, 790
As buds grow red when the snow-storms flee,
 From spring gathering up beneath,
Whose mild winds shake the elder brake,
And the wandering herdsmen know
That the white-thorn soon will blow: 795
Wisdom, Justice, Love, and Peace,
When they struggle to increase,
 Are to us as soft winds be
 To shepherd boys, the prophecy
Which begins and ends in thee. 800

IONE.

Where are the Spirits fled?

PANTHEA.

     Only a sense
Remains of them, like the omnipotence
Of music, when the inspired voice and lute
Languish, ere yet the responses are mute,
Which through the deep and labyrinthine soul,   805
Like echoes through long caverns, wind and roll.

PROMETHEUS.

How fair these air-born shapes! and yet I feel
Most vain all hope but love; and thou art far,
Asia! who, when my being overflowed,
Wert like a golden chalice to bright wine   810
Which else had sunk into the thirsty dust.
All things are still: alas! how heavily .
This quiet morning weighs upon my heart;
Though I should dream I could even sleep with grief
If slumber were denied not. I would fain   815
Be what it is my destiny to be,
The saviour and the strength of suffering man,
Or sink into the original gulph of things:
There is no agony, and no solace left;
Earth can console, Heaven can torment no more.   820

PANTHEA.

Hast thou forgotten one who watches thee
The cold dark night, and never sleeps but when
The shadow of thy spirit falls on her?

PROMETHEUS.

I said all hope was vain but love : thou lovest.

PANTHEA.

Deeply in truth; but the eastern star looks white,   825
And Asia waits in that far Indian vale
The scene of her sad exile; rugged once
And desolate and frozen, like this ravine;
But now invested with fair flowers and herbs,
And haunted by sweet airs and sounds, which flow   830
Among the woods and waters, from the æther
Of her transforming presence, which would fade
If it were mingled not with thine.   Farewell!

END OF THE FIRST ACT.

ACT II.

SCENE I. *Morning. A lovely Vale in the Indian Caucasus.*
ASIA *alone.*

ASIA.

From all the blasts of heaven thou hast descended :
Yes, like a spirit, like a thought, which makes
Unwonted tears throng to the horny eyes,
And beatings haunt the desolated heart,
Which should have learnt repose: thou hast descended   5
Cradled in tempests; thou dost wake, O Spring!
O child of many winds!   As suddenly
Thou comest as the memory of a dream,
Which now is sad because it hath been sweet;
Like genius, or like joy which riseth up   10
As from the earth, clothing with golden clouds
The desert of our life.

This is the season, this the day, the hour;
At sunrise thou shouldst come, sweet sister mine,
Too long desired, too long delaying, come!   15
How like death-worms the wingless moments crawl!
The point of one white star is quivering still
Deep in the orange light of widening morn
Beyond the purple mountains : through a chasm
Of wind-divided mist the darker lake   20
Reflects it: now it wanes: it gleams again
As the waves fade, and as the burning threads
Of woven cloud unravel in pale air:
'T is lost! and through yon peaks of cloud-like snow
The roseate sunlight quivers: hear I not   25
The Æolian music of her sea-green plumes
Winnowing the crimson dawn?

PANTHEA *enters.*

I feel, I see
Those eyes which burn through smiles that fade in tears,
Like stars half quenched in mists of silver dew.
Belovèd and most beautiful, who wearest   30
The shadow of that soul by which I live,
How late thou art! the spherèd sun had climbed
The sea; my heart was sick with hope, before
The printless air felt thy belated plumes.

PANTHEA.

Pardon, great Sister! but my wings were faint   35
With the delight of a remembered dream,
As are the noon-tide plumes of summer winds
Satiate with sweet flowers. I was wont to sleep
Peacefully, and awake refreshed and calm
Before the sacred Titan's fall, and thy   40

Unhappy love, had made, through use and pity,
Both love and woe familiar to my heart
As they had grown to thine: erewhile I slept
Under the glaucous caverns of old Ocean
Within dim bowers of green and purple moss,   45
Our young Ione's soft and milky arms
Locked then, as now, behind my dark, moist hair,
While my shut eyes and cheek were pressed within
The folded depth of her life-breathing bosom:
But not as now, since I am made the wind   50
Which fails beneath the music that I bear
Of thy most wordless converse; since dissolved
Into the sense with which love talks, my rest
Was troubled and yet sweet; my waking hours
Too full of care and pain.

ASIA.

       Lift up thine eyes,   55
And let me read thy dream.

PANTHEA.

       As I have said
With our sea-sister at his feet I slept.
The mountain mists, condensing at our voice
Under the moon, had spread their snowy flakes,
From the keen ice shielding our linkèd sleep.   60
Then two dreams came. One, I remember not.
But in the other his pale wound-worn limbs
Fell from Prometheus, and the azure night
Grew radiant with the glory of that form
Which lives unchanged within, and his voice fell   65
Like music which makes giddy the dim brain,
Faint with intoxication of keen joy:
" Sister of her whose footsteps pave the world

"With loveliness — more fair than aught but her,
"Whose shadow thou art — lift thine eyes on me."   70
I lifted them: the overpowering light
Of that immortal shape was shadowed o'er   ,
By love; which, from his soft and flowing limbs,
And passion-parted lips, and keen, faint eyes,
Steamed forth like vaporous fire; an atmosphere   75
Which wrapped me in its all-dissolving power,
As the warm æther of the morning sun
Wraps ere it drinks some cloud of wandering dew.
I saw not, heard not, moved not, only felt
His presence flow and mingle through my blood   80
Till it became his life, and his grew mine,
And I was thus absorbed, until it passed,
And like the vapours when the sun sinks down,
Gathering again in drops upon the pines,
And tremulous as they, in the deep night   85
My being was condensed; and as the rays
Of thought were slowly gathered, I could hear
His voice, whose accents lingered ere they died
Like footsteps of weak melody: thy name
Among the many sounds alone I heard   90
Of what might be articulate; though still
I listened through the night when sound was none.
Ione wakened then, and said to me:
"Canst thou divine what troubles me to-night?
"I always knew what I desired before,   95
"Nor ever found delight to wish in vain.
"But now I cannot tell thee what I seek;
"I know not; something sweet, since it is sweet
"Even to desire; it is thy sport, false sister;
"Thou hast discovered some enchantment old,   100
"Whose spells have stolen my spirit as I slept
"And mingled it with thine: for when just now

" We kissed, I felt within thy parted lips
" The sweet air that sustained me, and the warmth
" Of the life-blood, for loss of which I faint, 105
",Quivered between our intertwining arms."
I answered not, for the Eastern star grew pale,
But fled to thee.

ASIA.

   Thou speakest, but thy words
Are as the air : I feel them not : Oh, lift
Thine eyes, that I may read his written soul ! 110

PANTHEA.

I lift them though they droop beneath the load
Of that they would express : what canst thou see
But thine own fairest shadow imaged there ?

ASIA.

Thine eyes are like the deep, blue, boundless heaven
Contracted to two circles underneath 115
Their long, fine lashes ; dark, far, measureless,
Orb within orb, and line through line inwoven.

PANTHEA.

Why lookest thou as if a spirit passed ?

ASIA.

There is a change : beyond their inmost depth
I see a shade, a shape : 't is He, arrayed 120
In the soft light of his own smiles, which spread
Like radiance from the cloud-surrounded moon.
Prometheus, it is thine ! depart not yet !
Say not those smiles that we shall meet again
Within that bright pavilion which their beams 125

Shall build on the waste world? The dream is told.
What shape is that between us? Its rude hair
Roughens the wind that lifts it, its regard
Is wild and quick, yet 't is a thing of air
For through its gray robe gleams the golden dew   130
Whose stars the noon has quenched not.

DREAM.
                    Follow! Follow!
          PANTHEA.
It is mine other dream.

                    ASIA.

                    It disappears.

          PANTHEA.

It passes now into my mind.   Methought
As we sate here, the flower-infolding buds
Burst on yon lightning-blasted almond-tree,   135
When swift from the white Scythian wilderness
A wind swept forth wrinkling the Earth with frost:
I looked, and all the blossoms were blown down;
But on each leaf was stamped, as the blue bells
Of Hyacinth tell Apollo's written grief,   140
O, FOLLOW, FOLLOW!
                    ASIA.

                    As you speak, your words
Fill, pause by pause, my own forgotten sleep
With shapes.   Methought among the lawns together
We wandered, underneath the young gray dawn,
And multitudes of dense white fleecy clouds   145
Were wandering in thick flocks along the mountains
Shepherded by the slow, unwilling wind;
And the white dew on the new bladed grass,

Just piercing the dark earth, hung silently:
And there was more which I remember not: 150
But on the shadows of the morning clouds,
Athwart the purple mountain slope, was written
FOLLOW, O, FOLLOW! as they vanished by,
And on each herb, from which Heaven's dew had
    fallen,
The like was stamped, as with a withering fire. 155
A wind arose among the pines; it shook
The clinging music from their boughs, and then
Low, sweet, faint sounds, like the farewell of ghosts,
Were heard: OH, FOLLOW, FOLLOW, FOLLOW ME!
And then I said: " Panthea, look on me." 160
But in the depth of those belovèd eyes
Still I saw, FOLLOW, FOLLOW!

ECHO.
Follow, follow!

PANTHEA.

The crags, this clear spring morning, mock our voices
As they were spirit-tongued.

ASIA.
It is some being
Around the crags. What fine clear sounds! O, list! 165

ECHOES (*unseen*).

Echoes we: listen!
We cannot stay:
As dew-stars glisten
Then fade away —
    Child of Ocean! 170

Asia.

Hark! Spirits speak. The liquid responses
Of their aërial tongues yet sound.

Panthea.

                I hear.

Echoes.

O, follow, follow,
   As our voice recedeth
Through the caverns hollow,   175
   Where the forest spreadeth:

(*More distant.*)

O, follow, follow!
Through the caverns hollow,
As the song floats thou pursue,
Where the wild bee never flew,   180
Through the noontide darkness deep,
By the odour-breathing sleep
Of faint night flowers, and the waves
At the fountain-lighted caves,
While our music, wild and sweet,   185
Mocks thy gently falling feet,
   Child of Ocean!

Asia.

Shall we pursue the sound? It grows more faint
And distant.

Panthea.

List! the strain floats nearer now.

ECHOES.

In the world unknown   190
  Sleeps a voice unspoken ;
By thy step alone
  Can its rest be broken ;
Child of Ocean !

ASIA.

How the notes sink upon the ebbing wind !   195

ECHOES.

O, follow, follow !
  Through the caverns hollow,
As the song floats thou pursue,
  By the woodland noon-tide dew;
By the forests, lakes, and fountains   200
Through the many-folded mountains ;
To the rents, and gulphs, and chasms,
Where the Earth reposed from spasms,
On the day when He and thou
  Parted, to commingle now;   205
Child of Ocean !

ASIA.

Come, sweet Panthea, link thy hand in mine,
And follow, ere the voices fade away.

SCENE II. *A Forest, intermingled with Rocks and Caverns.* ASIA
and PANTHEA *pass into it. Two young Fauns are sitting on a
Rock, listening.*

SEMICHORUS I. OF SPIRITS.

The path through which that lovely twain
  Have passed, by cedar, pine, and yew,

And each dark tree that ever grew,
Is curtained out from Heaven's wide blue;
Nor sun, nor moon, nor wind, nor rain,   5
    Can pierce its interwoven bowers,
Nor aught, save where some cloud of dew,
Drifted along the earth-creeping breeze,
Between the trunks of the hoar trees,
    Hangs each a pearl in the pale flowers   10
Of the green laurel, blown anew;
And bends, and then fades silently,
One frail and fair anemone :
Or when some star of many a one
That climbs and wanders through steep night,   15
Has found the cleft through which alone
Beams fall from high those depths upon
Ere it is borne away, away,
By the swift Heavens that cannot stay,
It scatters drops of golden light,   20
Like lines of rain that ne'er unite :
And the gloom divine is all around,
And underneath is the mossy ground;

SEMICHORUS II.

There the voluptuous nightingales,
    Are awake through all the broad noon-day.   25
When one with bliss or sadness fails,
    And through the windless ivy-boughs,
    Sick with sweet love, droops dying away
On its mate's music-panting bosom;
Another from the swinging blossom,   30
    Watching to catch the languid close   .
Of the last strain, then lifts on high
The wings of the weak melody,

'Till some new strain of feeling bear
    The song, and all the woods are mute ;   35
When there is heard through the dim air
The rush of wings, and rising there
    Like many a lake-surrounded flute,
Sounds overflow the listener's brain
So sweet, that joy is almost pain.   40

SEMICHORUS I.

There those enchanted eddies play
    Of echoes, music-tongued, which draw,
    By Demogorgon's mighty law,
    With melting rapture, or sweet awe,
All spirits on that secret way;   45
    As inland boats are driven to Ocean
Down streams made strong with mountain-thaw:
    And first there comes a gentle sound
    To those in talk or slumber bound,
    And wakes the destined.   Soft emotion   50
Attracts, impels them: those who saw
    Say from the breathing earth behind
    There steams a plume-uplifting wind
Which drives them on their path, while they
    Believe their own swift wings and feet   55
The sweet desires within obey:
And so they float upon their way,
Until, still sweet, but loud and strong,
The storm of sound is driven along,
    Sucked up and hurrying: as they fleet   60
    Behind, its gathering billows meet
And to the fatal mountain bear
Like clouds amid the yielding air.

FIRST FAUN.

Canst thou imagine where those spirits live
Which make such delicate music in the woods? 65
We haunt within the least frequented caves
And closest coverts, and we know these wilds,
Yet never meet them, though we hear them oft:
Where may they hide themselves?

SECOND FAUN.

                    'T is hard to tell:
I have heard those more skilled in spirits say, 70
The bubbles, which the enchantment of the sun
Sucks from the pale faint water-flowers that pave
The oozy bottom of clear lakes and pools,
Are the pavilions where such dwell and float
Under the green and golden atmosphere 75
Which noon-tide kindles through the woven leaves;
And when these burst, and the thin fiery air,
The which they breathed within those lucent domes,
Ascends to flow like meteors through the night,
They ride on them, and rein their headlong speed, 80
And bow their burning crests, and glide in fire
Under the waters of the earth again.

FIRST FAUN.

If such live thus, have others other lives,
Under pink blossoms or within the bells
Of meadow flowers, or folded violets deep, 85
Or on their dying odours, when they die,
Or in the sunlight of the spherèd dew?

Second Faun.

Aye, many more which we may well divine.
But, should we stay to speak, noontide would come,
And thwart Silenus find his goats undrawn,　　　　　90
And grudge to sing those wise and lovely songs
Of fate, and chance, and God, and Chaos old,
And Love, and the chained Titan's woful doom,
And how he shall be loosed, and make the earth
One brotherhood: delightful strains which cheer　　95
Our solitary twilights, and which charm
To silence the unenvying nightingales.

Scene III. *A Pinnacle of Rock among Mountains.* Asia *and* Panthea.

Panthea.

Hither the sound has borne us — to the realm
Of Demogorgon, and the mighty portal,
Like a volcano's meteor-breathing chasm,
Whence the oracular vapour is hurled up
Which lonely men drink wandering in their youth,　　5
And call truth, virtue, love, genius, or joy,
That maddening wine of life, whose dregs they drain
To deep intoxication; and uplift,
Like Mænads who cry aloud, Evoe! Evoe!
The voice which is contagion to the world.　　　　10

Asia.

Fit throne for such a Power! Magnificent!
How glorious art thou, Earth! And if thou be
The shadow of some spirit lovelier still,
Though evil stain its work, and it should be
Like its creation, weak yet beautiful,　　　　　15

I could fall down and worship that and thee.
Even now my heart adoreth : Wonderful !
Look, sister, ere the vapour dim thy brain :
Beneath is a wide plain of billowy mist,
As a lake, paving in the morning sky,   20
With azure waves which burst in silver light,
Some Indian vale.   Behold it, rolling on
Under the curdling winds, and islanding
The peak whereon we stand, midway, around,
Encinctured by the dark and blooming forests,   25
Dim twilight-lawns, and stream-illumined caves,
And wind-enchanted shapes of wandering mist :
And far on high the keen sky-cleaving mountains
From icy spires of sun-like radiance fling
The dawn, as lifted Ocean's dazzling spray,   30
From some Atlantic islet scattered up,
Spangles the wind with lamp-like water-drops.
The vale is girdled with their walls, a howl
Of cataracts from their thaw-cloven ravines
Satiates the listening wind, continuous, vast,   35
Awful as silence.   Hark! the rushing snow!
The sun-awakened avalanche! whose mass,
Thrice sifted by the storm, had gathered there
Flake after flake, in heaven-defying minds
As thought by thought is piled, till some great truth   40
Is loosened, and the nations echo round,
Shaken to their roots, as do the mountains now.

PANTHEA.

Look how the gusty sea of mist is breaking
In crimson foam, even at our feet ! it rises
As Ocean at the enchantment of the moon   45
Round foodless men wrecked on some oozy isle.

ASIA.

The fragments of the cloud are scattered up;
The wind that lifts them disentwines my hair;
Its billows now sweep o'er mine eyes; my brain
Grows dizzy; I see thin shapes within the mist.   50

PANTHEA.

A countenance with beckoning smiles: there burns
An azure fire within its golden locks!
Another and another: hark! they speak!

SONG OF SPIRITS.

To the deep, to the deep,
        Down, down!   55
Through the shade of sleep,
Through the cloudy strife
Of Death and of Life;
Through the veil and the bar
Of things which seem and are   60
Even to the steps of the remotest throne,
        Down, down!

While the sound whirls around,
        Down, down!
As the fawn draws the hound,   65
As the lightning the vapour,
As a weak moth the taper;
Death, despair; love, sorrow;
Time both; to-day, to-morrow;
As steel obeys the spirit of the stone,   70
        Down, down!

Through the gray, void abysm,
   Down, down!
Where the air is no prism,
And the moon and stars are not,   75
And the cavern-crags wear not
The radiance of Heaven,
Nor the gloom to Earth given,
Where there is one pervading, one alone,
   Down, down!   80

In the depth of the deep
   Down, down!
Like veiled lightning asleep,
Like the spark nursed in embers,
The last look Love remembers,   85
Like a diamond, which shines
On the dark wealth of mines,
A spell is treasured but for thee alone.
   Down, down!

We have bound thee, we guide thee;   90
   Down, down!
With the bright form beside thee;
Resist not the weakness,
Such strength is in meekness
That the Eternal, the Immortal,   95
Must unloose through life's portal
The snake-like Doom coiled underneath his
  throne
   By that alone.

SCENE IV. *The Cave of* DEMOGORGON. ASIA *and* PANTHEA.

PANTHEA.

What veilèd form sits on that ebon throne?

ASIA.
The veil has fallen.

PANTHEA.

I see a mighty darkness
Filling the seat of power, and rays of gloom
Dart round, as light from the meridian sun,
Ungazed upon and shapeless; neither limb,   5
Nor form, nor outline; yet we feel it is
A living Spirit.

DEMOGORGON.

Ask what thou wouldst know.

ASIA.

What canst thou tell?

DEMOGORGON.

All things thou dar'st demand.

ASIA.

Who made the living world?

DEMOGORGON.

God.

ASIA.
Who made all
That it contains? thought, passion, reason, will,   10
Imagination?

DEMOGORGON.

God : Almighty God.

ASIA.

Who made that sense which, when the winds of spring
In rarest visitation, or the voice
Of one belovèd heard in youth alone,
Fills the faint eyes with falling tears which dim　　　15
The radiant looks of unbewailing flowers,
And leaves this peopled earth a solitude
When it returns no more?

DEMOGORGON.
　　　　Merciful God.

ASIA.

And who made terror, madness, crime, remorse,
Which from the links of the great chain of things,　　20
To every thought within the mind of man
Sway and drag heavily, and each one reels
Under the load towards the pit of death;
Abandoned hope, and love that turns to hate;
And self-contempt, bitterer to drink than blood;　　25
Pain, whose unheeded and familiar speech
Is howling, and keen shrieks, day after day;
And Hell, or the sharp fear of Hell?

DEMOGORGON.
　　　　　　He reigns.
ASIA.

Utter his name: a world pining in pain
Asks but his name: curses shall drag him down.　　30

DEMOGORGON.

He reigns.

ASIA.

I feel, I know it : who?

DEMOGORGON.

He reigns.

ASIA.

Who reigns? There was the Heaven and Earth at first,
And Light and Love; then Saturn, from whose throne
Time fell, an envious shadow: such the state
Of the earth's primal spirits beneath his sway,   35
As the calm joy of flowers and living leaves
Before the wind or sun has withered them,
And semivital worms; but he refused
The birthright of their being, knowledge, power,
The skill which wields the elements, the thought   40
Which pierces this dim universe like light,
Self-empire, and the majesty of love;
For thirst of which they fainted. Then Prometheus
Gave wisdom, which is strength, to Jupiter,
And with this law alone, " Let man be free,"   45
Clothed him with the dominion of wide Heaven.
To know nor faith, nor love, nor law; to be
Omnipotent but friendless is to reign;
And Jove now reigned; for on the race of man
First famine, and then toil, and then disease,   50
Strife, wounds, and ghastly death unseen before,
Fell; and the unseasonable seasons drove
With alternating shafts of frost and fire,
Their shelterless, pale tribes to mountain caves:
And in their desert hearts fierce wants he sent,   55
And mad disquietudes, and shadows idle

Of unreal good, which levied mutual war,
So ruining the lair wherein they raged.
Prometheus saw, and waked the legioned hopes
Which sleep within folded Elysian flowers,   60
Nepenthe, Moly, Amaranth, fadeless blooms,
That they might hide with thin and rainbow wings
The shape of Death; and Love he sent to bind
The disunited tendrils of that vine
Which bears the wine of life, the human heart;   65
And he tamed fire which, like some beast of prey,
Most terrible, but lovely, played beneath
The frown of man; and tortured to his will
Iron and gold, the slaves and signs of power,
And gems and poisons, and all subtlest forms   70
Hidden beneath the mountains and the waves.
He gave man speech, and speech created thought,
Which is the measure of the universe;
And Science struck the thrones of earth and heaven,
Which shook, but fell not; and the harmonious mind   75
Poured itself forth in all-prophetic song;
And music lifted up the listening spirit
Until it walked, exempt from mortal care,
Godlike, o'er the clear billows of sweet sound;
And human hands first mimicked and then mocked,   80
With moulded limbs more lovely than its own,
The human form, till marble grew divine;
And mothers, gazing, drank the love men see
Reflected in their race, behold, and perish.
He told the hidden power of herbs and springs,   85
And Disease drank and slept.   Death grew like sleep.
He taught the implicated orbits woven
Of the wide-wandering stars; and how the sun
Changes his lair, and by what secret spell
The pale moon is transformed, when her broad eye   90

Gazes not on the interlunar sea :
He taught to rule, as life directs the limbs,
The tempest-wingèd chariots of the Ocean,
And the Celt knew the Indian. Cities then
Were built, and through their snow-like columns flowed   95
The warm winds, and the azure æther shone,
And the blue sea and shadowy hills were seen.
Such, the alleviations of his state,
Prometheus gave to man, for which he hangs
Withering in destined pain: but who rains down   100
Evil, the immedicable plague, which, while
Man looks on his creation like a God
And sees that it is glorious, drives him on
The wreck of his own will, the scorn of earth,
The outcast, the abandoned, the alone?   105
Not Jove: while yet his frown shook heaven, aye, when
His adversary from adamantine chains
Cursed him, he trembled like a slave. Declare
Who is his master? Is he too a slave?

DEMOGORGON.

All spirits are enslaved which serve things evil: 110
Thou knowest if Jupiter be such or no.

ASIA.

Whom calledst thou God?

DEMOGORGON.

       I spoke but as ye speak,
For Jove is the supreme of living things.

ASIA.

Who is the master of the slave?

DEMOGORGON.

                    If the abysm
Could vomit forth its secrets.   But a voice   115
Is wanting, the deep truth is imageless;
For what would it avail to bid thee gaze
On the revolving world?   What to bid speak
Fate, Time, Occasion, Chance and Change?   To these
All things are subject but eternal Love.   120

ASIA.

So much I asked before, and my heart gave
The response thou hast given; and of such truths
Each to itself must be the oracle.
One more demand; and do thou answer me
As mine own soul would answer, did it know   125
That which I ask.   Prometheus shall arise
Henceforth the sun of this rejoicing world:
When shall the destined hour arrive?

DEMOGORGON.
                            Behold!
ASIA.

The rocks are cloven, and through the purple night
I see cars drawn by rainbow-wingèd steeds   130
Which trample the dim winds: in each there stands
A wild-eyed charioteer urging their flight.
Some look behind, as fiends pursued them there,
And yet I see no shapes but the keen stars:
Others, with burning eyes, lean forth, and drink   135
With eager lips the wind of their own speed,
As if the thing they loved fled on before,
And now, even now, they clasped it.   Their bright locks
Stream like a comet's flashing hair: they all
Sweep onward.

DEMOGORGON.

These are the immortal Hours,   140
Of whom thou didst demand. One waits for thee.

ASIA.

A spirit with a dreadful countenance
Checks its dark chariot by the craggy gulph.
Unlike thy brethren, ghastly charioteer,
Who art thou? Whither wouldst thou bear me? Speak! 145

SPIRIT.

I am the shadow of a destiny
More dread than is my aspect: ere yon planet
Has set, the darkness which ascends with me
Shall wrap in lasting night heaven's kingless throne.

ASIA.

What meanest thou?

PANTHEA.

That terrible shadow floats   150
Up from its throne, as may the lurid smoke
Of earthquake-ruined cities o'er the sea.
Lo! it ascends the car; the coursers fly
Terrified: watch its path among the stars
Blackening the night!

ASIA.

Thus I am answered: strange!   155

PANTHEA.

See, near the verge, another chariot stays;
An ivory shell inlaid with crimson fire,
Which comes and goes within its sculptured rim

Of delicate strange tracery; the young spirit
That guides it has the dove-like eyes of hope;   160
How its soft smiles attract the soul! as light
Lures wingèd insects through the lampless air.

SPIRIT.

My coursers are fed with the lightning,
     They drink of the whirlwind's stream,
And when the red morning is brightning   165
     They bathe in the fresh sunbeam;
     They have strength for their swiftness I deem,
Then ascend with me, daughter of Ocean.

I desire: and their speed makes night kindle;
     I fear: they outstrip the Typhoon;   170
Ere the cloud piled on Atlas can dwindle
     We encircle the earth and the moon:
     We shall rest from long labours at noon:
Then ascend with me, daughter of Ocean.

SCENE V.   *The Car pauses within a Cloud on the Top of a snowy
     Mountain.*   ASIA, PANTHEA, *and the* SPIRIT OF THE HOUR.

SPIRIT.

On the brink of the night and the morning
     My coursers are wont to respire;
But the Earth has just whispered a warning
     That their flight must be swifter than fire:
     They shall drink the hot speed of desire!   5

ASIA.

Thou breathest on their nostrils, but my breath
Would give them swifter speed.

SPIRIT.
Alas! it could not.

PANTHEA.

Oh Spirit! pause, and tell whence is the light
Which fills the cloud? the sun is yet unrisen.

SPIRIT.

The sun will rise not until noon. Apollo   10
Is held in heaven by wonder; and the light
Which fills this vapour, as the aërial hue
Of fountain-gazing roses fills the water,
Flows from thy mighty sister.

PANTHEA.
Yes, I feel —

ASIA.

What is it with thee, sister? Thou art pale.   15

PANTHEA.

How thou art changed! I dare not look on thee;
I feel but see thee not. I scarce endure
The radiance of thy beauty. Some good change
Is working in the elements, which suffer
Thy presence thus unveiled. The Nereids tell   20
That on the day when the clear hyaline
Was cloven at thy uprise, and thou didst stand
Within a veinèd shell, which floated on
Over the calm floor of the crystal sea,
Among the Ægean isles, and by the shores   25
Which bear thy name; love, like the atmosphere
Of the sun's fire filling the living world,
Burst from thee, and illumined earth and heaven

And the deep ocean and the sunless caves
And all that dwells within them; till grief cast   30
Eclipse upon the soul from which it came:
Such art thou now; nor is it I alone,
Thy sister, thy companion, thine own chosen one,
But the whole world which seeks thy sympathy.
Hear'st thou not sounds i' the air which speak the love   35
Of all articulate beings?   Feel'st thou not
The inanimate winds enamoured of thee?   List!

                            (*Music.*)

Asia.

Thy words are sweeter than aught else but his
Whose echoes they are: yet all love is sweet,
Given or returned.   Common as light is love,   40
And its familiar voice wearies not ever.
Like the wide heaven, the all-sustaining air,
It makes the reptile equal to the God:
They who inspire it most are fortunate,
As I am now; but those who feel it most   45
Are happier still, after long sufferings,
As I shall soon become.

Panthea.

         List! Spirits speak.

Voice *in the Air, singing.*

Life of Life! thy lips enkindle
   With their love the breath between them;
And thy smiles before they dwindle   50
   Make the cold air fire; then screen them
In those looks, where whoso gazes
Faints, entangled in their mazes.

Child of Light! thy limbs are burning
　　Through the vest which seems to hide them;　　　55
As the radiant lines of morning
　　Through the clouds ere they divide them;
And this atmosphere divinest
Shrouds thee wheresoe'er thou shinest.

Fair are others; none beholds thee,　　　　　60
　　But thy voice sounds low and tender
Like the fairest, for it folds thee
　　From the sight, that liquid splendour,
And all feel, yet see thee never,
As I feel now, lost for ever!　　　　　　65

Lamp of Earth! where'er thou movest
　　Its dim shapes are clad with brightness,
And the souls of whom thou lovest
　　Walk upon the winds with lightness,
Till they fail, as I am failing,　　　　　70
Dizzy, lost, yet unbewailing!

ASIA.

My soul is an enchanted boat,
　　Which, like a sleeping swan, doth float
Upon the silver waves of thy sweet singing;
　　And thine doth like an angel sit　　　75
　　Beside a helm conducting it,
Whilst all the winds with melody are ringing.
　　It seems to float ever, for ever,
　　Upon that many-winding river,
　　Between mountains, woods, abysses,　　80
　　A paradise of wildernesses!
Till, like one in slumber bound,

Borne to the ocean, I float down, around,
Into a sea profound, of ever-spreading sound :

    Meanwhile thy spirit lifts its pinions   85
    In music's most serene dominions;
Catching the winds that fan that happy heaven.
    And we sail on, away, afar,
    Without a course, without a star,
But by the instinct of sweet music driven ;   90
    Till through Elysian garden islets
    By thee, most beautiful of pilots,
    Where never mortal pinnace glided,
    The boat of my desire is guided :
Realms where the air we breathe is love,   95
Which in the winds and on the waves doth move,
Harmonizing this earth with what we feel above.

    We have passed Age's icy caves,
    And Manhood's dark and tossing waves,
And Youth's smooth ocean, smiling to betray: 100
    Beyond the glassy gulphs we flee
    Of shadow-peopled Infancy,
Through Death and Birth, to a diviner day;
    A paradise of vaulted bowers,
    Lit by downward-gazing flowers,   105
    And watery paths that wind between
    Wildernesses calm and green,
Peopled by shapes too bright to see,
And rest, having beheld ; somewhat like thee ;
Which walk upon the sea, and chaunt melodiously !   110

    END OF THE SECOND ACT.

ACT III.

SCENE I. *Heaven.* JUPITER *on his Throne;* THETIS *and the other Deities assembled.*

JUPITER.

Ye congregated powers of heaven, who share
The glory and the strength of him ye serve,
Rejoice! henceforth I am omnipotent.
All else had been subdued to me; alone
The soul of man, like unextinguished fire,   5
Yet burns towards heaven with fierce reproach and doubt,
And lamentation, and reluctant prayer,
Hurling up insurrection, which might make
Our antique empire insecure, though built
On eldest faith, and hell's coeval, fear;   10
And though my curses through the pendulous air,
Like snow on herbless peaks, fall flake by flake,
And cling to it; though under my wrath's night
It climb the crags of life, step after step,
Which wound it, as ice wounds unsandalled feet,   15
It yet remains supreme o'er misery,
Aspiring, unrepressed, yet soon to fall:
Even now have I begotten a strange wonder,
That fatal child, the terror of the earth,
Who waits but till the destined hour arrive,   20
Bearing from Demogorgon's vacant throne
The dreadful might of ever-living limbs
Which clothed that awful spirit unbeheld,
To redescend, and trample out the spark.
Pour forth heaven's wine, Idæan Ganymede,   25
And let it fill the Dædal cups like fire,
And from the flower-inwoven soil divine
Ye all-triumphant harmonies arise,

As dew from earth under the twilight stars :
Drink! be the nectar circling through your veins   30
The soul of joy, ye ever-living Gods,
Till exultation burst in one wide voice
Like music from Elysian winds.

                                             And thou
Ascend beside me, veilèd in the light
Of the desire which makes thee one with me,   35
Thetis, bright image of eternity!
When thou didst cry, " Insufferable might!
"God! Spare me! I sustain not the quick flames,
"The penetrating presence; all my being,
"Like him whom the Numidian seps did thaw   40
"Into a dew with poison, is dissolved,
"Sinking through its foundations:" even then
Two mighty spirits, mingling, made a third
Mightier than either, which, unbodied now,
Between us floats, felt, although unbeheld,   45
Waiting the incarnation, which ascends,
(Hear ye the thunder of the fiery wheels
Griding the winds?) from Demogorgon's throne.
Victory! victory! Feel'st thou not, O world,
The earthquake of his chariot thundering up   50
Olympus?

[*The Car of the* Hour *arrives.* DEMOGORGON *descends,
and moves towards the Throne of* JUPITER.

Awful shape, what art thou? Speak!

DEMOGORGON.

Eternity.   Demand no direr name.
Descend, and follow me down the abyss.
I am thy child, as thou wert Saturn's child;
Mightier than thee: and we must dwell together   55

Henceforth in darkness.   Lift thy lightnings not.
The tyranny of heaven none may retain,
Or reassume, or hold, succeeding thee:
Yet if thou wilt, as 't is the destiny
Of trodden worms to writhe till they are dead,   60
Put forth thy might.

JUPITER.

Detested prodigy!
Even thus beneath the deep Titanian prisons
I trample thee! thou lingerest?
                                Mercy! mercy!
No pity, no release, no respite! Oh,
That thou wouldst make mine enemy my judge,   65
Even where he hangs, seared by my long revenge,
On Caucasus! he would not doom me thus.
Gentle, and just, and dreadless, is he not
The monarch of the world?   What then art thou?
No refuge! no appeal!
                              Sink with me then,   70
We two will sink on the wide waves of ruin,
Even as a vulture and a snake outspent
Drop, twisted in inextricable fight,
Into a shoreless sea.   Let hell unlock
Its mounded oceans of tempestuous fire,   75
And whelm on them into the bottomless void
This desolated world, and thee, and me,
The conqueror and the conquered, and the wreck
Of that for which they combated.
                                  Ai! Ai!
The elements obey me not.   I sink   80
Dizzily down, ever, for ever, down.
And, like a cloud, mine enemy above
Darkens my fall with victory! Ai, Ai!

SCENE II. *The Mouth of a great River in the Island Atlantis.*
OCEAN *is discovered reclining near the Shore;* APOLLO *stands
beside him.*

OCEAN.

He fell, thou sayest, beneath his conqueror's frown?

APOLLO.

Aye, when the strife was ended which made dim
The orb I rule, and shook the solid stars,
The terrors of his eye illumined heaven
With sanguine light, through the thick ragged skirts   5
Of the victorious darkness, as he fell:
Like the last glare of day's red agony,
Which, from a rent among the fiery clouds,
Burns far along the tempest-wrinkled deep.

OCEAN.

He sunk to the abyss? To the dark void?   10

APOLLO.

An eagle so caught in some bursting cloud
On Caucasus, his thunder-baffled wings
Entangled in the whirlwind, and his eyes
Which gazed on the undazzling sun, now blinded
By the white lightning, while the ponderous hail   15
Beats on his struggling form, which sinks at length
Prone, and the aërial ice clings over it.

OCEAN.

Henceforth the fields of Heaven-reflecting sea
Which are my realm will heave, unstained with blood,
Beneath the uplifting winds, like plains of corn   20
Swayed by the summer air; my streams will flow

Round many-peopled continents, and round
Fortunate isles; and from their glassy thrones
Blue Proteus and his humid nymphs shall mark
The shadow of fair ships, as mortals see   25
The floating bark of the light-laden moon
With that white star, its sightless pilot's crest,
Borne down the rapid sunset's ebbing sea;
Tracking their path no more by blood and groans,
And desolation, and the mingled voice   30
Of slavery and command; but by the light   ⸰
Of wave-reflected flowers, and floating odours,
And music soft, and mild, free, gentle voices,
And sweetest music, such as spirits love.

APOLLO.

And I shall gaze not on the deeds which make   35
My mind obscure with sorrow, as eclipse
Darkens the sphere I guide; but list, I hear
The small, clear, silver lute of the young Spirit
That sits i' the morning star.

OCEAN.

     Thou must away;
Thy steeds will pause at even, till when farewell: 40
The loud deep calls me home even now to feed it
With azure calm out of the emerald urns
Which stand for ever full beside my throne.
Behold the Nereids under the green sea,
Their wavering limbs, borne on the wind-like stream,   45
Their white arms lifted o'er their streaming hair
With garlands pied and starry sea-flower crowns,
Hastening to grace their mighty sister's joy.

(*A sound of waves is heard.*)

It is the unpastured sea hungering for calm.
Peace, monster; I come now. Farewell.

ATHENE APOLLO.

          Farewell.   50

SCENE III. *Caucasus.* PROMETHEUS, HERCULES, IONE, *the* EARTH,
   SPIRITS, ASIA, *and* PANTHEA, *borne in the Car with the* SPIRIT
   OF THE HOUR.

HERCULES *unbinds* PROMETHEUS, *who descends.*

HERCULES.

Most glorious among spirits, thus doth strength
To wisdom, courage, and long-suffering love,
And thee, who art the form they animate,
Minister like a slave.

PROMETHEUS.

          Thy gentle words
Are sweeter even than freedom long desired   5
And long delayed.
          Asia, thou light of life,
Shadow of beauty unbeheld: and ye,
Fair sister nymphs, who made long years of pain
Sweet to remember, through your love and care:
Henceforth we will not part. There is a cave,   10
All overgrown with trailing odorous plants,
Which curtain out the day with leaves and flowers,
And paved with veinèd emerald, and a fountain
Leaps in the midst with an awakening sound.
From its curved roof the mountain's frozen tears   15
Like snow, or silver, or long diamond spires,
Hang downward, raining forth a doubtful light:
And there is heard the ever-moving air,

Whispering without from tree to tree, and birds,
And bees; and all around are mossy seats,   20
And the rough walls are clothed with long soft grass;
A simple dwelling, which shall be our own;
Where we will sit and talk of time and change,
As the world ebbs and flows, ourselves unchanged.
What can hide man from mutability?   25
And if ye sigh, then I will smile; and thou,
Ione, shall chaunt fragments of sea-music,
Until I weep, when ye shall smile away
The tears she brought, which yet were sweet to shed.
We will entangle buds and flowers and beams   30
Which twinkle on the fountain's brim, and make
Strange combinations out of common things,
Like human babes in their brief innocence;
And we will search, with looks and words of love,
For hidden thoughts, each lovelier than the last,   35
Our unexhausted spirits; and like lutes
Touched by the skill of the enamoured wind,
Weave harmonies divine, yet ever new,
From difference sweet where discord cannot be;
And hither come, sped on the charmèd winds,   40
Which meet from all the points of heaven, as bees
From every flower aërial Enna feeds,
At their known island-homes in Himera,
The echoes of the human world, which tell
Of the low voice of love, almost unheard,   45
And dove-eyed pity's murmured pain, and music,
Itself the echo of the heart, and all
That tempers or improves man's life, now free;
And lovely apparitions, dim at first,
Then radiant, as the mind, arising bright   50
From the embrace of beauty, whence the forms
Of which these are the phantoms, casts on them

The gathered rays which are reality,
Shall visit us, the progeny immortal
Of Painting, Sculpture, and rapt Poesy,　　　　55
And arts, though unimagined, yet to be.
The wandering voices and the shadows these
Of all that man becomes, the mediators
Of that best worship love, by him and us
Given and returned; swift shapes and sounds, which grow　60
More fair and soft as man grows wise and kind,
And veil by veil, evil and error fall:
Such virtue has the cave and place around.

　　　　　　(*Turning to the* Spirit of the Hour.)

For thee, fair Spirit, one toil remains.　Ione,
Give her that curvèd shell, which Proteus old　　　　65
Made Asia's nuptial boon, breathing within it
A voice to be accomplished, and which thou
Didst hide in grass under the hollow rock.

Ione.

Thou most desired Hour, more loved and lovely
Than all thy sisters, this is the mystic shell;　　　　70
See the pale azure fading into silver
Lining it with a soft yet glowing light:
Looks it not like lulled music sleeping there?

Spirit.

It seems in truth the fairest shell of Ocean:
Its sound must be at once both sweet and strange.　　　75

Prometheus.

Go, borne over the cities of mankind
On whirlwind-footed coursers: once again
Outspeed the sun around the orbèd world;

And as thy chariot cleaves the kindling air,
Thou breathe into the many-folded shell, 80
Loosening its mighty music; it shall be
As thunder mingled with clear echoes: then
Return; and thou shalt dwell beside our cave.
And thou, O, Mother Earth! —

THE EARTH.

I hear, I feel;
Thy lips are on me, and thy touch runs down 85
Even to the adamantine central gloom
Along these marble nerves; 'tis life, 'tis joy,
And through my withered, old, and icy frame
The warmth of an immortal youth shoots down
Circling. Henceforth the many children fair 90
Folded in my sustaining arms; all plants,
And creeping forms, and insects rainbow-winged,
And birds, and beasts, and fish, and human shapes,
Which drew disease and pain from my wan bosom,
Draining the poison of despair, shall take 95
And interchange sweet nutriment; to me
Shall they become like sister-antelopes
By one fair dam, snow-white and swift as wind,
Nursed among lilies near a brimming stream.
The dew-mists of my sunless sleep shall float 100
Under the stars like balm: night-folded flowers
Shall suck unwithering hues in their repose:
And men and beasts in happy dreams shall gather
Strength for the coming day, and all its joy:
And death shall be the last embrace of her 105
Who takes the life she gave, even as a mother
Folding her child, says, " Leave me not again."

ASIA.

Oh, mother! wherefore speak the name of death?
Cease they to love, and move, and breathe, and speak,
Who die?

THE EARTH.

It would avail not to reply: 110
Thou art immortal, and this tongue is known
But to the uncommunicating dead.
Death is the veil which those who live call life:
They sleep, and it is lifted: and meanwhile
In mild variety the seasons mild 115
With rainbow-skirted showers, and odorous winds,
And long blue meteors cleansing the dull night,
And the life-kindling shafts of the keen sun's
All-piercing bow, and the dew-mingled rain
Of the calm moonbeams, a soft influence mild, 120
Shall clothe the forests and the fields, aye, even
The crag-built deserts of the barren deep,
With ever-living leaves, and fruits, and flowers.
And thou! There is a cavern where my spirit
Was panted forth in anguish whilst thy pain 125
Made my heart mad, and those who did inhale it
Became mad too, and built a temple there,
And spoke, and were oracular, and lured
The erring nations round to mutual war,
And faithless faith, such as Jove kept with thee; 130
Which breath now rises, as amongst tall weeds
A violet's exhalation, and it fills
With a serener light and crimson air
Intense, yet soft, the rocks and woods around;
It feeds the quick growth of the serpent vine, 135
And the dark linkèd ivy tangling wild,

And budding, blown, or odour-faded blooms
Which star the winds with points of coloured light,
As they rain through them, and bright golden globes
Of fruit, suspended in their own green heaven,   140
And through their veinèd leaves and amber stems
The flowers whose purple and translucid bowls
Stand ever mantling with aërial dew,
The drink of spirits: and it circles round,
Like the soft waving wings of noonday dreams,   145
Inspiring calm and happy thoughts, like mine,
Now thou art thus restored.   This cave is thine.
Arise! Appear!

(A Spirit rises in the likeness of a winged child.)

    This is my torch-bearer;
Who let his lamp out in old time with gazing
On eyes from which he kindled it anew   150
With love, which is as fire, sweet daughter mine,
For such is that within thine own.   Run, wayward,
And guide this company beyond the peak
Of Bacchic Nysa, Mænad-haunted mountain,
And beyond Indus and its tribute rivers,   155
Trampling the torrent streams and glassy lakes
With feet unwet, unwearied, undelaying,
And up the green ravine, across the vale,
Beside the windless and crystalline pool,
Where ever lies, on unerasing waves,   160
The image of a temple, built above,
Distinct with column, arch, and architrave,
And palm-like capital, and over-wrought,
And populous most with living imagery,
Praxitelean shapes, whose marble smiles   165
Fill the hushed air with everlasting love.
It is deserted now, but once it bore

Thy name, Prometheus; there the emulous youths
Bore to thy honour through the divine gloom
The lamp which was thine emblem ; even as those   170
Who bear the untransmitted torch of hope
Into the grave, across the night of life,
As thou hast borne it most triumphantly
To this far goal of Time.   Depart, farewell.
Beside that temple is the destined cave.   175

SCENE IV. *A Forest. In the background a Cave.* PROMETHEUS,
    ASIA, PANTHEA, IONE, *and the* SPIRIT OF THE EARTH.

IONE.

Sister, it is not earthly: how it glides
Under the leaves! how on its head there burns
A light, like a green star, whose emerald beams
Are twined with its fair hair! how, as it moves,
The splendour drops in flakes upon the grass!   5
Knowest thou it?

PANTHEA.

It is the delicate spirit
That guides the earth through heaven.   From afar
The populous constellations call that light
The loveliest of the planets; and sometimes
It floats along the spray of the salt sea,   10
Or makes its chariot of a foggy cloud,
Or walks through fields or cities while men sleep,
Or o'er the mountain tops, or down the rivers,
Or through the green waste wilderness, as now,
Wondering at all it sees.   Before Jove reigned   15
It loved our sister Asia, and it came
Each leisure hour to drink the liquid light
Out of her eyes, for which it said it thirsted

As one bit by a dipsas, and with her
It made its childish confidence, and told her   20
All it had known or seen, for it saw much,
Yet idly reasoned what it saw; and called her, —
For whence it sprung it knew not, nor do I, —
"Mother, dear mother."

THE SPIRIT OF THE EARTH (*running to* ASIA).

Mother, dearest mother ;
May I then talk with thee as I was wont?   25
May I then hide my eyes in thy soft arms,
After thy looks have made them tired of joy?
May I then play beside thee the long noons,
When work is none in the bright silent air?

ASIA.

I love thee, gentlest being, and henceforth   30
Can cherish thee unenvied : speak, I pray :
Thy simple talk once solaced, now delights.

SPIRIT OF THE EARTH.

Mother, I am grown wiser, though a child
Cannot be wise like thee, within this day;
And happier too; happier and wiser both.   35
Thou knowest that toads, and snakes, and loathly worms,
And venomous and malicious beasts, and boughs
That bore ill berries in the woods, were ever
An hindrance to my walks o'er the green world :
And that, among the haunts of humankind,   40
Hard-featured men, or with proud, angry looks,
Or cold, staid gait, or false and hollow smiles,
Or the dull sneer of self-loved ignorance,
Or other such foul masks, with which ill thoughts

Hide that fair being whom we spirits call man;   45
And women too, ugliest of all things evil,
(Though fair, even in a world where thou art fair,
When good and kind, free and sincere like thee,)
When false or frowning made me sick at heart
To pass them, though they slept, and I unseen.   50
Well, my path lately lay through a great city
Into the woody hills surrounding it :
A sentinel was sleeping at the gate :
When there was heard a sound, so loud, it shook
The towers amid the moonlight, yet more sweet   55
Than any voice but thine, sweetest of all;
A long, long sound, as it would never end :
And all the inhabitants leapt suddenly
Out of their rest, and gathered in the streets,
Looking in wonder up to Heaven, while yet   60
The music pealed along.   I hid myself
Within a fountain in the public square,
Where I lay like the reflex of the moon
Seen in a wave under green leaves ; and soon
Those ugly human shapes and visages   65
Of which I spoke as having wrought me pain,
Passed floating through the air, and fading still
Into the winds that scattered them ; and those
From whom they passed seemed mild and lovely forms
After some foul disguise had fallen, and all   70
Were somewhat changed, and after brief surprise
And greetings of delighted wonder, all
Went to their sleep again : and when the dawn
Came, wouldst thou think that toads, and snakes, and
      efts,
Could e'er be beautiful ? yet so they were,   75
And that with little change of shape or hue :
All things had put their evil nature off :

I cannot tell my joy, when o'er a lake
Upon a drooping bough with night-shade twined,
I saw two azure halcyons clinging downward   80
And thinning one bright bunch of amber berries,
With quick long beaks, and in the deep there lay
Those lovely forms imaged as in a sky ;
So with my thoughts full of these happy changes,
We meet again, the happiest change of all.   85

ASIA.

And never will we part, till thy chaste sister
Who guides the frozen and inconstant moon
Will look on thy more warm and equal light
Till her heart thaw like flakes of April snow
And love thee.

SPIRIT OF THE EARTH.

What ; as Asia loves Prometheus?   90

ASIA.

Peace, wanton, thou art yet not old enough.
Think ye by gazing on each other's eyes
To multiply your lovely selves, and fill
With spherèd fires the interlunar air?

SPIRIT OF THE EARTH.

Nay, mother, while my sister trims her lamp   95
'Tis hard I should go darkling.

ASIA.
Listen ; look !

The SPIRIT OF THE HOUR *enters.*

PROMETHEUS.

We feel what thou hast heard and seen : yet speak.

Spirit of the Hour.

Soon as the sound had ceased whose thunder filled
The abysses of the sky and the wide earth,
There was a change: the impalpable thin air   100
And the all-circling sunlight were transformed,
As if the sense of love dissolved in them
Had folded itself round the spherèd world.
My vision then grew clear, and I could see
Into the mysteries of the universe :   105
Dizzy as with delight I floated down,
Winnowing the lightsome air with languid plumes,
My coursers sought their birth-place in the sun,
Where they henceforth will live exempt from toil
Pasturing flowers of vegetable fire,   110
And where my moonlike car will stand within
A temple, gazed upon by Phidian forms
Of thee, and Asia, and the Earth, and me,
And you fair nymphs looking the love we feel;
In memory of the tidings it has borne ;   115
Beneath a dome fretted with graven flowers,
Poised on twelve columns of resplendent stone,
And open to the bright and liquid sky.
Yoked to it by an amphisbenic snake
The likeness of those wingèd steeds will mock   120
The flight from which they find repose.   Alas,
Whither has wandered now my partial tongue
When all remains untold which ye would hear?
As I have said, I floated to the earth :
It was, as it is still, the pain of bliss   125
To move, to breathe, to be; I wandering went
Among the haunts and dwellings of mankind,
And first was disappointed not to see
Such mighty change as I had felt within

Expressed in outward things ; but soon I looked,   130
And behold, thrones were kingless, and men walked
One with the other even as spirits do,
None fawned, none trampled ; hate, disdain, or fear,
Self-love or self-contempt, on human brows,
No more inscribed, as o'er the gate of hell,   135
" All hope abandon ye who enter here ; "
None frowned, none trembled, none with eager fear
Gazed on another's eye of cold command,
Until the subject of the tyrant's will
Became, worse fate, the abject of his own,   140
Which spurred him, like an outspent horse, to death.
None wrought his lips in truth-entangling lines
Which smiled the lie his tongue disdained to speak ;
None, with firm sneer, trod out in his own heart
The sparks of love and hope till there remained   145
Those bitter ashes, a soul self-consumed,
And the wretch crept a vampire among men,
Infecting all with his own hideous ill ;
None talked that common, false, cold, hollow talk
Which makes the heart deny the *yes* it breathes,   150
Yet question that unmeant hypocrisy
With such a self-mistrust as has no name.
And women, too, frank, beautiful, and kind
As the free heaven which rains fresh light and dew
On the wide earth, passed ; gentle radiant forms,   155
From custom's evil taint exempt and pure ;
Speaking the wisdom once they could not think,
Looking emotions once they feared to feel,
And changed to all which once they dared not be,
Yet being now, made earth like heaven ; nor pride,   160
Nor jealousy, nor envy, nor ill shame,
The bitterest of those drops of treasured gall,
Spoilt the sweet taste of the nepenthe, love.

Thrones, altars, judgment-seats, and prisons; wherein,
And beside which, by wretched men were borne   165
Sceptres, tiaras, swords, and chains, and tomes
Of reasoned wrong, glozed on by ignorance,
Were like those monstrous and barbaric shapes,
The ghosts of a no more remembered fame,
Which, from their unworn obelisks, look forth   170
In triumph o'er the palaces and tombs
Of those who were their conquerors: mouldering round
Those imaged to the pride of kings and priests,
A dark yet mighty faith, a power as wide
As is the world it wasted, and are now   175
But an astonishment; even so the tools
And emblems of its last captivity,
Amid the dwellings of the peopled earth,
Stand, not o'erthrown, but unregarded now.
And those foul shapes, abhorred by god and man,   180
Which, under many a name and many a form
Strange, savage, ghastly, dark and execrable,
Were Jupiter, the tyrant of the world ;
And which the nations, panic-stricken, served
With blood, and hearts broken by long hope, and love   185
Dragged to his altars soiled and garlandless,
And slain among men's unreclaiming tears,
Flattering the thing they feared, which fear was hate,
Frown, mouldering fast, o'er their abandoned shrines:
The painted veil, by those who were, called life,   190
Which mimicked, as with colours idly spread,
All men believed and hoped, is torn aside ;
The loathsome mask has fallen, the man remains
Sceptreless, free, uncircumscribed, but man ;
Equal, unclassed, tribeless, and nationless,   195
Exempt from awe, worship, degree, the king
Over himself; just, gentle, wise: but man ;

Passionless; no, yet free from guilt or pain,
Which were, for his will made or suffered them,
Nor yet exempt, though ruling them like slaves,   200
From chance, and death, and mutability,
The clogs of that which else might oversoar
The loftiest star of unascended heaven,
Pinnacled dim in the intense inane.

END OF THE THIRD ACT.

ACT IV.

SCENE, *a Part of the Forest near the Cave of* PROMETHEUS. PAN-
THEA *and* IONE *are sleeping: they awaken gradually during
the first song.*

V OICE *of unseen Spirits.*

The pale stars are gone!
For the sun, their swift shepherd,
To their folds them compelling,
In the depths of the dawn,
Hastes, in meteor-eclipsing array, and they flee   5
Beyond his blue dwelling,
As fawns flee the leopard.
But where are ye?

A Train of dark Forms and Shadows passes by confusedly, singing.

Here, oh, here:
We bear the bier   . 10
Of the Father of many a cancelled year!
Spectres we
Of the dead Hours be,
We bear Time to his tomb in eternity.

Strew, oh, strew   15
Hair, not yew!
Wet the dusty pall with tears, not dew!
Be the faded flowers
Of Death's bare bowers
Spread on the corpse of the King of Hours!   20

Haste, oh, haste!
As shades are chased,
Trembling, by day, from heaven's blue waste.
We melt away,
Like dissolving spray,   25
From the children of a diviner day,
With the lullaby
Of winds that die
On the bosom of their own harmony!

IONE.

What dark forms were they?   30

PANTHEA.

The past Hours weak and gray,
With the spoil which their toil
Raked together
From the conquest but One could foil.

IONE.

Have they passed?

PANTHEA.

They have passed;   35
They outspeeded the blast, —
While 't is said, they are fled:

IONE.

Whither, oh, whither?

PANTHEA.

To the dark, to the past, to the dead.

VOICE *of unseen Spirits.*

Bright clouds float in heaven, 40
Dew-stars gleam on earth,
Waves assemble on ocean,
They are gathered and driven
By the storm of delight, by the panic of glee!
They shake with emotion, 45
They dance in their mirth.
But where are ye?

The pine boughs are singing
Old songs with new gladness,
The billows and fountains 50
Fresh music are flinging,
Like the notes of a spirit from land and from sea;
The storms mock the mountains
With the thunder of gladness.
But where are ye? 55

IONE.

What charioteers are these?

PANTHEA.

Where are their chariots?

SEMICHORUS OF HOURS.

The voice of the Spirits of Air and of Earth
Have drawn back the figured curtain of sleep
Which covered our being and darkened our birth
In the deep.

A VOICE.

In the deep?

SEMICHORUS II.

Oh, below the deep.   60

SEMICHORUS I.

An hundred ages we had been kept
   Cradled in visions of hate and care,
And each one who waked as his brother slept,
   Found the truth —

SEMICHORUS II.

Worse than his visions were !

SEMICHORUS I.

We have heard the lute of Hope in sleep;   65
   We have known the voice of Love in dreams, .
We have felt the wand of Power, and leap —

SEMICHORUS II.

As the billows leap in the morning beams!

CHORUS.

Weave the dance on the floor of the breeze,
   Pierce with song heaven's silent light,   70
Enchant the day that too swiftly flees,
   To check its flight ere the cave of night.

Once the hungry Hours were hounds
   Which chased the day like a bleeding deer,
And it limped and stumbled with many wounds   75
   Through the nightly dells of the desert year.

But now, oh weave the mystic measure
   Of music, and dance, and shapes of light,
Let the Hours, and the spirits of might and pleasure,
   Like the clouds and sunbeams, unite.

A Voice.

Unite! 80

Panthea.

See, where the Spirits of the human mind
Wrapped in sweet sounds, as in bright veils, approach.

Chorus of Spirits.

We join the throng
Of the dance and the song,
By the whirlwind of gladness borne along; 85
As the flying-fish leap
From the Indian deep,
And mix with the sea-birds, half asleep.

Chorus of Hours.

Whence come ye, so wild and so fleet,
For sandals of lightning are on your feet, 90
And your wings are soft and swift as thought,
And your eyes are as love which is veilèd not?

Chorus of Spirits.

We come from the mind
Of human kind
Which was late so dusk, and obscene, and blind; 95
Now 't is an ocean
Of clear emotion,
A heaven of serene and mighty motion.

From that deep abyss
Of wonder and bliss, 100
Whose caverns are crystal palaces;
From those skiey towers
Where Thought's crowned powers
Sit watching your dance, ye happy Hours!

From the dim recesses105
　　Of woven caresses,
Where lovers catch ye by your loose tresses ;
　　From the azure isles,
　　Where sweet Wisdom smiles,
Delaying your ships with her syren wiles.110

　　From the temples high
　　Of Man's ear and eye,
Roofed over Sculpture and Poesy ;
　　From the murmurings
　　Of the unsealed springs115
Where Science bedews his Dædal wings.

　　Years after years,
　　Through blood, and tears,
And a thick hell of hatreds, and hopes, and fears,
　　We waded and flew,120
　　And the islets were few
Where the bud-blighted flowers of happiness grew.

　　Our feet now, every palm,
　　Are sandalled with calm,
And the dew of our wings is a rain of balm ;125
　　And, beyond our eyes,
　　The human love lies
Which makes all it gazes on Paradise.

CHORUS OF SPIRITS AND HOURS.

Then weave the web of the mystic measure ;
From the depths of the sky and the ends of the earth,130
　　Come, swift Spirits of might and of pleasure,
Fill the dance and the music of mirth,
　　As the waves of a thousand streams rush by
　　To an ocean of splendour and harmony !

CHORUS OF SPIRITS.

Our spoil is won, 135
Our task is done,
We are free to dive, or soar, or run ;
Beyond and around,
Or within the bound
Which clips the world with darkness round. 140

We 'll pass the eyes
Of the starry skies
Into the hoar deep to colonize :
Death, Chaos, and Night,
From the sound of our flight, 145
Shall flee, like mist from a tempest's might.

And Earth, Air, and Light,
And the Spirit of Might,
Which drives round the stars in their fiery flight ;
And Love, Thought, and Breath, 150
The powers that quell Death,
Wherever we soar shall assemble beneath.

And our singing shall build
In the void's loose field
A world for the Spirit of Wisdom to wield ; 155
We will take our plan
From the new world of man,
And our work shall be called the Promethean.

CHORUS OF HOURS.

Break the dance, and scatter the song ;
Let some depart, and some remain. 160

SEMICHORUS I.

We, beyond heaven, are driven along :

SEMICHORUS II.

Us the enchantments of earth retain:

SEMICHORUS I.

Ceaseless, and rapid, and fierce, and free,
With the Spirits which build a new earth and sea,
And a heaven where yet heaven could never be.   165

SEMICHORUS II.

Solemn, and slow, and serene, and bright,
Leading the Day and outspeeding the Night,
With the powers of a world of perfect light.

SEMICHORUS I.

We whirl, singing loud, round the gathering sphere,
Till the trees, and the beasts, and the clouds appear   170
From its chaos made calm by love, not fear.

SEMICHORUS II.

We encircle the ocean and mountains of earth,
And the happy forms of its death and birth
Change to the music of our sweet mirth.

CHORUS OF HOURS AND SPIRITS.

Break the dance, and scatter the song,   175
   Let some depart, and some remain,
Wherever we fly we lead along
In leashes, like starbeams, soft yet strong,
   The clouds that are heavy with love's sweet rain.

PANTHEA.

Ha! they are gone!

IONE.

          Yet feel you no delight   180
From the past sweetness?

PANTHEA.

As the bare green hill
When some soft cloud vanishes into rain,
Laughs with a thousand drops of sunny water
To the unpavilioned sky!

IONE.

Even whilst we speak
New notes arise. What is that awful sound? 185

PANTHEA.

'Tis the deep music of the rolling world
Kindling within the strings of the waved air,
Æolian modulations.

IONE.

Listen too,
How every pause is filled with under-notes,
Clear, silver, icy, keen awakening tones, 190
Which pierce the sense, and live within the soul,
As the sharp stars pierce winter's crystal air
And gaze upon themselves within the sea.

PANTHEA.

But see where through two openings in the forest
Which hanging branches overcanopy, 195
And where two runnels of a rivulet,
Between the close moss violet-inwoven,
Have made their path of melody, like sisters
Who part with sighs that they may meet in smiles,
Turning their dear disunion to an isle 200
Of lovely grief, a wood of sweet sad thoughts;
Two visions of strange radiance float upon
The ocean-like enchantment of strong sound,

Which flows intenser, keener, deeper yet
Under the ground and through the windless air.   205

IONE.

I see a chariot like that thinnest boat,
In which the mother of the months is borne
By ebbing night into her western cave,
When she upsprings from interlunar dreams,
O'er which is curved an orblike canopy   210
Of gentle darkness, and the hills and woods
Distinctly seen through that dusk airy veil,
Regard like shapes in an enchanter's glass;
Its wheels are solid clouds, azure and gold,
Such as the genii of the thunder-storm   215
Pile on the floor of the illumined sea
When the sun rushes under it; they roll
And move and grow as with an inward wind;
Within it sits a wingèd infant, white
Its countenance, like the whiteness of bright snow,   220
Its plumes are as feathers of sunny frost,
Its limbs gleam white, through the wind-flowing folds
Of its white robe, woof of ætherial pearl.
Its hair is white, the brightness of white light
Scattered in strings; yet its two eyes are heavens   225
Of liquid darkness, which the Deity
Within seems pouring, as a storm is poured
From jaggèd clouds, out of their arrowy lashes,
Tempering the cold and radiant air around,
With fire that is not brightness; in its hand   230
It sways a quivering moon-beam, from whose point
A guiding power directs the chariot's prow
Over its wheelèd clouds, which as they roll
Over the grass, and flowers, and waves, wake sounds,
Sweet as a singing rain of silver dew.   235

PANTHEA.

And from the other opening in the wood
Rushes, with loud and whirlwind harmony,
A sphere, which is as many thousand spheres,
Solid as crystal, yet through all its mass
Flow, as through empty space, music and light: 240
Ten thousand orbs involving and involved,
Purple and azure, white, and green, and golden,
Sphere within sphere; and every space between
Peopled with unimaginable shapes,
Such as ghosts dream dwell in the lampless deep,   245
Yet each inter-transpicuous, and they whirl
Over each other with a thousand motions,
Upon a thousand sightless axles spinning,
And with the force of self-destroying swiftness,
Intensely, slowly, solemnly roll on,   250
Kindling with mingled sounds, and many tones,
Intelligible words and music wild.
With mighty whirl the multitudinous orb
Grinds the bright brook into an azure mist
Of elemental subtlety, like light;   255
And the wild odour of the forest flowers,
The music of the living grass and air,
The emerald light of leaf-entangled beams
Round its intense yet self-conflicting speed,
Seem kneaded into one aërial mass   260
Which drowns the sense.   Within the orb itself,
Pillowed upon its alabaster arms,
Like to a child o'erwearied with sweet toil,
On its own folded wings, and wavy hair,
The Spirit of the Earth is laid asleep,   265
And you can see its little lips are moving,
Amid the changing light of their own smiles,
Like one who talks of what he loves in dream.

IONE.

'Tis only mocking the orb's harmony.

PANTHEA.

And from a star upon its forehead, shoot,　　　　270
Like swords of azure fire, or golden spears
With tyrant-quelling myrtle overtwined,
Embleming heaven and earth united now,
Vast beams like spokes of some invisible wheel
Which whirl as the orb whirls, swifter than thought,　　275
Filling the abyss with sun-like lightnings,
And perpendicular now, and now transverse,
Pierce the dark soil, and as they pierce and pass,
Make bare the secrets of the earth's deep heart ;
Infinite mine of adamant and gold,　　　　280
Valueless stones, and unimagined gems,
And caverns on crystàlline columns poised
With vegetable silver overspread ;
Wells of unfathomed fire, and water springs
Whence the great sea, even as a child is fed,　　285
Whose vapours clothe earth's monarch mountain-tops
With kingly, ermine snow.　The beams flash on
And make appear the melancholy ruins
Of cancelled cycles ; anchors, beaks of ships ;
Planks turned to marble ; quivers, helms, and spears,　　290
And gorgon-headed targes, and the wheels
Of scythèd chariots, and the emblazonry
Of trophies, standards, and armorial beasts,
Round which death laughed, sepulchred emblems
Of dead destruction, ruin within ruin !　　　　295
The wrecks beside of many a city vast,
Whose population which the earth grew over
Was mortal, but not human ; see, they lie,

Their monstrous works, and uncouth skeletons,
Their statues, homes and fanes; prodigious shapes   300
Huddled in gray annihilation, split,
Jammed in the hard, black deep; and over these,
The anatomies of unknown wingèd things,
And fishes which were isles of living scale,
And serpents, bony chains, twisted around   305
The iron crags, or within heaps of dust
To which the tortuous strength of their last pangs
Had crushed the iron crags; and over these
The jaggèd alligator, and the might
Of earth-convulsing behemoth, which once   310
Were monarch beasts, and on the slimy shores,
And weed-overgrown continents of earth,
Increased and multiplied like summer worms
On an abandoned corpse, till the blue globe
Wrapped deluge round it like a cloke, and they   315
Yelled, gasped, and were abolished; or some God
Whose throne was in a comet, passed, and cried
Be not! And like my words they were no more.

The Earth.

The joy, the triumph, the delight, the madness!
The boundless, overflowing, bursting gladness,   320
The vapourous exultation not to be confined!
Ha! ha! the animation of delight
Which wraps me, like an atmosphere of light,
And bears me as a cloud is borne by its own wind.

The Moon.

Brother mine, calm wanderer,   325
Happy globe of land and air,
Some Spirit is darted like a beam from thee,
Which penetrates my frozen frame,

And passes with the warmth of flame,
With love, and odour, and deep melody   330
Through me, through me !

The Earth.

Ha ! Ha ! the caverns of my hollow mountains,
My cloven fire-crags, sound-exulting fountains
Laugh with a vast and inextinguishable laughter.
The oceans, and the deserts, and the abysses,   335
And the deep air's unmeasured wildernesses,
Answer from all their clouds and billows, echoing after.

They cry aloud as I do. Sceptred curse,
Who all our green and azure universe
Threatenedst to muffle round with black destruction,
    sending   340
A solid cloud to rain hot thunder-stones,
And splinter and knead down my children's bones,
All I bring forth, to one void mass battering and
    blending :

Until each crag-like tower, and storied column,
Palace, and obelisk, and temple solemn,   345
My imperial mountains crowned with cloud, and snow,
    and fire ;
My sea-like forests, every blade and blossom
Which finds a grave or cradle in my bosom,
Were stamped by thy strong hate into a lifeless mire.

How art thou sunk, withdrawn, covered, drunk up   350
By thirsty nothing, as the brackish cup
Drained by a desert-troop, a little drop for all ;
And from beneath, around, within, above,
Filling thy void annihilation, love
Burst in like light on caves cloven by the thunder-ball. 355

The Moon.

The snow upon my lifeless mountains
Is loosened into living fountains,
My solid oceans flow, and sing, and shine:
    A spirit from my heart bursts forth,
    It clothes with unexpected birth   360
My cold bare bosom: Oh! it must be thine
      On mine, on mine!

    Gazing on thee I feel, I know
    Green stalks burst forth, and bright flowers grow,
And living shapes upon my bosom move: 365
    Music is in the sea and air,
    Wingèd clouds soar here and there,
Dark with the rain new buds are dreaming of:
      'T is love, all love!

The Earth.

    It interpenetrates my granite mass,   370
    Through tangled roots and trodden clay doth pass,
Into the utmost leaves and delicatest flowers;
    Upon the winds, among the clouds 't is spread,
    It wakes a life in the forgotten dead,
They breathe a spirit up from their obscurest bowers.   375

    And like a storm bursting its cloudy prison
    With thunder, and with whirlwind, has arisen
Out of the lampless caves of unimagined being:
    With earthquake shock and swiftness making
      shiver
    Thought's stagnant chaos, unremoved for ever,   380
Till hate, and fear, and pain, light-vanquished shadows,
    fleeing,

Leave Man, who was a many-sided mirror,
Which could distort to many a shape of error,
This true fair world of things, a sea reflecting love ;
    Which over all his kind as the sun's heaven   385
    Gliding o'er ocean, smooth, serene, and even
Darting from starry depths radiance and life, doth
    move,

Leave Man, even as a leprous child is left,
Who follows a sick beast to some warm cleft .
Of rocks, through which the might of healing springs is
    poured;   390
    Then when it wanders home with rosy smile,
    Unconscious, and its mother fears awhile
It is a spirit, then, weeps on her child restored.

Man, oh, not men! a chain of linkèd thought,
Of love and might to be divided not,   395
Compelling the elements with adamantine stress;
    As the sun rules, even with a tyrant's gaze,
    The unquiet republic of the maze
Of planets, struggling fierce towards heaven's free wil-
    derness.

Man, one harmonious soul of many a soul,   400
    Whose nature is its own divine control,
Where all things flow to all, as rivers to the sea ;
    Familiar acts are beautiful through love ;
    Labour, and pain, and grief, in life's green grove
Sport like tame beasts, — none knew how gentle they
    could be !   405

His will, with all mean passions, bad delights,
    And selfish cares, its trembling satellites,
A spirit ill to guide, but mighty to obey,

Is as a tempest-wingèd ship, whose helm
Love rules, through waves which dare not over-
    whelm,   410
Forcing life's wildest shores to own its sovereign sway.

All things confess his strength. Through the cold
    mass
Of marble and of colour his dreams pass;
Bright threads whence mothers weave the robes their
    children wear ;
    Language is a perpetual Orphic song,   415
    Which rules with Dædal harmony a throng
Of thoughts and forms, which else senseless and shape-
    less were.

The lightning is his slave ; heaven's utmost deep
Gives up her stars, and like a flock of sheep
They pass before his eye, are numbered, and roll on !   420
    The tempest is his steed, he strides the air;
    And the abyss shouts from her depth laid bare,
Heaven, hast thou secrets? Man unveils me ; I have
    none.
                THE MOON.

The shadow of white death has passed
From my path in heaven at last,   425
A clinging shroud of solid frost and sleep;
    And through my newly-woven bowers,
    Wander happy paramours,
Less mighty, but as mild as those who keep
    Thy vales more deep.   430

              THE EARTH.

As the dissolving warmth of dawn may fold
A half unfrozen dew-globe, green, and gold,

And crystalline, till it becomes a wingèd mist,
    And wanders up the vault of the blue day,
    Outlives the noon, and on the sun's last ray   435
Hangs o'er the sea, a fleece of fire and amethyst.

The Moon.

    Thou art folded, thou art lying
    In the light which is undying
Of thine own joy, and heaven's smile divine;
    All suns and constellations shower   440
    On thee a light, a life, a power
Which doth array thy sphere ; thou pourest thine
    On mine, on mine !

The Earth.

    I spin beneath my pyramid of night,
    Which points into the heavens dreaming delight,   445
Murmuring victorious joy in my enchanted sleep ;
    As a youth lulled in love-dreams faintly sighing,
    Under the shadow of his beauty lying,
Which round his rest a watch of light and warmth
    doth keep.

The Moon.

    As in the soft and sweet eclipse,   450
    When soul meets soul on lovers' lips,
High hearts are calm, and brightest eyes are dull ;
    So when thy shadow falls on me,
    Then am I mute and still, by thee
Covered ; of thy love, Orb most beautiful,   455
    Full, oh, too full !

    Thou art speeding round the sun
    Brightest world of many a one ;

Green and azure sphere which shinest
With a light which is divinest 460
Among all the lamps of Heaven
To whom life and light is given;
I, thy crystal paramour
Borne beside thee by a power
Like the polar Paradise, 465
Magnet-like of lovers' eyes;
I, a most enamoured maiden
Whose weak brain is overladen
With the pleasure of her love,
Maniac-like around thee move 470
Gazing, an insatiate bride,
On thy form from every side
Like a Mænad, round the cup
Which Agave lifted up
In the weird Cadmæan forest. 475
Brother, wheresoe'er thou soarest
I must hurry, whirl and follow
Through the heavens wide and hollow,
Sheltered by the warm embrace
Of thy soul from hungry space, 480
Drinking from thy sense and sight
Beauty, majesty, and might,
As a lover or a chameleon
Grows like what it looks upon,
As a violet's gentle eye 485
Gazes on the azure sky
Until its hue grows like what it beholds,
As a gray and watery mist
Glows like solid amethyst
Athwart the western mountain it enfolds, 490
When the sunset sleeps
Upon its snow.

The Earth.

And the weak day weeps
That it should be so.

Oh, gentle Moon, the voice of thy delight 495
Falls on me like thy clear and tender light
Soothing the seaman, borne the summer night,
   Through isles for ever calm;
Oh, gentle Moon, thy crystal accents pierce
The caverns of my pride's deep universe, 500
Charming the tiger joy, whose tramplings fierce
   Made wounds which need thy balm.

Panthea.

I rise as from a bath of sparkling water,
A bath of azure light, among dark rocks,
Out of the stream of sound.

Ione.

             Ah me! sweet sister, 505
The stream of sound has ebbed away from us,
And you pretend to rise out of its wave,
Because your words fall like the clear, soft dew
Shaken from a bathing wood-nymph's limbs and hair.

Panthea.

Peace! peace! A mighty Power, which is as darkness, 510
Is rising out of Earth, and from the sky
Is showered like night, and from within the air
Bursts, like eclipse which had been gathered up
Into the pores of sunlight: the bright visions,
Wherein the singing spirits rode and shone, 515
Gleam like pale meteors through a watery night.

IONE.

There is a sense of words upon mine ear.

PANTHEA.

An universal sound like words: Oh, list!

DEMOGORGON.

Thou, Earth, calm empire of a happy soul,
   Sphere of divinest shapes and harmonies,   520
Beautiful orb! gathering as thou dost roll
   The love which paves thy path along the skies:

THE EARTH.

I hear: I am as a drop of dew that dies.

DEMOGORGON.

Thou, Moon, which gazest on the nightly Earth
   With wonder, as it gazes upon thee;   525
Whilst each to men, and beasts, and the swift birth
   Of birds, is beauty, love, calm, harmony:

THE MOON.

I hear: I am a leaf shaken by thee!

DEMOGORGON.

Ye kings of suns and stars, Dæmons and Gods,
   Ætherial Dominations, who possess   530
Elysian, windless, fortunate abodes
   Beyond Heaven's constellated wilderness:

A VOICE *from above.*

Our great Republic hears, we are bless'd, and bless.

DEMOGORGON.

Ye happy dead, whom beams of brightest verse
  Are clouds to hide, not colours to portray,   535
Whether your nature is that universe
  Which once ye saw and suffered —

A VOICE *from beneath.*

                  Or as they
Whom we have left, we change and pass away.

DEMOGORGON.

Ye elemental Genii, who have homes
  From man's high mind even to the central stone   540
Of sullen lead ; from Heaven's star-fretted domes
  To the dull weed some sea-worm battens on :

A CONFUSED VOICE.

We hear : thy words waken Oblivion.

DEMOGORGON.

Spirits, whose homes are flesh : ye beasts and birds,
  Ye worms, and fish ; ye living leaves and buds :   545
Lightning and wind ; and ye untameable herds,
  Meteors and mists, which throng air's solitudes:

A VOICE.

Thy voice to us is wind among still woods.

DEMOGORGON.

Man, who wert once a despot and a slave ;
  A dupe and a deceiver ; a decay;   550
A traveller from the cradle to the grave
  Through the dim night of this immortal day :

ALL.

Speak: thy strong words may never pass away.

DEMOGORGON.

This is the day, which down the void abysm
At the Earth-born's spell yawns for Heaven's despotism, 555
  And Conquest is dragged captive through the deep :
Love, from its awful throne of patient power
In the wise heart, from the last giddy hour
  Of dead endurance, from the slippery, steep,
And narrow verge of crag-like agony, springs 560
And folds over the world its healing wings.

Gentleness, Virtue, Wisdom, and Endurance,
These are the seals of that most firm assurance
  Which bars the pit over Destruction's strength;
And if, with infirm hand, Eternity, 565
Mother of many acts and hours, should free
  The serpent that would clasp her with his length;
These are the spells by which to re-assume
An empire o'er the disentangled doom.

To suffer woes which Hope thinks infinite; 570
To forgive wrongs darker than death or night;
  To defy Power, which seems omnipotent;
To love, and bear; to hope till Hope creates
From its own wreck the thing it contemplates;
  Neither to change, nor falter, nor repent; 575
This, like thy glory, Titan, is to be
Good, great and joyous, beautiful and free;
This is alone Life, Joy, Empire, and Victory.

SONNET: ENGLAND IN 1819.

An old, mad, blind, despised, and dying king, —
Princes, the dregs of their dull race, who flow
Through public scorn, — mud from a muddy spring, —
Rulers who neither see, nor feel, nor know,
But leech-like to their fainting country cling,   5
Till they drop, blind in blood, without a blow, —
A people starved and stabbed in the untilled field, —
An army, which liberticide and prey
Makes as a two-edged sword to all who wield:
Golden and sanguine laws which tempt and slay;   10
Religion Christless, Godless — a book sealed;
A Senate, — Time's worst statute unrepealed, —
Are graves, from which a glorious Phantom may
Burst, to illumine our tempestuous day.

                                                    1819.

SONG TO THE MEN OF ENGLAND.

I.

Men of England, wherefore plough
For the lords who lay ye low?
Wherefore weave with toil and care
The rich robes your tyrants wear?

II.

Wherefore feed, and clothe, and save,   5
From the cradle to the grave,
Those ungrateful drones who would
Drain your sweat — nay, drink your blood?

III.

Wherefore, Bees of England, forge
Many a weapon, chain, and scourge,   10
That these stingless drones may spoil
The forced produce of your toil?

IV.

Have ye leisure, comfort, calm,
Shelter, food, love's gentle balm?
Or what is it ye buy so dear   15
With your pain and with your fear?

V.

The seed ye sow, another reaps;
The wealth ye find, another keeps;
The robes ye weave, another wears;
The arms ye forge, another bears.   20

VI.

Sow seed, — but let no tyrant reap;
Find wealth, — let no impostor heap;
Weave robes, — let not the idle wear;
Forge arms, — in your defence to bear.

VII.

Shrink to your cellars, holes, and cells;   25
In halls ye deck another dwells.
Why shake the chains ye wrought? Ye see
The steel ye tempered glance on ye.

VIII.

With plough and spade, and hoe and loom,
Trace your grave, and build your tomb,   30
And weave your winding-sheet, till fair
England be your sepulchre.   1819.

ODE TO THE WEST WIND.

I.

O, WILD West Wind, thou breath of Autumn's being,
Thou, from whose unseen presence the leaves dead
Are driven, like ghosts from an enchanter fleeing,

Yellow, and black, and pale, and hectic red,
Pestilence-stricken multitudes : O, thou,   5
Who chariotest to their dark wintry bed

The wingèd seeds, where they lie cold and low,
Each like a corpse within its grave, until
Thine azure sister of the spring shall blow

Her clarion o'er the dreaming earth, and fill   10
(Driving sweet buds like flocks to feed in air)
With living hues and odours plain and hill :

Wild Spirit, which art moving every where;
Destroyer and preserver ; hear, O, hear !

II.

Thou on whose stream, 'mid the steep sky's commotion,   15
Loose clouds like earth's decaying leaves are shed,
Shook from the tangled boughs of Heaven and Ocean,

Angels of rain and lightning: there are spread
On the blue surface of thine airy surge,
Like the bright hair uplifted from the head   20

Of some fierce Mænad, even from the dim verge
Of the horizon to the zenith's height
The locks of the approaching storm.   Thou dirge

Of the dying year, to which this closing night
Will be the dome of a vast sepulchre,   25
Vaulted with all thy congregated might

Of vapours, from whose solid atmosphere
Black rain, and fire, and hail will burst : O, hear !

III.

Thou who didst waken from his summer dreams
The blue Mediterranean, where he lay,   30
Lulled by the coil of his crystàlline streams,

Beside a pumice isle in Baiæ's bay,
And saw in sleep old palaces and towers
Quivering within the wave's intenser day,

All overgrown with azure moss and flowers   35
So sweet, the sense faints picturing them ! Thou
For whose path the Atlantic's level powers

Cleave themselves into chasms, while far below
The sea-blooms and the oozy woods which wear
The sapless foliage of the ocean, know   40

Thy voice, and suddenly grow gray with fear,
And tremble and despoil themselves : O, hear !

IV.

If I were a dead leaf thou mightest bear ;
If I were a swift cloud to fly with thee ;
A wave to pant beneath thy power, and share   45

The impulse of thy strength, only less free
Than thou, O, uncontrollable ! If even
I were as in my boyhood, and could be

The comrade of thy wanderings over heaven,
As then, when to outstrip thy skiey speed   50
Scarce seemed a vision; I would ne'er have striven

As thus with thee in prayer in my sore need.   .
Oh! lift me as a wave, a leaf, a cloud!
I fall upon the thorns of life! I bleed!

A heavy weight of hours has chained and bowed   55
One too like thee : tameless, and swift, and proud.

                    v.

Make me thy lyre, even as the forest is :
What if my leaves are falling like its own!
The tumult of thy mighty harmonies

Will take from both a deep, autumnal tone,   60
Sweet though in sadness.   Be thou, spirit fierce,
My spirit!   Be thou me, impetuous one!

Drive my dead thoughts over the universe
Like withered leaves to quicken a new birth!
And, by the incantation of this verse,   65

Scatter, as from an unextinguished hearth
Ashes and sparks, my words among mankind!
Be through my lips to unawakened earth

The trumpet of a prophecy! O, wind,
If Winter comes, can Spring be far behind?   70

                                   1819.

THE INDIAN SERENADE.

I.

I ARISE from dreams of thee
In the first sweet sleep of night,
When the winds are breathing low,
And the stars are shining bright:
I arise from dreams of thee,   5
And a spirit in my feet
Hath led me — who knows how?
To thy chamber window, Sweet!

II.

The wandering airs they faint
On the dark, the silent stream —   10
The Champak odours fail
Like sweet thoughts in a dream;
The nightingale's complaint,
It dies upon her heart; —
As I must on thine,   15
O! belovèd as thou art!

III.

O lift me from the grass!
I die! I faint! I fail!
Let thy love in kisses rain
On my lips and eyelids pale.   20
My cheek is cold and white, alas!
My heart beats loud and fast; —
Oh! press it to thine own again,
Where it will break at last.

1819.

SOPHIA.

I.

THOU art fair, and few are fairer
  Of the Nymphs of earth or ocean;
They are robes that fit the wearer —
  Those soft limbs of thine, whose motion
Ever falls and shifts and glances   5
As the life within them dances.

II.

Thy deep eyes, a double Planet,
  Gaze the wisest into madness
With soft clear fire, — the winds that fan it
  Are those thoughts of tender gladness   10
Which, like Zephyrs on the billow,
Make thy gentle soul their pillow.

III.

If whatever face thou paintest
  In those eyes grows pale with pleasure,
If the fainting soul is faintest   15
  When it hears thy harp's wild measure,
Wonder not that when thou speakest
Of the weak my heart is weakest.

IV.

As dew beneath the wind of morning,
  As the sea which Whirlwinds waken,   20
As the birds at thunder's warning,
  As aught mute yet deeply shaken,
As one who feels an unseen spirit
Is my heart when thine is near it.

                     1819.

LOVE'S PHILOSOPHY.

I.

THE Fountains mingle with the River
  And the Rivers with the Ocean,
The winds of Heaven mix for ever
  With a sweet emotion;
Nothing in the world is single;   5
  All things by a law divine
In one spirit meet and mingle.
  Why not I with thine? —

II.

See the mountains kiss high Heaven
  And the waves clasp one another;   10
No sister-flower would be forgiven
  If it disdained its brother,
And the sunlight clasps the earth
  And the moonbeams kiss the sea:
What is all this sweet work worth   15
  If thou kiss not me?

                    1819.

ODE TO HEAVEN.

CHORUS OF SPIRITS.

First Spirit.

PALACE-ROOF of cloudless nights!
Paradise of golden lights!
  Deep, immeasurable, vast,
Which art now, and which wert then
  Of the present and the past,   5

Of the eternal where and when,
 Presence-chamber, temple, home,
 Ever-canopying dome,
Of acts and ages yet to come !

Glorious shapes have life in thee,   10
Earth, and all earth's company;
 Living globes which ever throng
Thy deep chasms and wildernesses ;
 And green worlds that glide along ;
And swift stars with flashing tresses ;   15
 And icy moons most cold and bright,
 And mighty suns beyond the night,
 Atoms of intensest light.

Even thy name is as a god,
Heaven ! for thou art the abode   20
 Of that power which is the glass
Wherein man his nature sees.
 Generations as they pass
Worship thee with bended knees.
 Their unremaining gods and they   25
 Like a river roll away :
 Thou remainest such alway.

Second Spirit.

Thou art but the mind's first chamber,
Round which its young fancies clamber,
 Like weak insects in a cave,   30
Lighted up by stalactites ;
 But the portal of the grave,
Where a world of new delights
 Will make thy best glories seem
 But a dim and noonday gleam   35
 From the shadow of a dream !

Third Spirit.

Peace! the abyss is wreathed with scorn
At your presumption, atom-born!
　What is heaven? and what are ye
Who its brief expanse inherit? 40
　What are suns and spheres which flee
With the instinct of that spirit
　Of which ye are but a part?
Drops which Nature's mighty heart
Drives through thinnest veins. Depart! 45

What is heaven? a globe of dew,
Filling in the morning new
　Some eyed flower whose young leaves waken
On an unimagined world:
　Constellated suns unshaken, 50
Orbits measureless, are furled
　In that frail and fading sphere,
　With ten millions gathered there,
　To tremble, gleam, and disappear.

December, 1819.

THE SENSITIVE PLANT.

PART FIRST.

A SENSITIVE Plant in a garden grew,
And the young winds fed it with silver dew,
And it opened its fan-like leaves to the light,
And closed them beneath the kisses of night.

And the Spring arose on the garden fair, 5
Like the Spirit of Love felt every where;
And each flower and herb on Earth's dark breast
Rose from the dreams of its wintry rest.

But none ever trembled and panted with bliss
In the garden, the field, or the wilderness,   10
Like a doe in the noon-tide with love's sweet want,
As the companionless Sensitive Plant.

The snow-drop, and then the violet,
Arose from the ground with warm rain wet,
And their breath was mixed with fresh odour, sent   15
From the turf, like the voice and the instrument.

Then the pied wind-flowers and the tulip tall,
And narcissi, the fairest among them all,
Who gaze on their eyes in the stream's recess,
Till they die of their own dear loveliness ;   20

And the Naiad-like lily of the vale,
Whom youth makes so fair and passion so pale,
That the light of its tremulous bells is seen
Through their pavilions of tender green ;

And the hyacinth purple, and white, and blue,   25
Which flung from its bells a sweet peal anew
Of music so delicate, soft, and intense,
It was felt like an odour within the sense :

And the rose like a nymph to the bath addressed,
Which unveiled the depth of her glowing breast,   30
Till, fold after fold, to the fainting air
The soul of her beauty and love lay bare :

And the wand-like lily, which lifted up,
As a Mænad, its moonlight-coloured cup,
Till the fiery star, which is its eye,   35
Gazed through clear dew on the tender sky ;

And the jessamine faint, and the sweet tuberose,
The sweetest flower for scent that blows ;
And all rare blossoms from every clime
Grew in that garden in perfect prime.   40

And on the stream whose inconstant bosom
Was prankt under boughs of embowering blossom,
With golden and green light, slanting through
Their heaven of many a tangled hue,

Broad water lilies lay tremulously,   45
And starry river-buds glimmered by,
And around them the soft stream did glide and dance
With a motion of sweet sound and radiance.

And the sinuous paths of lawn and of moss,
Which led through the garden along and across,   50
Some open at once to the sun and the breeze,
Some lost among bowers of blossoming trees,

Were all paved with daisies and delicate bells
As fair as the fabulous asphodels,
And flowrets which drooping as day drooped too   55
Fell into pavilions, white, purple, and blue,
To roof the glow-worm from the evening dew.

And from this undefiled Paradise
The flowers (as an infant's awakening eyes
Smile on its mother, whose singing sweet   60
Can first lull, and at last must awaken it),

When Heaven's blithe winds had unfolded them,
As mine-lamps enkindle a hidden gem,
Shone smiling to Heaven, and every one
Shared joy in the light of the gentle sun ;   65

For each one was interpenetrated
With the light and the odour its neighbour shed,
Like young lovers whom youth and love make dear
Wrapped and filled by their mutual atmosphere.

But the Sensitive Plant, which could give small fruit   70
Of the love which it felt from the leaf to the root,   .
Received more than all, it loved more than ever,
Where none wanted but it, could belong to the giver :

For the Sensitive Plant has no bright flower;
Radiance and odour are not its dower ;   75
It loves, even like Love ; its deep heart is full ;
It desires what it has not, the beautiful !

The light winds which from unsustaining wings
Shed the music of many murmurings ;
The beams which dart from many a star   80
Of the flowers whose hues they bear afar ;

The plumèd insects swift and free,
Like golden boats on a sunny sea,
Laden with light and odour, which pass
Over the gleam of the living grass ;   85

The unseen clouds of the dew, which lie
Like fire in the flowers till the sun rides high,
Then wander like spirits among the spheres,
Each cloud faint with the fragrance it bears ;

The quivering vapours of dim noontide,   90
Which like a sea o'er the warm earth glide,
In which every sound, and odour, and beam,
Move, as reeds in a single stream ;

Each and all like ministering angels were
For the Sensitive Plant sweet joy to bear,   95
Whilst the lagging hours of the day went by
Like windless clouds o'er a tender sky.

And when evening descended from heaven above,
And the Earth was all rest, and the air was all love,
And delight, though less bright, was far more deep,   100
And the day's veil fell from the world of sleep,

And the beasts, and the birds, and the insects were
          drowned
In an ocean of dreams without a sound;
Whose waves never mark, though they ever impress
The light sand which paves it, consciousness ;   105

(Only overhead the sweet nightingale
Ever sang more sweet as the day might fail,
And snatches of its Elysian chant
Were mixed with the dreams of the Sensitive Plant.)

The Sensitive Plant was the earliest   110
Up-gathered into the bosom of rest ;
A sweet child weary of its delight,
The feeblest and yet the favourite,
Cradled within the embrace of night.

PART SECOND.

There was a Power in this sweet place,
An Eve in this Eden ; a ruling grace
Which to the flowers, did they waken or dream,
Was as God is to the starry scheme.

A Lady, the wonder of her kind,   5
Whose form was upborne by a lovely mind

Which, dilating, had moulded her mien and motion
Like a sea-flower unfolded beneath the ocean,

Tended the garden from morn to even :
And the meteors of that sublunar heaven,   10
Like the lamps of the air when night walks forth,
Laughed round her footsteps up from the Earth !

She had no companion of mortal race,
But her tremulous breath and her flushing face
Told, whilst the morn kissed the sleep from her eyes,   15
That her dreams were less slumber than Paradise :

As if some bright Spirit for her sweet sake
Had deserted heaven while the stars were awake,
As if yet around her he lingering were,
Though the veil of daylight concealed him from her.   20

Her step seemed to pity the grass it pressed;
You might hear by the heaving of her breast,
That the coming and going of the wind
Brought pleasure there and left passion behind.

And wherever her airy footstep trod,   25
Her trailing hair from the grassy sod
Erased its light vestige, with shadowy sweep,
Like a sunny storm o'er the dark green deep.

I doubt not the flowers of that garden sweet
Rejoiced in the sound of her gentle feet;   30
I doubt not they felt the spirit that came
From her glowing fingers through all their frame.

She sprinkled bright water from the stream
On those that were faint with the sunny beam;
And out of the cups of the heavy flowers   35
She emptied the rain of the thunder showers.

She lifted their heads with her tender hands,
And sustained them with rods and ozier bands;
If the flowers had been her own infants she
Could never have nursed them more tenderly.   40

And all killing insects and gnawing worms,
And things of obscene and unlovely forms,
She bore in a basket of Indian woof,
Into the rough woods far aloof,

In a basket, of grasses and wild flowers full,   45
The freshest her gentle hands could pull
For the poor banished insects, whose intent,
Although they did ill, was innocent.

But the bee and the beamlike ephemeris
Whose path is the lightning's, and soft moths that kiss   50
The sweet lips of the flowers, and harm not, did she
Make her attendant angels be.

And many an antenatal tomb,
Where butterflies dream of the life to come,
She left clinging round the smooth and dark   55
Edge of the odorous cedar bark.

This fairest creature from earliest spring
Thus moved through the garden ministering
All the sweet season of summer tide,
And ere the first leaf looked brown — she died !   60

PART THIRD.

Three days the flowers of the garden fair
Like stars when the moon is awakened were,
Or the waves of Baiæ, ere luminous
She floats up through the smoke of Vesuvius.

And on the fourth, the Sensitive Plant   5
Felt the sound of the funeral chaunt,
And the steps of the bearers, heavy and slow,
And the sobs of the mourners, deep and low ;

The weary sound and the heavy breath,
And the silent motions of passing death,   10
And the smell, cold, oppressive, and dank,
Sent through the pores of the coffin plank ;

The dark grass, and the flowers among the grass,
Were bright with tears as the crowd did pass ;
From their sighs the wind caught a mournful tone,   15
And sate in the pines, and gave groan for groan.

The garden, once fair, became cold and foul,
Like the corpse of her who had been its soul,
Which at first was lovely as if in sleep,
Then slowly changed, till it grew a heap   20
To make men tremble who never weep.

Swift summer into the autumn flowed,
And frost in the mist of morning rode,
Though the noonday sun looked clear and bright,
Mocking the spoil of the secret night.   25

The rose leaves, like flakes of crimson snow,
Paved the turf and the moss below.
The lilies were drooping, and white, and wan,
Like the head and the skin of a dying man.

And Indian plants, of scent and hue   30
The sweetest that ever were fed on dew,
Leaf by leaf, day after day,
Were massed into the common clay.

And the leaves, brown, yellow, and gray, and red,
And white with the whiteness of what is dead, 35
Like troops of ghosts on the dry wind passed;
Their whistling noise made the birds aghast.

And the gusty winds waked the wingèd seeds,
Out of their birthplace of ugly weeds,
Till they clung round many a sweet flower's stem, 40
Which rotted into the earth with them.

The water-blooms under the rivulet
Fell from the stalks on which they were set;
And the eddies drove them here and there,
As the winds did those of the upper air. 45

Then the rain came down, and the broken stalks,
Were bent and tangled across the walks;
And the leafless net-work of parasite bowers
Massed into ruin; and all sweet flowers.

Between the time of the wind and the snow, 50
All loathliest weeds began to grow,
Whose coarse leaves were splashed with many a speck,
Like the water-snake's belly and the toad's back.

And thistles, and nettles, and darnels rank,
And the dock, and henbane, and hemlock dank, 55
Stretched out its long and hollow shank,
And stifled the air till the dead wind stank.

And plants, at whose names the verse feels loath,
Filled the place with a monstrous undergrowth,
Prickly, and pulpous, and blistering, and blue, 60
Livid, and starred with a lurid dew.

And agarics, and fungi, with mildew and mould
Started like mist from the wet ground cold;
Pale, fleshy, as if the decaying dead
With a spirit of growth had been animated!   65

Their moss rotted off them, flake by flake,
Till the thick stalk stuck like a murderer's stake,
Where rags of loose flesh yet tremble on high,
Infecting the winds that wander by.

Spawn, weeds, and filth, a leprous scum,   70
Made the running rivulet thick and dumb
And at its outlet flags huge as stakes
Dammed it up with roots knotted like water-snakes.

And hour by hour, when the air was still,
The vapours arose which have strength to kill: 75
At morn they were seen, at noon they were felt,
At night they were darkness no star could melt.

And unctuous meteors from spray to spray
Crept and flitted in broad noon-day
Unseen; every branch on which they alit   80
By a venomous blight was burned and bit.

The Sensitive Plant like one forbid
Wept, and the tears within each lid
Of its folded leaves which together grew
Were changed to a blight of frozen glue.   85

For the leaves soon fell, and the branches soon
By the heavy axe of the blast were hewn;
The sap shrank to the root through every pore
As blood to a heart that will beat no more.

For Winter came: the wind was his whip: 90
One choppy finger was on his lip:
He had torn the cataracts from the hills
And they clanked at his girdle like manacles;

His breath was a chain which without a sound
The earth, and the air, and the water bound;   95
He came, fiercely driven, in his chariot-throne,
By the tenfold blasts of the arctic zone.

Then the weeds which were forms of living death
Fled from the frost to the earth beneath.
Their decay and sudden flight from frost   100
Was but like the vanishing of a ghost!

And under the roots of the Sensitive Plant
The moles and the dormice died for want:
The birds dropped stiff from the frozen air
And were caught in the branches naked and bare.   105

First there came down a thawing rain
And its dull drops froze on the boughs again;
Then there steamed up a freezing dew
Which to the drops of the thaw-rain grew;

And a northern whirlwind, wandering about   110
Like a wolf that had smelt a dead child out,
Shook the boughs thus laden, and heavy and stiff,
And snapped them off with his rigid griff.

When winter had gone and spring came back
The Sensitive Plant was a leafless wreck;   115
But the mandrakes, and toadstools, and docks, and
       darnels,
Rose like the dead from their ruined charnels.

Conclusion.

Whether the Sensitive Plant, or that
Which within its boughs like a spirit sat
Ere its outward form had known decay,
Now felt this change, I cannot say.

Whether that Lady's gentle mind,　　　　　5
No longer with the form combined
Which scattered love, as stars do light,
Found sadness, where it left delight,

I dare not guess; but in this life
Of error, ignorance, and strife,　　　　　10
Where nothing is, but all things seem,
And we the shadows of the dream,

It is a modest creed, and yet
Pleasant if one considers it,
To own that death itself must be,　　　　　15
Like all the rest, a mockery.

That garden sweet, that Lady fair,
And all sweet shapes and odours there,
In truth have never passed away:
'Tis we, 'tis ours, are changed; not they.　　　　　20

For love, and beauty, and delight,
There is no death nor change: their might
Exceeds our organs, which endure
No light, being themselves obscure.

1820.

THE CLOUD.

I BRING fresh showers for the thirsting flowers,
    From the seas and the streams ;
I bear light shade for the leaves when laid
    In their noon-day dreams.
From my wings are shaken the dews that waken   5
    The sweet buds every one,
When rocked to rest on their mother's breast,
    As she dances about the sun.
I wield the flail of the lashing hail,
    And whiten the green plains under,   10
And then again I dissolve it in rain,
    And laugh as I pass in thunder.

I sift the snow on the mountains below,
    And their great pines groan aghast;
And all the night 't is my pillow white,   15
    While I sleep in the arms of the blast.
Sublime on the towers of my skiey bowers,
    Lightning my pilot sits ;
In a cavern under is fettered the thunder, —
    It struggles and howls at fits ;   20
Over earth and ocean, with gentle motion,
    This pilot is guiding me,
Lured by the love of the genii that move
    In the depths of the purple sea ;
Over the rills, and the crags, and the hills,   25
    Over the lakes and the plains,
Wherever he dream, under mountain or stream,
    The Spirit he loves remains ;
And I all the while bask in heaven's blue smile,
    Whilst he is dissolving in rains.   30

The sanguine sunrise, with his meteor eyes,
  And his burning plumes outspread,
Leaps on the back of my sailing rack,
  When the morning star shines dead,
As on the jag of a mountain crag,   35
  Which an earthquake rocks and swings,
An eagle alit one moment may sit
  In the light of its golden wings.
And when sunset may breathe, from the lit sea beneath,
  Its ardours of rest and of love,   40
And the crimson pall of eve may fall
  From the depth of heaven above,
With wings folded I rest, on mine airy nest,
  As still as a brooding dove.

That orbèd maiden with white fire laden,   45
  Whom mortals call the moon,
Glides glimmering o'er my fleece-like floor,
  By the midnight breezes strewn;
And wherever the beat of her unseen feet,
  Which only the angels hear,   50
May have broken the woof of my tent's thin roof,
  The stars peep behind her and peer;
And I laugh to see them whirl and flee,
  Like a swarm of golden bees,
When I widen the rent in my wind-built tent, 55
  Till the calm rivers, lakes, and seas,
Like strips of the sky fallen through me on high,
  Are each paved with the moon and these.

I bind the sun's throne with a burning zone,
  And the moon's with a girdle of pearl; 60
The volcanoes are dim, and the stars reel and swim,
  When the whirlwinds my banner unfurl.

From cape to cape, with à bridge-like shape,
    Over a torrent sea,
Sunbeam-proof, I hang like a roof,   65
    The mountains its columns be.
The triumphal arch through which I march
    With hurricane, fire, and snow,
When the powers of the air are chained to my chair,
    Is the million-coloured bow ;   70
The sphere-fire above its soft colours wove,
    While the moist earth was laughing below.

I am the daughter of earth and water,
    And the nursling of the sky;
I pass through the pores of the ocean and shores ;   75
    I change, but I cannot die.
For after the rain when, with never a stain,
    The pavilion of heaven is bare,
And the winds and sunbeams with their convex gleams
    Build up the blue dome of air,   80
I silently laugh at my own cenotaph,
    And out of the caverns of rain,
Like a child from the womb, like a ghost from the
    tomb,
    I arise and unbuild it again.

                 1820.

TO A SKYLARK.

Hail to thee, blithe spirit !
    Bird thou never wert,
    That from heaven, or near it,
    Pourest thy full heart
In profuse strains of unpremeditated art.   5

Higher still and higher
  From the earth thou springest
Like a cloud of fire ;
  The blue deep thou wingest,
And singing still dost soar, and soaring ever singest.   10

In the golden lightning
  Of the sunken sun,
O'er which clouds are brightning,
  Thou dost float and run;
Like an unbodied joy whose race is just begun.   15

The pale purple even
  Melts around thy flight ;
Like a star of heaven
  In the broad day-light
Thou art unseen, but yet I hear thy shrill delight,   20

Keen as are the arrows
  Of that silver sphere,
Whose intense lamp narrows
  In the white dawn clear,
Until we hardly see, we feel that it is there.   25

All the earth and air
  With thy voice is loud,
As, when night is bare,
  From one lonely cloud
The moon rains out her beams, and heaven is overflowed. 30

What thou art we know not ;
  What is most like thee?
From rainbow clouds there flow not
  Drops so bright to see
As from thy presence showers a rain of melody.   35

Like a poet hidden
  In the light of thought,
Singing hymns unbidden,
  Till the world is wrought
To sympathy with hopes and fears it heeded not: 40

Like a high-born maiden
  In a palace tower,
Soothing her love-laden
  Soul in secret hour
With music sweet as love, which overflows her bower: 45

Like a glow-worm golden
  In a dell of dew,
Scattering unbeholden
  Its aërial hue
Among the flowers and grass which screen it from the view: 50

Like a rose embowered
  In its own green leaves,
By warm winds deflowered,
  Till the scent it gives
Makes faint with too much sweet these heavy-wingèd
      thieves.   55

Sound of vernal showers
  On the twinkling grass,
Rain-awakened flowers,
  All that ever was
Joyous, and clear, and fresh, thy music doth surpass.   60

Teach us, sprite or bird,
  What sweet thoughts are thine;
I have never heard
  Praise of love or wine
That panted forth a flood of rapture so divine: 65

Chorus Hymenæal,
    Or triumphal chaunt,
Matched with thine, would be all
    But an empty vaunt,
A thing wherein we feel there is some hidden want.   70

    What objects are the fountains
      Of thy happy strain?
    What fields, or waves, or mountains?
      What shapes of sky or plain?
What love of thine own kind? what ignorance of pain?   75

    With thy clear keen joyance
      Languor cannot be —
    Shadow of annoyance
      Never came near thee:
Thou lovest — but ne'er knew love's sad satiety.   80

    Waking or asleep,
      Thou of death must deem
    Things more true and deep
      Than we mortals dream,
Or how could thy notes flow in such a crystal stream?   85

    We look before and after
      And pine for what is not:
    Our sincerest laughter
      With some pain is fraught;
Our sweetest songs are those that tell of saddest thought.   90

    Yet if we could scorn
      Hate, and pride, and fear;
    If we were things born
      Not to shed a tear,
I know not how thy joy we ever should come near.   95

Better than all measures
Of delightful sound —
Better than all treasures
That in books are found —
Thy skill to poet were, thou scorner of the ground!   100

Teach me half the gladness
That thy brain must know,
Such harmonious madness
From my lips would flow,
The world should listen then — as I am listening now.   105

1820.

ODE TO LIBERTY.

Yet, Freedom, yet thy banner torn but flying,
Streams like a thunder-storm against the wind.

BYRON.

I.

A GLORIOUS people vibrated again
   The lightning of the nations : Liberty
From heart to heart, from tower to tower, o'er Spain,
   Scattering contagious fire into the sky,
Gleamed.   My soul spurned the chains of its dismay,   5
      And, in the rapid plumes of song,
      Clothed itself, sublime and strong ;
As a young eagle soars the morning clouds among,
   Hovering in verse o'er its accustomed prey ;
      Till from its station in the heaven of fame   10
   The Spirit's whirlwind rapt it, and the ray
      Of the remotest sphere of living flame
Which paves the void was from behind it flung,
   As foam from a ship's swiftness, when there came
A voice out of the deep : I will record the same.   15

II.

The Sun and the serenest Moon sprang forth:
  The burning stars of the abyss were hurled
Into the depths of heaven. The Dædal earth,
  That island in the ocean of the world,
Hung in its cloud of all-sustaining air: 20
     But this divinest universe
     Was yet a chaos and a curse,
For thou wert not: but power from worst producing worse,
  The spirit of the beasts was kindled there,
    And of the birds, and of the watery forms,   25
    And there was war among them, and despair
     Within them, raging without truce or terms:
The bosom of their violated nurse
  Groaned, for beasts warred on beasts, and worms on
    worms,
  And men on men; each heart was as a hell of storms. 30

III.

Man, the imperial shape, then multiplied
  His generations under the pavilion
Of the Sun's throne: palace and pyramid,
  Temple and prison, to many a swarming million,
Were, as to mountain-wolves their ragged caves.   35
     This human living multitude
     Was savage, cunning, blind, and rude,
For thou wert not; but o'er the populous solitude,
  Like one fierce cloud over a waste of waves
    Hung Tyranny; beneath, sate deified   40
  The sister-pest, congregator of slaves;
    Into the shadow of her pinions wide
Anarchs and priests who feed on gold and blood,
  Till with the stain their inmost souls are dyed,
    Drove the astonished herds of men from every side. 45

IV.

The nodding promontories, and blue isles,
　And cloud-like mountains, and dividuous waves
Of Greece, basked glorious in the open smiles
　Of favouring heaven: from their enchanted caves
Prophetic echoes flung dim melody.　　　　　　　50
　　　On the unapprehensive wild
　　　The vine, the corn, the olive mild,
Grew savage yet, to human use unreconciled ;
　And, like unfolded flowers beneath the sea,
　　Like the man's thought dark in the infant's brain,　55
　Like aught that is which wraps what is to be,
　　Art's deathless dreams lay veiled by many a vein
Of Parian stone ; and, yet a speechless child,
　Verse murmured, and Philosophy did strain
　Her lidless eyes for thee ; when o'er the Ægean main　60

V.

Athens arose : a city such as vision
　Builds from the purple crags and silver towers
Of battlemented cloud, as in derision
　Of kingliest masonry : the ocean-floors
Pave it ; the evening sky pavilions it ;　　　　　65
　　　Its portals are inhabited
　　　By thunder-zonèd winds, each head
Within its cloudy wings with sunfire garlanded,
　A divine work ! Athens diviner yet
　　Gleamed with its crest of columns, on the will　70
　Of man, as on a mount of diamond, set ;
　　For thou wert, and thine all-creative skill
Peopled with forms that mock the eternal dead
　In marble immortality, that hill
　Which was thine earliest throne and latest oracle.　75

VI.

Within the surface of Time's fleeting river
  Its wrinkled image lies, as then it lay
Immovably unquiet, and for ever
  It trembles, but it cannot pass away !
The voices of thy bards and sages thunder   80
    With an earth-awakening blast
    Through the caverns of the past;
Religion veils her eyes; Oppression shrinks aghast:
  A wingèd sound of joy, and love, and wonder,
    Which soars where Expectation never flew,   85
  Rending the veil of space and time asunder !
    One ocean feeds the clouds, and streams, and dew;
One sun illumines heaven; one spirit vast
  With life and love makes chaos ever new,
  As Athens doth the world with thy delight renew.   90

VII.

Then Rome was, and from thy deep bosom fairest,
  Like a wolf-cub from a Cadmæan Mænad,
She drew the milk of greatness, though thy dearest
  From that Elysian food was yet unweanèd;
And many a deed of terrible uprightness   95
    By thy sweet love was sanctified;
    And in thy smile, and by thy side,
 Saintly Camillus lived, and firm Atilius died.
  But when tears stained thy robe of vestal whiteness,
    And gold profaned thy capitolian throne,   100
  Thou didst desert, with spirit-wingèd lightness,
    The senate of the tyrants: they sunk prone
Slaves of one tyrant : Palatinus sighed
  Faint echoes of Ionian song; that tone
  Thou didst delay to hear, lamenting to disown.   105

VIII.

From what Hyrcanian glen or frozen hill,
  Or piny promontory of the Arctic main,
Or utmost islet inaccessible,
  Didst thou lament the ruin of thy reign,
Teaching the woods, and waves, and desert rocks,   110
    And every Naiad's ice-cold urn,
    To talk in echoes sad and stern,
Of that sublimest lore which man had dared unlearn?
  For neither didst thou watch the wizard flocks
    Of the Scald's dreams, nor haunt the Druid's sleep. 115
  What if the tears rained through thy shattered locks
    Were quickly dried? for thou didst groan, not weep
When from its sea of death to kill and burn,
  The Galilean serpent forth did creep,
  And made thy world an undistinguishable heap.   120

IX.

A thousand years the Earth cried, Where art thou?
  And then the shadow of thy coming fell
On Saxon Alfred's olive-cinctured brow:
  And many a warrior-peopled citadel,
Like rocks which fire lifts out of the flat deep,   125
      Arose in sacred Italy,
      Frowning o'er the tempestuous sea
Of kings, and priests, and slaves, in tower-crowned majesty;
    That multitudinous anarchy did sweep,
      And burst around their walls, like idle foam,   130
    Whilst from the human spirit's deepest deep
      Strange melody with love and awe struck dumb
Dissonant arms; and Art, which cannot die,
    With divine wand traced on our earthly home
    Fit imagery to pave heaven's everlasting dome.   135

x.

Thou huntress swifter than the Moon! thou terror
  Of the world's wolves! thou bearer of the quiver,
Whose sunlike shafts pierce tempest-wingèd Error,
  As light may pierce the clouds when they dissever
In the calm regions of the orient day!   140
      Luther caught thy wakening glance;
      Like lightning, from his leaden lance
Reflected, it dissolved the visions of the trance
  In which, as in a tomb, the nations lay;
    And England's prophets hailed thee as their queen, 145
  In songs whose music cannot pass away,
    Though it must flow for ever: not unseen
Before the spirit-sighted countenance
  Of Milton didst thou pass, from the sad scene
  Beyond whose night he saw, with a dejected mien.   150

XI.

The eager hours and unreluctant years
  As on a dawn-illumined mountain stood,
Trampling to silence their loud hopes and fears,
  Darkening each other with their multitude,
And cried aloud, Liberty! Indignation   155
      Answered Pity from her cave;
      Death grew pale within the grave,
And Desolation howled to the destroyer, Save!
  When like heaven's sun girt by the exhalation
    Of its own glorious light, thou didst arise,   160
  Chasing thy foes from nation unto nation
    Like shadows: as if day had cloven the skies
At dreaming midnight o'er the western wave,
  Men started, staggering with a glad surprise,
  Under the lightnings of thine unfamiliar eyes.   165

XII.

Thou heaven of earth ! what spells could pall thee then,
  In ominous eclipse? a thousand years
Bred from the slime of deep oppression's den
  Dyed all thy liquid light with blood and tears,
Till thy sweet stars could weep the stain away ;   170
    How like Bacchanals of blood
    Round France, the ghastly vintage, stood
Destruction's sceptred slaves, and Folly's mitred brood !
  When one, like them, but mightier far than they,
    The Anarch of thine own bewildered powers   175
  Rose : armies mingled in obscure array,
    Like clouds with clouds, darkening the sacred bowers
Of serene heaven.   He, by the past pursued,
  Rests with those dead, but unforgotten hours,
Whose ghosts scare victor kings in their ancestral towers. 180

XIII.

England yet sleeps : was she not called of old?
  Spain calls her now, as with its thrilling thunder
Vesuvius wakens Ætna, and the cold
  Snow-crags by its reply are cloven in sunder :
O'er the lit waves every Æolian isle   185
    From Pithecusa to Pelorus
    Howls, and leaps, and glares in chorus :
They cry, Be dim ; ye lamps of heaven suspended o'er us.
  Her chains are threads of gold, she need but smile
    And they dissolve ; but Spain's were links of steel, 190
  Till bit to dust by virtue's keenest file.
    Twins of a single destiny ! appeal
To the eternal years enthroned before us,
  In the dim West ; impress us from a seal,
All ye have thought and done ! Time cannot dare conceal. 195

XIV.

Tomb of Arminius! render up thy dead,
  Till, like a standard from a watch-tower's staff,
His soul may stream over the tyrant's head;
  Thy victory shall be his epitaph,
Wild Bacchanal of truth's mysterious wine,   200
      King-deluded Germany,
      His dead spirit lives in thee.
Why do we fear or hope? thou art already free!
  And thou, lost Paradise of this divine
      And glorious world! thou flowery wilderness!   205
  Thou island of eternity! thou shrine
      Where desolation clothed with loveliness,
Worships the thing thou wert! O Italy,
  Gather thy blood into thy heart; repress
  The beasts who make their dens thy sacred palaces. 210

XV.

O, that the free would stamp the impious name
  Of KING into the dust! or write it there,
So that this blot upon the page of fame
  Were as a serpent's path, which the light air
Erases, and the flat sands close behind!   215
      Ye the oracle have heard:
      Lift the victory-flashing sword,
And cut the snaky knots of this foul gordian word,
  Which weak itself as stubble, yet can bind
      Into a mass, irrefragably firm,   220
  The axes and the rods which awe mankind;
      The sound has poison in it, 'tis the sperm
Of what makes life foul, cankerous, and abhorred;
  Disdain not thou, at thine appointed term,
  To set thine armèd heel on this reluctant worm.   225

XVI.

O, that the wise from their bright minds would kindle
  Such lamps within the dome of this dim world,
That the pale name of PRIEST might shrink and dwindle
  Into the hell from which it first was hurled,
A scoff of impious pride from fiends impure ;   230
      Till human thoughts might kneel alone
      Each before the judgment-throne
Of its own aweless soul, or of the power unknown !
    O, that the words which make the thoughts obscure
      From which they spring, as clouds of glimmering dew 235
    From a white lake blot heaven's blue portraiture,
      Were stripped of their thin masks and various hue
And frowns and smiles and splendours not their own,
      Till in the nakedness of false and true
    They stand before their Lord, each to receive its due. 240

XVII.

He who taught man to vanquish whatsoever
  Can be between the cradle and the grave
Crowned him the King of Life.   O vain endeavour !
  If on his own high will, a willing slave,
He has enthroned the oppression and the oppressor.   245
      What if earth can clothe and feed
      Amplest millions at their need,
And power in thought be as the tree within the seed?
    O, what if Art, an ardent intercessor,
      Driving on fiery wings to Nature's throne,   250
    Checks the great mother stooping to caress her,
      And cries : Give me, thy child, dominion
Over all height and depth? if Life can breed
    New wants, and wealth from those who toil and groan
    Rend of thy gifts and hers a thousand fold for one.   255

Come Thou, but lead out of the inmost cave
 Of man's deep spirit, as the morning-star
Beckons the Sun from the Eoan wave,
  Wisdom. I hear the pennons of her car
Self-moving, like cloud charioted by flame ;   260
   Comes she not, and come ye not,
   Rulers of eternal thought,
To judge, with solemn truth, life's ill-apportioned lot ?
  Blind Love, and equal Justice, and the Fame
   Of what has been, the Hope of what will be ? 265
  O, Liberty ! if such could be thy name
   Wert thou disjoined from these, or they from thee :
If thine or theirs were treasures to be bought
  By blood or tears, have not the wise and free
  Wept tears, and blood like tears? The solemn harmony 270

Paused, and the spirit of that mighty singing
 To its abyss was suddenly withdrawn;
Then, as a wild swan, when sublimely winging
 Its path athwart the thunder-smoke of dawn,
Sinks headlong through the aërial golden light   275
   On the heavy sounding plain,
   When the bolt has pierced its brain;
As summer clouds dissolve, unburthened of their rain;
  As a far taper fades with fading night,
   As a brief insect dies with dying day,   280
  My song, its pinions disarrayed of might,
   Drooped ; o'er it closed the echoes far away
Of the great voice which did its flight sustain,
  As waves which lately paved his watery way
  Hiss round a drowner's head in their tempestuous play. 285
  Spring, 1820.

ARETHUSA.

I.

ARETHUSA arose
From her couch of snows
In the Acroceraunian mountains, —
From cloud and from crag,
With many a jag,   5
Shepherding her bright fountains.
　　She leapt down the rocks,
　　With her rainbow locks
Streaming among the streams; —
　　Her steps paved with green   10
　　The downward ravine
Which slopes to the western gleams:
　　And gliding and springing
　　She went, ever singing,
In murmurs as soft as sleep;   15
　　The Earth seemed to love her,
　　And Heaven smiled above her,
As she lingered towards the deep.

II.

　　Then Alpheus bold,
　　On his glacier cold,   20
With his trident the mountains strook
　　And opened a chasm
　　In the rocks; — with the spasm
All Erymanthus shook.
　　And the black south wind   25
　　It concealed behind
The urns of the silent snow,
　　And earthquake and thunder
　　Did rend in sunder

The bars of the springs below: 30
    The beard and the hair
    Of the River-god were
Seen through the torrent's sweep,
    As he followed the light
    Of the fleet nymph's flight   35
To the brink of the Dorian deep.

III.

"Oh, save me! Oh, guide me!
    And bid the deep hide me,
For he grasps me now by the hair!"
    The loud Ocean heard,   40
    To its blue depth stirred,
And divided at her prayer;
    And under the water
    The Earth's white daughter
Fled like a sunny beam;   45
    Behind her descended
    Her billows, unblended
With the brackish Dorian stream : —
    Like a gloomy stain
    On the emerald main   50
Alpheus rushed behind, —
    As an eagle pursuing
    A dove to its ruin
Down the streams of the cloudy wind.

IV.

    Under the bowers   55
    Where the Ocean Powers
Sit on their pearlèd thrones,
    Through the coral woods
    Of the weltering floods,

Over heaps of unvalued stones;   60
    Through the dim beams
    Which amid the streams
Weave a net-work of coloured light;
    And under the caves,
    Where the shadowy waves   65
Are as green as the forest's night : —
    Outspeeding the shark
    And the sword-fish dark,
Under the ocean foam,
    And up through the rifts   70
    Of the mountain clifts
They passed to their Dorian home.

v.

    And now from their fountains
    In Enna's mountains,
Down one vale where the morning basks,   75
    Like friends once parted
    Grown single-hearted,
They ply their watery tasks.
    At sunrise they leap
    From their cradles steep   80
In the cave of the shelving hill;
    At noon-tide they flow
    Through the woods below
And the meadows of Asphodel;
    And at night they sleep   85
    In the rocking deep
Beneath the Ortygian shore; —
    Like spirits that lie
    In the azure sky
When they love but live no more.   90

1820.

TO ——

I.

I FEAR thy kisses, gentle maiden,
  Thou needest not fear mine;
My spirit is too deeply laden
  Ever to burthen thine.

II.

I fear thy mien, thy tones, thy motion,   5
  Thou needest not fear mine;
Innocent is the heart's devotion
  With which I worship thine.

1820.

THE QUESTION.

I.

I DREAMED that, as I wandered by the way,
  Bare winter suddenly was changed to spring,
And gentle odours led my steps astray,
  Mixed with a sound of waters murmuring
Along a shelving bank of turf, which lay   5
  Under a copse, and hardly dared to fling
Its green arms round the bosom of the stream,
But kissed it and then fled, as thou mightest in dream.

II.

There grew pied wind-flowers and violets,
  Daisies, those pearled Arcturi of the earth,   10
The constellated flower that never sets;
  Faint oxlips; tender bluebells, at whose birth
The sod scarce heaved; and that tall flower that wets
  (Like a child, half in tenderness and mirth)

Its mother's face with heaven's collected tears,　　　15
When the low wind, its playmate's voice, it hears.

III.

And in the warm hedge grew lush eglantine,
　　Green cowbind and the moonlight-coloured May,
And cherry-blossoms, and white cups, whose wine
　　Was the bright dew, yet drained not by the day;　　20
And wild roses, and ivy serpentine,
　　With its dark buds and leaves, wandering astray;
And flowers azure, black, and streaked with gold,
Fairer than any wakened eyes behold.

IV.

And nearer to the river's trembling edge　　　25
　　There grew broad flag-flowers, purple prankt with
　　　　white,
And starry river-buds among the sedge,
　　And floating water-lilies, broad and bright,
Which lit the oak that overhung the hedge
　　With moonlight beams of their own watery light;　　30
And bulrushes and reeds of such deep green
As soothed the dazzled eye with sober sheen.

V.

Methought that of these visionary flowers
　　I made a nosegay, bound in such a way
That the same hues, which in their natural bowers　　35
　　Were mingled or opposed, the like array
Kept these imprisoned children of the Hours
　　Within my hand, — and then, elate and gay,
I hastened to the spot whence I had come,
That I might there present it! — oh! to whom?　　40

1820.

SONG OF PROSERPINE,

WHILE GATHERING FLOWERS ON THE PLAIN OF ENNA.

I.

SACRED Goddess, Mother Earth,
   Thou from whose immortal bosom
Gods and men and beasts have birth,
   Leaf and blade and bud and blossom,
Breathe thine influence most divine   5
On thine own child, Proserpine.

II.

If with mists of evening dew
   Thou dost nourish these young flowers
Till they grow, in scent and hue,
   Fairest children of the hours,   10
Breathe thine influence most divine
On thine own child, Proserpine.

                               1820.

HYMN OF APOLLO.

I.

THE sleepless Hours who watch me as I lie,
   Curtained with star-inwoven tapestries,
From the broad moonlight of the sky,
   Fanning the busy dreams from my dim eyes, —
Waken me when their Mother, the gray Dawn,   5
Tells them that dreams and that the moon is gone.

II.

Then I arise, and climbing Heaven's blue dome,
   I walk over the mountains and the waves,
Leaving my robe upon the ocean foam ;
   My footsteps pave the clouds with fire ; the caves 10
Are filled with my bright presence, and the air
Leaves the green earth to my embraces bare.

III.

The sunbeams are my shafts, with which I kill
   Deceit, that loves the night and fears the day ;
All men who do or even imagine ill   15
   Fly me, and from the glory of my ray
Good minds and open actions take new might,
Until diminished by the reign of night.

IV.

I feed the clouds, the rainbows and the flowers
   With their ætherial colours; the Moon's globe   20
And the pure stars in their eternal bowers
   Are cinctured with my power as with a robe ;
Whatever lamps on Earth or Heaven may shine,
Are portions of one power, which is mine.

V.

I stand at noon upon the peak of Heaven,   25
   Then with unwilling steps I wander down
Into the clouds of the Atlantic even ;
   For grief that I depart they weep and frown :
What look is more delightful than the smile
With which I soothe them from the western isle ?   30

VI.

I am the eye with which the Universe
  Beholds itself and knows itself divine ;
All harmony of instrument or verse,
  All prophecy, all medicine are mine,
All light of art or nature ; — to my song,   35
Victory and praise in their own right belong.

                                     1820.

HYMN OF PAN.

I.

From the forests and highlands
  We come, we come ;
From the river-girt islands,
  Where loud waves are dumb
    Listening to my sweet pipings.   5
The wind in the reeds and the rushes,
  The bees on the bells of thyme,
The birds on the myrtle bushes,
The cicale above in the lime,
And the lizards below in the grass,   10
Were as silent as ever old Tmolus was,
    Listening to my sweet pipings.

II.

Liquid Peneus was flowing,
  And all dark Tempe lay
In Pelion's shadow, outgrowing   15
  The light of the dying day,
    Speeded by my sweet pipings.

The Sileni, and Sylvans, and Fauns,
    And the Nymphs of the woods and waves,
To the edge of the moist river-lawns,   20
    And the brink of the dewy caves,
And all that did then attend and follow
Were silent with love, as you now, Apollo,
    With envy of my sweet pipings.

III.

I sang of the dancing stars,   25
    I sang of the dædal Earth,
And of Heaven — and the giant wars,
    And Love, and Death, and Birth, —
      And then I changed my pipings, —
Singing how down the vale of Menalus   30
    I pursued a maiden and clasped a reed :
Gods and men, we are all deluded thus !
    It breaks in our bosom and then we bleed:
All wept, as I think both ye now would,
If envy or age had not frozen your blood,   35
    At the sorrow of my sweet pipings.

                              1820.

LETTER TO MARIA GISBORNE.

                    LEGHORN, *July* 1, 1820.

THE spider spreads her webs, whether she be
In poet's tower, cellar, or barn, or tree ;
The silk-worm in the dark green mulberry leaves
His winding sheet and cradle ever weaves ;
So I, a thing whom moralists call worm,   5
Sit spinning still round this decaying form,

From the fine threads of rare and subtle thought —
No net of words in garish colours wrought
To catch the idle buzzers of the day —
But a soft cell, where when that fades away,   10
Memory may clothe in wings my living name
And feed it with the asphodels of fame,
Which in those hearts which must remember me
Grow, making love an immortality.

Whoever should behold me now, I wist,   15
Would think I were a mighty mechanist,
Bent with sublime Archimedean art
To breathe a soul into the iron heart
Of some machine portentous, or strange gin,
Which by the force of figured spells might win   20
Its way over the sea, and sport therein ;
For round the walls are hung dread engines, such
As Vulcan never wrought for Jove to clutch
Ixion or the Titan: — or the quick
Wit of that man of God, St. Dominic,   25
To convince Atheist, Turk or Heretic,
Or those in philanthropic council met,
Who thought to pay some interest for the debt
They owed to Jesus Christ for their salvation,
By giving a faint foretaste of damnation   30
To Shakespeare, Sidney, Spenser and the rest
Who made our land an island of the bless'd,
When lamp-like Spain, who now relumes her fire
On Freedom's hearth, grew dim with Empire: —
With thumbscrews, wheels, with tooth and spike and jag, 35
Which fishers found under the utmost crag
Of Cornwall and the storm-encompassed isles,
Where to the sky the rude sea rarely smiles
Unless in treacherous wrath, as on the morn

When the exulting elements in scorn   40
Satiated with destroyed destruction, lay
Sleeping in beauty on their mangled prey,
As panthers sleep; — and other strange and dread
Magical forms the brick floor overspread——
Proteus transformed to metal did not make   45
More figures, or more strange ; nor did he take
Such shapes of unintelligible brass,
Or heap himself in such a horrid mass
Of tin and iron not to be understood;
And forms of unimaginable wood,   50
To puzzle Tubal Cain and all his brood:
Great screws, and cones, and wheels, and groovèd
        blocks,
The elements of what will stand the shocks
Of wave and wind and time. — Upon the table
More knacks and quips there be than I am able   55
To catalogize in this verse of mine: —
A pretty bowl of wood — not full of wine,
But quicksilver; that dew which the gnomes drink
When at their subterranean toil they swink,
Pledging the dæmons of the earthquake, who   60
Reply to them in lava — cry halloo !
And call out to the cities o'er their head, —
Roofs, towers and shrines, the dying and the dead,
Crash through the chinks of earth — and then all
        quaff
Another rouse, and hold their sides and laugh.   65
This quicksilver no gnome has drunk — within
The walnut bowl it lies, veinèd and thin,
In colour like the wake of light that stains
The Tuscan deep, when from the moist moon rains
The inmost shower of its white fire — the breeze   70
Is still — blue heaven smiles over the pale seas.

And in this bowl of quicksilver — for I
Yield to the impulse of an infancy
Outlasting manhood — I have made to float
A rude idealism of a paper boat, —   75
A hollow screw with cogs — Henry will know
The thing I mean and laugh at me, — if so
He fears not I should do more mischief. — Next
Lie bills and calculations much perplexed,
With steam-boats, frigates, and machinery quaint   80
Traced over them in blue and yellow paint.
Then comes a range of mathematical
Instruments, for plans nautical and statical;
A heap of rosin, a queer broken glass
With ink in it; — a china cup that was   85
What it will never be again, I think,
A thing from which sweet lips were wont to drink
The liquor doctors rail at — and which I
Will quaff in spite of them — and when we die
We 'll toss up who died first of drinking tea,   90
And cry out, — "heads or tails?" where'er we be.
Near that a dusty paint-box, some odd hooks,
A half-burnt match, an ivory block, three books,
Where conic sections, spherics, logarithms,
To great Laplace, from Saunderson and Sims,   95
Lie heaped in their harmonious disarray
Of figures, — disentangle them who may.
Baron de Tott's Memoirs beside them lie,
And some odd volumes of old chemistry.
Near those a most inexplicable thing,   100
With lead in the middle — I 'm conjecturing
How to make Henry understand; but no —
I 'll leave, as Spenser says, with many mo,
This secret in the pregnant womb of time,
Too vast a matter for so weak a rhyme.   105

And here like some weird Archimage sit I,
Plotting dark spells, and devilish enginery,
The self-impelling steam-wheels of the mind
Which pump up oaths from clergymen, and grind
The gentle spirit of our meek reviews   110
Into a powdery foam of salt abuse,
Ruffling the ocean of their self-content; —
I sit — and smile or sigh as is my bent,
But not for them — Libeccio rushes round
With an inconstant and an idle sound;   115
I heed him more than them — the thunder-smoke
Is gathering on the mountains, like a cloke
Folded athwart their shoulders broad and bare;
The ripe corn under the undulating air
Undulates like an ocean; — and the vines   120
Are trembling wide in all their trellised lines —
The murmur of the awakening sea doth fill
The empty pauses of the blast; — the hill
Looks hoary through the white electric rain,
And from the glens beyond, in sullen strain,   125
The interrupted thunder howls; above
One chasm of heaven smiles, like the eye of Love
On the unquiet world; — while such things are,
How could one worth your friendship heed the war
Of worms? the shriek of the world's carrion jays,   130
Their censure, or their wonder, or their praise?

You are not here! the quaint witch Memory sees
In vacant chairs, your absent images,
And points where once you sat, and now should be
But are not. — I demand if ever we   135
Shall meet as then we met; and she replies,
Veiling in awe her second-sighted eyes; —
" I know the past alone — but summon home

"My sister Hope, — she speaks of all to come."
But I, an old diviner, who knew well   140
Every false verse of that sweet oracle,
Turned to the sad enchantress once again,
And sought a respite from my gentle pain,
In citing every passage o'er and o'er
Of our communion — how on the sea-shore   145
We watched the ocean and the sky together,
Under the roof of blue Italian weather;
How I ran home through last year's thunder-storm,
And felt the transverse lightning linger warm
Upon my cheek — and how we often made   150
Feasts for each other, where good will outweighed
The frugal luxury of our country cheer,
As well it might, were it less firm and clear
Than ours must ever be; — and how we spun
A shroud of talk to hide us from the sun   155
Of this familiar life, which seems to be
But is not, — or is but quaint mockery
Of all we would believe, and sadly blame
The jarring and inexplicable frame
Of this wrong world: — and then anatomize   160
The purposes and thoughts of men whose eyes
Were closed in distant years; — or widely guess
The issue of the earth's great business,
When we shall be as we no longer are —
Like babbling gossips safe, who hear the war   165
Of winds, and sigh, but tremble not; — or how
You listened to some interrupted flow
Of visionary rhyme, — in joy and pain
Struck from the inmost fountains of my brain,
With little skill perhaps; — or how we sought   170
Those deepest wells of passion or of thought
Wrought by wise poets in the waste of years,

Staining their sacred waters with our tears;
Quenching a thirst ever to be renewed!
Or how I, wisest lady! then indued   175
The language of a land which now is free,
And, winged with thoughts of truth and majesty,
Flits round the tyrant's sceptre like a cloud,
And bursts the peopled prisons, and cries aloud,
"My name is Legion!"—that majestic tongue,   180
Which Calderon over the desert flung
Of ages and of nations; and which found
An echo in our hearts, and with the sound
Startled oblivion;—thou wert then to me
As is a nurse—when inarticulately   185
A child would talk as its grown parents do.
If living winds the rapid clouds pursue,
If hawks chase doves through the ætherial way,
Huntsmen the innocent deer, and beasts their prey,
Why should not we rouse with the spirit's blast   190
Out of the forest of the pathless past
These recollected pleasures?
      You are now
In London, that great sea, whose ebb and flow
At once is deaf and loud, and on the shore
Vomits its wrecks, and still howls on for more.   195
Yet in its depth what treasures! You will see
That which was Godwin,—greater none than he
Though fallen—and fallen on evil times—to stand
Among the spirits of our age and land,
Before the dread tribunal of *to-come*   200
The foremost,—while Rebuke cowers pale and dumb.
You will see Coleridge—he who sits obscure
In the exceeding lustre and the pure
Intense irradiation of a mind
Which, with its own internal lightning blind,   205

Flags wearily through darkness and despair —
A cloud-encircled meteor of the air,
A hooded eagle among blinking owls. ——
You will see Hunt — one of those happy souls
Which are the salt of the earth, and without whom   210
This world would smell like what it is — a tomb ;
Who is, what others seem; his room no doubt
Is still adorned by many a cast from Shout,
With graceful flowers tastefully placed about ;
And coronals of bay from ribbons hung,   215
And brighter wreaths in neat disorder flung ;
The gifts of the most learn'd among some dozens
Of female friends, sisters-in-law and cousins.
And there is he with his eternal puns,
Which beat the dullest brain for smiles, like duns   220
Thundering for money at a poet's door ;
Alas ! it is no use to say, "I'm poor!" —
Or oft in graver mood, when he will look
Things wiser than were ever read in book,
Except in Shakespeare's wisest tenderness. —   225
You will see Hogg, — and I cannot express
His virtues, — though I know that they are great,
Because he locks, then barricades the gate
Within which they inhabit ; — of his wit
And wisdom, you 'll cry out when you are bit.   230
He is a pearl within an oyster-shell,
One of the richest of the deep ; — and there
Is English Peacock with his mountain fair
Turned into a Flamingo ; — that shy bird
That gleams i' the Indian air — have you not heard,   235
When a man marries, dies, or turns Hindoo,
His best friends hear no more of him ? — but you
Will see him, and will like him too, I hope,
With the milk-white Snowdonian Antelope

Matched with this cameleopard : — his fine wit   240
Makes such a wound, the knife is lost in it ;
A strain too learnèd for a shallow age,
Too wise for selfish bigots, let his page,
Which charms the chosen spirits of the time,
Fold itself up for the serener clime   245
Of years to come, and find its recompense
In that just expectation. — Wit and sense,
Virtue and human knowledge, all that might
Make this dull world a business of delight,
Are all combined in Horace Smith. — And these,   250
With some exceptions, which I need not tease
Your patience by descanting on, — are all
You and I know in London.
                I recall
My thoughts, and bid you look upon the night.
As water does a sponge, so the moonlight   255
Fills the void, hollow, universal air : —
What see you ? — unpavilioned heaven is fair
Whether the moon, into her chamber gone,
Leaves midnight to the golden stars, or wan
Climbs with diminished beams the azure steep ;   260
Or whether clouds sail o'er the inverse deep,
Piloted by the many-wandering blast,
And the rare stars rush through them dim and fast : ——
All this is beautiful in every land. ——
But what see you beside? — a shabby stand   265
Of Hackney coaches — a brick house or wall
Fencing some lonely court, white with the scrawl
Of our unhappy politics ; — or worse —
A wretched woman reeling by, whose curse
Mixed with the watchman's, partner of her trade,   270
You must accept in place of serenade ; —
Or yellow haired Pollonia, murmuring

To Henry some unutterable thing.
I see a chaos of green leaves and fruit
Built round dark caverns, even to the root   275
Of the living stems that feed them — in whose bowers
There sleep in their dark dew the folded flowers;
Beyond, the surface of the unsickled corn
Trembles not in the slumbering air, and, borne
In circles quaint, and ever-changing dance,   280
Like wingèd stars the fire-flies flash and glance,
Pale in the open moonshine; but each one
Under the dark trees seems a little sun,
A meteor tamed, a fixed star gone astray
From the silver regions of the milky way; —   285
Afar the Contadino's song is heard,
Rude, but made sweet by distance — and a bird
Which cannot be the Nightingale, and yet
I know none else that sings so sweet as it
At this late hour; — and then all is still ——   290
Now Italy or London, which you will!

    Next winter you must pass with me; I 'll have
My house by that time turned into a grave
Of dead despondence and low-thoughted care,
And all the dreams which our tormentors are;   295
Oh! that Hunt, Hogg, Peacock and Smith were there,
With every thing belonging to them fair! —
We will have books, Spanish, Italian, Greek;
And ask one week to make another week
As like his father as I 'm unlike mine,   300
Which is not his fault, as you may divine.
Though we eat little flesh and drink no wine,
Yet let 's be merry: we 'll have tea and toast,
Custards for supper, and an endless host
Of syllabubs and jellies and mince-pies,   305

And other such lady-like luxuries, —
Feasting on which we will philosophize!
And we 'll have fires out of the Grand Duke's wood,
To thaw the six weeks' winter in our blood.
And then we 'll talk ; — what shall we talk about? 310
Oh ! there are themes enough for many a bout
Of thought-entangled descant ; — as to nerves —
With cones and parallelograms and curves
I 've sworn to strangle them if once they dare
To bother me — when you are with me there. 315
And they shall never more sip laudanum,
From Helicon or Himeros ; — well, come ;
And, in despite of God and of the devil,
We 'll make our friendly philosophic revel
Outlast the leafless time ; till buds and flowers 320
Warn the obscure inevitable hours,
Sweet meeting by sad parting to renew ; —
"To-morrow to fresh woods and pastures new."

ODE TO NAPLES.

EPODE I. a.

I STOOD within the city disinterred,
　　And heard the autumnal leaves like light footfalls
Of spirits passing through the streets, and heard
　　The Mountain's slumberous voice at intervals
　　　Thrill through those roofless halls; 5
The oracular thunder penetrating shook
　　The listening soul in my suspended blood;
I felt that Earth out of her deep heart spoke —
　　I felt, but heard not : — through white columns glowed
　　　The isle-sustaining Ocean-flood, 10

A plane of light between two Heavens of azure:
    Around me gleamed many a bright sepulchre
Of whose pure beauty, Time, as if his pleasure
Were to spare Death, had never made erasure;
    But every living lineament was clear   15
    As in the sculptor's thought; and there
The wreaths of stony myrtle, ivy and pine,
    Like winter leaves o'ergrown by moulded snow,
    Seemed only not to move and grow
Because the crystal silence of the air   20
    Weighed on their life; even as the Power divine
    Which then lulled all things, brooded upon mine.

EPODE II. *a.*

        Then gentle winds arose
        With many a mingled close
Of wild Æolian sound and mountain-odour keen;   25
        And where the Baian ocean
        Welters with air-like motion,
Within, above, around its bowers of starry green,
    Moving the sea-flowers in those purple caves
        Even as the ever stormless atmosphere   30
            Floats o'er the Elysian realm,
    It bore me like an Angel, o'er the waves
        Of sunlight, whose swift pinnace of dewy air
            No storm can overwhelm;
            I sailed, where ever flows   35
            Under the calm Serene
            A spirit of deep emotion
            From the unknown graves
            Of the dead kings of Melody.
Shadowy Aornos darkened o'er the helm   40
The horizontal æther; heaven stripped bare
Its depths over Elysium, where the prow

Made the invisible water white as snow;
From that Typhæan mount, Inarime,
   There streamed a sunlight vapour, like the standard   45
      Of some ætherial host;
      Whilst from all the coast,
   Louder and louder, gathering round, there wandered
Over the oracular woods and divine sea
Prophesyings which grew articulate —   , 50
They seize me — I must speak them — be they fate!

STROPHE a. I.

Naples! thou Heart of men which ever pantest
   Naked, beneath the lidless eye of heaven!
Elysian City which to calm enchantest
   The mutinous air and sea: they round thee, even   55
   As sleep round Love, are driven!
Metropolis of a ruined Paradise
   Long lost, late won, and yet but half regained!
Bright Altar of the bloodless sacrifice,
   Which armèd Victory offers up unstained   60
   To Love, the flower-enchained!
Thou which wert once, and then didst cease to be,
Now art, and henceforth ever shalt be, free,
   If Hope, and Truth, and Justice can avail,
      Hail, hail, all hail!   65

STROPHE β. 2.

   Thou youngest giant birth
   Which from the groaning earth
Leap'st, clothed in armour of impenetrable scale!
   Last of the Intercessors!
   Who 'gainst the Crowned Transgressors   70
Pleadest before God's love! Arrayed in Wisdom's mail,

Wave thy lightning lance in mirth,
Nor let thy high heart fail,
Though from their hundred gates the leagued Oppressors,
With hurried legions move!   75
Hail, hail, all hail!

ANTISTROPHE α.

What though Cimmerian Anarchs dare blaspheme
Freedom and thee? thy shield is as a mirror
To make their blind slaves see, and with fierce gleam
To turn his hungry sword upon the wearer;   80
A new Actæon's error
Shall theirs have been — devoured by their own hounds!
Be thou like the imperial Basilisk
Killing thy foe with unapparent wounds!
Gaze on oppression, till at that dread risk   85
Aghast she pass from the Earth's disk:
Fear not, but gaze — for freemen mightier grow,
And slaves more feeble, gazing on their foe;
If Hope and Truth and Justice may avail,
Thou shalt be great. — All hail!   90

ANTISTROPHE β. 2.

From Freedom's form divine,
From Nature's inmost shrine,
Strip every impious gawd, rend Error veil by veil:
O'er Ruin desolate,
O'er Falsehood's fallen state,   95
Sit thou sublime, unawed; be the Destroyer pale!
And equal laws be thine,
And wingèd words let sail,
Freighted with truth even from the throne of God:
That wealth, surviving fate,   100
Be thine. — All hail!

ANTISTROPHE α. γ.

Didst thou not start to hear Spain's thrilling pæan
From land to land re-echoed solemnly,
Till silence became music ? From the Ææan
    To the cold Alps, eternal Italy   105
    Starts to hear thine ! The Sea
Which paves the desert streets of Venice laughs
  In light and music ; widowed Genoa wan
By moonlight spells ancestral epitaphs,
    Murmuring, where is Doria ? fair Milan,   110
    Within whose veins long ran
The viper's palsying venom, lifts her heel
To bruise his head. The signal and the seal
  (If Hope and Truth and Justice can avail)
Art Thou of all these hopes. — O hail !   115

ANTISTROPHE β. γ.

    Florence ! beneath the sun,
    Of cities fairest one,
Blushes within her bower for Freedom's expectation :
    From eyes of quenchless hope
    Rome tears the priestly cope,   120
As ruling once by power, so now by admiration,
    As athlete stripped to run
    From a remoter station
For the high prize lost on Philippi's shore : —
  As then Hope, Truth, and Justice did avail,   125
So now may Fraud and Wrong ! O hail !

EPODE I. β.

Hear ye the march as of the Earth-born Forms
  Arrayed against the ever-living Gods ?
The crash and darkness of a thousand storms
  Bursting their inaccessible abodes   130
    Of crags and thunder-clouds ?

See ye the banners blazoned to the day,
  Inwrought with emblems of barbaric pride?
Dissonant threats kill Silence far away;
    The serene Heaven which wraps our Eden wide   135
      With iron light is dyed;
The Anarchs of the North lead forth their legions
    Like Chaos o'er creation, uncreating;
An hundred tribes nourished on strange religions
And lawless slaveries, — down the aërial regions   140
    Of the white Alps, desolating,
    Famished wolves that bide no waiting,
Blotting the glowing footsteps of old glory,
Trampling our columned cities into dust,
      Their dull and savage lust   145
    On Beauty's corse to sickness satiating —
They come!   The fields they tread look black and hoary
With fire — from their red feet the streams run gory!

EPODE II. β.

    Great Spirit, deepest Love!
    Which rulest, and dost move   •   150
All things which live and are, within the Italian shore;
    Who spreadest heaven around it,
    Whose woods, rocks, waves, surround it,
Who sittest in thy star, o'er Ocean's western floor;
Spirit of beauty! at whose soft command   155
    The sunbeams and the showers distil its foison
    From the Earth's bosom chill;
O bid those beams be each a blinding brand
    Of lightning! bid those showers be dews of poison!
      Bid the Earth's plenty kill!   160
      Bid thy bright Heaven above,
      Whilst light and darkness bound it,
      Be their tomb who planned
      To make it ours and thine!

Or, with thine harmonizing ardours fill 165
And raise thy sons, as o'er the prone horizon
Thy lamp feeds every twilight wave with fire —
Be man's high hope and unextinct desire
The instrument to work thy will divine!
  Then clouds from sunbeams, antelopes from leopards, 170
    And frowns and fears from Thee,
    Would not more swiftly flee
  Than Celtic wolves from the Ausonian shepherds. —
Whatever, Spirit, from thy starry shrine
  Thou yieldest or withholdest, Oh let be 175
This city of thy worship ever free!

August 17-25, 1820.

GOOD NIGIIT.

I.

Good night? ah! no; the hour is ill
  Which severs those it should unite;
Let us remain together still,
  Then it will be *good* night.

II.

How can I call the lone night good, 5
  Though thy sweet wishes wing its flight?
Be it not said, thought, understood,
  Then it will be *good* night.

III.

To hearts which near each other move
  From evening close to morning light, 10
The night is good; because, my love,
  They never *say* good night.

1820.

THE WORLD'S WANDERERS.

I.

TELL me, thou star, whose wings of light
Speed thee in thy fiery flight,
In what cavern of the night
　　　Will thy pinions close now?

II.

Tell me, moon, thou pale and gray　　　　　5
Pilgrim of heaven's homeless way,
In what depth of night or day
　　　Seekest thou repose now?

III.

Weary wind, who wanderest
Like the world's rejected guest,　　　　　10
Hast thou still some secret nest
　　　On the tree or billow?

　　　　　　　　　　　　　1820.

TO THE MOON.

ART thou pale for weariness
Of climbing heaven and gazing on the earth,
　　　Wandering companionless
Among the stars that have a different birth, —
And ever changing, like a joyless eye　　　　　5
That finds no object worth its constancy?

　　　　　　　　　　　　　1820.

TIME LONG PAST.

I.

LIKE the ghost of a dear friend dead
    Is Time long past.
A tone which is now forever fled,
A hope which is now forever past,
A love so sweet it could not last,   5
    Was Time long past.

II.

There were sweet dreams in the night
    Of Time long past:
And, was it sadness or delight,
Each day a shadow onward cast   10
Which made us wish it yet might last —
    That Time long past.

III.

There is regret, almost remorse,
    For Time long past.
'T is like a child's belovèd corse   15
A father watches, till at last
Beauty is like remembrance, cast
    From Time long past.

                   1820.

SONNET.

YE hasten to the grave!   What seek ye there,
Ye restless thoughts and busy purposes
Of the idle brain, which the world's livery wear?
O thou quick heart which pantest to possess
All that pale Expectation feigneth fair!   5

Thou vainly curious mind which wouldest guess
Whence thou didst come, and whither thou must go,
And all that never yet was known would know —
Oh, whither hasten ye, that thus ye press,
With such swift feet life's green and pleasant path,　　　10
Seeking, alike from happiness and woe,
A refuge in the cavern of gray death?
O heart, and mind, and thoughts, what thing do you
Hope to inherit in the grave below?

　　　　　　　　　　　　　　　　1820.

DIRGE FOR THE YEAR.

I.

ORPHAN hours, the year is dead, —
　Come and sigh, come and weep!
Merry hours, smile instead,
　For the year is but asleep.
See, it smiles as it is sleeping,　　　　　5
Mocking your untimely weeping.

II.

As an earthquake rocks a corse
　In its coffin in the clay,
So White Winter, that rough nurse,
　Rocks the death-cold year to-day;　　　10
Solemn hours! wail aloud
For your mother in her shroud.

III.

As the wild air stirs and sways
　The tree-swung cradle of a child,
So the breath of these rude days　　　　15
　Rocks the year: — be calm and mild,

Trembling hours,—she will arise
With new love within her eyes.

IV.

January gray is here,
 Like a sexton by her grave;   20
February bears the bier,
 March with grief doth howl and rave,
And April weeps—but, O, ye hours,
 Follow with May's fairest flowers.

January 1, 1821.

TIME.

UNFATHOMABLE Sea! whose waves are years,
 Ocean of Time, whose waters of deep woe
Are brackish with the salt of human tears!
 Thou shoreless flood, which in thy ebb and flow
Claspest the limits of mortality!   5
 And sick of prey, yet howling on for more,
Vomitest thy wrecks on its inhospitable shore;
 Treacherous in calm, and terrible in storm,
  Who shall put forth on thee,
  Unfathomable Sea?   10

1821.

TO NIGHT.

I.

SWIFTLY walk o'er the western wave,
   Spirit of Night!
Out of the misty eastern cave,
Where all the long and lone daylight,

Thou wovest dreams of joy and fear,   5
Which make thee terrible and dear, —
      Swift be thy flight !

II.

Wrap thy form in a mantle gray,
      Star in-wrought !
Blind with thine hair the eyes of Day;   10
Kiss her until she be wearied out,
Then wander o'er city, and sea, and land,
Touching all with thine opiate wand —
      Come, long sought !

III.

When I arose and saw the dawn,   15
      I sighed for thee ;
When light rode high, and the dew was gone,
And noon lay heavy on flower and tree,
And the weary Day turned to his rest,
Lingering like an unloved guest,   20
      I sighed for thee.

IV.

Thy brother Death came, and cried,
      Wouldst thou me ?
Thy sweet child Sleep, the filmy-eyed,
Murmured like a noon-tide bee,   25
Shall I nestle near thy side ?
Wouldst thou me ? — And I replied,
      No, not thee !

V.

Death will come when thou art dead,
      Soon, too soon —   30

Sleep will come when thou art fled ;
Of neither would I ask the boon
I ask of thee, belovèd Night —
Swift be thine approaching flight,
      Come soon, soon !   35
               1821.

FROM THE ARABIC : AN IMITATION.

I.

My faint spirit was sitting in the light
    Of thy looks, my love ;
  It panted for thee like the hind at noon
    For the brooks, my love.
Thy barb whose hoofs outspeed the tempest's flight   5
    Bore thee far from me ;
  My heart, for my weak feet were weary soon,
    Did companion thee.

II.

Ah ! fleeter far than fleetest storm or steed,
    Or the death they bear,   10
  The heart which tender thought clothes like a dove
    With the wings of care ;
In the battle, in the darkness, in the need,
    Shall mine cling to thee,
  Nor claim one smile for all the comfort, love,   15
    It may bring to thee.
               1821.

TO EMILIA VIVIANI.

MADONNA, wherefore hast thou sent to me
  Sweet basil and mignonette,
Embleming love and health, which never yet
In the same wreath might be?
    Alas, and they are wet !   5
Is it with thy kisses or thy tears?
    For never rain or dew
    Such fragrance drew
From plant or flower—the very doubt endears
    My sadness ever new,   10
The sighs I breathe, the tears I shed for thee.

Send the stars light, but send not love to me,
  In whom love ever made
Health like a heap of embers soon to fade.

March, 1821.

EPIPSYCHIDION.

VERSES ADDRESSED TO THE NOBLE AND UNFORTUNATE LADY,

EMILIA V——,

NOW IMPRISONED IN THE CONVENT OF ——.

L'anima amante si slancia fuori del creato, e si crea nel infinito un Mondo tutto per essa, diverso assai da questo oscuro e pauroso baratro.

HER OWN WORDS.

1821.

My Song, I fear that thou wilt find but few
Who fitly shall conceive thy reasoning,
Of such hard matter dost thou entertain ;
Whence, if by misadventure, chance should bring
Thee to base company, (as chance may do,)
Quite unaware of what thou dost contain,
I prithee, comfort thy sweet self again,
My last delight ! tell them that they are dull,
And bid them own that thou art beautiful.

EPIPSYCHIDION.

ADVERTIZEMENT.

THE Writer of the following Lines died at Florence, as he was preparing for a voyage to one of the wildest of the Sporades, which he had bought, and where he had fitted up the ruins of an old building, and where it was his hope to have realized a scheme of life, suited perhaps to that happier 5 and better world of which he is now an inhabitant, but hardly practicable in this. His life was singular; less on account of the romantic vicissitudes which diversified it, than the ideal tinge which it received from his own character and feelings. The present Poem, like the Vita Nuova of Dante, is sufficiently 10 intelligible to a certain class of readers without a matter-of-fact history of the circumstances to which it relates; and to a certain other class it must ever remain incomprehensible, from a defect of a common organ of perception for the ideas of which it treats. Not but that, *gran vergogna sarebbe a colui,* 15 *che rimasse cosa sotto veste di figura, o di colore rettorico: e domandato non sapesse denudare le sue parole da cotal veste, in guisa che avessero verace intendimento.* The present poem appears to have been intended by the Writer as the dedication to some longer one. The stanza on 20 the opposite page is almost a literal translation from Dante's famous Canzone

Voi, ch' intendendo, il terzo ciel movete, etc.

The presumptuous application of the concluding lines to his own composition will raise a smile at the expense of my 25 unfortunate friend: be it a smile not of contempt, but pity.

S.

EPIPSYCHIDION.

Sweet Spirit! Sister of that orphan one,
Whose empire is the name thou weepest on,
In my heart's temple I suspend to thee
These votive wreaths of withered memory.

Poor captive bird! who, from thy narrow cage,   5
Pourest such music, that it might assuage
The rugged hearts of those who prisoned thee,
Were they not deaf to all sweet melody;
This song shall be thy rose: its petals pale
Are dead, indeed, my adored Nightingale!   10
But soft and fragrant is the faded blossom,
And it has no thorn left to wound thy bosom.

High, spirit-wingèd Heart! who dost for ever
Beat thine unfeeling bars with vain endeavour,
Till those bright plumes of thought, in which arrayed   15
It over-soared this low and worldly shade,
Lie shattered; and thy panting, wounded breast
Stains with dear blood its unmaternal nest!
I weep vain tears: blood would less bitter be,
Yet poured forth gladlier, could it profit thee.   20

Seraph of Heaven! too gentle to be human,
Veiling beneath that radiant form of Woman
All that is insupportable in thee
Of light, and love, and immortality!
Sweet Benediction in the eternal Curse!   25
Veiled Glory of this lampless Universe!
Thou Moon beyond the clouds! Thou living Form
Among the Dead! Thou Star above the Storm!

Thou Wonder, and thou Beauty, and thou Terror!
Thou Harmony of Nature's art! Thou Mirror   30
In whom, as in the splendour of the Sun,
All shapes look glorious which thou gazest on!
Aye, even the dim words which obscure thee now
Flash, lightning-like, with unaccustomed glow;
I pray thee that thou blot from this sad song   35
All of its much mortality and wrong,
With those clear drops, which start like sacred dew
From the twin lights thy sweet soul darkens through,
Weeping, till sorrow becomes ecstasy:
Then smile on it, so that it may not die.   40

    I never thought before my death to see
Youth's vision thus made perfect. Emily,
I love thee; though the world by no thin name
Will hide that love from its unvalued shame.
Would we two had been twins of the same mother!   45
Or, that the name my heart lent to another
Could be a sister's bond for her and thee,
Blending two beams of one eternity!
Yet were one lawful and the other true,
These names, though dear, could paint not, as is due, 50
How beyond refuge I am thine. Ah me!
I am not thine: I am a part of *thee.*

    Sweet Lamp! my moth-like Muse has burnt its wings;
Or, like a dying swan who soars and sings,
Young Love should teach Time, in his own gray style, 55
All that thou art. Art thou not void of guile,
A lovely soul formed to be bless'd and bless?
A well of sealed and secret happiness,
Whose waters like blithe light and music are,
Vanquishing dissonance and gloom? A Star   60

Which moves not in the moving Heavens, alone?
A smile amid dark frowns? a gentle tone
Amid rude voices? a belovèd light?
A Solitude, a Refuge, a Delight?
A Lute, which those whom love has taught to play   65
Make music on, to soothe the roughest day
And lull fond grief asleep? a buried treasure?
A cradle of young thoughts of wingless pleasure?
A violet-shrouded grave of Woe? — I measure
The world of fancies, seeking one like thee,   70
And find — alas! mine own infirmity.

She met me, Stranger, upon life's rough way,
And lured me towards sweet Death; as Night by Day,
Winter by Spring, or Sorrow by swift Hope,
Led into light, life, peace.   An antelope,   75
In the suspended impulse of its lightness,
Were less ætherially light: the brightness
Of her divinest presence trembles through
Her limbs, as underneath a cloud of dew
Embodied in the windless Heaven of June   80
Amid the splendour-wingèd stars, the Moon
Burns, inextinguishably beautiful:
And from her lips, as from a hyacinth full
Of honey-dew, a liquid murmur drops,
Killing the sense with passion; sweet as stops   85
Of planetary music heard in trance.
In her mild lights the starry spirits dance,
The sun-beams of those wells which ever leap
Under the lightnings of the soul—too deep
For the brief fathom-line of thought or sense.   90
The glory of her being, issuing thence,
Stains the dead, blank, cold air with a warm shade
Of unentangled intermixture, made

By Love, of light and motion : one intense
Diffusion, one serene Omnipresence,   95
Whose flowing outlines mingle in their flowing
Around her cheeks and utmost fingers glowing
With the unintermitted blood, which there
Quivers, (as in a fleece of snow-like air
The crimson pulse of living morning quiver,)   100
Continuously prolonged, and ending never,
Till they are lost, and in that Beauty furled
Which penetrates and clasps and fills the world ;
Scarce visible from extreme loveliness.
Warm fragrance seems to fall from her light dress   105
And her loose hair ; and where some heavy tress
The air of her own speed has disentwined,
The sweetness seems to satiate the faint wind ;
And in the soul a wild odour is felt,
Beyond the sense, like fiery dews that melt   110
Into the bosom of a frozen bud.——
See where she stands ! a mortal shape indued
With love and life and light and deity,
And motion which may change but cannot die ;
An image of some bright Eternity ;   115
A shadow of some golden dream ; a Splendour
Leaving the third sphere pilotless ; a tender
Reflexion of the eternal Moon of Love
Under whose motions life's dull billows move ;
A Metaphor of Spring and Youth and Morning ;   120
A Vision like incarnate April, warning,
With smiles and tears, Frost the Anatomy
Into his summer grave.

               Ah, woe is me !
What have I dared ? where am I lifted ? how
Shall I descend, and perish not ? I know   125

That Love makes all things equal : I have heard
By mine own heart this joyous truth averred :
The spirit of the worm beneath the sod
In love and worship blends itself with God.

   Spouse! Sister! Angel! Pilot of the Fate   130
Whose course has been so starless! O too late
Belovèd! O too soon adored, by me!
For in the fields of immortality
My spirit should at first have worshipped thine,
A divine presence in a place divine;   135
Or should have moved beside it on this earth,
A shadow of that substance, from its birth;
But not as now :—I love thee; yes, I feel
That on the fountain of my heart a seal
Is set, to keep its waters pure and bright   140
For thee, since in those *tears* thou hast delight.
We—are we not formed, as notes of music are,
For one another, though dissimilar;
Such difference without discord, as can make
Those sweetest sounds, in which all spirits shake   145
As trembling leaves in a continuous air?

   Thy wisdom speaks in me, and bids me dare
Beacon the rocks on which high hearts are wrecked.
I never was attached to that great sect,
Whose doctrine is, that each one should select   150
Out of the crowd a mistress or a friend,
And all the rest, though fair and wise, commend
To cold oblivion, though 't is in the code
Of modern morals, and the beaten road
Which those poor slaves with weary footsteps tread,   155
Who travel to their home among the dead
By the broad highway of the world, and so

With one chained friend, perhaps a jealous foe,
The dreariest and the longest journey go.

True Love in this differs from gold and clay, 160
That to divide is not to take away.
Love is like understanding, that grows bright,
Gazing on many truths; 'tis like thy light,
Imagination! which from earth and sky,
And from the depths of human phantasy, 165
As from a thousand prisms and mirrors, fills
The Universe with glorious beams, and kills
Error, the worm, with many a sun-like arrow
Of its reverberated lightning.   Narrow
The heart that loves, the brain that contemplates, 170
The life that wears, the spirit that creates
One object, and one form, and builds thereby
A sepulchre for its eternity.

Mind from its object differs most in this:
Evil from good; misery from happiness; 175
The baser from the nobler; the impure
And frail, from what is clear and must endure.
If you divide suffering and dross, you may
Diminish till it is consumed away;
If you divide pleasure and love and thought, 180
Each part exceeds the whole; and we know not
How much, while any yet remains unshared,
Of pleasure may be gained, of sorrow spared:
This truth is that deep well, whence sages draw
The unenvied light of hope; the eternal law 185
By which those live, to whom this world of life
Is as a garden ravaged, and whose strife
Tills for the promise of a later birth
The wilderness of this Elysian earth.

There was a Being whom my spirit oft   190
Met on its visioned wanderings, far aloft,
In the clear golden prime of my youth's dawn,
Upon the fairy isles of sunny lawn,
Amid the enchanted mountains, and the caves
Of divine sleep, and on the air-like waves   195
Of wonder-level dream, whose tremulous floor
Paved her light steps ; — on an imagined shore,
Under the gray beak of some promontory
She met me, robed in such exceeding glory,
That I beheld her not.   In solitudes   200
Her voice came to me through the whispering woods,
And from the fountains, and the odours deep
Of flowers, which, like lips murmuring in their sleep
Of the sweet kisses which had lulled them there,
Breathed but of *her* to the enamoured air ;   205
And from the breezes whether low or loud,
And from the rain of every passing cloud,
And from the singing of the summer-birds,
And from all sounds, all silence.   In the words
Of antique verse and high romance, — in form,   210
Sound, colour — in whatever checks that Storm
Which with the shattered present chokes the past;
And in that best philosophy, whose taste
Makes this cold common hell, our life, a doom
As glorious as a fiery martyrdom ;   215
Her Spirit was the harmony of truth. —

Then, from the caverns of my dreamy youth
I sprang, as one sandalled with plumes of fire,
And towards the loadstar of my one desire,
I flitted, like a dizzy moth, whose flight   220
Is as a dead leaf's in the owlet light,
When it would seek in Hesper's setting sphere

A radiant death, a fiery sepulchre,
As if it were a lamp of earthly flame.—
But She, whom prayers or tears then could not tame,   225
Passed, like a God throned on a wingèd planet,
Whose burning plumes to tenfold swiftness fan it,
Into the dreary cone of our life's shade ;
And as a man with mighty loss dismayed,
I would have followed, though the grave between   230
Yawned like a gulph whose spectres are unseen :
When a voice said :—" O Thou of hearts the weakest,
" The phantom is beside thee whom thou seekest."
Then I—"where ? " the world's echo answered "where !"
And in that silence, and in my despair,   235
I questioned every tongueless wind that flew
Over my tower of mourning, if it knew
Whither 't was fled, this soul out of my soul ;
And murmured names and spells which have control
Over the sightless tyrants of our fate ;   240
But neither prayer nor verse could dissipate
The night which closed on her ; nor uncreate
That world within this Chaos, mine and me,
Of which she was the veiled Divinity,
The world I say of thoughts that worshipped her :   245
And therefore I went forth, with hope and fear
And every gentle passion sick to death,
Feeding my course with expectation's breath,
Into the wintry forest of our life ;
And struggling through its error with vain strife,   250
And stumbling in my weakness and my haste,
And half bewildered by new forms, I passed
Seeking among those untaught foresters
If I could find one form resembling hers,
In which she might have masked herself from me.   255
There,—One, whose voice was venomed melody,

Sate by a well, under blue night-shade bowers ;
The breath of her false mouth was like faint flowers,
Her touch was as electric poison, — flame
Out of her looks into my vitals came,   260
And from her living cheeks and bosom flew
A killing air, which pierced like honey-dew
Into the core of my green heart, and lay
Upon its leaves ; until, as hair grown gray
O'er a young brow, they hid its unblown prime   265
With ruins of unseasonable time.

    In many mortal forms I rashly sought
The shadow of that idol of my thought.
And some were fair — but beauty dies away :
Others were wise — but honeyed words betray :   270
And One was true — oh ! why not true to me ?
Then, as a hunted deer that could not flee,
I turned upon my thoughts, and stood at bay,
Wounded and weak and panting ; the cold day
Trembled, for pity of my strife and pain.   275
When, like a noon-day dawn, there shone again
Deliverance.   One stood on my path who seemed
As like the glorious shape which I had dreamed,
As is the Moon, whose changes ever run
Into themselves, to the eternal Sun ;   280
The cold chaste Moon, the Queen of Heaven's bright isles,
Who makes all beautiful on which she smiles,
That wandering shrine of soft yet icy flame
Which ever is transformed, yet still the same,
And warms not but illumines.   Young and fair   285
As the descended Spirit of that sphere,
She hid me, as the Moon may hide the night
From its own darkness, until all was bright
Between the Heaven and Earth of my calm mind,

And, as a cloud charioted by the wind,   290
She led me to a cave in that wild place,
And sate beside me, with her downward face
Illumining my slumbers, like the Moon
Waxing and waning o'er Endymion.
And I was laid asleep, spirit and limb,   295
And all my being became bright or dim
As the Moon's image in a summer sea,
According as she smiled or frowned on me ;
And there I lay, within a chaste cold bed :
Alas, I then was nor alive nor dead :—   300
For at her silver voice came Death and Life,
Unmindful each of their accustomed strife,
Masked like twin babes, a sister and a brother,
The wandering hopes of one abandoned mother,
And through the cavern without wings they flew,   305
And cried " Away, he is not of our crew."
I wept, and though it be a dream, I weep.

What storms then shook the ocean of my sleep,
Blotting that Moon, whose pale and waning lips
Then shrank as in the sickness of eclipse ;—   310
And how my soul was as a lampless sea,
And who was then its Tempest; and when She,
The Planet of that hour, was quenched, what frost
Crept o'er those waters, till from coast to coast
The moving billows of my being fell   315
Into a death of ice, immovable ;—
And then— what earthquakes made it gape and split,
The white Moon smiling all the while on it,
These words conceal :—If not, each word would be
The key of staunchless tears. Weep not for me !   320

At length, into the obscure Forest came
The Vision I had sought through grief and shame.

Athwart that wintry wilderness of thorns
Flashed from her motion splendour like the Morn's,
And from her presence life was radiated   325
Through the gray earth and branches bare and dead;
So that her way was paved, and roofed above
With flowers as soft as thoughts of budding love;
And music from her respiration spread
Like light, — all other sounds were penetrated   330
By the small, still, sweet spirit of that sound,
So that the savage winds hung mute around;
And odours warm and fresh fell from her hair
Dissolving the dull cold in the frore air:
Soft as an Incarnation of the Sun,   335
When light is changed to love, this glorious One
Floated into the cavern where I lay,
And called my Spirit, and the dreaming clay
Was lifted by the thing that dreamed below
As smoke by fire, and in her beauty's glow   340
I stood, and felt the dawn of my long night
Was penetrating me with living light:
I knew it was the Vision veiled from me
So many years — that it was Emily.

Twin Spheres of light who rule this passive Earth,   345
This world of love, this *me;* and into birth
Awaken all its fruits and flowers, and dart
Magnetic might into its central heart;
And lift its billows and its mists, and guide
By everlasting laws each wind and tide   350
To its fit cloud, and its appointed cave;
And lull its storms, each in the craggy grave
Which was its cradle, luring to faint bowers
The armies of the rainbow-wingèd showers;
And, as those married lights, which from the towers   355

Of Heaven look forth and fold the wandering globe
In liquid sleep and splendour, as a robe;
And all their many-mingled influence blend,
If equal, yet unlike, to one sweet end;—
So ye, bright regents, with alternate sway   360
Govern my sphere of being, night and day!
Thou, not disdaining even a borrowed might;
Thou, not eclipsing a remoter light;
And, through the shadow of the seasons three,
From Spring to Autumn's sere maturity,   365
Light it into the Winter of the tomb,
Where it may ripen to a brighter bloom.
Thou too, O Comet beautiful and fierce,
Who drew the heart of this frail Universe
Towards thine own; till, wrecked in that convulsion,   370
Alternating attraction and repulsion,
Thine went astray and that was rent in twain;
Oh, float into our azure heaven again!
Be there love's folding-star at thy return;
The living Sun will feed thee from its urn   375
Of golden fire; the Moon will veil her horn
In thy last smiles; adoring Even and Morn
Will worship thee with incense of calm breath
And lights and shadows; as the star of Death
And Birth is worshipped by those sisters wild   380
Called Hope and Fear—upon the heart are piled
Their offerings,—of this sacrifice divine
A World shall be the altar.

                 Lady mine,
Scorn not these flowers of thought, the fading birth
Which from its heart of hearts that plant puts forth   385
Whose fruit, made perfect by thy sunny eyes,
Will be as of the trees of Paradise.

The day is come, and thou wilt fly with me.
To whatsoe'er of dull mortality
Is mine, remain a vestal sister still;   390
To the intense, the deep, the imperishable,
Not mine but me, henceforth be thou united
Even as a bride, delighting and delighted.
The hour is come :—the destined Star has risen
Which shall descend upon a vacant prison.   395
The walls are high, the gates are strong, thick set
The sentinels — but true love never yet
Was thus constrained : it overleaps all fence:
Like lightning, with invisible violence
Piercing its continents; like Heaven's free breath,   400
Which he who grasps can hold not: liker Death,
Who rides upon a thought, and makes his way
Through temple, tower, and palace, and the array
Of arms : more strength has Love than he or they;
For it can burst his charnel, and make free   405
The limbs in chains, the heart in agony,
The soul in dust and chaos.
                    Emily,
A ship is floating in the harbour now,
A wind is hovering o'er the mountain's brow;
There is a path on the sea's azure floor,   410
No keel has ever ploughed that path before;
The halcyons brood around the foamless isles ;
The treacherous Ocean has forsworn its wiles;
The merry mariners are bold and free:
Say, my heart's sister, wilt thou sail with me?   415
Our bark is as an albatross, whose nest
Is a far Eden of the purple East;
And we between her wings will sit, while Night
And Day, and Storm, and Calm, pursue their flight,
Our ministers, along the boundless Sea,   420

Treading each other's heels, unheededly.
It is an isle under Ionian skies,
Beautiful as a wreck of Paradise;
And, for the harbours are not safe and good,
This land would have remained a solitude   425
But for some pastoral people native there,
Who from the Elysian, clear, and golden air
Draw the last spirit of the age of gold, —
Simple and spirited, innocent and bold.
The blue Ægean girds this chosen home,   430
With ever-changing sound and light and foam,
Kissing the sifted sands and caverns hoar;
And all the winds wandering along the shore
Undulate with the undulating tide:
There are thick woods where sylvan forms abide;   435
And many a fountain, rivulet, and pond,
As clear as elemental diamond,
Or serene morning air; and far beyond,
The mossy tracks made by the goats and deer
(Which the rough shepherd treads but once a year,)   440
Pierce into glades, caverns, and bowers, and halls
Built round with ivy, which the waterfalls
Illumining, with sound that never fails
Accompanying the noon-day nightingales;
And all the place is peopled with sweet airs;   445
The light clear element which the isle wears
Is heavy with the scent of lemon-flowers,
Which floats like mist laden with unseen showers
And falls upon the eyelids like faint sleep;
And from the moss violets and jonquils peep,   450
And dart their arrowy odour through the brain
Till you might faint with that delicious pain.
And every motion, odour, beam, and tone,
With that deep music is in unison:

Which is a soul within the soul—they seem   455
Like echoes of an antenatal dream. —
It is an isle 'twixt Heaven, Air, Earth, and Sea,
Cradled, and hung in clear tranquillity;
Bright as that wandering Eden Lucifer,
Washed by the soft blue Oceans of young air.   460
It is a favoured place.   Famine or Blight,
Pestilence, War and Earthquake, never light
Upon its mountain-peaks ; blind vultures, they
Sail onward far upon their fatal way :
The wingèd storms, chaunting their thunder-psalm   465
To other lands, leave azure chasms of calm
Over this isle, or weep themselves in dew,
From which its fields and woods ever renew
Their green and golden immortality.
And from the sea there rise, and from the sky   470
There fall, clear exhalations, soft and bright,
Veil after veil, each hiding some delight,
Which Sun or Moon or zephyr draw aside,
Till the isle's beauty, like a naked bride
Glowing at once with love and loveliness,   475
Blushes and trembles at its own excess :
Yet, like a buried lamp, a Soul no less
Burns in the heart of this delicious isle,
An atom of th' Eternal, whose own smile
Unfolds itself, and may be felt, not seen,   480
O'er the gray rocks, blue waves, and forests green,
Filling their bare and void interstices. —
But the chief marvel of the wilderness
Is a lone dwelling, built by whom or how
None of the rustic island-people know :   485
'T is not a tower of strength, though with its height
It overtops the woods ; but, for delight,
Some wise and tender Ocean-King, ere crime

Had been invented, in the world's young prime,
Reared it, a wonder of that simple time,   490
An envy of the isles, a pleasure-house
Made sacred to his sister and his spouse.
It scarce seems now a wreck of human art,
But, as it were, Titanic ; in the heart
Of Earth having assumed its form, then grown   495
Out of the mountains, from the living stone,
Lifting itself in caverns light and high :
For all the antique and learnèd imagery
Has been erased, and in the place of it
The ivy and the wild-vine interknit   500
The volumes of their many-twining stems ;
Parasite flowers illume with dewy gems
The lampless halls, and when they fade, the sky
Peeps through their winter-woof of tracery
With Moon-light patches, or star atoms keen,   505
Or fragments of the day's intense serene ; —
Working mosaic on their Parian floors.
And, day and night, aloof, from the high towers
And terraces, the Earth and Ocean seem
To sleep in one another's arms, and dream   510
Of waves, flowers, clouds, woods, rocks, and all that we
Read in their smiles, and call reality.

This isle and house are mine, and I have vowed
Thee to be lady of the solitude. —
And I have fitted up some chambers there   515
Looking towards the golden Eastern air,
And level with the living winds, which flow
Like waves above the living waves below. —
I have sent books and music there, and all
Those instruments with which high spirits call   520
The future from its cradle, and the past

Out of its grave, and make the present last
In thoughts and joys which sleep, but cannot die,
Folded within their own eternity.
Our simple life wants little, and true taste   525
Hires not the pale drudge Luxury, to waste
The scene it would adorn, and therefore, still,
Nature, with all her children, haunts the hill.
The ring-dove, in the embowering ivy, yet
Keeps up her love-lament, and the owls flit   530
Round the evening tower, and the young stars glance
Between the quick bats in their twilight dance ;
The spotted deer bask in the fresh moon-light
Before our gate, and the slow, silent night
Is measured by the pants of their calm sleep.   535
Be this our home in life, and when years heap
Their withered hours, like leaves, on our decay,
Let us become the over-hanging day,
The living soul of this Elysian isle,
Conscious, inseparable, one.   Meanwhile   540
We two will rise, and sit, and walk together,
Under the roof of blue Ionian weather,
And wander in the meadows, or ascend
The mossy mountains, where the blue heavens bend
With lightest winds, to touch their paramour ;   545
Or linger, where the pebble-paven shore,
Under the quick, faint kisses of the sea
Trembles and sparkles as with ecstasy, —
Possessing and possessed by all that is
Within that calm circumference of bliss,   550
And by each other, till to love and live
Be one : — or, at the noontide hour, arrive
Where some old cavern hoar seems yet to keep
The moonlight of the expired night asleep,
Through which the awakened day can never peep ;   555

A veil for our seclusion, close as Night's,
Where secure sleep may kill thine innocent lights;
Sleep, the fresh dew of languid love, the rain
Whose drops quench kisses till they burn again.
And we will talk, until thought's melody   560
Become too sweet for utterance, and it die
In words, to live again in looks, which dart
With thrilling tone into the voiceless heart,
Harmonizing silence without a sound.
Our breath shall intermix, our bosoms bound,   565
And our veins beat together; and our lips,
With other eloquence than words, eclipse
The soul that burns between them; and the wells
Which boil under our being's inmost cells,
The fountains of our deepest life, shall be   570
Confused in passion's golden purity,
As mountain-springs under the morning Sun.
We shall become the same, we shall be one
Spirit within two frames, oh! wherefore two?
One passion in twin-hearts, which grows and grew, 575
Till like two meteors of expanding flame,
Those spheres instinct with it become the same
Touch, mingle, are transfigured; ever still
Burning, yet ever inconsumable:
In one another's substance finding food,   580
Like flames too pure and light and unimbued
To nourish their bright lives with baser prey,
Which point to Heaven and cannot pass away:
One hope within two wills, one will beneath
Two overshadowing minds, one life, one death,   585
One Heaven, one Hell, one immortality,
And one annihilation. Woe is me!
The wingèd words on which my soul would pierce
Into the height of love's rare Universe

Are chains of lead around its flight of fire. —   590
I pant, I sink, I tremble, I expire!

Weak Verses, go, kneel at your Sovereign's feet,
And say: — "We are the masters of thy slave;
"What wouldest thou with us and ours and thine?"
Then call your sisters from Oblivion's cave,   595
All singing loud: "Love's very pain is sweet,
"But its reward is in the world divine
"Which, if not here, it builds beyond the grave."
So shall ye live when I am there.   Then haste
Over the hearts of men, until ye meet   600
Marina, Vanna, Primus, and the rest,
And bid them love each other and be bless'd:
And leave the troop which errs, and which reproves,
And come and be my guest, — for I am Love's.

TO ———.

Music, when soft voices die,
Vibrates in the memory —
Odours, when sweet violets sicken,
Live within the sense they quicken.
Rose-leaves, when the rose is dead,   5
Are heaped for the beloved's bed;
And so thy thoughts, when thou art gone,
Love itself shall slumber on.

1821.

SONG.

I.

RARELY, rarely, comest thou,
  Spirit of Delight!
Wherefore hast thou left me now
  Many a day and night?
Many a weary night and day   5
'T is since thou art fled away.

II.

How shall ever one like me
  Win thee back again?
With the joyous and the free
  Thou wilt scoff at pain.   10
Spirit false! thou hast forgot
All but those who need thee not.

III.

As a lizard with the shade
  Of a trembling leaf,
Thou with sorrow art dismayed;   15
  Even the sighs of grief
Reproach thee, that thou art not near,
And reproach thou wilt not hear.

IV.

Let me set my mournful ditty
  To a merry measure,   20
Thou wilt never come for pity,
  Thou wilt come for pleasure.
Pity then will cut away
Those cruel wings, and thou wilt stay.

V.

I love all that thou lovest,   25
  Spirit of Delight!
The fresh Earth in new leaves dressed,
  And the starry night;
Autumn evening, and the morn
When the golden mists are born.   30

VI.

I love snow, and all the forms
  Of the radiant frost;
I love waves, and winds, and storms,
  Every thing almost
Which is Nature's, and may be   35
Untainted by man's misery.

VII.

I love tranquil solitude,
  And such society
As is quiet, wise and good;
  Between thee and me   40
What difference? but thou dost possess
The things I seek, not love them less.

VIII.

I love Love — though he has wings,
  And like light can flee,
But above all other things,   45
  Spirit, I love thee —
Thou art love and life! O come,
Make once more my heart thy home.

                  1821.

MUTABILITY.

I.

THE flower that smiles to-day
    To-morrow dies;
All that we wish to stay
    Tempts and then flies.
What is this world's delight?   5
Lightning that mocks the night,
    Brief even as bright.

II.

Virtue, how frail it is!
    Friendship how rare!
Love, how it sells poor bliss   10
    For proud despair!
But we, though soon they fall,
Survive their joy, and all
    Which ours we call.

III.

Whilst skies are blue and bright.   15
    Whilst flowers are gay,
Whilst eyes that change ere night
    Make glad the day;
Whilst yet the calm hours creep,
Dream thou — and from thy sleep   20
    Then wake to weep.

1821.

ADONAIS:

AN ELEGY ON THE DEATH OF JOHN KEATS, AUTHOR
OF ENDYMION, HYPERION, &c.

Ἀστὴρ πρὶν μὲν ἔλαμπες ἐνὶ ζώοισιν ἑῶος.
Νῦν δὲ θανὼν λάμπεις ἕσπερος ἐν φθιμένοις.

PLATO.

1821.

PREFACE.

Φάρμακον ἦλθε, Βίων, ποτὶ σὸν στόμα, φάρμακον εἶδες·
Πῶς τευ τοῖς χείλεσσι ποτέδραμε, κοὐκ ἐγλυκάνθη;
Τίς δὲ βροτὸς τοσσοῦτον ἀνάμερος ἢ κεράσαι τοι,
Ἢ δοῦναι λαλέοντι τὸ φάρμακον; ἔκφυγεν ᾠδάν.

MOSCHUS, Epitaph. Bion.

It is my intention to subjoin to the London edition of this poem, a criticism upon the claims of its lamented object to be classed among the writers of the highest genius who have adorned our age. My known repugnance to the narrow principles of taste on which several of his earlier compositions 5 were modelled prove[s] at least that I am an impartial judge. I consider the fragment of *Hyperion* as second to nothing that was ever produced by a writer of the same years.

John Keats died at Rome of a consumption, in his twenty-fourth year, on the —— of —— 1821; and was buried in the 10 romantic and lonely cemetery of the Protestants in that city, under the pyramid which is the tomb of Cestius, and the massy walls and towers, now mouldering and desolate, which formed the circuit of ancient Rome. The cemetery is an open space among the ruins covered in winter with violets and daisies. It 15 might make one in love with death, to think that one should be buried in so sweet a place.

The genius of the lamented person to whose memory I have dedicated these unworthy verses, was not less delicate and fragile than it was beautiful; and, where cankerworms abound, 20 what wonder if its young flower was blighted in the bud? The savage criticism on his *Endymion*, which appeared in the *Quarterly Review*, produced the most violent effect on his susceptible mind; the agitation thus originated ended in the rupture of a blood-vessel in the lungs; a rapid consumption 25 ensued, and the succeeding acknowledgments from more candid critics, of the true greatness of his powers, were ineffectual to heal the wound thus wantonly inflicted.

It may be well said that these wretched men know not
30 what they do. They scatter their insults and their slanders
without heed as to whether the poisoned shaft lights on a heart
made callous by many blows, or one like Keats's, composed
of more penetrable stuff. One of their associates is, to my
knowledge, a most base and unprincipled calumniator. As to
35 *Endymion,* — was it a poem, whatever might be its defects, to
be treated contemptuously by those who had celebrated, with
various degrees of complacency and panegyric, *Paris,* and
Woman, and *A Syrian Tale,* and Mrs. Lefanu, and Mr. Bar-
rett, and Mr. Howard Payne, and a long list of the illustrious
40 obscure? Are these the men who, in their venal good nature,
presumed to draw a parallel between the Rev. Mr. Milman and
Lord Byron? What gnat did they strain at here, after having
swallowed all those camels? Against what woman taken in
adultery, dares the foremost of these literary prostitutes to cast
45 his opprobrious stone? Miserable man! you, one of the meanest, have wantonly defaced one of the noblest specimens of
the workmanship of God. Nor shall it be your excuse that,
murderer as you are, you have spoken daggers, but used none.
The circumstances of the closing scene of poor Keats's
50 life were not made known to me until the Elegy was ready for
the press. I am given to understand that the wound which his
sensitive spirit had received from the criticism of *Endymion*
was exasperated by the bitter sense of unrequited benefits; the
poor fellow seems to have been hooted from the stage of life,
55 no less by those on whom he had wasted the promise of his
genius, than those on whom he had lavished his fortune and
his care. He was accompanied to Rome, and attended in his last
illness, by Mr. Severn, a young artist of the highest promise,
who, I have been informed, "almost risked his own life, and
60 sacrificed every prospect to unwearied attendance upon his
dying friend." Had I known these circumstances before the
completion of my poem, I should have been tempted to add
my feeble tribute of applause to the more solid recompense
which the virtuous man finds in the recollection of his own
65 motives. Mr. Severn can dispense with a reward from "such

stuff as dreams are made of." His conduct is a golden augury
of the success of his future career — may the unextinguished
Spirit of his illustrious friend animate the creations of his
pencil, and plead against Oblivion for his name!

ADONAIS.

I.

I WEEP for Adonais — he is dead!
O, weep for Adonais! though our tears
Thaw not the frost which binds so dear a head!
And thou, sad Hour, selected from all years
To mourn our loss, rouse thy obscure compeers,   5
And teach them thine own sorrow, say: with me
Died Adonais; till the Future dares
Forget the Past, his fate and fame shall be
An echo and a light unto eternity.

II.

Where wert thou, mighty Mother, when he lay,   10
When thy Son lay, pierced by the shaft which flies
In darkness? where was lorn Urania
When Adonais died?   With veilèd eyes,
'Mid listening Echoes, in her Paradise
She sate, while one, with soft enamoured breath,   15
Rekindled all the fading melodies,
With which, like flowers that mock the corse beneath,
He had adorned and hid the coming bulk of death.

III.

O, weep for Adonais — he is dead!
Wake, melancholy Mother, wake and weep!   20
Yet wherefore?   Quench within their burning bed

Thy fiery tears, and let thy loud heart keep,
Like his, a mute and uncomplaining sleep ;
For he is gone, where all things wise and fair
Descend ; — oh, dream not that the amorous Deep   25
Will yet restore him to the vital air ;
Death feeds on his mute voice, and laughs at our despair.

IV.

Most musical of mourners, weep again !
Lament anew, Urania ! — He died,
Who was the Sire of an immortal strain,   30
Blind, old, and lonely, when his country's pride,
The priest, the slave, and the liberticide,
Trampled and mocked with many a loathèd rite
Of lust and blood ; he went, unterrified,
Into the gulph of death ; but his clear Sprite   35
Yet reigns o'er earth ; the third among the sons of light.

V.

Most musical of mourners, weep anew !
Not all to that bright station dared to climb ;
And happier they their happiness who knew,
Whose tapers yet burn through that night of time   40
In which suns perished ; others more sublime,
Struck by the envious wrath of man or God,
Have sunk, extinct in their refulgent prime ;
And some yet live, treading the thorny road,
Which leads, through toil and hate, to Fame's serene abode. 45

VI.

But now, thy youngest, dearest one has perished,
The nursling of thy widowhood, who grew,
Like a pale flower by some sad maiden cherished,
And fed with true love tears, instead of dew ;

Most musical of mourners, weep anew !   50
Thy extreme hope, the loveliest and the last,
The bloom, whose petals, nipped before they blew,
Died on the promise of the fruit, is waste ;
The broken lily lies — the storm is overpast.

VII.

To that high Capital, where kingly Death   55
Keeps his pale court in beauty and decay,
He came ; and bought, with price of purest breath,
A grave among the eternal. — Come away !
Haste, while the vault of blue Italian day
Is yet his fitting charnel-roof ! while still   60
He lies, as if in dewy sleep he lay ;
Awake him not ! surely he takes his fill
Of deep and liquid rest, forgetful of all ill.

VIII.

He will awake no more, oh, never more ! —
Within the twilight chamber spreads apace,   65
The shadow of white Death, and at the door
Invisible Corruption waits to trace
His extreme way to her dim dwelling-place ;
The eternal Hunger sits, but pity and awe
Soothe her pale rage, nor dares she to deface   70
So fair a prey, till darkness, and the law
Of change, shall o'er his sleep the mortal curtain draw.

IX.

O, weep for Adonais ! — The quick Dreams,
The passion-wingèd Ministers of thought,
Who were his flocks, whom near the living streams   75
Of his young spirit he fed, and whom he taught

The love which was its music, wander not, —
Wander no more, from kindling brain to brain,
But droop there, whence they sprung ; and mourn their lot
Round the cold heart, where, after their sweet pain,   80
They ne'er will gather strength, or find a home again.

X.

And one with trembling hands clasps his cold head,
And fans him with her moonlight wings, and cries :
" Our love, our hope, our sorrow, is not dead ;
" See, on the silken fringe of his faint eyes,   85
" Like dew upon a sleeping flower, there lies
" A tear some Dream has loosened from his brain."
Lost Angel of a ruined Paradise !
She knew not 't was her own ; as with no stain
She faded, like a cloud which had outwept its rain.   90

XI.

One from a lucid urn of starry dew
Washed his light limbs as if embalming them ;
Another clipped her profuse locks, and threw
The wreath upon him, like an anadem,
Which frozen tears instead of pearls begem ;   95
Another in her wilful grief would break
Her bow and wingèd reeds, as if to stem
A greater loss with one which was more weak ;
And dull the barbèd fire against his frozen cheek.

XII.

Another Splendour on his mouth alit,   100
That mouth, whence it was wont to draw the breath
Which gave it strength to pierce the guarded wit,
And pass into the panting heart beneath
With lightning and with music : the damp death

Quenched its caress upon his icy lips;   105
And, as a dying meteor stains a wreath
Of moonlight vapour, which the cold night clips,
It flushed through his pale limbs, and passed to its eclipse.

XIII.

And others came . . . Desires and Adorations,
Wingèd Persuasions and veiled Destinies,   110
Splendours, and Glooms, and glimmering Incarnations
Of hopes and fears, and twilight Phantasies;
And Sorrow, with her family of Sighs,
And Pleasure, blind with tears, led by the gleam
Of her own dying smile instead of eyes,   115
Came in slow pomp; — the moving pomp might seem
Like pageantry of mist on an autumnal stream.

XIV.

All he had loved, and moulded into thought,
From shape, and hue, and odour, and sweet sound,
Lamented Adonais.   Morning sought   120
Her eastern watch-tower, and her hair unbound,
Wet with the tears which should adorn the ground,
Dimmed the aërial eyes that kindle day;
Afar the melancholy thunder moaned,
Pale Ocean in unquiet slumber lay,   125
And the wild winds flew round, sobbing in their dismay.

XV.

Lost Echo sits amid the voiceless mountains,
And feeds her grief with his remembered lay,
And will no more reply to winds or fountains,
Or amorous birds perched on the young green spray,   130
Or herdsman's horn, or bell at closing day;
Since she can mimic not his lips, more dear

Than those for whose disdain she pined away
Into a shadow of all sounds : — a drear
Murmur, between their songs, is all the woodmen hear.   135

XVI.

Grief made the young Spring wild, and she threw down
Her kindling buds, as if she Autumn were,
Or they dead leaves ; since her delight is flown
For whom should she have waked the sullen year ?
To Phœbus was not Hyacinth so dear   140
Nor to himself Narcissus, as to both
Thou, Adonais : wan they stand and sere
Amid the faint companions of their youth,
With dew all turned to tears ; odour, to sighing ruth.

XVII.

Thy spirit's sister, the lorn nightingale,   145
Mourns not her mate with such melodious pain ;
Not so the eagle, who like thee could scale
Heaven, and could nourish in the sun's domain
Her mighty youth with morning, doth complain,
Soaring and screaming round her empty nest,   150
As Albion wails for thee : the curse of Cain
Light on his head who pierced thy innocent breast,
And scared the angel soul that was its earthly guest !

XVIII.

Ah woe is me ! Winter is come and gone,
But grief returns with the revolving year ;   155
The airs and streams renew their joyous tone ;
The ants, the bees, the swallows reappear ;
Fresh leaves and flowers deck the dead Seasons' bier ;
The amorous birds now pair in every brake,
And build their mossy homes in field and brere ;   160

And the green lizard, and the golden snake,
Like unimprisoned flames, out of their trance awake.

XIX.

Through wood and stream and field and hill and Ocean
A quickening life from the Earth's heart has burst
As it has ever done, with change and motion   165
From the great morning of the world when first
God dawned on Chaos; in its stream immersed
The lamps of Heaven flash with a softer light;
All baser things pant with life's sacred thirst;
Diffuse themselves; and spend in love's delight   170
The beauty and the joy of their renewèd might.

XX.

The leprous corpse touched by this spirit tender
Exhales itself in flowers of gentle breath;
Like incarnations of the stars, when splendour
Is changed to fragrance, they illumine death   175
And mock the merry worm that wakes beneath;
Naught we know, dies. Shall that alone which knows
Be as a sword consumed before the sheath
By sightless lightning? — th' intense atom glows
A moment, then is quenched in a most cold repose.   180

XXI.

Alas! that all we loved of him should be,
But for our grief, as if it had not been,
And grief itself be mortal! Woe is me!
Whence are we, and why are we? of what scene
The actors or spectators? Great and mean   185
Meet massed in death, who lends what life must borrow.
As long as skies are blue, and fields are green,
Evening must usher night, night urge the morrow,
Month follow month with woe, and year wake year to sorrow.

XXII.

He will awake no more, oh, never more!   190
"Wake thou," cried Misery, "childless Mother, rise
"Out of thy sleep, and slake, in thy heart's core,
"A wound more fierce than his with tears and sighs."
And all the Dreams that watched Urania's eyes,
And all the Echoes whom their sister's song   195
Had held in holy silence, cried: "Arise!"
Swift as a Thought by the snake Memory stung,
From her ambrosial rest the fading Splendour sprung.

XXIII.

She rose like an autumnal Night, that springs
Out of the East, and follows wild and drear   200
The golden Day, which, on eternal wings,
Even as a ghost abandoning a bier,
Had left the Earth a corpse.   Sorrow and fear
So struck, so roused, so rapt Urania;
So saddened round her like an atmosphere   205
Of stormy mist; so swept her on her way
Even to the mournful place where Adonais lay.

XXIV.

Out of her secret Paradise she sped,
Through camps and cities rough with stone, and steel,
And human hearts, which to her aëry tread   210
Yielding not, wounded the invisible
Palms of her tender feet where'er they fell:
And barbèd tongues, and thoughts more sharp than
    they,
Rent the soft Form they never could repel,
Whose sacred blood, like the young tears of May,   215
Paved with eternal flowers that undeserving way.

XXV.

In the death chamber for a moment Death,
Shamed by the presence of that living Might,
Blushed to annihilation, and the breath
Revisited those lips, and life's pale light   220
Flashed through those limbs, so late her dear delight.
"Leave me not wild and drear and comfortless,
"As silent lightning leaves the starless night!
"Leave me not!" cried Urania: her distress
Roused Death: Death rose and smiled, and met her vain
     caress.   ·   225

XXVI.

"Stay yet awhile! speak to me once again;
"Kiss me, so long but as a kiss may live;
"And in my heartless breast and burning brain
"That word, that kiss shall all thoughts else survive,
"With food of saddest memory kept alive,   230
"Now thou art dead, as if it were a part
"Of thee, my Adonais! I would give
"All that I am to be as thou now art!
"But I am chained to Time, and cannot thence depart!

XXVII.

"Oh gentle child, beautiful as thou wert,   235
"Why didst thou leave the trodden paths of men
"Too soon, and with weak hands though mighty heart
"Dare the unpastured dragon in his den?
"Defenceless as thou wert, oh where was then
"Wisdom the mirrored shield, or scorn the spear?   240
"Or hadst thou waited the full cycle, when
"Thy spirit should have filled its crescent sphere,
"The monsters of life's waste had fled from thee like deer.

XXVIII.

"The herded wolves, bold only to pursue;
"The obscene ravens, clamorous o'er the dead;   245
"The vultures to the conqueror's banner true,
"Who feed where Desolation first has fed,
"And whose wings rain contagion;— how they fled,
"When like Apollo, from his golden bow,
"The Pythian of the age one arrow sped   250
"And smiled!— The spoilers tempt no second blow;
"They fawn on the proud feet that spurn them lying low.

XXIX.

"The sun comes forth, and many reptiles spawn;
"He sets, and each ephemeral insect then
"Is gathered into death without a dawn,   255
"And the immortal stars awake again;
"So is it in the world of living men:
"A godlike mind soars forth, in its delight
"Making earth bare and veiling heaven, and when
"It sinks, the swarms that dimmed or shared its light 260
"Leave to its kindred lamps the spirit's awful night."

XXX.

Thus ceased she: and the mountain shepherds came,
Their garlands sere, their magic mantles rent;
The Pilgrim of Eternity, whose fame
Over his living head like Heaven is bent,   265
An early but enduring monument,
Came, veiling all the lightnings of his song
In sorrow; from her wilds Ierne sent
The sweetest lyrist of her saddest wrong,
And love taught grief to fall like music from his tongue. 270

XXXI.

Midst others of less note, came one frail Form,
A phantom among men, companionless
As the last cloud of an expiring storm
Whose thunder is its knell; he, as I guess,
Had gazed on Nature's naked loveliness,   275
Actæon-like, and now he fled astray
With feeble steps o'er the world's wilderness,
And his own thoughts, along that rugged way,
Pursued, like raging hounds, their father and their prey.

XXXII.

A pardlike Spirit beautiful and swift —   280
A Love in desolation masked; — a Power
Girt round with weakness; — it can scarce uplift
The weight of the superincumbent hour;
It is a dying lamp, a falling shower,
A breaking billow; — even whilst we speak   285
Is it not broken?   On the withering flower
The killing sun smiles brightly; on a cheek
The life can burn in blood, even while the heart may break.

XXXIII.

His head was bound with pansies overblown,
And faded violets, white, and pied, and blue;   290
And a light spear topped with a cypress cone,
Round whose rude shaft dark ivy tresses grew
Yet dripping with the forest's noonday dew,
Vibrated, as the ever-beating heart
Shook the weak hand that grasped it; of that crew   295
He came the last, neglected and apart;
A herd-abandoned deer struck by the hunter's dart.

XXXIV.

All stood aloof, and at his partial moan
Smiled through their tears; well knew that gentle band
Who in another's fate now wept his own;   300
As, in the accents of an unknown land,
He sung new sorrow; sad Urania scanned
The Stranger's mien, and murmured: "who art thou?"
He answered not, but with a sudden hand ·
Made bare his branded and ensanguined brow,   305
Which was like Cain's or Christ's — Oh ! that it should
    be so!

XXXV.

What softer voice is hushed over the dead?
Athwart what brow is that dark mantle thrown?
What form leans sadly o'er the white death-bed,
In mockery of monumental stone,   310
The heavy heart heaving without a moan?
If it be He, who, gentlest of the wise,
Taught, soothed, loved, honoured the departed one,
Let me not vex with inharmonious sighs
The silence of that heart's accepted sacrifice.   315

XXXVI.

Our Adonais has drunk poison — oh !
What deaf and viperous murderer could crown
Life's early cup with such a draught of woe?
The nameless worm would now itself disown:
It felt, yet could escape the magic tone   320
Whose prelude held all envy, hate, and wrong,
But what was howling in one breast alone,
Silent with expectation of the song,
Whose master's hand is cold, whose silver lyre unstrung.

XXXVII.

Live thou, whose infamy is not thy fame!   325
Live! fear no heavier chastisement from me,
Thou noteless blot on a remembered name!
But be thyself, and know thyself to be!
And ever at thy season be thou free
To spill the venom when thy fangs o'erflow: 330
Remorse and Self-contempt shall cling to thee;
Hot Shame shall burn upon thy secret brow,
And like a beaten hound tremble thou shalt — as now.

XXXVIII.

Nor let us weep that our delight is fled
Far from these carrion kites that scream below;   335
He wakes or sleeps with the enduring dead;
Thou canst not soar where he is sitting now. —
Dust to the dust! but the pure spirit shall flow
Back to the burning fountain whence it came,
A portion of the Eternal, which must glow   340
Through time and change, unquenchably the same,
Whilst thy cold embers choke the sordid hearth of shame.

XXXIX.

Peace, peace! he is not dead, he doth not sleep —
He hath awakened from the dream of life —
'T is we who, lost in stormy visions, keep   345
With phantoms an unprofitable strife,
And in mad trance strike with our spirit's knife
Invulnerable nothings. — *We* decay
Like corpses in a charnel; fear and grief
Convulse us and consume us day by day,   350
And cold hopes swarm like worms within our living clay.

XL.

He has outsoared the shadow of our night;
Envy and calumny and hate and pain,
And that unrest which men miscall delight,
Can touch him not and torture not again;   355
From the contagion of the world's slow stain
He is secure, and now can never mourn
A heart grown cold, a head grown gray in vain;
Nor, when the spirit's self has ceased to burn,
With sparkless ashes load an unlamented urn.   360

XLI.

He lives, he wakes — 't is Death is dead, not he;
Mourn not for Adonais. — Thou young Dawn
Turn all thy dew to splendour, for from thee
The spirit thou lamentest is not gone;
Ye caverns and ye forests, cease to moan!   365
Cease ye faint flowers and fountains, and thou Air
Which like a mourning veil thy scarf hadst thrown
O'er the abandoned Earth, now leave it bare
Even to the joyous stars which smile on its despair!

XLII.

He is made one with Nature: there is heard   370
His voice in all her music, from the moan
Of thunder, to the song of night's sweet bird;
He is a presence to be felt and known
In darkness and in light, from herb and stone,
Spreading itself where'er that Power may move   375
Which has withdrawn his being to its own;
Which wields the world with never wearied love,
Sustains it from beneath, and kindles it above.

XLIII.

He is a portion of the loveliness
Which once he made more lovely: he doth bear   380
His part, while the one Spirit's plastic stress
Sweeps through the dull dense world, compelling there
All new successions to the forms they wear;
Torturing th' unwilling dross that checks its flight
To its own likeness, as each mass may bear;   385
And bursting in its beauty and its might
From trees and beasts and men into the Heaven's light.

XLIV.

The splendours of the firmament of time
May be eclipsed, but are extinguished not;
Like stars to their appointed height they climb   390
And death is a low mist which cannot blot
The brightness it may veil.   When lofty thought
Lifts a young heart above its mortal lair,
And love and life contend in it, for what
Shall be its earthly doom, the dead live there   395
And move like winds of light on dark and stormy air.

XLV.

The inheritors of unfulfilled renown
Rose from their thrones, built beyond mortal thought,
Far in the Unapparent.   Chatterton
Rose pale, his solemn agony had not   400
Yet faded from him; Sidney, as he fought
And as he fell and as he lived and loved
Sublimely mild, a Spirit without spot,
Arose; and Lucan, by his death approved:
Oblivion as they rose shrank like a thing reproved.   405

XLVI.

And many more, whose names on Earth are dark
But whose transmitted effluence cannot die
So long as fire outlives the parent spark,
Rose, robed in dazzling immortality.
" Thou art become as one of us," they cry,   410
" It was for thee yon kingless sphere has long
" Swung blind in unascended majesty,
"Silent alone amid an Heaven of Song.
" Assume thy wingèd throne, thou Vesper of our throng ! "

XLVII.

Who mourns for Adonais? oh come forth   415
Fond wretch! and know thyself and him aright.
Clasp with thy panting soul the pendulous Earth;
As from a centre, dart thy spirit's light
Beyond all worlds, until its spacious might
Satiate the void circumference : then shrink   420
Even to a point within our day and night ;
And keep thy heart light lest it make thee sink
When hope has kindled hope, and lured thee to the brink.

XLVIII.

Or go to Rome, which is the sepulchre,
O, not of him, but of our joy: 't is naught   425
That ages, empires, and religions there
Lie buried in the ravage they have wrought;
For such as he can lend, — they borrow not
Glory from those who made the world their prey;
And he is gathered to the kings of thought   430
Who waged contention with their time's decay,
And of the past are all that cannot pass away.

XLIX.

Go thou to Rome, — at once the Paradise,
The grave, the city, and the wilderness ;
And where its wrecks like shattered mountains rise,   435
And flowering weeds and fragrant copses dress
The bones of Desolation's nakedness
Pass, till the Spirit of the spot shall lead
Thy footsteps to a slope of green access
Where, like an infant's smile, over the dead,   440
A light of laughing flowers along the grass is spread.

L.

And gray walls moulder round, on which dull Time
Feeds, like slow fire upon a hoary brand ;
And one keen pyramid with wedge sublime,
Pavilioning the dust of him who planned   445
This refuge for his memory, doth stand
Like flame transformed to marble ; and beneath,
A field is spread, on which a newer band
Have pitched in Heaven's smile their camp of death
Welcoming him we lose with scarce extinguished breath. 450

LI.

Here pause : these graves are all too young as yet
To have outgrown the sorrow which consigned
Its charge to each ; and if the seal is set,
Here, on one fountain of a mourning mind,
Break it not thou ! too surely shalt thou find   455
Thine own well full, if thou returnest home,
Of tears and gall.   From the world's bitter wind
Seek shelter in the shadow of the tomb.
What Adonais is, why fear we to become ?

LII.

The One remains, the many change and pass ;　　460
Heaven's light forever shines, Earth's shadows fly ;
Life, like a dome of many-coloured glass,
Stains the white radiance of Eternity,
Until Death tramples it to fragments. — Die,
If thou wouldst be with that which thou dost seek !　　465
Follow where all is fled ! — Rome's azure sky,
Flowers, ruins, statues, music, words, are weak
The glory they transfuse with fitting truth to speak.

LIII.

Why linger, why turn back, why shrink, my Heart?
Thy hopes are gone before : from all things here　　470
They have departed ; thou shouldst now depart!
A light is past from the revolving year,
And man, and woman ; and what still is dear
Attracts to crush, repels to make thee wither.
The soft sky smiles, — the low wind whispers near ;　　475
'T is Adonais calls! oh, hasten thither,
No more let Life divide what Death can join together.

LIV.

That Light whose smile kindles the Universe,
That Beauty in which all things work and move,
That Benediction which the eclipsing Curse　　480
Of birth can quench not, that sustaining Love
Which, through the web of being blindly wove
By man and beast and earth and air and sea,
Burns bright or dim, as each are mirrors of
The fire for which all thirst, now beams on me,　　485
Consuming the last clouds of cold mortality.

LV.

The breath whose might I have invoked in song
Descends on me; my spirit's bark is driven,
Far from the shore, far from the trembling throng
Whose sails were never to the tempest given ;   490
The massy earth and spherèd skies are riven!
I am borne darkly, fearfully, afar :
Whilst burning through the inmost veil of Heaven,
The soul of Adonais, like a star,
Beacons from the abode where the Eternal are.   495

SONNET: POLITICAL GREATNESS.

NOR happiness, nor majesty, nor fame,
Nor peace, nor strength, nor skill in arms or arts,
Shepherd those herds whom tyranny makes tame ;
Verse echoes not one beating of their hearts,
History is but the shadow of their shame,   5
Art veils her glass, or from the pageant starts
As to oblivion their blind millions fleet,
Staining that Heaven with obscene imagery
Of their own likeness.   What are numbers knit
By force or custom?   Man who man would be,   10
Must rule the empire of himself ; in it
Must be supreme, establishing his throne
On vanquished will, quelling the anarchy
Of hopes and fears, being himself alone.

1821.

THE AZIOLA.

I.

"Do you not hear the Aziola cry?
　　Methinks she must be nigh,"
　　　Said Mary, as we sate
In dusk, ere stars were lit, or candles brought;
　　　And I, who thought　　　　　　　　5
　　This Aziola was some tedious woman,
　　　Asked, "Who is Aziola?"　How elate
I felt to know that it was nothing human,
　　No mockery of myself to fear or hate:
　　　And Mary saw my soul,　　　　　10
And laughed, and said, "Disquiet yourself not;
　　　'T is nothing but a little downy owl."

II.

Sad Aziola! many an eventide
　　Thy music I had heard
By wood and stream, meadow and mountain-side,　15
　　And fields and marshes wide,
Such as nor voice, nor lute, nor wind, nor bird,
　　The soul ever stirred;
Unlike and far sweeter than them all.
Sad Aziola! from that moment I　　　　20
　　Loved thee and thy sad cry.

　　　　　　　　　　　　　　　1821.

A LAMENT.

I.

Oh, world! oh, life! oh, time!
On whose last steps I climb
　　Trembling at that where I had stood before;

When will return the glory of your prime?
  No more — O, never more !   5

II.

Out of the day and night
A joy has taken flight ;
  Fresh spring, and summer, and winter hoar,
Move my faint heart with grief, but with delight
  No more — O, never more !   10

              1821.

REMEMBRANCE.

I.

SWIFTER far than summer's flight —
Swifter far than youth's delight —
Swifter far than happy night,
    Art thou come and gone —
As the wood when leaves are shed,   5
As the night when sleep has fled,
As the heart when joy is dead,
    I am left lone, alone.

II.

The swallow summer comes again —
The owlet night resumes his reign —   10
But the wild-swan youth is fain
    To fly with thee, false as thou.
My heart each day desires the morrow ;
Sleep itself is turned to sorrow ;
Vainly would my winter borrow   15
    Sunny leaves from any bough.

III.

Lilies for a bridal bed —
Roses for a matron's head —
Violets for a maiden dead —
    Pansies let *my* flowers be :   20
On the living grave I bear
Scatter them without a tear —
·Let no friend, however dear,
    Waste one hope, one fear for me.

                       1821.

TO-MORROW.

WHERE art thou, beloved To-morrow?
  When young and old and strong and weak,
Rich and poor, through joy and sorrow,
  Thy sweet smiles we ever seek, —
In thy place — ah ! well-a-day !   5
We find the thing we fled — To-day.

                       1821.

LINES.

IF I walk in Autumn's even
  While the dead leaves pass,
If I look on Spring's soft heaven, —
  Something is not there which was.
Winter's wondrous frost and snow,   5
Summer's clouds, where are they now?

                       1821.

TO ———.

I.

ONE word is too often profaned
    For me to profane it,
One feeling too falsely disdained
    For thee to disdain it.
One hope is too like despair   5
    For prudence to smother,
And pity from thee more dear
    Than that from another.

II.

I can give not what men call love,
    But wilt thou accept not   10
The worship the heart lifts above
    And the Heavens reject not,—
The desire of the moth for the star,
    Of the night for the morrow,
The devotion to something afar   15
    From the sphere of our sorrow?

1821.

TO ———.

I.

WHEN passion's trance is overpast,
If tenderness and truth could last
Or live, whilst all wild feelings keep
Some mortal slumber, dark and deep,
I should not weep, I should not weep!   5

II.

It were enough to feel, to see
Thy soft eyes gazing tenderly,
And dream the rest—and burn and be
The secret food of fires unseen,
Couldst thou but be as thou hast been   10

III.

After the slumber of the year
The woodland violets re-appear,
All things revive in field or grove
And sky and sea, but two, which move
And form all others, life and love.   15

1821.

A BRIDAL SONG.

I.

THE golden gates of Sleep unbar
   Where Strength and Beauty met together
Kindle their image like a star
   In a sea of glassy weather.
Night, with all thy stars look down, —   5
   Darkness, weep thy holiest dew, —
Never smiled the inconstant moon
      On a pair so true.
Let eyes not see their own delight ; —
Haste, swift Hour, and thy flight   10
      Oft renew.

II.

Fairies, sprites, and angels keep her !
   Holy stars, permit no wrong !

And return to wake the sleeper,
     Dawn, — ere it be long
Oh joy! oh fear! what will be done
In the absence of the sun!
     Come along!

         1821.

SONG FROM HELLAS.

LIFE may change, but it may fly not;
Hope may vanish, but can die not;
Truth be veiled, but still it burneth;
Love repulsed, — but it returneth!

Yet were life a charnel where
Hope lay coffined with Despair;
Yet were truth a sacred lie,
Love were lust —

     If Liberty
Lent not life its soul of light,
Hope its iris of delight,
Truth its prophet's robe to wear,
Love its power to give and bear.

CHORUS FROM HELLAS.

THE young moon has fed
     Her exhausted horn,
         With the sunset's fire:
The weak day is dead,
     But the night is not born;

And, like loveliness panting with wild desire
  While it trembles with fear and delight,
  Hesperus flies from awakening night,
And pants in its beauty and speed with light
  Fast flashing, soft, and bright.   10
Thou beacon of love! thou lamp of the free!
      Guide us far, far away,
To climes where now veiled by the ardour of day
      Thou art hidden
    From waves on which weary noon,   15
    Faints in her summer swoon,
    Between Kingless continents sinless as Eden,
    Around mountains and islands inviolably
    Prankt on the sapphire sea.
                    1821.

FINAL CHORUS FROM HELLAS.

THE world's great age begins anew,
  The golden years return,
The earth doth like a snake renew
  Her winter weeds outworn:
Heaven smiles, and faiths and empires gleam,   5
Like wrecks of a dissolving dream.

A brighter Hellas rears its mountains
  From waves serener far;
A new Peneus rolls his fountains
  Against the morning-star.   10
Where fairer Tempes bloom, there sleep
Young Cyclads on a sunnier deep.

A loftier Argo cleaves the main,
  Fraught with a later prize;

Another Orpheus sings again,   15
   And loves, and weeps, and dies.
A new Ulysses leaves once more.
Calypso for his native shore.

O, write no more the tale of Troy,
   If earth Death's scroll must be!   20
Nor mix with Laian rage the joy
   Which dawns upon the free:
Although a subtler Sphinx renew
Riddles of death Thebes never knew.

Another Athens shall arise,   25
   And to remoter time
Bequeath, like sunset to the skies,
   The splendour of its prime;
And leave, if naught so bright may live,
All earth can take or Heaven can give.   30

Saturn and Love their long repose
   Shall burst, more bright and good
Than all who fell, than One who rose,
   Than many unsubdued:
Not gold, not blood, their altar dowers,   35
But votive tears and symbol flowers.

O cease! must hate and death return?
   Cease! must men kill and die?
Cease! drain not to its dregs the urn
   Of bitter prophecy.   40
The world is weary of the past,
O might it die or rest at last!

                           1821.

TO EDWARD WILLIAMS.

I.

The serpent is shut out from paradise.
    The wounded deer must seek the herb no more
      In which its heart-cure lies:
    The widowed dove must cease to haunt a bower
Like that from which its mate with feignèd sighs   5
      Fled in the April hour.
    I too must seldom seek again
Near happy friends a mitigated pain.

II.

Of hatred I am proud, — with scorn content;
    Indifference, that once hurt me, now is grown   10
      Itself indifferent.
    But, not to speak of love, pity alone
Can break a spirit already more than bent.
      The miserable one
    Turns the mind's poison into food, —   15
Its medicine is tears, — its evil good.

III.

Therefore, if now I see you seldomer,
    Dear friends, dear *friend!* know that I only fly
      Your looks, because they stir
    Griefs that should sleep, and hopes that cannot die: 20
The very comfort that they minister
      I scarce can bear, yet I,
    So deeply is the arrow gone,
Should quickly perish if it were withdrawn.

IV.

When I return to my cold home, you ask   25
    Why I am not as I have ever been.

You spoil me for the task
   Of acting a forced part in life's dull scene, —
Of wearing on my brow the idle mask
     Of author, great or mean,   30
   In the world's carnival. I sought
Peace thus, and but in you I found it not.

v.

Full half an hour, to-day, I tried my lot
   With various flowers, and every one still said,
     " She loves me —— loves me not."   35
And if this meant a vision long since fled —
If it meant fortune, fame, or peace of thought —
     If it meant, — but I dread
   To speak what you may know too well :
Still there was truth in the sad oracle.   40

vi.

The crane o'er seas and forests seeks her home ;
   No bird so wild but has its quiet nest,
     When it no more would roam ;
   The sleepless billows on the ocean's breast
Break like a bursting heart, and die in foam,   45
     And thus at length find rest.
   Doubtless there is a place of peace
Where *my* weak heart and all its throbs will cease.

vii.

I asked her, yesterday, if she believed
   That I had resolution. One who *had*   50
     Would ne'er have thus relieved
   His heart with words, — but what his judgment bade
Would do, and leave the scorner unrelieved.
     These verses are too sad
   To send to you, but that I know,   55
Happy yourself, you feel another's woe.   1821.

SONG.

" A widow bird sate mourning for her love
    Upon a wintry bough ;
The frozen wind crept on above,
    The freezing stream below.

" There was no leaf upon the forest bare,   5
    No flower upon the ground,
And little motion in the air
    Except the mill-wheel's sound."

                1821.

THE MAGNETIC LADY TO HER PATIENT.

I.

" Sleep, sleep on ! forget thy pain ;
    My hand is on thy brow,
My spirit on thy brain,
My pity on thy heart, poor friend ;
    And from my fingers flow   5
The powers of life, and like a sign,
    Seal thee from thine hour of woe,
And brood on thee, but may not blend
      With thine.

II.

" Sleep, sleep on ! I love thee not;   10
    But when I think that he
Who made and makes my lot
As full of flowers as thine of weeds,
    Might have been lost like thee,
And that a hand which was not mine   15

Might then have charmed his agony
As I another's — my heart bleeds
    For thine.

III.

" Sleep, sleep, and with the slumber of
    The dead and the unborn   20
Forget thy life and love ;
Forget that thou must wake for ever ;
    Forget the world's dull scorn ;
Forget lost health, and the divine
    Feelings which died in youth's brief morn ;   25
And forget me, for I can never
    Be thine.

IV.

" Like a cloud big with a May shower,
    My soul weeps healing rain,
On thee, thou withered flower ;   30
It breathes mute music on thy sleep ;
    Its odour calms thy brain ;
Its light within thy gloomy breast
    Spreads like a second youth again.
By mine thy being is to its deep   35
    Possessed.

V.

" The spell is done.   How feel you now ? "
    " Better — Quite well," replied
The sleeper. — " What would do
You good when suffering and awake ?   40
    What cure your head and side ? —"
"What would cure, that would kill me, Jane :
    And as I must on earth abide
Awhile, yet tempt me not to break
    My chain."   1822.   45

LINES.

I.

WHEN the lamp is shattered
The light in the dust lies dead –
When the cloud is scattered
The rainbow's glory is shed.
When the lute is broken, 5
Sweet tones are remembered not ;
When the lips have spoken,
Loved accents are soon forgot.

II.

As music and splendour
Survive not the lamp and the lute, 10
The heart's echoes render
No song when the spirit is mute, —
No song but sad dirges,
Like the wind through a ruined cell,
Or the mournful surges 15
That ring the dead seaman's knell.

III.

When hearts have once mingled
Love first leaves the well-built nest, —
The weak one is singled
To endure what it once possessed. 20
O, Love ! who bewailest
The frailty of all things here,
Why choose you the frailest
For your cradle, your home and your bier ?

IV.

Its passions will rock thee 25
As the storms rock the ravens on high :

Bright reason will mock thee,
Like the sun from a wintry sky.
From thy nest every rafter
Will rot, and thine eagle home   30
Leave thee naked to laughter,
When leaves fall and cold winds come.

1822.

TO JANE—THE INVITATION.

Best and brightest, come away!
Fairer far than this fair Day,
Which, like thee to those in sorrow,
Comes to bid a sweet good-morrow
To the rough Year just awake   5
In its cradle on the brake.
The brightest hour of unborn Spring,
Through the winter wandering,
Found, it seems, the halcyon Morn
To hoar February born;   10
Bending from Heaven, in azure mirth,
It kissed the forehead of the Earth,
And smiled upon the silent sea,
And bade the frozen streams be free,
And waked to music all their fountains, 15
And breathed upon the frozen mountains,
And like a prophetess of May
Strewed flowers upon the barren way,
Making the wintry world appear
Like one on whom thou smilest, dear.   20

Away, away, from men and towns,
To the wild wood and the downs—

To the silent wilderness
Where the soul need not repress
Its music lest it should not find   25
An echo in another's mind,
While the touch of Nature's art
Harmonizes heart to heart.
I leave this notice on my door
For each accustomed visitor : —   30
"I am gone into the fields
To take what this sweet hour yields; —
Reflexion, you may come to-morrow,
Sit by the fireside with Sorrow. —
You with the unpaid bill, Despair, —   35
You tiresome verse-reciter, Care, —
I will pay you in the grave, —
Death will listen to your stave.
Expectation too, be off!
To-day is for itself enough ;   40
Hope, in pity mock not Woe
With smiles, nor follow where I go ;
Long having lived on thy sweet food,
At length I find one moment's good
After long pain — with all your love,   45
This you never told me of."

Radiant Sister of the Day,
Awake! arise! and come away!
To the wild woods and the plains,
And the pools where winter rains   50
Image all their roof of leaves,
Where the pine its garland weaves
Of sapless green and ivy dun
Round stems that never kiss the sun;
Where the lawns and pastures be,   55

And the sand-hills of the sea ;—
Where the melting hoar-frost wets
The daisy-star that never sets,
And wind-flowers, and violets,
Which yet join not scent to hue,   60
Crown the pale year weak and new ;
When the night is left behind
In the deep east, dun and blind,
And the blue noon is over us,
And the multitudinous   65
Billows murmur at our feet,
Where the earth and ocean meet,
And all things seem only one
In the universal sun.

February, 1822.

TO JANE — THE RECOLLECTION.

I.

Now the last day of many days,
    All beautiful and bright as thou,
      The loveliest and the last, is dead,
Rise, Memory, and write its praise !
Up to thy wonted work ! come, trace   5
      The epitaph of glory fled, —
For now the Earth has changed its face,
    A frown is on the Heaven's brow.

II.

We wandered to the Pine Forest
      That skirts the Ocean's foam,   10
The lightest wind was in its nest,
      The tempest in its home.

The whispering waves were half asleep,
    The clouds were gone to play,
And on the bosom of the deep,   15
    The smile of Heaven lay ;
It seemed as if the hour were one
    Sent from beyond the skies,
Which scattered from above the sun
    A light of Paradise.   20

III.

We paused amid the pines that stood
    The giants of the waste,
Tortured by storms to shapes as rude
    As serpents interlaced,
And soothed by every azure breath,   25
    That under heaven is blown,
To harmonies and hues beneath,
    As tender as its own ;
Now all the tree-tops lay asleep,
    Like green waves on the sea,   30
As still as in the silent deep
    The ocean woods may be.

IV.

How calm it was ! — the silence there
    By such a chain was bound
That even the busy woodpecker   35
    Made stiller by her sound
The inviolable quietness ;
    The breath of peace we drew
With its soft motion made not less
    The calm that round us grew.   40
There seemed from the remotest seat
    Of the white mountain waste,

To the soft flower beneath our feet,
    A magic circle traced, —
A spirit interfused around,   45
    A thrilling silent life,
To momentary peace it bound
    Our mortal nature's strife ; —
And still I felt the centre of
    The magic circle there   50
Was one fair form that filled with love
    The lifeless atmosphere.

v.

We paused beside the pools that lie
    Under the forest bough ;
Each seemed as 't were a little sky   55
    Gulphed in a world below ;
A firmament of purple light,
    Which in the dark earth lay,
More boundless than the depth of night,
    And purer than the day —   60
In which the lovely forests grew
    As in the upper air,
More perfect both in shape and hue
    Than any spreading there.
There lay the glade and neighbouring lawn,   65
    And through the dark green wood
The white sun twinkling like the dawn
    Out of a speckled cloud.
Sweet views which in our world above
    Can never well be seen,   70
Were imaged by the water's love
    Of that fair forest green.
And all was interfused beneath
    With an elysian glow,

An atmosphere without a breath,   75
    A softer day below.
Like one beloved the scene had lent
    To the dark water's breast
Its every leaf and lineament
    With more than truth expressed;   80
Until an envious wind crept by,
    Like an unwelcome thought,
Which from the mind's too faithful eye
    Blots one dear image out.
Though thou art ever fair and kind,   85
    The forests ever green,
Less oft is peace in Shelley's mind,
    Than calm in waters seen.

February, 1822.

WITH A GUITAR, TO JANE.

ARIEL to Miranda. —Take
This slave of Music, for the sake
Of him who is the slave of thee,
And teach it all the harmony
In which thou canst, and only thou,   5
Make the delighted spirit glow,
Till joy denies itself again,
And, too intense, is turned to pain;
For by permission and command
Of thine own Prince Ferdinand,   10
Poor Ariel sends this silent token
Of more than ever can be spoken;
Your guardian spirit, Ariel, who,
From life to life, must still pursue
Your happiness; — for thus alone   15

Can Ariel ever find his own.
From Prospero's enchanted cell,
As the mighty verses tell,
To the throne of Naples, he
Lit you o'er the trackless sea,   20
Flitting on, your prow before,
Like a living meteor.
When you die, the silent Moon,
In her interlunar swoon,
Is not sadder in her cell   25
Than deserted Ariel.
When you live again on earth,
Like an unseen star of birth,
Ariel guides you o'er the sea
Of life from your nativity.   30
Many changes have been run,
Since Ferdinand and you begun
Your course of love, and Ariel still
Has tracked your steps, and served your will;
Now, in humbler, happier lot,   35
This is all remembered not;
And now, alas! the poor sprite is
Imprisoned, for some fault of his,
In a body like a grave;—
From you he only dares to crave,   40
For his service and his sorrow,
A smile to-day, a song to-morrow.

The artist who this idol wrought,
To echo all harmonious thought,
Felled a tree, while on the steep   45
The woods were in their winter sleep,
Rocked in that repose divine
On the wind-swept Apennine;

And dreaming, some of Autumn past,
And some of Spring approaching fast,   50
And some of April buds and showers,
And some of songs in July bowers,
And all of love ; and so this tree, —
O that such our death may be ! —
Died in sleep, and felt no pain,   55
To live in happier form again :
From which, beneath Heaven's fairest star,
The artist wrought this loved Guitar,
And taught it justly to reply,
To all who question skilfully,   60
In language gentle as thine own ;
Whispering in enamoured tone
Sweet oracles of woods and dells,
And summer winds in sylvan cells ;
For it had learnt all harmonies   65
Of the plains and of the skies,
Of the forests and the mountains,
And the many-voicèd fountains ;
The clearest echoes of the hills,
The softest notes of falling rills,   70
The melodies of birds and bees,
The murmuring of summer seas,
And pattering rain, and breathing dew,
And airs of evening ; and it knew
That seldom-heard mysterious sound,   75
Which, driven on its diurnal round,
As it floats through boundless day,
Our world enkindles on its way —
All this it knows, but will not tell
To those who cannot question well   80
The spirit that inhabits it ;
It talks according to the wit

Of its companions; and no more
Is heard than has been felt before,
By those who tempt it to betray   85
These secrets of an elder day:
But sweetly as its answers will
Flatter hands of perfect skill,
It keeps its highest, holiest tone
For our belovèd Jane alone.   90

                                        1822.

TO JANE.

I.

THE keen stars were twinkling,
And the fair moon was rising among them,
        Dear Jane!
The guitar was tinkling,
But the notes were not sweet till you sung them   5
        Again.

II.

As the moon's soft splendour
        O'er the faint cold starlight of heaven
                Is thrown,
        So your voice most tender   10
To the strings without soul had then given
                Its own.

III.

The stars will awaken,
Though the moon sleep a full hour later,
                To-night;   15
        No leaf will be shaken
Whilst the dews of your melody scatter
                Delight.

Though the sound overpowers,
Sing again, with your dear voice revealing   20
   A tone
Of some world far from ours,
Where music and moonlight and feeling
   Are one.

           1822.

———

LINES WRITTEN IN THE BAY OF LERICI.

SHE left me at the silent time
When the moon had ceased to climb
The azure path of Heaven's steep,
And like an albatross asleep,
Balanced on her wings of light,   5
Hovered in the purple night,
Ere she sought her ocean nest
In the chambers of the West.
She left me, and I stayed alone
Thinking over every tone   10
Which, though silent to the ear,
The enchanted heart could hear,
Like notes which die when born, but still
Haunt the echoes of the hill ;
And feeling ever — O too much ! —   15
The soft vibration of her touch,
As if her gentle hand, even now.
Lightly trembled on my brow ;
And thus, although she absent were,
Memory gave me all of her   20
That even Fancy dares to claim : —
Her presence had made weak and tame

All passions, and I lived alone
In the time which is our own;
The past and future were forgot,   25
As they had been, and would be, not.
But soon, the guardian angel gone,
The dæmon reassumed his throne
In my faint heart.   I dare not speak
My thoughts, but thus disturbed and weak   30
I sat and saw the vessels glide
Over the ocean bright and wide,
Like spirit-wingèd chariots sent
O'er some serenest element
For ministrations strange and far;   35
As if to some Elysian star
Sailed for drink to medicine
Such sweet and bitter pain as mine.
And the wind that winged their flight
From the land came fresh and light,   40
And the scent of wingèd flowers,
And the coolness of the hours
Of dew, and sweet warmth left by day,
Were scattered o'er the twinkling bay.
And the fisher with his lamp   45
And spear about the low rocks damp
Crept, and struck the fish which came
To worship the delusive flame.
Too happy they, whose pleasure sought
Extinguishes all sense and thought   50
Of the regret that pleasure leaves,
Destroying life alone, not peace!

                                    1822.

LINES.

I.

WE meet not as we parted,
  We feel more than all may see,
My bosom is heavy-hearted,
  And thine full of doubt for me.
  One moment has bound the free.   5

II.

That moment is gone for ever,
  Like lightning that flashed and died,
Like a snow-flake upon the river,
  Like a sunbeam upon the tide,
  Which the dark shadows hide.   10

III.

That moment from time was singled
  As the first of a life of pain,
The cup of its joy was mingled
  — Delusion too sweet though vain!
  Too sweet to be mine again.   15

IV.

Sweet lips, could my heart have hidden
  That its life was crushed by you,
Ye would not have then forbidden
  The death which a heart so true
  Sought in your briny dew.   20

V.

   *   *   *   *
    *   *   *   *
   *   *   *   *

Methinks too little cost
For a moment so found, so lost!   22

1822.

A DIRGE.

Rough wind, that moanest loud
    Grief too sad for song;
Wild wind, when sullen cloud
    Knells all the night long;
Sad storm, whose tears are vain,
Bare woods, whose branches stain,
Deep caves and dreary main,
    Wail, for the world's wrong!

1822.

EPITAPH.

These are two friends whose lives were undivided;
So let their memory be, now they have glided
Under the grave; let not their bones be parted,
For their two hearts in life were single-hearted.

1822.

NOTES.

—•••—

ALASTOR.

THE circumstances in which this poem was written serve to throw light upon its meaning. "Already at twenty-three Shelley was disillusioned of some eager and exorbitant hopes; the first great experiment of his heart had proved a failure; his boyish ardour for the enfranchisement of a people had been without result; his literary efforts had met with little sympathy or recognition; and, during the early months of the year, he had felt how frail was his hold on life, and had almost confronted that mystery which lies behind the veil of mortal existence" (Dowden's *Life*, Vol. I, p. 530). "In the spring of 1815," says Mrs. Shelley in her note on this poem, "an eminent physician pronounced that he was dying rapidly of a consumption." The mood reflected in *Alastor* is the mood in which Shelley regarded his own past, with death staring him in the face. As he looks back on his life, he notes especially its isolation and apparent fruitlessness. He feels that he has been a creature alone and apart, pursuing aims which the mass of men do not understand, and thus cut off from the wholesome and stimulating sympathy of his fellows. This "self-centred seclusion," as he explains in the Preface to the poem, is not the result of a cold or egoistic nature; he does not belong to the class described in the second paragraph of the Preface. IIis isolation is caused by the loftiness of his ideal and by his perfect devotion to it. IIe neglected attainable but imperfect good for the sake of ideal perfections which forever escape his grasp. One form of this devotion to the ideal is the desire for complete sympathy of mind and feeling, such as would be afforded by a woman in perfect harmony with his own highest self; it is this aspect of his eager but vain quest which is made especially prominent in *Alastor*.

These experiences, then, of Shelley's spiritual life and this mood in which he regards them, form the substance of the poem; the poet does not, however, describe these things directly: he symbolizes them in the wanderings of an imaginary hero, and the intangible feelings and experiences of which we have spoken are concretely shadowed forth in descriptions of scenery. But these descriptions do not stand in the poem solely on account of their symbolic import; the poet delights in them for their own sake, and so will the appreciative reader. To follow the course of a stream on foot or by boat was always to Shelley a peculiarly fascinating employment. In 1814 he had "visited some of the more magnificent scenes of Switzerland, and returned to England from Lucerne by the Reuss and Rhine. This river-navigation enchanted him. In his favourite poem of *Thalaba* his imagination had been excited by the description of such a voyage" (Mrs. Shelley's note). In the beginning of September, 1815, immediately before writing *Alastor*, he had followed in a wherry the course of the Thames from Windsor almost to its source. The poem itself was written at Bishopsgate, on the borders of Windsor forest, amidst whose oaks he spent a great part of his time. From the stores of natural beauty thus accumulated in his mind, he shaped the scenery of the poem. But he does not realistically reproduce what he has observed. He modifies and combines elements derived from actual nature in order to reflect his own feelings and moods. But, although the journey of the hero symbolizes Shelley's own life, and the different scenes suggest the character of its various experiences, the reader must not attempt to press the symbolism too far. *Alastor* is not an allegory like the first two books of the *Faery Queen;* each circumstance does not have a definite allegorical meaning. But, rather, the poet, in the vaguer fashion of a musical composer, suggests and stimulates certain frames of mind and feeling through the use of concrete imagery. To appreciate the poem, we must catch its varying tone and spirit, not too inquisitively search for secondary senses.

The blank verse of *Alastor* is evidently affected by the study of Wordsworth (cf. *Tintern Abbey*, for example), and the influence of the elder poet is apparent also occasionally in individual phrases: "natural piety" (l. 3), "obstinate questionings" (l. 26), "too deep for tears" (l. 713). Southey's *Thalaba*, as Mrs. Shelley points out, was also a factor in the composition of *Alastor*, and Shelley may have read and got hints from Volney's *Genie des Tombeaux*.[1]

2 33. The lines with which the Preface closes are from Wordsworth's *Excursion*, Book I. Shelley misquotes; the original has " And they " not " And those."

---

[1] Sources, parallel passages, etc., have been collected by Dr. Ackermann and M. Beljame ; see the Bibliography at end of this volume.

Alastor is a Greek word meaning an evil genius. Peacock, who suggested the title, explains, in his *Memoirs of Shelley*, that the poem is so called because the spirit of solitude is here treated as a spirit of evil. *Alastor* is *not* the name of the hero.

3 1–9. The poet invokes the inspiration of Nature.

3 2. **Mother :** Nature.

3 16. **This boast:** the claims which the poet makes for himself in the preceding conditional clauses.

3 18. **Mother :** see l. 2.

4 46. **modulate :** be in harmony with.

4 50–66. A description of the hero; the most marked peculiarity of his life is its isolation.

5 60–63. Cf. Longfellow's *Excelsior.*

5 67–128. At l. 67 the narrative of the hero's life begins; it embodies, partly in symbols, Shelley's spiritual autobiography, — his alienation from the opinions of those about him and his pursuit of truth through the study of science and of ancient literature.

6 93. **Frequent :** thronged; cf. *Paradise Lost*, I, l. 797.

6 101. Shelley himself preferred a purely vegetable diet, and advocated abstinence from animal food in a note to *Queen Mab*, subsequently printed as a separate pamphlet.

6 118–120. M. Beljame in his edition of *Alastor*, p. 92, points out that Shelley had probably in mind the zodiac of Denderah, a ruined town of Upper Egypt, celebrated for a temple "with noble portico supported by twenty-four columns. The walls, columns, etc., are covered with figures and hieroglyphics. . . . On the ceiling of the portico are numerous mythological figures arranged in zodiacal fashion." In Volney's *Ruines des Tombeaux* mention is made of the zodiac of Denderah.

6 120. This line refers to the hieroglyphics.

7 129–139. These lines symbolize the neglect of human sympathy and affection. Note how purely ideal the framework of the poem is; we do not, even in imagination, feel that these events and scenes have any reality.

7 140–191. Upon the poet's mind bursts the conception of ideal perfection and beauty embodied in female form. Nothing will satisfy him but the finding of the counterpart of this ideal in the actual world. The search for this counterpart becomes the passion of his life, and is symbolized in the further wanderings of the hero. Cf. ll. 190–255 of *Epipsychidion.*

7 141. **Carmanian :** Carmania (modern Kerman), an eastern province of Persia, containing a frightful salt desert.

7 142. The mountains where the Indus and Oxus rise are the Hindu-Kush.

7 145. **the vale of Cashmire** is the valley of the Upper Jhelum in northern India, proverbial for its beauty and fertility.

9 193-6. An example of Shelley's power of suggesting a vast landscape.

9 211-222. If the ideal is unattainable in this life, may it not be ours after death?

9 219. **Conduct:** this is the reading of the original edition. Rossetti conjectures *conducts*, which seems natural, as "vault" is the subject; but Forman suggests that "Shelley meant us to understand the rather outré construction, 'Does the bright arch lead, while does death's blue vault conduct,' etc."

9 213-219. The connection of the two ideas here expressed seems to be: "If the beautiful reflection in the water allures to something so unlike itself as the black depths beneath, may not the ugly vault of death lead to something as unlike itself, — to the beautiful ideal world?"

10 227 ff. Such a conflict between an eagle and a serpent is described at length in stanzas viii ff. of *The Revolt of Islam*, I.

10 240. **Aornos:** in ancient times one of the chief cities of Bactria, near the northern foot of the Hindu-Kush Mountains. This and other of the proper names in the passage are evidently derived from the poet's reading in classical literature.

Petra: the Petra referred to is probably the city situated on a lofty cliff in Sogdiana, mentioned in Quintus Curtius as taken by Alexander the Great.

10 242. **Balk:** the modern name of Bactra, a city situated somewhat to the east of Aornos. These two places are mentioned as the greatest cities of Bactria in Arrian's *Expedition of Alexander* (M. Beljame's edition, p. 112).

where the desolated tombs, etc.: at Arbela, namely, a city in Adiabene in Assyria; the Emperor Caracalla dispersed the contents of the tombs of the Parthian kings to the winds (see *Dion Cassius*, lxxviii, 1, cited by M. Beljame, p. 113).

10 255-271. Cf. Longfellow's *Excelsior*.

11 272. **Chorasmian shore:** in ancient times the Chorasmii dwelt to the south of the Aral Sea, and one would suppose that the shore of this lake is referred to. The description of the voyage and the reference to the Caucasus (l. 377) would, however, lead us to suppose that the poet had in his mind the Caspian Sea. M. Beljame seems to

think that the shore of the Aral Sea is here referred to, but the Caspian in "sea-shore" of l. 275. This would obviate the difficulty referred to below; but it is improbable that the writer would so abruptly omit all reference to the wanderer's journey from the Aral to the Caspian. In truth, it is needless to trouble ourselves to follow on the map the course of the hero's wanderings; the poet selected, doubtless, from his memories of classical history and literature, euphonious names which had suitable associations, more or less vague.

11 272-5. The hero first pauses where the marshes begin, a point which may be roughly called the shore; then a strong impulse urges him to the actual shore, — the margin of the sea.

12 293. **Its precious charge**: the vision described in ll. 148-191.

12 294. **a shadowy lure**: the hope that the ideal might be found beyond death.

13 338-9. Cf. ll. 3-4 of *A Summer-evening Church-yard*, —

> And pallid evening twines its beaming hair
> In duskier braids around the languid eyes of day.

13 340 ff. In describing the voyage in the boat, Shelley had evidently in mind *Thalaba*, XI, stanzas 34 ff.

14 363. The sea discharges itself through an underground passage which the boat follows; at l. 370 river and boat emerge into the open air.

14 374-412. The flood plunges down a vast chasm, but a puff of wind carries the boat safely into a quiet cove. Here the hero leaves the boat; the rest of his journeying is on foot.

15 412-413. Shelley seems sometimes to have decked his hair in this fashion; see Introduction, p. lx.

15 412-420. Careless of everything else, he is driven onward by his yearning for the ideal.

15 420 ff. A typical Shelleyan forest, with its vastness and eerie mystery; cf. the similar description in *Rosalind and Helen*, ll. 95 ff.

16 445-8. The patches of sky seen through the foliage, by daylight or moonlight, change their shapes with the movement of the boughs.

16 455-7. Cf. *A Summer-evening Church-yard*, ll. 5-6.

17 457-468. Shelley is wont to dwell with particular delight on reflections of scenery in the water; see *To Jane — The Recollection*, ll. 53 ff.

17 479-491. The hero feels himself in communion with the all-pervading spirit of nature, but is drawn onward by the sense of the ideal.

17 484-6. Forman explains this: "The spirit, assuming for speech the undulating woods, etc., held commune with the poet."

17 489-490. The eyes which he had beheld in dream still seemed to hover over him.

18 493. The hero now follows the downward course of a rivulet which has its source in the well mentioned in l. 457.

19 528. **windlestrae**: the stalks of certain grasses; the ordinary form is "windlestraw." Scott (*Old Mortality*, chap. vi) makes Lady Bellenden say: "I had rather the rigs of Tillietudlem bare naething but windlestraes and sandy lavrocks."

19 533-9. Here the poet seems to indicate the meaning of his symbolism.

19 535. **irradiate**: shining, brilliant.

19 543-550. This obscure passage has been much discussed. Mr. Rossetti explains: "Rocks rose, lifting their pinnacles; and the precipice (precipitous sides or archway) of the ravine, obscuring the said ravine with its shadow, did unclose (opened, was rifted), aloft, amid toppling stones," etc. The interpretation of 'disclosed' seems farfetched.

Mr. Swinburne says (*Essays and Studies*, p. 197): "I suspect the word 'its' to be wrong, and either a blind slip of the pen or a printer's error. If it is not and we are to assume that there is any break in the sentence, the parenthesis must surely extend thus far: 'its precipice obscuring the ravine'; *i.e.*, the rocks opened or 'disclosed' where the precipices above the ravine obscured it. But I take 'disclosed' to be the participle: 'its precipice darkened the ravine (which was) disclosed above.' The sentence is left hanging loose and ragged, short by a line at least, and never wound up to any end at all. Such a sentence we, too, certainly find, once at least, in the *Prometheus Unbound*, II, iv, 12-18."

Mr. Forman suggests, but does not read, "amidst precipices," for "and its precipices"; he further connects 'obscuring' with 'rocks,' 'disclosed' (as a participle) with 'ravine,' 'amid toppling stones,' etc., with 'lifted.'

Professor Dowden, in a letter quoted in the preface to Mr. Dobell's reprint of *Alastor*, explains the passage as follows: "As the ravine narrows, its rocky sides rise in height, so that the ravine grows dark below from the sheer height of its precipitous sides; but above, in the rocky heights, can be discerned openings in the crags, and caverns, amid which the voice of the stream echoes. Such is the sense I get, and I extract it from Shelley's text by considering the relative '*which*' following '*rocks*' as nominative, not only to the verb '*lifted*,' but also to the verb '*disclosed*'; and this verb '*disclosed*' has as its accusative or object the words 'black gulphs and yawning caves.' The words 'its precipice obscuring the ravine,' I take to be parenthetical, and as meaning *the height of its rocky sides darkening the ravine.* Pointed thus, my meaning may be clearer:

> On every side now rose
> Rocks, which, in unimaginable forms
> Lifted their black and barren pinnacles
> In the light of evening, and (its precipice
> Obscuring the ravine) disclosed above
> ('Mid toppling stones) black gulphs, etc.

I separate '*toppling stones*,' as governed by the preposition ''*mid,*' from '*black gulphs,*' etc., which is governed by the verb '*disclosed.*' '*Above*' is an adverb, not a preposition, and means *in the upper region.*"

The objection to Professor Dowden's explanation is the putting of the "black gulphs" and "yawning caves" at the *top* of the ravine. But either this explanation or Mr. Swinburne's suggestion that the sentence is left unfinished seems to be the best solution of the difficulty.

20 589–596. **One human step**: the step of the hero. *One voice* must also be the hero's voice, though, as Mr. Rossetti says (*Shelley Society's Note Book*, p. 22), "It is rather anomalous to say that his own voice led his form." Mr. Rossetti suggests, as a possible explanation, that, since the voice "inspired the echoes," it may have been by following the echoes that the hero found the nook.

21 602–5. **its mountains**: the mountains on the "horizon's verge." The moon was low in the horizon; its light flowed from behind the mountains, and illuminated the mist which filled the atmosphere.

21 610. **sightless**: invisible; cf. *Epipsychidion*, l. 240.

21 611. **Skeleton**: the "Skeleton" is Death, as we see from l. 619.

21 612. **its**: the career of the storm mentioned in l. 610.

21 619–624. The meaning of this passage appears to be that if Death will devour all that Ruin has made ready for him, he will be satisfied, and will no more make sudden and violent attacks. Men would, in that case, die by the natural slow processes of age, like flowers.

22 650. **divided**: the horns of the moon are divided by the intervention of a "jagged hill," as is shown by l. 654.

23 667–671. The hero is compared to a lute, a bright stream, a dream of youth; the lute is "still," the stream is "dark and dry," the dream is "unremembered."

23 672. Medea: the daughter of Aëtes, king of Colchis, and wife of Jason, the winner of the Golden Fleece; she possessed magical powers. In this reference to her "wondrous alchemy," the poet is thinking of Ovid's *Metamorphoses*, VII, 257–285, where it is related that under the influence of Medea's incantation: Vernat humus, floresque et mollia pabula surgunt (l. 284).

23 676. the chalice: of immortality.

23 677. one living man: the Wandering Jew, to whom immortality was given as a curse. The Wandering Jew was often in Shelley's mind; in boyhood he wrote a poem on the subject; and the Jew figures, also, both in *Queen Mab* and in *Hellas*.

23 678. Vessel of deathless wrath: cf. Romans, ix. 22: "What if God, willing to shew his wrath and to make his power known, endured with much long-suffering the vessels of wrath fitted to destruction."

23 681. the dream: that there is an elixir of life.

24 709–710. speak, etc.: show their lack of power by their feeble attempts to image this woe.

24 712. deep for tears:

> To me the meanest flower that blows can give
> Thoughts that do often lie too deep for tears.
> (Wordsworth's *Ode on Intimations of Immortality*.)

A SUMMER-EVENING CHURCH-YARD.

"The summer evening that suggested to him the poem written in the church-yard of Lechlade occurred during his voyage up the Thames, in the autumn of 1815" (Mrs. Shelley's note). For a description of this voyage, see Dowden's *Life*, Vol. I, pp. 526–530.

25 13. aërial Pile: the clouds above the setting sun.

LINES ("The cold earth slept below").

Given under the title "November, 1815," in *The Literary Pocket-book* for 1823. "There can be no great rashness in suggesting that the subject of the poem is the death of Harriet Shelley, who drowned herself on the 9th of November, 1816. In that case, *1815* and *raven hair* were used as a disguise, Harriet's hair having been a light brown" (Forman's note).

26 17. raven: Mrs. Shelley's edition reads *tangled*.

TO WORDSWORTH.

In the earlier stages of the French Revolution Wordsworth strongly sympathized with the party of progress; subsequently he became intensely conservative. The events of the time and the innate tendencies of Wordsworth's mind sufficiently account for this change ; but some radical enthusiasts of the day regarded him as a deserter, and his acceptance of an appointment under the government in 1813 caused an outburst of indignation against him among these more ardent spirits. The change in Wordsworth's attitude to political questions also suggested Browning's *Lost Leader*.

HYMN TO INTELLECTUAL BEAUTY.

Mrs. Shelley tells us that this poem was conceived during Shelley's voyage with Lord Byron around the Lake of Geneva in the summer of 1816. In the conception of " Intellectual Beauty " we have a thought characteristic of Shelley and recurring continually in his works. The idea is borrowed from Plato, and will be best grasped through the reading of Diotima's speech in Plato's *Symposium*, as translated by Shelley himself (see in Forman's edition of the *Prose Works*, Vol. III, especially pp. 219-222). In this speech Diotima explains how the love of beautiful objects leads on to the love of the beautiful in soul and thought, and, finally, to the conception of universal beauty, of perfect abstract beauty, " eternal, unproduced, indestructible; neither subject to increase nor decay; not, like other things, partly beautiful and partly deformed; not at one time beautiful and at another time not; not beautiful in relation to one thing and deformed in relation to another; not here beautiful and there deformed ; not beautiful in the estimation of one person and deformed in that of another; nor can this supreme beauty be figured to the imagination like a beautiful face, or beautiful hands, or any portion of the body, nor like any discourse, nor any science. Nor does it subsist in any other that lives and is, either in earth, or in heaven, or in any other place ; but it is eternally uniform and consistent, and monoeidic with itself. All other things are beautiful through a participation of it, with this condition, that, although they are subject to production and decay, it never becomes more or less, or endures any change. When any one, ascending from the correct system of Love, begins to contemplate this supreme beauty, he already touches the consummation of his labour. For such as discipline themselves upon this system, or are conducted by another beginning to ascend through these transitory objects which are beautiful, towards that which is beauty itself, proceeding as on steps from the love of one form to that of two, and from that of two, to that of all forms which are beautiful; and from beautiful forms to beautiful habits and institutions, and from institutions to beautiful doctrines; until, from the meditation of many doctrines, they arrive at that which is nothing else than the doctrine of supreme beauty itself, in the knowledge and contemplation of which at length they repose."

Through the perception of such beauty, the soul receives, according to Shelley, its highest and best stimulus. The desire of this beauty lifts us above the petty and ignoble. Unfortunately, it is only at times that we are fully conscious of it. Its absence is lamented, and its power celebrated in the *Hymn* before us. It will be noted that there is a certain parallelism between this poem and Wordsworth's *Ode on Intimations of Immortality;* in the latter Wordsworth laments the vanishing in mature life of the perception of the divine beauty of the universe.

28 5. **shower** is a verb here.

28 25-36. The attempts to solve the mystery of the universe have failed; nothing serves to lighten the world except the perception of the beauty which lies behind it.

28 26. **these responses:** the responses to the questions of stanza ii.

29 45. The simile seems scarcely appropriate.

29 49-52. Cf. *Alastor*, ll. 23-29.

29 50-51. Shelley probably pronounced 'pursuing' *pursuin'*; at the present time in England this is at once a fashionable and a vulgar error. The same imperfect rhyme is found in Wordsworth, *e.g.*, *Ode on Intimations of Immortality*, ll. 43-46.

30 73 ff. Compare the opening of the last stanza of Wordsworth's *Ode on the Intimations of Immortality.*

ON FANNY GODWIN.

Fanny Godwin (daughter of Mary Wollstonecraft and adopted by William Godwin, hence the elder half-sister of Mary Shelley) poisoned herself October 9, 1816. She was of a tender, melancholy nature, and the only reason she assigned for her act was that she brought trouble to others. Shelley had seen her a short time before her death.

OZYMANDIAS.

First published in *The Examiner* of January 11, 1818. The Greek historian Diodorus gives an account of the statue referred to in the poem. It was reputed, he says, the largest in Egypt, the foot exceeding seven cubits in length; the inscription was, "I am Ozymandias, king of kings ; if any one wishes to know what I am and where I lie, let him surpass me in some of my exploits " (see *Diodorus*, I, 47; or Wilkinson's *Ancient Egypt*, Vol. I, chap. ii).

The freedom, or even carelessness, of Shelley's treatment of the laws of the regular sonnet and the success of the poem, notwithstanding, are characteristic of his art. Presumably, lines 2 and 4, 9 and 11 are intended to rhyme.

31 7. **survive**: inasmuch as they are depicted on the features of the statue.

31 8. **The hand**: of the sculptor.

them: the passions.

the heart: of the monarch.

PASSAGE OF THE APENNINES.

32 9. **lay**: note the violation of grammar for the sake of rhyme, and cf. Byron's *Childe Harold*, IV, l. 1620.

LINES WRITTEN AMONG THE EUGANEAN HILLS.

This poem was written at a villa near Este where the Shelleys lived for a short time during the autumn of 1818. "We looked from the garden," writes Mrs. Shelley, "over the plains of Lombardy, bounded to the west by the far Apennines, while to the east the horizon was lost in misty distance." A few weeks before this poem was written the Shelleys had been in Venice, where Byron was then living. There their infant daughter died. Sorrow and ill health combined to make this a season of deep depression to the poet.

34 43. **are**: the grammar is defective.

34 45–65. These lines contain a concrete illustration of the assertions in the passage immediately preceding.

34 47-48. The bones still occupy the position which was given to them when the unhappy wretch stretched himself out for the last time.

35 71-89. " I saw once from a tower that overlooked two rookeries, this very thing. The moment the sun's disk had fully climbed over the edge of a distant wood, the whole band of rooks, from both their homes, silent before, rose, all the birds together, with a great 'hail,' into the air, and, hovering for a second or two, streamed down the wind towards the sun " (Stopford Brooke's note).

36 97. **Amphitrite**: a daughter of Oceanus.

36 114. If there is a reference to any particular temple here, it is probably that at Delphi, where Apollo chiefly uttered his oracles; in a Greek temple there would not be a *dome.*

37 122-133. Venice was at this time under the dominion of Austria.

38 152. **Celtic Anarch**: Austria. The Celts for a long time represented the northern barbarians to the Romans, and here the term Celtic seems to be applied vaguely to the northern barbarians as distinguished from the natives of Italy.

38 167-205. This passage on Byron was interpolated after the MS. of the poem had been sent to the printer.

39 195. **Scamander**: a river near Troy.

39 200-1. Arqua, where Petrarch, the great Italian poet (1304-74) lived, died, and is buried, is in the neighborhood.

39 206. It will be noted that the poem follows the course of the day.

40 219-230. These lines refer to Italy being under foreign domination.

40 238. In speaking of Sin and Death here, the poet is probably thinking of these personages as described in *Paradise Lost*, II, ll. 648 ff.

40 239. **Ezzelin**: Ezzelino da Romano (1194-1259), a famous Ghibelline chief. In the *Divine Comedy* he is represented by Dante as among the tyrants who are expiating the sin of cruelty.

42 292. **The point,** etc.: the zenith.

42 296-8. The reference is to the coloring of foliage by the action of frost.

42 315-319. The poet has been saying that the plains, leaves, vines, etc., and even his own sad spirit, are all interpenetrated and lightened " by the glory of the sky." What that " glory of the sky " is he does not venture to define ; whether it is love, or light, etc., or the universal spirit of beauty which exists in all these things, or something which the poet's own mind bestows upon external objects, — that mind which by its imaginative power lends life to the dead universe. The whole

passage is a poetic expression for the fact that Shelley, as he gazes upon the scene, forgets the sadness of his life, and feels the joy and beauty of the world about him; there is, in addition, a suggestion of Shelley's mystical philosophy.

43 333. **its**: the antecedent is "the frail bark of this lone being."

43 342-373. Cf. the description of the island in *Epipsychidion*, ll. 422 ff.

SONNET ("Lift not the painted veil").

Although the phenomena of life are merely the superficial appearances which conceal the real forces that lie beneath, do not seek to penetrate beyond the former. All that you will attain will be vague conjectures which spring from your hopes and fears.

44 1. The same metaphor is employed in the *Essay on Life* (*Prose Works*, Vol. II, p. 259) in speaking of the philosophical theory that nothing exists except as it is perceived, — a theory held by the poet himself.

44 6. **sightless**: invisible; frequently used in this sense by Shelley; cf. *Alastor*, l. 610.

STANZAS WRITTEN IN DEJECTION.

Speaking of the period when this poem was composed, Mrs. Shelley says: "At this time Shelley suffered greatly in health. . . . Constant and poignant physical suffering exhausted him; and though he preserved the appearance of cheerfulness, and often greatly enjoyed our wanderings in the environs of Naples, and our excursions on its sunny sea, yet many hours were passed when his thoughts shadowed by illness, became gloomy, and then he escaped to solitude, and in verses which he hid from fear of wounding me, poured forth morbid but too natural bursts of discontent and sadness. . . . We lived in utter solitude — and such is often not the nurse of cheerfulness." Medwin connects this poem with the fate of the mysterious lady who is said to have followed the poet from England to Naples, and to have died there (see Dowden's *Life*, Vol. II, p. 252).

46 22. Shelley may have had some particular "sage" in mind, but such content is a common attribute of sages, — of the Stoics, for example.

47 37–45. Some might lament me, should I die, as I shall lament the departure of this beautiful day; but the memory of the day will be a source of joy — not so, the memory of me.

———

PROMETHEUS UNBOUND.

The First Act of *Prometheus Unbound* was written at Este (see Introduction, p. lxiii) in the autumn of 1818, when the memory of the passage through the Alps in the previous spring was fresh in the poet's mind, and was completed, or nearly so, early in October. In a letter from Milan of April 30, he writes that he has on his journey read two or three plays of Euripides (see Dowden's *Life*, Vol. II, p. 201), and Mrs. Shelley says: "The Greek tragedians were his most familiar companions in his wanderings, and the sublime majesty of Æschylus filled him with wonder and delight" (Dowden's *Life*, Vol. II, p. 239). The Second and Third Acts were written in Rome, especially among the ruins of the Baths of Caracalla (see Preface, p. 50, and Introduction, pp. lxiv, v), during the early months of the year 1819. On April 6 he writes to Peacock : "My Prometheus is just finished, and in a month or two I shall send it. It is a drama with characters and mechanism of a kind yet unattempted, and I think the execution is better than any of my former attempts." The Fourth Act was an afterthought, written at Florence during the latter part of the same year.

In this work Shelley makes use of an old Greek myth already employed for dramatic purposes by Æschylus in his *Prometheus Bound*. To this work of Æschylus the poem of Shelley is indebted for its general form, for the situation and scenery of the First Act, and for some individual phrases and passages.[1] Although Shelley's *Prometheus* approaches rather the type of Greek tragedy than of the English national drama, it does not attempt, as *Samson Agonistes*, accurately to reproduce the form of a Greek play. It is, further, not a drama in the ordinary sense ; the poet himself indicates this in calling it a "*lyrical* drama." It is a poem which depicts through characters and dialogues, not external life, but the general conceptions of the writer's mind and the feelings which these conceptions awaken in him. Here Shelley gives a view of

---

[1] See Dr. R. Ackermann's *Studien über Shelley's Prometheus Unbound* in *Englische Studien*, Band xvi, for a collection of original and parallel passages from Æschylus, etc.; also the comparison between the two plays in Miss Scudder's edition.

the history of the universe, past and to come, as Milton gives another view of the same subject in *Paradise Lost*. The *Prometheus* gives expression to philosophical ideas which were current in France before the Revolution in the form which they took in Shelley's mind ; *Paradise Lost*, to the philosophy of Puritanism as conceived by Milton.

Upon the meaning of the poem, the following extract from Mrs. Shelley's notes will serve to throw some light : " The prominent feature of Shelley's theory of the destiny of the human species was, that evil is not inherent in the system of the creation, but an accident that might be expelled. This also forms a portion of Christianity; God made earth and man perfect, till he, by his fall

'Brought death into the world and all our woe.'

Shelley believed that mankind had only to will that there should be no evil, and there would be none. It is not my part in these notes to notice the arguments that have been urged against this opinion, but to mention the fact that he entertained it, and was indeed attached to it with fervent enthusiasm. That man could be so perfectionized as to be able to expel evil from his own nature, and from the greater part of the creation, was the cardinal point of his system. And the subject he loved best to dwell on, was the image of One warring with the Evil Principle, oppressed not only by it, but by all, even the good, who were deluded into considering evil a necessary portion of humanity. A victim full of fortitude and hope, and the spirit of triumph emanating from a reliance on the ultimate omnipotence of good. Such he had depicted in his last poem [*The Revolt of Islam*], when he made Laon the enemy and the victim of tyrants. He now took a more idealized image of the same subject. He followed certain classical authorities in figuring Saturn as the good principle, Jupiter the usurping evil one, and Prometheus as the regenerator, who unable to bring mankind back to primitive innocence, used knowledge as a weapon to defeat evil, by leading mankind beyond the state wherein they are sinless through ignorance, to that in which they are virtuous through wisdom. Jupiter punished the temerity of the Titan by chaining him to a rock of Caucasus, and causing a vulture to devour his still renewed heart. There was a prophecy afloat in heaven portending the fall of Jove, the secret of averting which was known only to Prometheus; and the god offered freedom from torture on condition of its being communicated to him. According to the mythological story, this referred to the offspring of Thetis, who was destined to be greater than his father. Prometheus at last bought pardon for his crime of enriching mankind with his gifts, by revealing the prophecy. Hercules killed the vulture and set him free, and Thetis was married to Peleus, the father of Achilles.

Shelley adapted the catastrophe of this story to his peculiar views. The son, greater than his father, born of the nuptial of Jupiter and Thetis, was to dethrone Evil, and bring back a happier reign than that of Saturn. Prometheus defies the power of his enemy, and endures centuries of torture, till the hour arrives when Jove, blind to the real event, but darkly guessing that some great good to himself will flow, espouses Thetis. At the moment, the Primal Power of the world drives him from his usurped throne, and Strength in the person of Hercules, liberates Humanity, typified in Prometheus, from the tortures generated by evil done or suffered. Asia, one of the Oceanides, is the wife of Prometheus, — she was, according to other mythological interpretations, the same as Venus and Nature. When the Benefactor of Mankind is liberated, Nature resumes the beauty of her prime, and is united to her husband, the emblem of the human race, in perfect and happy union. In the Fourth Act, the poet gives further scope to his imagination, and idealizes the forms of creation, such as we know them, instead of such as they appeared to the Greeks. Maternal Earth, the mighty Parent, is superseded by the Spirit of the Earth — the guide of our planet through the realms of the sky — while his fair and weaker companion and attendant, the Spirit of the Moon, receives bliss from the annihilation of Evil in the superior sphere."

Such are the main ideas expressed or implied in this drama. Men lived originally in a state of nature, without social organization and institutions. This period, which the nineteenth century regards as one of violence and misery, Rousseau and his school depicted as a time of innocence and bliss. In the ancient myth, Shelley found an analogue for this phase of human history in the Golden Age of the reign of Saturn. But, if men were then innocent and happy, they were also childish and undeveloped. In course of time came progress; they acquired the arts of life, material comforts, political institutions, religious conceptions. So far good; but, unfortunately, all ideas and institutions have a tendency to crystallize, to survive their usefulness, to cramp the individual and to hinder the further development of society, — to produce, in short, tyranny, social, political, and religious. It was this pernicious side of established things that almost exclusively held the attention of the thinkers who stimulated the French Revolution. The iniquitous conditions amidst which they lived led them to regard all institutions as evil, and not only as an evil, but as the source of all other evil. Could men but rid themselves of these, human nature — fundamentally good, as was assumed — would regain the innocence and happiness of the Golden Age. Shelley, in this poem, personifies institutions, or authority, as Jupiter, who, in accordance with the views just unfolded, is identical with the principle of evil. His overthrow is necessary for the regeneration of mankind. Now, as this school of thinkers identified authority and established power with the source of evil, so they naturally found in their antithesis — revolution or liberty — the principle of good. In the nineteenth century, we regard liberty as desirable, because it is a condition necessary for the development of good; but, for the typical thought of the eighteenth century, it was an ultimate and highest good. So with Shelley: Prometheus, the opponent of Jupiter, personifies the spirit of resistance, of revolution, and consequently, also, the spirit of good. Prometheus, as depicted in the ancient fable, was further adapted to Shelley's purpose, because he was represented, not merely as the assertor of freedom against the tyranny of Jove, but also as the benefactor of men, who bestowed upon them the arts of life. This very spirit of revolution and of beneficence it was which raised men above the undeveloped condition of a state of nature, by originating the organization of men, — a thing in itself highly beneficial, though in course of time it checked individual freedom and degenerated into tyranny. Hence, the poet represents (Act I, 380; II, iv, 43–45) Jupiter as deriving his power originally from Prometheus; who gave Jove all authority, provided men were left free. That is, institutions should be thoroughly plastic, not checking the liberty of individuals either in the internal sphere of thought or in the external sphere of action. But this condition imposed by Prometheus was not observed; hence tyranny and the consequent degradation of human nature. The second great period in the history of the race is thus inaugurated, — the period in which Shelley regarded himself as living, when evil is seated in the places of power, and good is weak and shackled. This is the condition of things symbolically presented in Act I of the drama; the situation affords the poet an opportunity for the expression of those feelings with which he witnessed the injustice, the hatred, the sufferings of men about him. The torments of Prometheus arise from the contemplation of misery and wickedness among men, especially from the perception of that saddest fact that evil is often the outcome of good intentions; as illustrated, for example, in Shelley's view, by the history of Christianity and of the French Revolution (Act I, 498–655).

In the First Act the main action (if action it may be called) as distinguished from the situation, lies in the revoking of the curse. The
poet in this emphasizes a needful change in the spirit of revolution, —
the change from hatred and violence to the spirit of meekness and love
(cf. the quotation from a letter of Shelley, p. lxvi of this volume).

In the old myth, Prometheus was espoused to an ocean nymph;
Shelley calls her Asia. Asia represents the ideal, the ideal which had
been attained in the Golden Age, when Prometheus and Asia dwelt
together; and which will be attained again when evil is finally over-
thrown. This ideal for which the highest natures yearn, that which
encourages them in their struggle with evil, is, for Shelley, the spirit of
beauty, as we see in the *Hymn to Intellectual Beauty* and elsewhere.
This spirit is in the *Adonais* identified with the Uranian Venus. The
conception embodied in Asia is, therefore, wide and elastic; as are the
conceptions embodied in Jupiter and Prometheus. Asia is beauty, love,
the ideal; again she is the feminine type as related to the masculine
Prometheus; so she is feeling as opposed to intellect or wisdom. In
Æschylus, Prometheus is comforted by the presence of the Ocean-
idæ; so in Shelley's poem, the two sisters of Asia, Panthea and Ione,
soothe and encourage the hero and act as messengers between him
and Asia. Their functions indicate that they represent faith and hope,
and, with Asia, make up the familiar triad, faith, hope, and love.

Of the Second Act, Asia is the central figure. In her relation to
Prometheus, she is primarily the ideal, the spirit of beauty; but in her
independent action, she is rather the impersonation of love, or, more
broadly, of the emotional nature of man. The Second Act represents
her as pursuing and attaining truth; when she has attained it, the new
era begins. The two prerequisites of the new era are symbolized in the
respective attitudes of Asia and of Prometheus; when the emotional
nature of man is centred about the true, and when the revolutionary
spirit has learned to abjure violence, the overthrow of evil is assured.
Asia is stimulated in her quest by the visions of faith (Act II, sc. i).
The revelation of truth comes from Demogorgon.

Demogorgon is an important but very vague character in the drama.
Shelley's philosophy was mainly negative; its constructive ideas were
meagre; so the portion of the poem that symbolizes the reconstructive
and represents the future, is ill defined. The nature of the catastrophe
and of the force that brings it about are not clearly indicated; and,
apart from symbolism, the fall of Jupiter is not dramatically effective.

There is a tendency in Shelley, perceptible in the *Adonais*, for example,
towards dualism. On the one hand, there is the frame of the universe

—call it matter, force, or law — eternal and necessary existence. On the other hand, there is *spirit*, which works in and through this frame of things, as the soul works within the body — free, yet limited and hampered by its instrument. This fundamental fact behind all others, this fixed frame of the universe — necessity or fate — is shadowed forth in Demogorgon. From Demogorgon, then, *i.e.*, from an investigation of the constitution of the universe, of the fixed course of things, Asia learns the truths unfolded in the Fourth Scene. As the fundamental note of the First Act is patient endurance, so that of the Second Act is joyful advance and attainment.

The Third Act presents the catastrophe. Jupiter weds Thetis ; from the offspring of this union he expects some great advantage to himself. Instead of this, however, Demogorgon appears and drags Jupiter down into the unfathomable gulf. This appears to mean that tyranny by the full attainment of its own aims brings ruin upon itself; the fall of evil when it has reached a climax is involved in the very constitution of the universe. Demogorgon, *i.e.*, necessity, who has existed from all eternity, appears as the particular result of Jove's act, — is incarnated as the offspring of his union with Thetis. Evil having fallen, Prometheus is set free by Hercules (strength). Shelley's natural tendency is to disregard physical force, and the part of Hercules is not a prominent one, nor does he have any share in the overthrow of Jupiter, who falls rather by the inner necessity of his nature. The remainder of the poem is occupied with a description of the renovated universe and with a triumphal chorus to celebrate the reign of beauty and good.

This crude and hard outline of the meaning of the poem is given in order that the student may grasp more readily its general purpose and line of thought, and so be in a better position to appreciate its poetic beauties. But the *Prometheus* must not be regarded as a puzzle to be solved by ingenious interpretations, nor must the allegory be forced, especially in details. The poem is much more a medium for the expression of emotions with regard to certain great subjects than an expedient for the systematic statement of a philosophy.[1] Further, its greatness is lyric, not dramatic. In her introduction to the poem, Miss Scudder admirably says : " His [Shelley's] is not the Shakespearean power of dramatic construction, dependent on the clash of character with events ; neither is it exactly the intellectual power shown in a noble development of thought — experience like Tennyson's in *In Memoriam*. Shelley's power is more akin to that of the musician. . . . The unity of the poem then, since akin to the unity of music, is primarily emotional."

[1] Compare the poet's statement in the Preface (p. 53).

ACT I.

Scene. The scene suggested is similar to that of Æschylus's *Prometheus Vinctus.* Compare also Shelley's Journal, March 26, 1818 : "After dinner we ascended Les Échelles, winding along a road cut through perpendicular rocks, of immense elevation. . . . The rocks, which cannot be less than a thousand feet in perpendicular height, sometimes overhang the road on each side, and almost shut out the sky. The scene is like that described in the Prometheus of Æschylus : — vast rifts and caverns in the granite precipices ; wintry mountains with ice and snow above ; the loud sounds of unseen waters within the caverns, and walls of toppling rocks, only to be scaled as he describes, by the wingèd chariot of the ocean nymphs."

54 2. **But One :** Prometheus himself; cf. l. 265.

54 9. **eyeless in hate :** blind in thy hatred ; the phrase belongs to "thou" (l. 10).

54 15. The versification is defective ; Mr. Forman suggests that "empire" should be pronounced as a trisyllable, or that "empery" should be read ; cf. *Letter to Maria Gisborne,* l. 34.

55 25-52. Cf. Æschylus, *Prom. Vinct.,* ll. 88-99.

ὦ δῖος αἰθὴρ καὶ ταχύπτεροι πνοαί,
ποταμῶν τε πηγαὶ ποντίων τε κυμάτων
ἀνήριθμον γέλασμα, παμμῆτόρ τε γῆ,
καὶ τὸν πανόπτην κύκλον ἡλίου καλῶ·
ἴδεσθέ μ᾽ οἷα πρὸς θεῶν πάσχω θεός.

*   *   *   *   *

φεῦ φεῦ, τὸ παρὸν τό τ᾽ ἐπερχόμενον
πῆμα στενάχω.

55 32. **moon-freezing :** freezing in the moonlight.

55 34. **Heaven's wingèd hound :** The vulture, which, according to the old story, tore the entrails of Prometheus ; the phrase is a translation from Æschylus : Διὸς δέ τοι πτηνὸς κύων δαφοινὸς ἀετὸς (*Prom. Vinct.,* ll. 1021-2).

55 41-47. Cf. *Prom. Vinct.,* ll. 23-25.

56 53-59. The change from hatred to pity seems to be the first step towards the release of Prometheus.

56 54. Forman suggests that both metre and sense would be improved by the omission of "the."

56 62. **wrinkling :** shrivelling.

56 73-111. As the curse predicted the fall of the tyrant, the horror and misery of the speakers were not due to personal considerations ; it must have been the mere terror and awfulness of the curse that overcame them.

58 104. For the rhyme, cf. *Hymn to Intellectual Beauty*, ll. 50–51, with note.

58 124. **informs** : animates ; cf. Tennyson's *Freedom*, stanza i :

> O Thou so fair in summers gone,
> While yet thy fresh and virgin soul
> Informed the pillar'd Parthenon,
> The glittering Capitol.

59 137. **love** : probably for *lovest* (so Swinburne interprets) ; cf. *The Skylark*, l. 80, " Thou lovest, but ne'er *knew* love's sad satiety " ; also *Epipsychidion*, l. 369. It has been suggested that "love" is a noun, the subject of *is moving near ;* this seems feeble. Mr. Rossetti ingeniously suggests : *Jove — how cursed I him ?* but this is not in the style of Shelley. Mr. Forman interprets "love" in the first person, *I love.*

61 191-209. The idea of a world of shades may have been suggested by Plato's notion of archetypes. What purpose or deeper meaning Shelley had in introducing this idea into the poem is not very clear. All things which have existed, still continue to live in the past, as we say ; they maintain what may be called a shadowy existence, and may be evoked by memory ; so with Prometheus's curse, which is dead so far as its author is concerned. The source of the reference to Zoroaster has not been discovered. Shelley himself had a vision of his own spectre, but at a time subsequent to the writing of *Prometheus* (see Dowden's *Life*, Vol. II, p. 516).

62 212. **Hades or Typhon** : the former word is here used for Pluto, the presiding divinity of Hades, or the lower world, as in *Paradise Lost*, II, l. 964. *Typhon*, one of the monsters of the primitive world, is described by Prometheus himself (*Prom. Vinct.*, ll. 354 ff.) as hurled beneath Mount Ætna by Zeus for resisting the gods.

64 272-3. Authority gets the right from men to control them externally, but one man cannot confer on another the power of self-control or power over the *will* of others.

65 294. **Both** : both evil and good deeds.

65 295. **thou** and **solitude** are in the same construction as "universe " in the preceding line.

66 324. A serpent-cinctured wand: the rod entwined with two serpents borne by Mercury, and known as the *Caduceus.*

68 342. the Son of Maia: Mercury, the herald of Jove. The attitude of Mercury towards Prometheus is similar to that of Hephæstus in the *Prometheus Vinctus.*

68 346–7. Geryon, etc.: monsters of classical fable.

68 348–350. The Sphinx propounded a riddle to the Thebans as they passed, and slew those who could not guess it. At length Œdipus solved the riddle and delivered Thebes. He was rewarded with the hand of Queen Jocasta, — the two, although the fact was not known, being really mother and son. The consequence of this incestuous union was a series of dire calamities, which afforded favorite themes for Greek tragedy.

68 353. Cf. the words of Hephæstus in *Prom. Vinct.,* l. 19.

69 371–3. In Æschylus, also, Prometheus knows such a secret; see *Prom. Vinct.,* ll. 947–8.

69 375–6. The secret when revealed will be an intercessor on behalf of Prometheus. This is a striking example in miniature of Shelley's mythopœic faculty (cf. note on *The Cloud,* p. 341).

69 385. crystal-wingèd snow: cf. λευκοπτέρῳ νιφάδι (white-winged snow) in *Prom. Vinct.,* l. 993.

70 398. " Damocles having extolled the great felicity of Dionysius on account of his wealth and power, the tyrant invited him to try what his happiness really was, and placed him at a magnificent banquet, in the midst of which Damocles saw a naked sword suspended over his head by a single horsehair — a sight which quickly dispelled all his visions of happiness."

70 396–9. The only submission which Jupiter is willing to accept is the revelation of the destiny which is impending over him like the sword of Damocles; but that revelation would assure the power of Jupiter and the slavery of mankind.

70 403–5. Justice will not punish those who sin against her laws; those who sin inflict a more than sufficient punishment on themselves.

71 429–431. The same idea is contained in the *Prom. Vinct.,* ll. 966–9.

72 442. hollow: this adjective belongs to "they" (l. 440), not to "wings."

73 452–7. The Furies represent the various causes of pain and suffering among men.

74 483–491. The foul and evil ideas which arise in the mind are represented as springing from external influences, but are so subtly infused that the sufferer thinks they originate with himself; cf. the wide-spread notion of the suggestions of Satan and his ministers.

75 498–532. Various forms in which evil and misery exist among men are here indicated.

75 513–516. The dread of Hell makes men cruel.

77 539–545. The veil of futurity is torn, and Prometheus sees how evil comes out of good ; the perception of this is the keenest agony which he has to endure.

77 546. The reference is to the Founder of Christianity.

77 546–654. Particular instances of good resulting in evil are represented : (1st) the developments of Christianity in ll. 546–566, 586–631 ; (2d) the French Revolution and its consequences in ll. 567–577, 648–654.

80 618–631. The degradation of the inner nature is worse than the bodily anguish which has been described. In this passage we have a picture of the actual world as it appeared in Shelley's eyes.

81 634. The persistence of good in the heart of Prometheus enables him to rise superior to his torments.

82 657–670. The Spirits sent by the Earth to comfort Prometheus are embodiments of the joy which arises from good impulses, actions, etc. : the first Spirit tells of heroic action ; the second, of heroic self-sacrifice ; the third, of wisdom ; the fourth, of the creative power of the poetic imagination ; the fifth and sixth, of the beautiful ideals of love.

84 712. **Between :** the commas after " Between " and " cloud " are not in the original editions, but are inserted by Forman and Dowden to bring out the meaning of the passage. Forman considers " Be-tween " equivalent to *through*, and cites, for this sense of the word :
" Between one foliaged lattice twinkling fair " (*Alastor*, l. 464) and *The Cloud*, ll. 69, 70, for the image. The meaning would then be *through the rainbow's arch*. But Forman also suggests, what seems to be the true explanation, that " Between " means *between arch and sea*.

85 737–749. Professor Winchester notes how vividly suggestive of Shelley's own poetic temper this passage is ; *e.g.*, ll. 746–8, as regards material beauty.

86 765–770. Love in the actual world is followed by disappointment and pain ; so, at least, it had been in the poet's experience.

86 770. The punctuation is that of the original; if correct, " I wandered o'er " must mean *I continued my wanderings.* Mr. Forman believes that the punctuation subverts the sense, and that " I wandered o'er " is a relative clause describing " night."

86 772–5. Cf. " For Homer says, that the Goddess Calamity is deli-cate, and that her feet are tender. ' Her feet are soft,' he says, ' for she treads not upon the ground, but makes her paths upon the heads of men '" (Shelley's translation of *The Banquet* of Plato. Forman's edition, Vol. VII, p. 196).

88 807-833. The thoughts of the hero turn to Asia, and we are prepared for her appearance in the next act.

ACT II, SCENE I.

89 1-12. The similes in this passage are examples of the imagery referred to in the fourth paragraph of Shelley's Preface to the poem (see p. 50).

90 14. **thou** : Panthea.

90 26 **Æolian** : the music is produced by the wind, like that of the æolian harp. The adjective is derived from *Æolus*, the name of the god of the wind.

90 31. **that soul** : Prometheus.

90 38-55. In happier seasons, when the spirit attains its ideal, faith and hope are not needful ; but now Panthea (faith) is busily employed as a messenger between Asia and Prometheus.

91 62-92. In her first dream, Faith sees by anticipation the triumph of good.

92 93-106. Hope can only vaguely shape the picture of the ideal.

94 127-141. This second dream of Faith is a dream of the period of transition from present evil to future perfection   It is a "rude," "wild," and "quick" period of arduous pursuit.

94 140. The story goes that Apollo inadvertently killed Hyacinthus, whom he loved.   The latter was changed into a flower on whose leaves might be discerned the Greek interjection to express woe, AI.

95 165. "Mr. Rossetti suspects that *around* is a misprint for *among* or *amid*,— finding some difficulty in regard to a being 'around the crags.' My impression is that the word *around* is Shelley's, and that Asia simply means some diffused, elemental being, such as one would expect to find in a poem full of symbolic supernaturalism, — some spirit, perhaps, similar in character to those described by the Earth in ll. 658-661, Act I " (Forman's note).

ACT II, SCENE II.

The forest scene seems to symbolize human life, with its material beauty (described in *Semi-chorus* I), its emotional experiences (*Semi-chorus* II), and its intellectual impulses and perceptions (*Semi-chorus* III).

99 38. Like the music from a flute played on a lake.

99 50. **the destined** : the chosen few who seize the truth of things. The reading of the line is that of the MS. at Boscombe. In the first edition the line was printed, " And wakes the destined soft emotion." Mrs. Shelley in her first edition of 1839 inserted a colon after "destined " ; in her second edition this is changed to a comma.

99 62. **the fatal mountain** " is probably that to which Panthea and Asia are advancing, and where we find them at the beginning of the next scene " (Miss Scudder's note).

101 90. **thwart** : perverse, ill-tempered.

Silenus is associated, in ancient story, with the fauns and satyrs who represent the powers of nature ; Silenus had the gifts of song and prophecy.

ACT II, SCENE III.

Asia and Panthea have passed out of the world of ordinary experience represented by the forest of the previous scene, and rise to the arduous and lofty heights of thought symbolized by the mountainous scenery here presented.

101 9. **mænads** : the frenzied followers of Bacchus ; one of their cries was *Evoe*.

101 12-15. This hypothesis is in harmony with the revelations of Demogorgon in the next scene, as Asia herself says in ll. 121-2 of Scene iv.

102 40-42. An illustration of the species of imagery spoken of in the Preface, p. 50. The simile possibly gives an inkling of the symbolic meaning of the whole description.

103 54. The " Song of Spirits " shows that to attain truth we must get beyond the mere *phenomena*, the visible aspects of things, to the real, eternal world of which these are but shadows. Shelley found suggestions for this mysticism in the works of Plato and Berkeley.

104 74. Where the air is not a medium through which light passes, *i.e.*, where there is no light. The reference in "prism" is to the *use*, not to the *form* of the prism.

104 93-98. " The power of Demogorgon can be set free only when love has attained to utter self-abnegation " (Miss Scudder). In this last stanza we pass from the *intellectual* conditions of the successful pursuit of truth, to the *moral*.

ACT II, SCENE IV.

Demogorgon: this name is employed by various writers to designate a powerful and mysterious spirit. Milton (*Paradise Lost*, II,
l. 965), speaking of the "throne of Chaos" and of "Night eldest of
things," places beside it

> Orcus and Ades, and the dreaded name
> Of Demogorgon.

Spenser (*Faerie Queen*, I, l. 37) mentions "Great Gorgon, prince of
darkness and of night," Greene (*Friar Bacon and Friar Bungay*, XI,
l. 110), "Demogorgon, master of the fates." According to Lactantius,
an ancient commentator on Statius, Demogorgon is the origin and first
of all the gods, and is alluded to, though not named, both by Statius and
by Lucan in, *e.g., Pharsalia*, VI, ll. 496–9 and 744–8. See for the various
references Ackermann, *Englische Studien*, XVI, pp. 34–37. The ideas
connected with Demogorgon in earlier literature are, therefore, in harmony with the interpretation of this personage given in the introductory
note, p. 318–319.

106 12. **which** has no verb to complete it; this is probably due to
the author's oversight, not to corruption in the text.

106 12–18. Cf. this statement with the similar one in the *Essay on
Love* (Forman's edition, Vol. VII, p. 269).

106 28 ff. The ultimate source of evil is not traced to God, but to
some power of which nothing is known save that it is a power. Evil
comes from Jupiter, it is true; but Jupiter is in himself powerless, and
the evil which springs from him may, and will, in time be got rid of.
But there is more deeply implanted in the universe a mysterious source
of evil of which man knows nothing, and upon which he can exert no
influence. Shelley, as others, found the problem of the origin of evil
insoluble, and thrust it back into a vague and remote mystery.

107 32 ff. In this passage we have an embodiment in myth of
Shelley's ideas as to the history of the universe. First, there is dimly
indicated the existence of absolute, eternal entities. Then, with Saturn,
"from whose throne time fell," began the world of phenomena, the
actual world which appears to our senses. Originally mankind was
like a child, innocent and enjoying its existence, with self-conscious-
ness and intellectual power scarcely developed. With the growth of
the latter came wisdom and knowledge; men improved their conditions by inventing institutions, organizing themselves. Hence there
arose government and authority, symbolized in this poem as Jupiter.

Wisdom enthroned these on condition that men should not be enslaved by them, but should preserve the spirit of liberty, of free investigation; institutions must not blind or impede the spirit of man. But the natural tendency of authority is to evil (ll. 47-48). From the consequent degradation came the miseries of humanity. Then the spirit of man was roused to produce alleviations for his sad condition (l. 59),— ideas, feelings, inventions for increasing his bodily comfort, the discoveries of science, and the creations of art.

107 43-100. In Æschylus, also, Jupiter wins his sovereignty by the aid of Prometheus (*Prom. Vinct.*, ll. 219-223); and the benefits which, according to Asia, are conferred upon humanity by Prometheus are similar to those mentioned in the older drama. This whole passage may be compared with ll. 435-506 of the *Prometheus Vinctus.*

108 61. **Nepenthe** was a magic drug which caused forgetfulness of care and sorrow (see *Odyssey*, IV, 221).

Moly was the herb given by Hermes to Ulysses to preserve him against the spells of Circe (see *Odyssey*, X, 302-6, and cf. Milton, *Comus*, l. 636).

Amaranth: the word means originally *unfading*, and is used by Milton to designate one of the flowers inwoven in the crowns of the angels of Heaven:

> Immortal amarant, a flower which once
> In Paradise fast by the tree of Life
> Began to bloom, but soon for Man's offence
> To Heaven remov'd, where first it grew, there grows
> And flowers aloft shading the fount of Life.
>
> *Paradise Lost*, III, ll. 353-7.

108 80-84. Mr. Swinburne says (*Essays and Studies*, p. 198): "The simplest explanation here possible is, I believe, the right. Women with child gazing on statues (say on the Venus of Melos) bring forth children like them — children whose features reflect the passion of the gaze and perfection of the sculptured beauty; men, seeing, are consumed with love; 'perish' meaning simply '*deperire*'; cf. Virgil's well-worn version, 'ut vidi, ut perii.'" This interpretation may seem far-fetched, but is confirmed by Act IV, ll. 412-414.

109 91. **interlunar:** in the absence of the moon; a favorite word with Shelley, who found it in Milton's *Samson Agonistes*, l. 89

> Silent as the moon
> Hid in her vacant interlunar cave.

109 100. **rains**: this is the reading of Mrs. Shelley's editions, and is adopted by Rossetti, Dowden, and Woodberry. The editions published in Shelley's lifetime read *reigns*, which is retained by Forman, who says: "The statement made is that Jove does *not reign* down evil. If it were that he did not *rain* down evil, it would be contradictory of the whole conception of Jove in this poem." But the point in the passage before us is that Jove is not the ultimate source of evil; he, too, is enslaved.

109 112 ff. Understanding from Demogorgon's last reply that the power of Jupiter is not ultimate, Asia naturally reverts to "God," of whom Demogorgon had already spoken, and asks for a further description of God, so that she may know whether God is the ultimate cause.

In the following passage Shelley's meaning seems to be that, in the ordinary sense of the word "God," Jupiter is God ; he is supreme in the world of phenomena. But behind these phenomena lies absolute existence — the permanent laws and conditions of the universe to which all things are subject. Shelley finds language inadequate to express this mystery ; these absolute forces are not *personal;* he merely adumbrates them by words like "Fate," "Time," etc. (l. 119). This notion of a dim, inexplicable force behind everything else was held also by the Greeks in their conception of a Fate to which the gods themselves are subject. We find this idea expressed in the *Prom. Vinct.*, ll. 515–518:

> Χο. τίς οὖν ἀνάγκης ἐστὶν οἰακοστρόφος;
> Πρ. Μοῖραι τρίμορφοι μνήμονές τ' Ἐρινύες.
> Χο. τούτων ἄρα Ζεύς ἐστιν ἀσθενέστερος;
> Πρ. οὔκουν ἂν ἐκφύγοι γε τὴν πεπρωμένην,

which is thus translated by Plumptre:

> CHORUS. Who guides the helm, then, of necessity ?
> PROM. Fates triple-formed, Erinnyes unforgetting.
> CHORUS. Is Zeus, then, weaker in his might than these ?
> PROM. Not even he can 'scape the thing decreed.

Shelley makes an exception to this all-pervading power: Eternal Love is not subject to it. By this he seems to indicate that there is a spirit present in the universe, — a spirit in which men share, — which rises superior to all conditions and forces; just as many thinkers except from the dominion of necessity the will of rational creatures. Shelley, in short, conceives the universe here, as in the *Adonais*, to be dualistic: on the one hand, there is a sort of body, inert, and sometimes positively evil; and on the other, a spirit of Beauty and Love working in and through it, hampered by the body, yet rising superior to it.

110 121-2. Cf. Act II, iii, 12–16.

110 122-3. The poet means that no one can adequately express for another the ideas at which he has been hinting. Each one must interpret them in detail for himself.

111 142. This "spirit" is the spirit of the hour of Jupiter's doom.

111 156. This second spirit is that of the hour of Prometheus's release.

ACT II, SCENE V.

113 20-31. This passage, with its reference to the birth of Aphrodite (Venus) from the sea, serves to identify Asia in some measure with Venus, and, of course, with the *Uranian* Venus.

114 48. The "Voice" (in the stage direction) is doubtless the voice of Prometheus, who is also addressed in the song of Asia which follows.

114 52. **looks.** "It has been suggested to read *locks* instead of *looks*, but Mr. Garnett (*Relics of Shelley*, p. 98) settled the point by recording that 'in an Italian prose translation made by Shelley himself the disputed word is rendered *sguardi*'" (Forman's note).

Mr. Forman illustrates the meaning of these lines by the following quotation from a letter of Shelley to Peacock (April 6, 1819), where he says of Roman beauties: "The only inferior part are the eyes, which, though good and gentle, want the mazy depth of colour behind colour, with which the intellectual women of England and Germany entangle the heart in soul-inwoven labyrinths."

115 62. it: the liquid splendour in which thou art clothed. The " for " introduces the reason that " none beholds thee."

115 65. " The strange words 'lost for ever' express that passionate self-abandonment which possesses those that yearn after the unattainable ideal " (Todhunter, *A Study of Shelley*, p. 167).

115 72 ff. This song affords a wonderful example of the use of imagery, not as a symbol to be intellectually interpreted, but like notes of music, to suggest and stimulate a certain train of feeling, — the ineffable sense of the perfect satisfaction of every desire.

116 96. **and** is not in the original editions ; it is a conjecture of Mr. Rossetti; adopted by Forman and Dowden.

116 98-103. The periods of life are mentioned in reverse order, as if the spirit were moving backward to the infinite world from which it originally came.

116 108-110. The structure and rhythm of the last two lines are extraordinarily awkward; " rest " is in the same construction as " see "; "somewhat like thee " belongs to " shapes."

Act III, Scene I.

117 13. **night** is the reading of Mrs. Shelley's edition, adopted by Rossetti, Dowden, and Woodberry; *might* is the reading of the edition published in Shelley's lifetime, and is retained by Forman.

117 25. **Idæan Ganymede:** Ganymede was the cup-bearer of Jupiter. He was of Trojan descent, and was carried off from Mount Ida in the neighborhood of Troy.

117 26. **Dædal:** skilfully wrought. A favorite word with Shelley; cf. Act IV, ll. 116, 416; *Ode to Liberty*, l. 18; *Hymn of Pan*, l. 26, etc.

118 40. The allusion is to a passage in Lucan's *Pharsalia*, IX, ll. 763–788, which describes the death of a soldier by the bite of a *seps*, a species of poisonous serpent.

119 72-73. For a full description of such a conflict, see *The Revolt of Islam*, Canto I, vi–xiv.

Act III, Scene II.

120 11. "This speech is printed precisely as in Shelley's edition; but it is open to some doubt whether a line is not lost. We may, however, be meant to understand simply, 'an eagle *sinks* so *when* caught in some bursting cloud '" (Forman's note).

121 24. **Proteus:** a personage of ancient myth, the old man of the sea, who possessed prophetic gifts and the power of transforming himself into various shapes; see Virgil's *Georgics*, IV, 387–414.

Act III, Scene III.

122 10 ff. There is a similar description of a paradise in *Epipsychidion*, ll. 422 ff.

122 15-17. A description of stalactites.

123 42. **Enna:** a city in the centre of Sicily; cf. *Paradise Lost*, IV, ll. 268–271:

> Not that fair field
> Of Enna, where Proserpine gathering flowers,
> Herself a fairer flower by gloomy Dis
> Was gathered.

123 43. **Himera** was the name of a river in the neighborhood of Enna; in this passage the name appears to be transferred to the country.

123 49-53. The lovely creations of art shall visit us, less splendid at first, but afterwards radiant, when the mind of the artist, from familiarity with actual beauty, shall be able to give to the phantoms of the imagination the excellences which exist in reality.

124 64-68. Proteus (see note on III, ii, 24, above) had prophetic powers, and may, therefore, be appropriately represented as the giver of the trumpet which announces the inauguration of a new era.

125 85-104. The poet represents material nature as changing through some mysterious sympathy with the moral renovation of man.

125 105-114. The poet considers that men will still be subject to death and mutability (see l. 25 above, and ll. 200-1 of sc. iv).

126 110-114. ' Only those who have experienced death can understand what it is.' To Shelley death remained an inexplicable mystery. The most satisfactory view of it to him is that expressed in ll. 113-114 : What we call life is that which hides real existence from us ; we shall enter fully into life after we have died ; hence what we call *life* is, truly considered, *death*. Cf. the *Sonnet* on p. 44, and *Adonais*, stanzas xxxix, xli, and lii.

126 123. It is a question whether this is the same cavern as that described by Prometheus (l. 10 above), or a different one. The two descriptions may be due to inadvertence on the part of the poet.

127 154. **Nysa**: the legendary scene of the nurture of Bacchus, whose frenzied female followers were called Mænads.

127 161. Apparently a second temple beside the cave.

127 165. **Praxitelean shapes**: shapes possessing the perfection of the statues of Praxiteles, one of the greatest of Greek sculptors, who flourished about 464 B.C.

ACT III, SCENE IV.

Spirit of the Earth (stage direction): Mr. Rossetti says in his article on *Prometheus Unbound* (*Shelley Society Papers*): " My own opinion is that the Winged-child Spirit [introduced at the close of the last scene] and the Spirit of the Earth are probably not the same personage. . . . If the spirits are indeed two, as I think, they have a strange unity in duality; if they are one, they are an unaccountable duality in unity; for their recorded performances in the two scenes appear to be positively at odds *inter se*." To the present editor it seems probable that the poet intended one and the same character in the two scenes. In the *Spirit of the Earth* the poet represents the natural tendencies of the Earth as a whole (as in common talk we

speak of the spirit of an age, of a nation, etc.). These natural tendencies are innocent and good, and had free scope in the early Golden
Age (see ll. 15–16), but were still undeveloped when the reign of evil
came to check them. Hence, the Spirit was and still remains a child,
but has begun to grow again, and will, by and by, reach man's estate.
This natural good tendency of earthly things is a portion of the universal spirit of beauty and love; hence, its embodiment (the child) is
closely connected with Asia and calls her " mother."

129 19. **dipsas**: a serpent mentioned in Lucan's *Pharsalia*, IX,
l. 610, whose bite caused intense thirst.

129 24. The action of the Spirit here, as well as the previous conversation of Panthea and Ione, would lead us to suppose that it now
meets them for the first time instead of having accompanied them
" beyond the peak of Bacchic Nysa," etc. (sc. iii, l. 148 ff.), as the identification with the " Winged-child " of the previous scene implies.

130 54. The sounding of the shell is referred to (see Act III, iii,
64–83).

131 94. **interlunar air**: the air from which the moon is absent;
cf. note on Act II, iv, 91.

132 106. The punctuation of the text is that of the original. The
sense would be better indicated by putting, as Professor Woodberry
does, a semicolon at the end of the line: ' As I dizzy with delight
floated down, my coursers,' etc.

132 110. **Pasturing flowers** evidently means ' pasturing on flowers.'
Mr. Forman conjectures that *on* is omitted through inadvertence.

132 112. **Phidian**: cf. " Praxitelean " in III, iii, 165, above. Phidias
was the greatest of Greek sculptors; died 432 B.C.

132 119. **amphisbenic snake**: a snake with a head at each end.
Antique chariot spokes were sometimes made in this form, but Mr.
Forman is " inclined to think Shelley's own fancy adapted to this use
the prodigy found with the seps and the dipsas in Bk. IX of Lucan's
Pharsalia."

132 136. This is a translation of the inscription on the gate of Hell,
according to Dante's *Inferno*, III, 9.

132 149–152. The ordinary hollow talk of society, where one assents
from mere complacency to things which the heart denies; yet in this
assent there is no definite hypocritical purpose, although such behavior
leads to mistrust of our own sincerity.

134 164–179. This sentence is long-drawn and obscure, but the meaning becomes apparent on examination. The following interpretation is
by Professor Woodberry: " The emblems of Power and Faith stand in

the new world unregarded and mouldering memorials of a dead past, just as the Egyptian monuments imaged to a later time than their own a vanished monarchy and religion ; the fact that these monuments survive the new race and last into our still later time is an unnecessary and subordinate incident, inserted because it appealed to Shelley's imagination."

134 172. The punctuation is that of the original. Mr. Rossetti puts a comma after "conquerors" and a period after "round," and, consequently, connects "mouldering" with "palaces and tombs."

134 173. those refers to "monstrous and barbaric shapes."

imaged is the past tense (as Forman, Rossetti, and Woodberry interpret), not the past participle, as Mr. Swinburne supposes (*Essays and Studies*, p. 200).

134 190-2. Compare the opening lines of the *Sonnet*, on p. 44, and *Adonais*, ll. 462-5.

134 193-8. The colon after "man" (l. 194) and the period after "man" (l. 197) are inserted from Mr. Rossetti's emendations of the punctuation of the original editions, where there are no stops whatever after these words. These changes seem to be required by the sense, and are rendered more plausible by the fact that at the ends of lines stops are apt to fall out. Mr. Rossetti makes other changes in the punctuation of the passage which make the connection more obvious, but are not absolutely necessary. He prints :

> The man remains, —
> Sceptreless, free, uncircumscribed ; but man :
> Equal, unclassed, tribeless, and nationless,
> Exempt from awe, worship, degree, the king
> Over himself ; just, gentle, wise : but man.
> Passionless ? no ; yet free from guilt or pain, —

With no stops at the end of ll. 194 and 197, as the original editions read, the "but" in these two lines seems out of place. Mr. Forman and Professor Woodberry retain the punctuation of the original editions, and the former argues in behalf of it : " He [Mr. Rossetti] objects to this *but* on the ground that there is no antithesis, but the contrary, between the epithets which precede and follow it. If the *but* were what Mr. Rossetti takes it to be, this statement is obviously true ; but this must not be too hastily admitted. I leave the passage as I find it, because I see no great difficulty and suspect no corruption whatever, though the forms of expression are certainly eccentric. The *but* in dispute I take to be used in the common sense of *only, merely*. . . .

The insertion of a full stop at *man* in l. 197 seems to me to destroy the one great antithesis that the poet meant to express : I cannot think he meant, as Mr. Rossetti says, that man, though equal, the king over himself, etc., is still man. The antithesis which he seems to me to have meant to emphasize is man equal and thoroughly emancipated from artificial laws and restraints, but not man passionless, — man exempt from guilt and pain; but not from death and mutability."

134 194 ff. Note Shelley's dislike of all authority as brought out in the picture of perfected humanity; there is absolutely no social organization.

135 200-1. It is noteworthy that Shelley's conception of the highest perfection of which the universe is capable admits the existence of defects ; these, however, and even death itself, lose their terrors for mankind through the force of the individual will, through assuming the proper attitude of mind with regard to them.

ACT IV.

Act IV was an afterthought. Mrs. Shelley says : " At first he completed the drama in three acts. It was not till several months after, when at Florence, that he conceived that a fourth act, a sort of hymn of rejoicing in the fulfilment of the prophecies with regard to Prometheus, ought to be added to complete the composition." Panthea and Ione (Faith and Hope) are present throughout the act and serve to describe the scene and interpret the other characters.

135 1-39. The past is buried.

137 40-80. A new spirit rules all things.

139 93-128. The Spirits of the Human Mind tell of the pursuits of regenerated humanity.

140 116. **Dædal** : here, as usual, the word may be interpreted 'skilfully wrought' (see note on Act III, i, 26); but the word may perhaps be used with special reference to the wings which Dædalus invented and with which he soared heavenward.

142 180. The dialogue serves to divide the first and second lyrical interludes.

143 184. **unpavilioned sky** : the sky from the pavilion of clouds has vanished ; cf. *The Cloud*, l. 78.

143 202. **Two visions** : the chariot of the Earth and the chariot of the Moon.

144 206-235. Description of the Moon and her chariot.

144 213. **Regard** : look like; an odd use of the word as an intransitive verb.

144 221. Mr. Rossetti proposes to improve the versification by interchanging "feathers " and "plumes "; but the rhythm of the verse as it stands seems Shelleyan.

145 236–318. Description of the Earth and his chariot.

145 242. and before "green" is not in the original editions, but is inserted by Rossetti, followed by Forman.

146 272. tyrant-quelling myrtle : the epithet is doubtless suggested by the story of the Athenian heroes, Harmodius and Aristogeiton, who hid their swords in myrtle wreaths when they made their attack on the tyrant of their city, 514 B.C.

146 281. Valueless : invaluable ; cf. *unvalued* with the same meaning, *Arethusa*, l. 60.

147 302. If "over" means *outside of*, the strata are in the reverse order to the natural one.

147 325. Brother mine : the Earth who is the speaker in this dialogue is evidently not the same character as the Earth who appears in the first act. That "Earth" is feminine, the mother of the Titans, and corresponds to the Greek *Gaia*. The description of the figure of the Earth in the chariot (ll. 261–8 above) would correspond with the *Spirit of the Earth* in Act III, sc. iv, but the language of the speeches suits better the *Earth* of Act I. Mr. James Thomson (as quoted by Miss Scudder) asserts that the speaker in Act IV corresponds to neither of the earlier personifications, but is " our own natural Earth, the living enduring root of these and of all other conceptions, mythologic, imaginative, rational ; the animate World-sphere instinct with spirit, personified as masculine in relation to the feminine Moon." On the other hand, Mr. Forman has no " moral doubt that we should read *The Spirit of the Earth* and *The Spirit of the Moon*, for *The Earth* and *The Moon*," from this point onward ; because, " in the first place, *The Spirit of the Earth* and *The Spirit of the Moon* are introduced explicitly in the long speeches of Ione and Panthea, ll. 194–318, immediately preceding the choric dialogue in question. Secondly, this Spirit that guides the Earth is told by Asia, in Act III, sc. iv, that they will never part till his ' chaste sister who guides the frozen and inconstant moon ' shall love him ; and when he asks — ' What; as Asia loves Prometheus ? ' — the reply is, ' Peace, wanton, thou art yet not old enough ' : from which, I imagine, we are to assume that in the interval he has grown old enough, and the prophecy of love from *The Spirit of the Moon* is under fulfilment. Thirdly, Mrs. Shelley, in her first edition of 1839, inserted a new dramatis persona, *The Spirit of the Moon*, presumably from Shelley's list of errata; and there are no speeches but these of *The Moon* to assign to such a person."

149 370. **It :** love.

150 394-9. **Man, oh, not men !** Man considered as making a unity, not regarded as composed of individuals with conflicting interests; as a whole united by love, as the solar system is held in unity and order by the sun. The passage is interesting both as exhibiting Shelley's tendency to abstractions and his yearning for simplicity and unity, and also as a sort of anticipation of the socialistic ideal.

150 408. A spirit which it is difficult to guide, but which is strong in exacting obedience.

151 412-413. Man embodies his dreams in statuary and painting.

151 414. The idea here is the same as that explained in the note on ll. 83-84 of Act. II, sc. iv.

151 415. **Orphic:** perhaps here means no more than 'poetic.' Orpheus was the father of Greek poetry; but the adjective *Orphic* usually suggests poetry of a sacred or mystic character.

151 416. **Dædal:** see note on Act III, i, 26.

151 418. The preceding stanza speaks of man's artistic activity ; here reference is made to his skill in science.

151 432. **unfrozen :** this is the reading of Mrs. Shelley's editions (followed by Forman, Dowden, and Woodberry). Mr. Rossetti reads *infrozen*, following the editions published in Shelley's lifetime.

153 473. **Mænad :** see note on Act II, iii, 9.

153 474-5. **Agave** was the daughter of Cadmus, the mythical founder of Thebes. Shelley has in mind here those scenes of the *Bacchæ* of Euripides, where Agave is the leader of the Theban women in their Bacchic orgies.

156 534-8. Whether the dead become a portion of the all-pervading spirit of the universe (see *Adonais*, stanzas xlii, xliii), or utterly pass away.

156 551. Cf. Wordsworth's " She was a phantom of delight," l. 24 :

> A Traveller between life and death.

157 554-5. The day on which Heaven's despotism is to be swallowed up by the abyss, through the influence of Prometheus. Prometheus is called " earth-born " as being a Titan; the Titans were sons of Heaven and Earth.

157 562-578. Demogorgon sums up the moral of the drama. The virtues mentioned in l. 562 are the assurance that the happy era will be maintained ; and should evil (here represented as a serpent) once more gain the upper hand, these virtues afford the means of subduing it.

The final stanza expresses what, in Shelley's opinion, is the proper attitude, even in our own times, of those who desire the renovation of mankind.

SONNET: ENGLAND IN 1819.

9. There is a semicolon at the end of this line, in Mrs. Shelley's edition of 1839 (when this sonnet was first published), and a comma in her second edition. Both Mr. Forman and Professor Dowden read without any stop at the end of the line.

ODE TO THE WEST WIND.

Mr. Stopford Brooke says of this ode : " The emotion awakened by the approaching storm sets on fire other sleeping emotions in his heart, and the whole of his being bursts into flame around the first emotion. This is the manner of the genesis of all the noblest lyrics. He passes from magnificent union of himself with Nature and magnificent realization of her storm and peace, to equally great self-description, and then mingles all nature and himself together, that he may sing of the restoration of mankind. There is no song in the whole of our literature more passionate, more penetrative, more full of the force by which the idea and its form are united in one creation " (Preface to *Poems of Shelley*, p. xvii).

The *terza rima* (aba, bcb, cdc, etc.), employed in this poem, is but little used in English poetry. The suitability here of the stanza form to the theme should be noted. The series of sustained waves of feeling, each closing in an invocation, corresponds to the suspended rhyme of each triplet, resolved at the close of each fourth stanza by the couplet, with its sense of completeness.

THE INDIAN SERENADE.

There are several versions of this poem, all seemingly originating with Shelley himself. It appeared in print in *The Liberal*, 1822, under the title *Song, written for an Indian Air;* Mrs. Shelley published it among the *Posthumous Poems* as *Lines to an Indian Air.* In 1819 Shelley gave a MS. copy of the poem to Miss Sophia Stacey, and this MS. still exists; another MS., found on Shelley's person after his death, is described by Browning in a letter to Leigh Hunt; still another MS. is in the Harvard collection.

163 4. **shining:** "burning" in *The Liberal* and the Harvard MS.

163 11. So the line reads in *The Liberal*, the Harvard MS., and the *Posthumous Poems*; but "And the Champak's odours fail" in the reading of the Browning MS., followed by Forman; Dowden reads, "And the champak."

Champak: "this plant is mentioned as *chumpak* in Sketches of Hindoostan (p. 96), where Medwin explains that it is jasmine" (Forman's note).

163 15. So the line reads in *The Liberal* and *Posthumous Poems*, as also, apparently, in the Browning MS. The Harvard MS. and Mrs. Shelley's later edition read, "As I must die on thine"; this version is adopted by Woodberry.

163 16. So the line reads in the Browning MS., Harvard MS., and Mrs. Shelley's later edition; but *The Liberal* and the *Posthumous Poems* omit the "O."

163 23. This is the reading of the Browning MS., followed by Forman and Dowden; "press me to thine own" is found in *The Liberal;* "press it close to thine again" in the Harvard MS. and in Mrs. Shelley's editions.

SOPHIA.

These stanzas were addressed to Miss Sophia Stacey. "This lady," says Mr. Rossetti "was a ward of Mr. Parker, an uncle by marriage of Shelley, living in Bath. She saw a good deal of the poet and his wife in Italy from time to time, having lived three months in the same house with them in Florence. . . . She eventually married Captain J. P. Catty, R.E."

In the original MS. there are several cancelled readings. It is interesting to note the changes which the poet made: in l. 10 "tender" was originally *gentle;* in l. 11 "Zephyrs" was *the lightnings;* in l. 12 "gentle" was *softest;* in l. 14 "those" was *thine;* in l. 15 "soul" was *heart.*

LOVE'S PHILOSOPHY.

First published in *The Indicator*, December, 1819. In the following December Shelley gave a MS. copy of this poem to Miss Stacey. The text follows this MS., which still exists. "Mr. J. H. Dixon pointed out in *Notes and Queries* (in January, 1868) that the poem is traceable to a French song in eight lines, — 'Les vents baisent les nuages'" (Forman's note). The French song is not quoted in *Notes and Queries* (Jan. 25th), but Mr. Dixon states that Shelley's poem is an imitation, not a translation.

165 7. *The Indicator* and the Harvard MS. read, "In one another's being."

165 11. **Sister**: *The Indicator* reads, "leaf or."

165 15. In *The Indicator* this line stood, "What are all these kissings worth."

ODE TO HEAVEN.

Mrs. Shelley says in her Preface to *Essays, Letters*, etc. : "Shelley was a disciple of the Immaterial Philosophy of Berkeley. This theory gave unity and grandeur to his ideas, while it opened a wide field for his imagination. The creation, such as it was perceived by his mind — a unit in immensity — was slight and narrow compared with the interminable forms of thought that might exist beyond, to be perceived perhaps hereafter by his own mind; all of which are perceptible to other minds that fill the universe, not of space in the material sense, but of infinity in the immaterial one. Such ideas are, in some degree, developed in his poem entitled *Heaven*; and when he makes one of the interlocutors exclaim,

> Peace! the abyss is wreathed in scorn
> Of thy presumption, atom-born,

he expresses his despair of being able to conceive, far less express, all of variety, majesty, and beauty, which is veiled from our imperfect senses in the unknown realm, the mystery of which his poetic vision sought in vain to penetrate."

166 21-22. The power wherein man sees a reflection of his own nature; man's conception of God is based upon his knowledge of himself.

166 32. **But the portal**, etc. : this is in the same construction as "but the mind's first chamber," in l. 28.

This is primarily a descriptive poem. The poet, with evident delight and exquisite power, produces his picture of the garden and its mistress, and enters into and sympathizes with the imagined life of the flowers. Secondarily, this concrete picture is symbolic of other things. The Sensitive Plant, with its isolation, its intensity, its yearnings, is Shelley himself. The lady of the garden is the mystical Spirit of Beauty "whose smile kindles the universe." The change which comes over the garden and the Sensitive Plant at the approach of winter typifies the evil and ugly side of things, — death and the other ills which quench the joy of life. The Conclusion (as the close of *Adonais*) suggests that this change is transitory or unreal, that the Spirit of Beauty abides, and that the soul of man does not altogether pass away at death, but is united to the *one* spirit which is eternal.

The workmanship of the poem is very characteristic of Shelley. The freedom with which the laws of rhythm and rhyme are treated lends a wonderful charm. It will be noted that the music of the verse is subtly varied by varying the number of anapæstic substitutions for the regular iambs in different lines.

PART I.

168 17. **wind-flowers**: *i.e.*, anemones (derived from ἄνεμος, wind).

168 34. **Mænad**: a female follower of Dionysus inspired with Bacchic frenzy, bearing the *thyrsus*, a wand tipped with a pine cone.

170 72-73. The following is Mr. Swinburne's explanation of this obscure passage (*Essays and Studies*, pp. 185-6): "The plant, which could not prove by produce of any blossom the love it felt, received more of the light and odour mutually shed upon each other by its neighbour flowers than did any one among these, and thus, though powerless to show it, yet . . . felt more love than the flower which gave it gifts of light and odour could feel, having nothing to give back, as the others had, in return; all the more thankful and loving for the very barrenness and impotence of requital which made the gift a charity instead of an exchange." To the present writer it seems rather that "the giver" is the Sensitive Plant itself. The other flowers had as much love as they required (" Where none wanted but it "); but the Sensitive Plant felt more love for others than could ever be felt for it.

PART III.

173 1-4. The flowers were dimmed and overcast with gloom, as the stars when the moon shines out, or as the waves of the Bay of Naples when the moon is darkened by the smoke of Vesuvius.

173 3. **Baiæ**: a Roman watering-place on the Bay of Naples.

175 50-57. Mr. Rossetti changed the punctuation so as to connect "thistles . . . henbane" with "began to grow," and "hemlock" with "stretched." But Shelley was careless in matters of detail, and doubtless, as Mr. Forman says, his meaning was that all the plants mentioned ("thistles . . . hemlock") "stifled the air," while the hemlock, in addition to stifling the air, "stretched out," etc.

176 66-69. This stanza, which is found in the edition published by Shelley himself, was omitted by Mrs. Shelley, perhaps on the authority of a correction by the poet. Here and elsewhere we find in Shelley a morbid tendency towards the horrible.

176 82. **forbid**: accursed; as in *Macbeth*, I, iii, 21.

177 91. Seemingly another reminiscence of *Macbeth*, I, iii, 44-45:

> By each at once her choppy finger laying
> Upon her skinny lips.

177 113. **griff**: grip; a word not found elsewhere, apparently of Shelley's own invention.

THE CLOUD.

This poem consists of a series of imaginative statements of simple facts in regard to clouds. Shelley describes the Cloud as if it had a personal existence of its own. In modern poetry, as a rule, natural objects are described in connection with human life, either as influencing it or for the sake of embodying or reflecting the feelings of the poet. It is, however, characteristic of Shelley's genius that he has the power and the tendency to enter into the imaginary life of natural objects, instead of making them enter into man's life. Of this power, " *The Cloud* is the most perfect example," says Mr. Stopford Brooke. " It describes the life of the Cloud as it might have been a million of years before man came on earth. The ' sanguine Sunrise ' and the ' orbed Maiden,' the moon, who are the playmates of the Cloud, are pure elemental beings " (Preface to *Poems of Shelley*, p. xl).

179 15. **'t is :** *i.e.,* the snow is; the Cloud clings about the mountain, whose top is covered with snow.

179 21–30. What natural phenomenon is described in the poetical
language of these lines is by no means clear. Since the pilot is the
lightning, Shelley may, perhaps, have thought that the motion of
clouds is influenced by electric forces existing in the earth, and may
represent these forces here as "genii." The pilot moves the cloud over
that part of the earth where he dreams the spirit (the electric force)
remains. Through the influence of this force the pilot makes the rain
fall from the under surface of the cloud, while the upper surface is bask-
ing in the blue light of heaven.

180 53–54. The apparent motion of the stars whilst broken clouds
pass rapidly over them is here represented as a real motion.

180 58. **these :** the stars.

181 81. **cenotaph :** an empty tomb ; in this case the blue dome of
heaven.

TO A SKYLARK.

182 7–8. It has been proposed to change the punctuation in the text
(which is that of Shelley's edition) by transferring the semicolon from
the end of l. 8 to the end of l. 7. Professor Baynes says in regard
to this suggestion : " This is, however, a complete mistake, the critic
having failed to notice that in the opening verse of the poem the lark,
when first addressed by the poet, is already far up in the sky ; and that
in the second verse she continues to ascend further and further from
the earth, higher and higher into the air. The image ' like a cloud of
fire ' applies not to the appearance of the bird at all . . . but to the continuous motion upward, for the obvious reason that 'fire ascending
seeks the sun ' " (*Edinburgh Review,* April, 1871).

182 15. **unbodied** is the reading in Shelley's and Mrs Shelley's
editions. In the article just cited, Professor Baynes says : " In quoting
the poem Professor Craik changed *unbodied* into *embodied*, adding that
the latter was ' undoubtedly the true word, though always perverted
into *unbodied*, — as if joy were a thing that naturally wore a body.'. . .
The fatal objection to the proposed change is, that it is completely at
variance with the whole feeling, as well as with the entire conception of
the poem ; that it reverses the very epithet by which in this particular
stanza that conception is most vividly expressed. At the outset
Shelley addresses the Skylark as a spirit singing in the pure empyrean,

and ever soaring nearer to heaven's gate as she sings. He then apostrophizes the emancipated soul of melody on the celestial lightness and freedom in which it now expatiates. To the swift, sympathetic imagination of the poet, the scorner of the ground, floating far up in the golden light, had become an aërial rapture, a disembodied joy, a 'delighted spirit,' whose ethereal race had just begun."

182 21. **arrows:** the rays of light from the "star of heaven."

184 80. **knew** for *knew'st;* so *drew* for *drew'st* in *Epipsychidion,* l. 369.

ODE TO LIBERTY.

The occasion of this poem was an uprising in Spain, of which Mary Shelley writes in a letter to a friend, dated March 26, 1820 : "I suppose that you have heard the news — that the beloved Ferdinand has proclaimed the Constitution of 1812, and called the Cortes. The Inquisition is established, the dungeons opened, and the patriots pouring out. This is good. I should like to be in Madrid now."

The body of the poem consists of a review of the development of liberty (cf. Collins's *Ode to Liberty*), concluding with an exhortation to the nations.

The motto is from Byron's *Childe Harold,* IV, stanza xcviii.

185 St. i. Inspired by the uprisal in Spain, the poet's soul is rapt beyond the bounds of space and time, and hears a voice, represented as uttering stanzas ii–xviii.

185 1-2. Mr. Alfred Forman suggests a colon after "again," and a comma after "nations"; this change makes the meaning clearer, but the punctuation in the text is that of the original edition and of the Harvard MS. A similar use of *vibrate* as a transitive verb is found in a letter of Shelley to Hogg, recently printed by Mr. T. J. Wise: "I feel I touch the string which, if vibrated, excites acute pain."

185 9. **Hovering in verse:** Mr. Rossetti reads *inverse,* but the poet is thinking of the "soul," not of the "eagle"; cf. "in the rapid plumes of song," l. 6.

186 ii–iii. In the beginning liberty was not.

186 18. **Dædal:** marvellously contrived; see on *Prometheus,* Act III, i, 26.

186 41. **sister-pest:** *viz.,* religion.

187 iv. The germs of better things lay undeveloped in Greece.

187 47. **dividuous**: dividing.

187 v. At length Athens brought forth Liberty, which in turn begot Art.

187 70–71. **on the will of man** . . . **set**: a state based upon the wishes of its citizens.

187 74. **that hill**: the Acropolis of Athens.

188 vi. The influence of Athens survives, and inspires the world with the spirit of liberty.

188 78–79. A reminiscence, doubtless unconscious, of the opening verses of Wordsworth's *Stanzas on a Picture of Peele Castle:*

> I was thy neighbour once, thou rugged Pile!
> Four summer weeks I dwelt in sight of thee:
> I saw thee every day; and all the while
> Thy Form was sleeping on a glassy sea.
>
> So pure the sky, so quiet was the air!
> So like, so very like, was day to day!
> Whene'er I looked, thy Image still was there;
> It trembled, but it never passed away.

188 vii. Rome became the seat of Freedom, until cruelty and love of gold drove her away.

188 92–93. The reference is to the *Bacchæ* of Euripides, ll. 699–700, where the Cadmæan Mænads (the Theban followers of Bacchus) are described as nursing young wolves.

188 93–94. **though thy dearest**, etc.: Athens still cherished freedom.

188 98. **Camillus**: one of the heroes of republican Rome; his greatest achievement was the defeat (390 B.C.) of the Gauls under Brennus.

Atilius: better known as *Regulus;* he fought against Carthage, was made captive, and dissuaded the Senate (250 B.C.) from making a peace that would have saved his own life.

188 103–4. **Palatinus sighed**, etc.: Palatinus was one of the seven hills of Rome, and the original site of the city; subsequently it was the residence of Augustus and the succeeding emperors. The reference here is to the imitation of Greek poetry by Roman writers of the Empire, perhaps particularly to the imitation of the Ionian Homer in the *Æneid*, whose author, Virgil, enjoyed the patronage of Augustus.

189 viii. After the rise of the Empire at Rome the Spirit of Liberty vanished to some remote and unknown region.

189 106. **Hyrcanian**: Hyrcania was a Persian province on the shores of the Caspian.

189 114-115. Thou wert to be found neither among the Teutons nor among the Celts, the two great northern races of Europe.

189 119. **The Galilean serpent:** Christianity.

189 ix-x. In the time of Alfred the Spirit of Liberty reappeared, developed in the republican cities of Italy, which, under her influence, became the home of Art ; next, this same spirit is apparent in the work of Luther and of some Englishmen, — Milton, for example.

190 xi-xii. There followed a general revival of freedom, which, however, again suffered eclipse from the excesses of the French Revolution.

191 175. **The Anarch :** Napoleon.

191 xiii. Spain calls upon England to free herself, — a task much easier than that which Spain herself had undertaken.

191 185. **Æolian isle:** the name *Æolian* was applied to a group of islands to the northeast of Sicily.

191 186. **Pithecusa :** island at the entrance of the Bay of Naples.
Pelorus : a promontory northeast of Sicily.

191 189. **Her :** England's.

191 192-5. These obscure lines are variously interpreted. Mr. Swinburne (*Essays and Studies*, p. 189) says : " The poet bids the two nations, ' twins of a single destiny,' appeal to the years to come." The sense of what follows is, — Mr. Swinburne thinks, — " Impress us *with* all ye have thought and done, *which* time cannot dare conceal." Mr. Forman is inclined to read *as* for *us*. He says : " To me the poet seems to invoke England and Spain to rise together and appeal to the future of Republican America, to impress on them, as from a seal, all that had been and should be thought and done by Republicanism in America ; and that invocation is supported by the simple proposition that Time cannot dare conceal *anything*." Professor Woodberry in his note on the passage says : " The lines contain a twofold appeal : first, to the future, typified in America ; second, to the past, realized in Spanish and English history, or, by paraphrase, great ages that were and that Time will not dare forget, stamp on man's mind, with the clear and fixed impression of a seal, your image or memory. The difficulty arises from the condensation involved in the sudden identification of England and Spain with what they have thought and done, as being ideally what they essentially are, and in the abruptness with which the immortal memory of that achievement is then stated. The words ' all ye have thought and done ' are to be taken as in the case of address."

To the present editor the words " the eternal . . . West " seem to refer, not to the future, but to the past, — the years which have passed into the west with setting suns; the meaning of the second part of the passage is sufficiently indicated by Mr. Swinburne and Professor Wood-berry, though, as the former says, the construction falls to pieces.

192 xiv. Appeal to Germany and to Italy.

192 196. **Arminius :** the hero who, 9 A.D., maintained the liberties of Germany by checking the advance of the Romans beyond the Rhine.

192 200–1. The poet refers to Germany's freedom in speculative thought, which has inspired her with new ideas, although political free-dom is wanting.

192 xv–xvi. These stanzas are characteristic of the thought of Shelley and of the school to which he is inclined. Evil in the world is due mainly to bad government and to religion; men freed from these two influences would naturally become good.

193 xvii. Of what avail are skill and mastery of men if they volun-tarily make slaves of themselves?

193 248. **And power in thought,** etc.: ' If thought is capable of developing power, as the seed is capable of developing the tree,' or perhaps : ' If intellectual power is now to that which it will be as the seed is to the tree.'

193 249–255. Of what avail is it that man by his art becomes master of natural forces, if wealth can extort from the poor and suffering the benefits resulting from art and liberty in the proportion of a thousand to one ?

193 253–4. The cry of Art ends at " depth."

193 254–5. " Wealth " is the subject of " can rend "; " thy " means *Liberty's ;* " hers," *Art's.*

194 xviii. Liberty will come to the world and bring with her Wis-dom, etc.

194 258. **Eoan wave :** wave of dawn (Gk. ἠώς, dawn).

194 259. **her :** Wisdom's.

194 270. The words of the " voice out of the deep " (l. 15) end at " tears."

194 xix. The inspiration of the poetic seer vanishes.

ARETHUSA.

Arethusa was a fountain in the island of Ortygia near Syracuse in Sicily; Alpheus, a river in the Peloponnesus which in parts of its course flows underground. " This subterranean descent gave rise to the story about the river god Alpheus and the nymph Arethusa. The latter, pursued by Alpheus, was changed by Artemis into the fountain of Arethusa, but the god continued to pursue her under the sea, and attempted to mingle his stream with the fountain in Ortygia."

The reader will note the resemblance of this poem to *The Cloud* in general character and in versification.

195 3. **Acroceraunian mountains**: Acroceraunia was the ancient name of a promontory in Epirus, formed by the western extremity of a chain known as the *Ceraunii Montes*.

195 24. **Erymanthus**: a mountain of Arcadia in the Peloponnesus.

195 25–27. The south wind which Erymanthus concealed behind its snowy peaks.

196 52–53. For the rhyme, cf. *Hymn to Intellectual Beauty*, ll. 50–51, with note.

197 60. **unvalued**: inestimable; cf. "thy *unvalu'd* book" in Milton's *Epitaph on Shakespeare*.

197 74. **Enna**: see note on *Prometheus*, III, iii, 43.

197 87. **Ortygian**: see introductory note on this poem.

THE QUESTION.

198 9. **wind-flowers**: see note on *The Sensitive Plant*, l. 17.

198 10. **Arcturi**: Arcturus was the name of the constellation of the Little Bear, or of a star in it. This constellation never sets; hence the ever-blooming daisies are called *Arcturi* (cf. *To Jane — The Invitation*, l. 58).

198 13. The reference in "that tall flower" which drops dew upon the earth is uncertain; "the most likely suggestions are 'crown imperial,' large campanula, and tulip. See *The Sensitive Plant:* 'The pied wind-flowers and the tulip tall'" (Miss M. A. Wood's *Third Poetry Book*).

199 15. **heaven's collected**: so the existing MS. copies read, as also the text published in the poet's lifetime. Mrs. Shelley's edition reads *heaven-collected*, and she is followed by Forman.

SONG OF PROSERPINE.

Proserpine was the daughter of Demeter (the latter name probably signifies *mother-earth*), the goddess of the earth. Proserpine was carried off by the god of the lower world, but returned to spend a portion of each year with her mother. The story is told in Ovid's *Meta-morphoses*, V. Proserpine probably symbolizes the seed-corn, which is buried, but comes again to life.

Enna: see note on *Arethusa*, l. 4.

HYMN OF APOLLO.

This and the *Hymn of Pan* were written to be inserted in a drama by Edward Williams. Apollo and Pan were represented as contending before Tmolus for the prize in music. In this hymn Apollo appears as the sun god.

HYMN OF PAN.

Pan was the god of flocks and shepherds; he was the inventor of the shepherd's flute, which he constructed from a reed.

202 11. **Tmolus:** the god of Mount Tmolus in Lydia; he is said to have been judge of a musical contest between Apollo and Pan.

202 13–15. **Peneus, Tempe, Pelion:** a river, a valley, and a mountain in Thessaly.

203 18. **Sileni** (satyrs) in Greek mythology were followers of Bacchus; they dwelt in forests and partook somewhat of the nature of lower animals. *Fauns* were similar creatures of Latin mythology. *Sylvans*, spirits of the forest.

203 26. **dædal:** marvellously wrought; see on *Prometheus*, Act III, i, 26.

203 30. **Menalus:** a mountain in Arcadia sacred to Pan.

LETTER TO MARIA GISBORNE.

This was written as a friendly letter, probably without the slightest idea of its ever becoming public, and exhibits Shelley in an easy, familiar vein. It was first printed in the *Posthumous Poems* of 1824, but certain passages were omitted. A transcript in Mrs. Shelley's writing is in existence; as also, at Boscombe, a very illegible draft in Shelley's hand. Mrs. Shelley says: "He addressed the letter to Mrs. Gisborne from this house [at Leghorn], which was hers; he made a study of the workshop of her son, who was an engineer. Mrs. Gisborne had been a friend of my father in her younger days. She was a lady of great accomplishments, and charming from her frank and affectionate nature." For further particulars in regard to Mrs. Gisborne, see the Introduction, p. lxii, and Dowden's *Life*, Vol. II, p. 206.

203 1-14. Shelley represents himself as engaged in weaving poems, not to catch present applause, but lasting fame in the future.

204 13. **must** is the reading of the Boscombe MS., but *most* of Mrs. Shelley's transcript and the edition of 1824.

204 17. **Archimedean**: Archimedes of Syracuse (287-212 B.C.) was a famous mathematician and inventor of various mechanical appliances.

204 24. **Ixion or the Titan**: the Titan is Prometheus; both he and Ixion were submitted to tortures by Jupiter.

204 25. **St. Dominic**: a Spaniard who flourished in the beginning of the thirteenth century and founded the order of Dominican Friars; in the text there is reference to the part he took in the crusade against heretics.

204 27-43. The reference is to instruments of torture sent by the Spaniards in the Armada.

204 33-34. Referring to the uprisal in Spain in 1820; see notes on the *Ode to Liberty*, p. 343.

204 34. **Empire** is apparently used here as a trisyllable; cf. *Prometheus*, Act I, i, 15.

204 35. **With** is to be construed with "giving," l. 30.

205 59. **swink**: work; a common word in earlier English.

206 75. Forman and Dowden put a colon at the end of this line, without authority, and to the injury of the sense. The "hollow screw" is the "idealism of a paper boat"; otherwise, as Professor Woodberry notes, the word "mischief" (l. 80) is without application. Shelley was addicted to sailing paper boats on streams and ponds (see the Introduction, p. lvii).

206 81. **them**: the "bills and calculations" (l. 79).

206 93-95. Treatises by various mathematical writers, from Saunderson to Laplace, are strewed about. *Laplace*, distinguished French mathematician (1749-1827); *Saunderson*, a blind mathematician, professor at Cambridge in the early part of the last century; *Sims*, a mathematical instrument maker of the time (Ellis's *Concordance*); *Baron de Tott*, a diplomatist, traveller, and author, 1733-93.

206 103. **as Spenser says**: this clause applies to "with many mo," "mo" being a form of *more* frequently found in Spenser and other elder writers.

207 106–112. These lines refer to the opposition which Shelley's writings stirred up among the orthodox in literature and theology.

207 114. **Libeccio** : Italian name for the southwest wind.

208 146–7. Almost the same lines occur in *Epipsychidion*, ll. 41–42.

208 164. Mr. Forman paraphrases this line, "when we shall again be as once we were but no longer are," but adds that he is morally certain that Shelley meant to write, "when we shall be no longer as we are."

209 175–6. **indued** : put on, acquired ; Mrs. Gisborne instructed Shelley in Spanish.

209 181. **Calderon** : the greatest of Spanish dramatists (1600–81).

209 197. **Godwin** : the father of Mrs. Shelley, author of *Political Justice*, a book which exercised a profound influence upon Shelley's views (see the Introduction, pp. xxxii ff.).

210 209. **Hunt** : Leigh Hunt, the well-known writer and friend of Shelley.

210 213. **Shout** : according to Mr. Forman, an obscure manufacturer of casts in London at the time.

210 226. **Hogg** : Jefferson Hogg, the college friend and biographer of Shelley.

210 233. **Peacock** : Thomas Love Peacock, poet, novelist, and friend of Shelley.

his mountain fair : his mountain beauty, *i.e.*, the Welsh lady whom Peacock had this year married.

210 234. **Turned into a Flamingo** : Shelley, playing upon the name of his friend, says that he has turned from a peacock into a flamingo, because the latter is a shy bird, and since his marriage Peacock has scarcely allowed himself to be seen by his friends.

210 239. **Snowdonian Antelope** : again, Mrs. Peacock; *Snowdon* is the well-known *Welsh* mountain.

211 240. **cameleopard** : perhaps, as is suggested in Ellis's *Shelley Concordance*, a figurative expression for a tall, handsome person.

211 250. **Horace Smith**, another of Shelley's friends, was a wealthy London stock-broker with literary predilections; along with his brother James he wrote the famous *Rejected Addresses* which parodied the styles of various poets.

211 253. The writer now begins a description of the external scenes visible, at the moment, to Mrs. Gisborne and himself, respectively.

211 272. The editor is unable to identify "the yellow-haired Pollonia."

212 286. **Contadino** : an Italian peasant.

213 312. Shelley was subject to nervous attacks for which he took laudanum (see Dowden's *Life*, Vol. I, pp. 226, 433).

213 316-7. **Helicon**: a mountain in Bœotia, sacred to the Muses. **Himeros**: "Ἱμερος, from which the river Himera was named, is, with some slight shade of difference, a synonym for Love" (Shelley's note).

In these lines the poet seems to say that he will not soothe his nerves either with poetry or with love.

213 322. This is the last line of Milton's *Lycidas*.

ODE TO NAPLES.

The events which occasioned this ode are mentioned in the diary of Miss Clairmont, who was living with the Shelleys at the time, under date July 16, 1820: "Report of the Revolution at Naples. The people assembled round the palace [July 2] demanding a constitution; the king ordered his troops to fire and disperse the crowd; they refused, and he has now promised a constitution. The head of them is the Duke of Campo Chiaro. This is glorious, and is produced by the Revolution in Spain" (Dowden's *Life*, Vol. II, p. 342).

Mr. Swinburne says in regard to the designation of the parts of the ode as epodes, strophes, etc.: "They are, as far as I can see, hopelessly muddled; beginning with an Epode (after-song!)."

213 1. **the city disinterred**: Pompeii.

213 4. **The Mountain**: Vesuvius.

214 11. The light reflected from the surface of the Mediterranean, between the sky above and its image in the water below.

214 24. **close**: a musical cadence.

214 25. **Æolian sound**: perhaps 'with a sound like an Æolian harp.' "Æolian" is itself derived from *Æolus*, the name of the god of the winds.

214 26. **Baian ocean**: the neighboring part of the Mediterranean; see note on *The Sensitive Plant*, III, l. 3.

214 32. **It**: the reference is not clear, perhaps to "Power divine" (l. 21).

214 33. **whose** refers to "Angel."

214 35-43. These lines state in metaphorical terms that the poet is carried away by poetic inspiration.

214 40. **Aornos**: Ἄορνος λίμνη is applied to Lake Avernus, which, according to ancient story, was connected with the lower world. Hence, "Aornos" may here mean Hades, as opposed to Elysium in l. 42.

215 41. **that Typhæan mount, Inarime:** *Inarime* is a name of the island of Ischia, northwest of the Bay of Naples. It contained an active volcano; hence the monster *Typhœus* or *Typhon* was said to lie buried beneath it, as Enceladus beneath Ætna.

215 57. Cf. "Lost Angel of a ruined Paradise" in *Adonais*, l. 88.

215 58-61. These lines refer to the recent bloodless revolution.

216 77. **Cimmerian Anarchs:** the Cimmerii, according to Greek myth, dwelt in a land of perpetual darkness to the north; hence the fitness of applying the epithet here to the tyrannical governments of Europe, Austria, etc.

216 81. **Actæon:** a huntsman who saw Artemis (Diana) bathing and was thereupon pursued and devoured by his own hounds.

216 82. **Basilisk.** This mythical monster was able to slay by the look merely. The word is derived from the Greek word for 'king'; hence the epithet "imperial."

217 102. See introductory notes to this poem and to the *Ode to Liberty*.

217 110. **Doria:** Andrea Doria, a great Genoese admiral, who in the earlier part of the sixteenth century victoriously fought for the independence of the republic of Genoa.

217 124. **Philippi's shore:** the reference is to the battle of Philippi (42 B C.), where Brutus and Cassius, the representatives of republican principles, were defeated by Octavius.

217 127. **Earth-born Forms:** the Titans, who were children of the Earth, and made war on the gods.

218 137. **The Anarchs of the North:** Austria and other northern powers. The language of the context is doubtless suggested by the invasions of ancient Italy by northern barbarians.

218 149 ff. An appeal to the Spirit of Love and Beauty which the poet so often treats as a real entity.

219 173. **Ausonian:** Italian.

GOOD NIGHT.

This song first appeared in *The Literary Pocket-Book* for 1822. It was one of the poems given to Miss Stacey in December, 1820; this MS. still exists, and exhibits several variations from the version in this text.

219 1. Stacey MS. reads: "*Good-night?*" *No, love, the night is ill.*

219 5. Stacey MS. reads: *How were the night without thee good?*

219 9. Stacey MS. reads : *The hearts that on each other beat.*

219 11-12. Stacey MS. reads : *Have nights as good as they are sweet,*
But never say " good-night."

THE WORLD'S WANDERERS.

Mr. Forman conjectures that a stanza is lacking, of which the last line would have rhymed with "billow."

TIME LONG PAST.

221 17. Beauty comes from the past, as well as memories.

SONNET (" Ye hasten to the grave ").

This sonnet was first published in *The Literary Pocket-Book* for 1823. Two MSS. exist : one at Harvard ; the other was sold among the Ollier MSS.

221 1. **grave :** in the Ollier MS. *dead*, the reading of the earlier editions, is scored out, and *grave* substituted.

221 5. **pale Expectation:** the reading of the Ollier MS. ; elsewhere *anticipation.*

TO NIGHT.

223 1. **over:** in the Harvard MS. the reading *o'er* is found, which is adopted by Woodberry ; this makes the versification correspond to that of the first lines in the other stanzas.

224 19. **his :** Mr. Rossetti makes the plausible emendation *her*, on the ground that " Day " in stanza ii is a feminine impersonation. It is quite likely, however, that the conception of Day in the poet's mind had changed ; the masculine personification seems more suitable to the context here.

FROM THE ARABIC.

Medwin says that this is almost a translation from a passage in *Antar, a Bedoween Romance*, by Terrick Hamilton (London, 1819 and 1820).

TO EMILIA VIVIANI.

The first eleven lines of this poem were included in *Posthumous Poems*; the last three have been added since from the Boscombe MS. through Dr. Garnett.

EPIPSYCHIDION.

In the autumn of 1820, the Shelleys, who were then residing in Pisa, became acquainted with a young, beautiful, and sentimental Italian lady, Emilia Viviani, who was confined by her relatives in the convent of St. Anna. The acquaintance ripened into friendship. About the close of the year Mary Shelley writes in a letter to Leigh Hunt: "It is grievous to see this beautiful girl wearing out the best years of her life in an odious convent, where both mind and body are sick for want of appropriate exercise for each. I think she has great talent, if not genius — or if not an internal fountain how could she have acquired the mastery she has of her own language, which she writes so beautifully, or those ideas which lift her far above the rest of the Italians? She has not studied much, and now, hopeless from a five years' confinement, everything disgusts her, and she looks with hatred and distaste even on the alleviations of her situation. Her only hope is in marriage, which her parents tell her is concluded, although she has never seen the person intended for her." A week or two later Shelley writes to Miss Clairmont: "I see Emily sometimes, and whether her presence is the source of pleasure or pain to me, I am equally ill-fated in both. I am deeply interested in her destiny, and that interest can in no manner influence it. She is not, however, insensible to my sympathy, and she counts it among her alleviations. As much comfort as she receives from my attachment to her, *I lose.* There is no reason that you should fear any mixture of that which you call *love.* My conception of Emilia's talents augments every day. Her moral nature is fine, but not above circumstances; yet I think her tender and true, which is always something. How many are only one of these things at a time!" (Dowden's *Life*, Vol. II, p. 389).

Emilia's misfortunes, her beauty, her intellectual vivacity attracted Shelley. Her ardent, sentimental, and impressionable nature (see the extracts from her letters in Dowden's *Life*, Vol. II, pp. 373-7) caught and reflected Shelley's peculiar ideas and feelings, so that she seemed to him that complementary soul for which he had long been seeking, the pursuit of which is embodied in *Alastor*. " Emilia," says Professor Dowden (Vol. II, p. 378), " beautiful, spiritual, sorrowing, became for him a type and symbol of what Goethe names ' the eternal feminine,' a type and symbol of all that is most radiant and divine in nature, all that is most remote and unattainable, yet ever to be pursued — the ideal of beauty, truth, and love. She was at once a living and breathing woman, young, lovely, ardent, afflicted, and the avatar of the Ideal." *Epipsychidion* is the poetic embodiment of the feelings awakened by this supposed discovery of the " avatar of the Ideal." But his illusion in regard to Emilia was very brief. On February 16, 1821, he sent *Epipsychidion* with some shorter poems to his publisher, Ollier. " The longer poem," wrote Shelley, " I desire should not be considered as my own ; indeed, in a certain sense, it is a production of a portion of me already dead ; and in this sense the advertizement is no fiction. It is to be published simply for the esoteric few ; and I make its author a secret, to avoid the malignity of those who turn sweet food into poison, transforming all they touch into the corruption of their own nature." Again, he writes to Mrs. Gisborne, " The ' Epipsychidion ' is a mystery ; as to real flesh and blood, you know that I do not deal in these articles ; you might as well go to a gin-shop for a leg of mutton, as expect anything human and earthly from me. I desired Ollier not to circulate this piece except to the συνετοί, and even they, it seems, are inclined to approximate me to the circle of a servant-girl and her sweetheart." On another occasion he says : " The ' Epipsychidion ' I cannot look at ; the person whom it celebrates was a cloud instead of a Juno ; and poor Ixion starts from the Centaur that was the offspring of his own embrace. If you are curious, however, to hear what I am and have been, it will tell you something thereof. It is an idealized history of my own life and feelings. I think one is always in love with something or other ; the error — I confess it is not easy for spirits cased in flesh and blood to avoid it — consists in seeking in a mortal image the likeness of what is, perhaps, eternal."

The ideal, the pursuit of which is described in the poem before us, may be better understood through the following extract from Shelley's

Essay on Love, Prose Works, Vol. II, Forman's edition, pp. 268-9 : "If we reason, we would be understood; if we imagine, we would that the airy children of our brain were born anew in another's; if we feel, we would that another's nerves should vibrate to our own, that the beams of their eyes should kindle at once and mix and melt into our own; that lips of motionless ice should not reply to lips quivering and burn-ing with the heart's best blood. This is Love. . . . The discovery of its antitype ; the meeting with an understanding capable of clearly estimating our own; an imagination which should enter into, and seize upon the subtle and delicate peculiarities which we have delighted to cherish and unfold in secret ; with a frame whose nerves, like the chords of two exquisite lyres, strung to the accompaniment of one delightful voice, vibrate with vibrations of our own; and of a combina-tion of all these in such proportions as the type within demands; this is the invisible and unattainable point to which Love tends ; and to attain which it urges forth the powers of man to arrest the faintest shadow of that, without the possession of which there is no rest nor respite to the heart over which it rules." In another prose piece of Shelley, a fragment in Italian recovered by Dr. Garnett, the theme of *Epipsychidion* is treated (see Forman, *Prose Works*, Vol. III, pp. 83 ff. for this piece and Dr. Garnett's translation).

The influence of Plato, more particularly of the *Symposium* (see Shelley's translation in Forman's edition of the *Prose Works*, Vol. III), is evident in this poem, which also owes something to Dante, whose works Shelley had been diligently reading since his arrival in Italy. The passage translated from Dante's *Convito*, and the reference in the Advertizement to the *Vita Nuova* indicate a special connection between the *Epipsychidion* and these two works.[1]

227. **Motto**: the Italian motto on the title-page is from a little essay, *Il Vero Amore* (The True Love), written by Emilia after reading the *Symposium* of Plato. (This essay with a translation is given by Medwin in his *Life of Shelley*, Vol. II, quoted in Appendix of Forman's edition of the *Poetical Works*, Vol. II.) The following is Medwin's translation of the words quoted in the motto : " The soul of him who loves launches itself out of the created, and creates in the infinite a world for itself, and for itself alone, how different from this obscure and fearful den."

---

[1] Again, Dr. Ackermann's pamphlet may be consulted for an examination of sources in detail. An essay on the poem by Mr. Stopford Brooke is prefixed to the reprint of the original edition among the *Shelley Society's Publications*.

229. **Advertizement** : the poem was published anonymously, and the Advertizement is a description by Shelley of the imaginary writer.

229 15-18. The Italian quotation is from Dante's *Vita Nuova*, XXV, and is thus translated by Mr. Rossetti : " Great were his shame who should rhyme anything under a garb of metaphor or rhetorical colour, and then, being asked should be incapable of stripping his words of this garb so that they might have a veritable meaning."

229 21. **from Dante's famous Canzone** : the stanza translated is the last verse of the first Canzone of Dante's *Convito*.

Epipsychidion : " Shelley translates his title in the line, —

' Whither 't was fled *this soul out of my soul :* '

and the word *Epipsychidion* is coined by him to express the idea of that line. It might mean 'something which is placed on the soul,' as if to complete or crown it. Or it might be, and more probably was, intended by Shelley to be a diminutive of endearment from *Epipsyche*. There is no such Greek word as ἐπι-ψυχή. But Epipsyche would mean 'a soul upon a soul,' just as Epicycle, in the Ptolemaic astronomy, meant 'a circle upon a circle.' Such 'a soul on a soul ' might be para-phrased as 'a soul which is the complement of, or responsive to an-other soul,' *i.e.*, to the soul of the poet, so that each soul seeks to be united with that other, to be in harmony wherewith it has been created. This idea, many suggestions of which may be found in Plato, seems most clearly expressed in the lines near the end of the poem beginning, ' One passion in two hearts' " (Stopford Brooke's *Poems of Shelley*, pp. 329-330). In his *Essay on Love* Shelley speaks of " a soul within our soul," whose " antitype " is described in the quotation, p. 356, above.

230 1. The poem opens with an address to Emilia.

230 1-2. **that orphan one**, etc. : Emilia's spiritual sister is Mary Shelley, whose mother died in giving birth to her ; the *name* is Shelley's own name. In many letters from Emilia to Mary, the latter is ad-dressed as *Cara Sorella* (Dear Sister).

230 5. **thy narrow cage** : the convent of St. Anna, in which she was detained against her will.

230 21. The poet proceeds to identify Emilia with the Eternal Spirit of Beauty which rules the universe (cf. *Hymn to Intellectual Beauty*, the concluding stanzas of *Adonais*, etc.).

231 38. The soul is only dimly revealed through the eyes.

231 41-42. The ideal which he had formed in his youth (cf. *Alastor*).

231 43-44. The world will conceal by some gross name the true character of my love to you (see the *Advertizement,* and the extracts from Shelley's letters, p. 355).

231 44. **unvalued** : not regarded by the poet.

231 46. **another:** Mary.

231 48. Uniting two incarnations of the Eternal Beauty; cf. l. 115.

231 49. **one** refers to ll. 46-48 : if it were lawful that you should both be united to me by the same tie.

the other refers to l. 45 : if we had been sister and brother.

The passage gives a glimpse at the morbid aberration of Shelley's views in regard to the relations of the sexes which appears repeatedly both in his writings and his life.

231 55. **should teach Time, in his own gray style** : should express in the language of time, or the ordinary world, as distinguished from the language of the infinite and mystical world.

232 68. **Wingless,** and hence such as will not fly away.

232 71. **Mine own infirmity** : *viz.,* his inability to express what she is.

232 75. Note the correspondence of "light," "life," "peace," respectively, with the three preceding comparisons (ll. 73-74).

232 77 ff. "This is an extreme example of Shelley's attempt to clothe in some sensuous form his tenuous spiritual conceptions. The spiritual beauty of the woman is made to shed an actual halo, — an effluence, about her" (Professor Winchester).

232 86. **planetary music :** the fabulous music of the spheres.

232 87-89. In her eyes her emotions are seen, — the reflections of the changes which her soul undergoes.

233 100. **morning quiver:** Mr. Rossetti reads, *morn may quiver.* Mr. Forman considers this a case in which Shelley uses the subjunctive mood, and cites a similar case from the twenty-second stanza of *Laon and Cythna.* Mr. Alfred Forman suggests that Shelley felt "pulse " as a plural here.

233 117. In the ancient system of astronomy, the heavenly bodies were conceived as fastened in a series of transparent concentric spheres moving about the Earth. The sphere nearest the Earth was that of the Moon ; the second, that of Mercury ; the third, that of Venus; accordingly, Emilia is here identified with the goddess of love. The line is evidently suggested by the line of Dante quoted in the *Advertizement,* l. 23.

233 122. **Anatomy:** used in the sense of a withered, lifeless form; Shakespeare, *Comedy of Errors,* V, i, 238-9 :

A hungry lean-faced villain, a mere anatomy.

234 130. **Fate:** the poet's own fate.

234 142-6. For a similar conception of Love, see Shelley's *Essay on Love, Prose Works,* Forman's edition, Vol. II (quoted in part, p. 356).

234 148. **Beacon:** set a beacon upon.

234 153. **'t is:** the reading of the Boscombe MS. The ordinary reading is *it is.*

235 160-173. This passage is especially characteristic of the poet's views and temperament. It may be compared with the mystical doctrines of Diotima in Plato's *Symposium,* for example, with the following passage as translated by Shelley himself (*Prose Works,* Vol. III, p. 219): " He who aspires to love rightly, ought from his earliest youth to seek an intercourse with beautiful forms, and first to make a single form the object of his love, and therein to generate intellectual excellences. He ought, then, to consider that beauty in whatever form it resides is the brother of that beauty which subsists in another form; and if he ought to pursue that which is beautiful in form, it would be absurd to imagine that beauty is not one and the same thing in all forms, and would therefore remit much of his ardent preferences towards one, through his perception of the multitude of claims upon his love. . . ." Diotima goes on to describe how one should then rise above mere beauty of form, to beauty of soul, thence to beauty of conduct, of knowledge, and of wisdom, until finally " he who has been disciplined to this point of Love, by contemplating beautiful objects gradually, and in their order, now arriving at the end of all that concerns Love, on a sudden beholds a beauty wonderful in its nature." This beauty she proceeds to describe in the passage quoted in the introductory note to the *Hymn to Intellectual Beauty,* p. 309, above.

235 174. **in this :** *viz.,* in what follows, ll. 178-183.

235 186-9. The 'world of life' is good and beautiful, yet marred by ugliness ; a garden, yet ravaged ; an Elysium, yet a wilderness.

236 190. **a Being:** the poet's ideal; with the whole passage cf. *Alastor,* especially ll. 150-180.

236 221. **in the owlet light:** this phrase refers to the flight of the "dizzy moth," not to that of the "dead leaf." The epithet "owlet" is used to suggest the dim, uncanny light which the moth seeks to exchange for that of the Evening Star.

237 228. **cone:** the word is suggested by the form of the shadow cast by heavenly bodies.

237 240. **sightless:** invisible; cf. *Alastor,* l. 610.

237 253. **those untaught foresters :** "the dwellers in the wintry forest of our life " (l. 249).

237 256-266. Actual persons have been conjecturally mentioned as being in the poet's mind when writing the descriptions of those he encountered in his search for the ideal (see, for example, F. G. Fleay's article in *Poet Lore*, Vol. II, No. 5, and Dr. Ackermann's *Quellen*, etc.). Such identification, even when certain, is not needful for the understanding of the poem. Here we have a description of the merely sensual love. In Plato's *Symposium*, two Venuses and two kinds of love are spoken of (see Shelley's translation, *Prose Works*, Vol. III, pp. 176–7), the Uranian or Heavenly, and the Pandemian or Common. The latter sort of love does not elevate, but degrades, and is the species described in this passage.

238 262. **honey-dew,** though sweet, blights the leaves upon which it is formed.

238 271. Possibly Harriet may be referred to in this line.

238 277. **One :** Mary.

238 285-307. In metaphorical language Shelley describes Mary's influence upon him ; she brought him peace, but at the expense of the highest ideals. He sank into a kind of apathy, and lost his ardor for the ideal. He lived neither in the commonplace nor in the ideal world. The difference between the highest life and spiritual death became imperceptible to him.

239 308-320. He is roused from his lethargy by some violent and painful experiences, — perhaps those connected with the death of Harriet. Again comes a period of deadness and coldness, followed by further stormy experiences, of which "the Moon" knew nothing. These may be the mysterious troubles at Naples towards the close of 1818, of which there are hints in his biography and writings (see *Stanzas Written in Dejection*, with notes). "The Planet of the hour" in that case would perhaps be the noble and infatuated lady who, according to Medwin, followed Shelley from England to Naples and there died (see Dowden's *Life*, Vol. II, p. 252).

240 345. **Twin Spheres :** Emilia the sun, and Mary the moon.

241 368. **O Comet,** etc.: probably the same as "the Planet of that hour" (l. 313) ; but, if this be so, the identification of "the Planet of the hour" with the noble lady must be incorrect, since she was already dead. Mr. Fleay identifies the "Comet" with the "Constantia" addressed in several of the lyrical poems, and Constantia with Claire Clairmont (see Introduction, p. l).

241 369. **drew :** for *drew'st ;* cf. *To a Skylark*, l. 80.

241 372. **that:** "The heart of this frail universe" (l. 369), *i.e.*, the poet's own heart.

241 374. On thy return take thy place among these other spheres, as the Evening Star.

folding-star: cf. Milton's *Comus*, ll. 93–94:

> The star that bids the shepherd fold
> Now to the top of Heav'n doth hold.

241 381-3. **heart** is parallel to "World"; "offerings," to "sacrifice"; "Their" refers to "Hope and Fear." The offerings of Hope and Fear are piled upon the altar of the heart; the sacrifice divine, described in ll. 377–9, will be offered on the altar of the World.

242 388-393. The transcendental and mystical character of his feelings towards Emilia is emphasized in these lines.

242 392. **Not mine but me**: the body may be described as 'mine,' but 'me' is something deeper, my own personality, — it is to this that is used thou must be united.

242 400. **continents**: in the original sense, — 'that which contains'; cf. Shakespeare, *Midsummer-Night's Dream*, II, ii, 92, where the word is used of the banks of a river.

242 405. **it**: Love.

242 408. Cf. the quotation from a letter, Introduction, p. lxviii. The voyage contemplated, however, is not a voyage in space, the scenes described are not intended to represent anything actual ; description, as in *Alastor*, is employed to suggest conceptions of impalpable things, — feelings, yearnings, ideal conditions.

243 454. The punctuation, which is that of the original, is peculiar. Mr. Rossetti and Professor Woodberry substitute a comma for the semicolon, — a change which serves to make the meaning clearer.

244 459. **Lucifer**: the morning star ; the word literally means 'light-bearer.'

247 557. **kill thine**, etc. : close thy eyes.

248 601. **Marina** was a pet name for Mary. "Vanna" may be Mrs. Williams, and "Primus," Edward Williams or Lord Byron. The name Vanna was probably suggested by Dante's Monna Vanna.

TO — (" Music when soft voices die ").

248 7. **thoughts** is governed by "on" in the next line.

SONG (" Rarely, rarely, comest thou ").

250 41.   What difference except that thou dost possess, etc. ?

ADONAIS.

The two poets Shelley and Keats first met at the house of their common friend, Leigh Hunt, in 1817. They were not specially drawn to one another ; Keats, at least, was inclined to hold aloof from Shelley, and their acquaintance never ripened into intimacy.   In 1818 Keats's first notable poem, *Endymion*, was published.   Of it Shelley wrote in a private letter, dated September 6, 1819 : " Much praise is due to me for having read it, the author's intention appearing to be that no person should possibly get to the end of it.   Yet it is full of some of the highest and finest gleams of poetry : indeed, everything seems to be viewed by the mind of a poet which is described in it.   I think if he had printed about fifty pages of fragments from it, I should have been led to admire Keats as a poet more than I ought — of which there is now no danger." Of this poem there appeared a savage review in *The Quarterly* for April, 1818, — a review which doubtless made a very painful impression on Keats ; though it did not, as Shelley heard and believed, shorten the poet's life.   In the beginning of 1820 Keats had an attack of hemorrhage from the lungs, and by midsummer his disease had become so serious as to make a residence in a warmer climate imperative.   Having heard of this, Shelley, in a kindly letter of July 27, urged Keats to be his guest at Pisa.   The latter did not accept the invitation, although he went to Italy in September, first to Naples, then to Rome, where, in February, 1821, he died.   In the summer of 1820 Keats's last volume had been published, containing *Isabella, Hyperion, The Eve of St. Agnes*, etc.   *Hyperion* gave Shelley a new opinion as to Keats's powers.   He wrote to Mrs. Leigh Hunt, November 11, 1820: " Keats's new volume arrived to us, and the fragment called *Hyperion* promises for him that he is destined to become one of the first writers of the age.   His other things are imperfect enough, and, what is worse, written in a bad sort of style which is becoming fashionable among those who fancy that they are imitating Hunt and Wordsworth."   Again, he wrote to Peacock, February 15, 1821 : " His other poems are worth little ; but if *Hyperion* be not grand poetry, none has been produced by our contemporaries."   Soon after Keats's death Shelley wrote the *Adonais*.   On

June 5, 1821, he says : " I have been engaged these last days in compos-
ing a poem on the death of Keats, which will shortly be finished. .... It
is a highly wrought *piece of art*, and perhaps better in point of composition than anything I have written." In a letter of September 25 he
says: " The *Adonais* in spite of its mysticism is the least imperfect of my
compositions, and, as an image of my regret and honour for poor Keats,
I wish it to be so."

As suggested in the former of these two letters, the *Adonais* is somewhat artificial in form, following the model of the Greek pastoral elegy,
as does also the *Lycidas* of Milton, which was doubtless in Shelley's
mind as he wrote. To two Greek poems, Bion's *Elegy on the Death of
Adonis* and the *Epitaph on Bion* ascribed to Moschus, Shelley is especially indebted, both for general hints and for individual phrases and
passages. Of both these Greek poems Shelley made fragmentary trans-
lations, which are to be found in the collected editions of his works.
Apart from these, the general influence of Shelley's familiarity with
the Greek and Latin classics is, in the *Adonais*, more than usually
apparent.

The beauty and power of the *Adonais* do not lie in the truth and
intensity with which the feeling of grief is depicted. No strong tie of
affection bound the poets together. The interest of the theme for
Shelley, as for the reader, is in the resemblance between Keats's circumstances and those of his elegist. Like Keats, Shelley was a youthful
poet, inspired by genuine devotion to the beautiful, unrecognized, mis-
apprehended, and misrepresented. The possibility of early death,
which would make the parallelism complete (as the subsequent fact
does render it complete for the reader), was often present in Shelley's
mind. As in *Alastor*, so here the poet contemplates and embodies his
own lot if cut off in the immaturity of power and fame. In another's
fate he weeps his own. It is this personal note which lends the needed
sincerity and pathos to the highly wrought and sometimes rather fanciful expression of the poem. In addition, the subject brings up the
mystery of future existence and of the relation of the individual to the
universe. It is this which forms the substance of the later and finer
portion of the *Adonais*. Here the writer gives expression to a thought
which is akin to, if different from, thoughts which appear in Wordsworth's poetry (in *Tintern Abbey*, for example) and in the closing
lyrics of Tennyson's *In Memoriam*, — the idea of the presence of one
divine informing spirit in all nature, of which the soul of man is but a
single manifestation. It is significant that in the *Adonais* this one
spirit is conceived scarcely as a personal and moral force, — not as God,

but as a sort of vague abstraction or tendency, which makes, **not** primarily for righteousness, but for beauty and truth.

253.　**The motto**: Shelley elsewhere translates these lines :

> Thou wert the morning star among the living,
>   Ere thy fair light had fled ;
> Now, having died, thou art as Hesperus, giving
>   New splendour to the dead.

254.　**Preface**: the Greek lines prefixed are translated by Andrew Lang (*Theocritus, Bion, and Moschus, rendered into English Prose*) : "Poison came, Bion, to thy mouth — thou didst know poison. To such lips as thine did it come, and was not sweetened ? What mortal was so cruel that could mix poison for thee, or who could give thee the venom that heard thy voice ? Surely he had no music in his soul."

Adonais: this name is applied to Keats in order, apparently, to connect the poem with Bion's *Elegy on Adonis*. The opening lines of this elegy suggested the first stanza of *Adonais ;* it is thus translated by Shelley (Forman's edition, Vol. IV, p. 232) :

> I mourn for Adonis dead — loveliest Adonis —
> Dead, dead Adonis — and the Loves lament.
> Sleep no more, Venus, wrapped in purple woof —
> Make violet-stolèd queen, and weave the crown
> Of death, — 't is Misery calls, — for he is dead.

256 3.　**so dear a head**: a classic metonomy; cf. tam cari capitis (Horace, *Odes*, I, 24).

256 5.　Rouse the other hours which are not made memorable by the death of Adonais.

256 12.　**Urania**: the word literally means 'pertaining to heaven,' and was applied by the Greeks to the muse of astronomy. Milton, in the opening passage of *Paradise Lost*, abandons the Greek usage, and personifies under this name the highest poetic inspiration, the heavenly spirit (so also Tennyson, *In Memoriam*, xxxvii). Shelley here probably refers to Uranian Aphrodite (see p. 309), the spirit of heavenly love, which he regards as the regenerating force of the universe. This interpretation is confirmed by the fact that in Bion's elegy Aphrodite takes the part assigned to Urania in the present poem.

256 15.　**one**: one of the Echoes repeats to Urania the songs which Adonais composed in his last days

257 29–45.　The loss of Adonais recalls Urania's loss of other sons.

257 29–36.　The reference is to Milton.

257 35. **clear Sprite**: doubtless a reminiscence of the phrase in *Lycidas:* " Fame is the spur that the clear spirit doth raise."

257 36. **the third,** etc.: in his *Defence of Poetry* Shelley calls Homer the first, Dante the second, and Milton the third epic poet.

257 37–43. Not all poets belong to the highest order, and those are fortunate who, recognizing their own limitations, have devoted themselves to the lesser kinds of poetry to which they were suited, and so have produced works which still live, instead of wasting their energies on subjects too great for them. There are others who had the ability to produce great works, but through unfavorable circumstances were prevented from doing so. And some are now alive, struggling with various difficulties which stand in the way of success.

257 46–72. The poem returns to Adonais lying yet unburied at Rome.

257 47. **widowhood**: the age of Keats is, by this metaphor, represented as a time unfavorable to the highest sort of poetry.

257 48–49. An allusion to Keats's *Isabella, or the Pot of Basil,* where the heroine

> Hung over her sweet basil evermore
> And moistened it with tears unto the core.

258 55. **that high Capital**: Rome, which with its ruins and memories of the past seems the special seat of Death.

258 63. **liquid**: a classic use of the word; cf. Liquida nocte (*Æneid,* X, 272), Per aestatem liquidam (*Georg.* IV, 59) ; so Gray, *Ode on the Spring,* l. 27.

258 68. **His extreme way,** etc. : to mark out the path of Adonais, — the last path he will ever travel, — to the dwelling-place of Corruption.

258 69. **The eternal Hunger**: *i.e.,* Corruption.

258 73–120. The poet fancifully personifies the thoughts, desires, etc., of Adonais, and represents them as bewailing him. The passage is suggested by the elegy on Bion : " Thy sudden doom, O Bion, Apollo himself lamented, and the Satyrs mourned thee, and the Priapi in sable raiment, and the Panes sorrow for thy song, and the fountain fairies in the wood made moan, and their tears turned to rivers of waters " (Lang's translation). Mr. Rossetti also notes that " the trance of Adonis attended by Cupids forms an incident in Keats's own poem of *Endymion,* Book II."

258 75–76. This allegorical method of expression belongs to Pastoral Poetry ; cf. *Lycidas,* where the poet's studies at Cambridge are referred to in language describing the pursuits of shepherds.

259 80. **after their sweet pain**: after the pangs of their birth.

259 88. **a ruined Paradise**: the mind of the dead poet.

259 91–99. Cf. Bion's *Elegy on Adonis:* "He reclines, the delicate Adonis, in his raiment of purple, and around him the Loves are weeping and groaning aloud, clipping their locks for Adonis. And one upon his shafts, another on his bow, is treading, and one hath loosed the sandal of Adonis, and another hath broken his own feathered quiver, and one in a golden vessel bears water, and another laves the wound, and another, from behind him, with his wings is fanning Adonis."

259 102–4. **Which gave it strength,** etc.: *i.e.,* the intellect (of the reader), which is cautious in accepting ideas, is, nevertheless, captivated by the force and beauty which the poet lends to them.

259 104. **the damp death**: probably the damps of death on the lips of Adonais. Mr. Rossetti suggests that "the damp death" may be another name for the "Splendour" (l. 100); this "obtains some confirmation from the succeeding phrase about the 'dying metaphor.'"

260 107. **clips**: embraces, as often in Spenser and elsewhere.

260 120–153. Nature also mourns for Adonais.

Cf. the following passage from Lang's translation of the *Elegy on Bion:* "Ye flowers, now in sad clusters breathe yourselves away. Now redden, ye roses, in your sorrow, and now wax red, ye windflowers; now, thou hyacinth, whisper the letters on thee graven, and add a deeper *ai ai* to thy petals; he is dead, the beautiful singer. . . . Ye nightingales that lament among the thick leaves of the trees, tell ye to the Sicilian waters of Arethusa the tidings that Bion the herdsman is dead. . . . And Echo in the rocks laments that thou art silent, and no more she mimics thy voice. And in sorrow for thy fall the trees cast down their fruit, and all the flowers have faded."

260 127.   Ἀχὼ δ' ἐν πέτρῃσιν ὀδύρεται ὅττι σιωπῇ
    κοὐκέτι μιμεῖται τὰ σὰ χείλεα.

                         Epit. Bionis, l. 30.

261 133. The nymph Echo, according to Greek story, loved Narcissus, who was enamored of his own image reflected in the water; so that Echo pined away until she became a voice only.

261 140–4. The poet passes from the conception of Hyacinth and Narcissus as persons, to the conception of them as flowers; it is as flowers that they mourn for Adonais.

261 151–3. An allusion to the reviewer whose harsh criticism was supposed to have shortened Keats's life.

261 154–189. The thought of nature, upon which he has been dwelling, turns the writer's mind to that which spring is effecting about him, and to the contrast which the revival of nature presents with the finality of death in the individual man.

Cf. *Epit. Bionis*, ll. 106–111 :

> αἰαῖ ταὶ μαλάχαι μὲν ἐπὰν κατὰ κᾶπον ὄλωνται
> ἠδὲ τὰ χλωρὰ σέλινα τό τ' εὐθαλὲς οὖλον ἄνηθον,
> ὕστερον αὖ ζώονται καὶ εἰς ἔτος ἄλλο φύονται
> ἄμμες δ' οἱ μεγάλοι καὶ καρτεροί, οἱ σοφοὶ ἄνδρες,
> ὁππότε πρᾶτα θάνωμες ἀνάκοοι ἐν χθονὶ κοίλᾳ
> εὔδομες εὖ μάλα μακρὸν ἀτέρμονα νήγρετον ὕπνον,

thus translated by Lang: " Ah me ! when the mallows wither in the garden, and the green parsley and the curled tendrils of the anise, on a later day they live again, and spring in another year ; but we men, we the great and mighty or wise, when once we have died, in hollow earth we sleep, gone down into silence ; a right long, and endless, and unawakening sleep."

262 179. **sightless** : invisible ; cf. *Alastor*, 610.

262 186. **who lends**, etc. : *i.e.*, the living spirit animates that which belongs to death (*e.g.*, the soul animates the body) that which can only be used temporarily, and must return to death again.

262 188. **urge** : follow closely upon ; cf. urget diem nox et dies noctem (Horace, *Epodes*, XVII, 25).

263 190–225. Urania hastens to Rome to lament over the dead body.

263 195. **their sister's song** : the song of the Echo, mentioned in l. 15.

263 208–216. Cf. Shelley's translation of the elegy on Adonis :

> Aphrodite
> With hair unbound is wandering through the woods,
> Wildered, ungirt, unsandalled — the thorns pierce
> Her hastening feet and drink her sacred blood.

263 211–212. Cf. Virgil, *Ecl.*, X, 48–49 :

> Ah! te ne frigora laedant!
> Ah, tibi ne teneras glacies secet aspera plantas.

264 227. A translation of *Epit. Adon.*, l. 42 :

> τοσοῦτόν με φίλησον, ὅσον ζώει τὸ φίλημα.

264 228. **heartless** : not in the ordinary sense ; applied here because her heart has been given to Adonais.

264 235-261. These lines refer to the reviewer, and are an adaptation of a passage in the *Elegy on Adonis:* "For why, ah overbold! didst thou follow the chase, and, being so fair, why wert thou thus over-hardy to fight with beasts?"

264 238. **unpastured**: unfed; cf. *Æneid*, XII, 876: impastus leo.

264 240. **Wisdom the mirrored shield**: in stories of romance the polished shield is sometimes represented as dazzling the adversary in battle.

264 241-2. Until his genius had become fully matured.

265 245. **obscene**: in the classical sense, 'foul,' 'loathsome.'

265 249-251. The reference is to Byron, who, when his early verses were severely criticised in the *Edinburgh Review*, retaliated in a success-ful satire, *English Bards and Scotch Reviewers.*

Shelley has the Apollo Belvedere in mind; in this statue Apollo, according to one theory, is represented as having just discharged an arrow at the Python.

265 262-315. The fellow shepherds of Adonais; *i.e.*, poets contem-porary with Keats are represented as mourning his death.

265 264. **The Pilgrim of Eternity**: Byron; *Pilgrim* is suggested by *Childe Harold; Eternity*, a complimentary suggestion of the perma-nence of Byron's fame.

265 268. **Ierne**: Ireland.

265 269-270. Thomas Moore is meant. The special reference in "her saddest wrong" is not apparent.

The deep grief of Byron and Moore existed in the imagination of the poet only.

266 271. **one frail Form**: Shelley. The portrait of himself is note-worthy; observe the resemblance to the hero of *Alastor.*

266 275. Actæon saw Diana bathing, and was, in consequence, pur-sued and torn to pieces by his own hounds. So Shelley has penetrated too deeply into the mysteries of the universe; the thoughts to which his insight gives rise, torment him and separate him from the interests of ordinary life.

266 289-290. Cf. st. iii, *Remembrance* (p. 277), with note thereon.

266 291-2. This description is suggested by the equipment of a follower of Dionysus; see Euripides, *Bacchæ*, l. 80:

$$\text{ἀνὰ θύρσον τε τινάσσων κισσῷ τε στεφανωθεὶς}$$
$$\text{Διόνυσον θεραπεύει.}$$

267 298. **partial**: because, as is made clear in l. 300, Keats's lot resembled his own.

267 301. **accents of an unknown land**: this refers, probably, to the fact that Shelley's poetry gives expression to feelings and ideas remote from the understanding and sympathy of men in general. Mr. Rossetti suggests that the reference is to the poet's following a Greek model in the English tongue.

267 312. **He**: Leigh Hunt. The friendship between Keats and Hunt was much closer than that which connected him with the other poets mentioned.

267 316–333. The poet turns again to the reviewer. The passage is suggested by the lines from Moschus quoted at the beginning of the Preface (p. 254).

268 328, The heaviest punishment is to live thy degraded life, and to be conscious of the degraded life which thou livest.

268 334–396. In sts. xviii–xxii is the first reference in the poem to the import of death ; there the poet went no further than a suggestion, ' Naught we know dies, shall the spirit of man alone utterly perish?' (ll. 177–180). Here the poet returns to the subject in a more positive mood ; the spirit of Adonais is reunited to the one eternal spirit which animates and beautifies the universe.

268 343. There is a similar transition in *Lycidas*, 165 :

> Weep no more, woful shepherds, weep no more,
> For Lycidas, your sorrow, is not dead.

268 343–351. Similar ideas are to be found in the four closing stanzas of *The Sensitive Plant*. Mr. Rossetti also quotes from Plato's *Phædo* : " Death is merely the separation of soul and body. And this is the very consummation at which philosophy aims : the body hinders thought, — the mind attains truth by retiring into herself. Through no bodily sense does she perceive justice, beauty, goodness, and other ideas. The philosopher has a livelong quarrel with bodily desires, and he should welcome the release of his soul."

269 370–8. Cf. *In Memoriam*, xlvi.

273 379–387. Here Shelley conceives the universe as dualistic, matter and spirit : matter retards and is the source of imperfection and evil ; spirit gradually shapes it to higher ends.

270 397–414. Those who, like Keats, have died before attaining the full meed of glory welcome him to the eternal world : Chatterton, the poet, who in his eighteenth year (1770) committed suicide ; Sir Philip Sidney, poet, critic, and statesman, who in his thirty-third year died heroically on the field of Zutphen (1586) ; Lucan, the author of the epic poem *Pharsalia*, who, condemned by Nero for conspiracy, antici-

pated execution by a voluntary death, 65 A.D., when about twenty-six years old.

271 412. **blind**: dark ; cf. the similar use of the Latin *caecus.*

271 415–424. This obscure stanza bids the mourner consider the universe in all its vastness, and then he will be able to measure the insignificance of himself or of any other single individual. He will thus attain to a proper frame of mind ; for at first, when he is drawn on by the hope of immortality, to gaze from the brink of this earthly life over eternal existence, he may find it difficult to submit with resignation to the absorption of his own individuality into the Eternal Spirit.

The image of the material universe before the poet's mind in this stanza seems to be that of the older astronomy, adopted in *Paradise Lost :* the earth hanging in the centre surrounded by sphere after sphere, in each of which is fixed one of the heavenly bodies.

217 424–459. The poet turns to the earthly surroundings of the dead body.

217 424–5. It is only the body that is buried ; but it was through this body that the spirit of Keats became known to us ; thus the body may be said to have been the source of the joy which we felt in him.

272 435–7. The description of the Baths of Caracalla by Shelley, quoted pp. lxiv–v of the Introduction, illustrates these lines.

272 439–450. Description of the Protestant burial ground at Rome where Keats (and now Shelley) lies. Shelley speaks of it in a letter of December 22, 1818 : "The English burying-place is a green slope near the walls, under the pyramidal tomb of Cestius, and is, I think, the most beautiful and solemn cemetery I ever beheld. To see the sun shining on its bright grass, fresh, when we visited it, with autumnal dews, and hear the whispering of the wind among the leaves of the trees which have overgrown the tomb of Cestius, and the soil which is stirring in the sun-warm earth, and to mark the tombs, mostly of women and young people, who were buried there, one might, if one were to die, desire the sleep they seem to sleep."

272 444–7. The pyramid of Cestius, an ancient tomb referred to in the last note.

272 451–7. Shelley had doubtless in mind, while writing these lines, his beloved child William, who was buried in this cemetery (see Introduction, p. lxv).

272 453–5. If the grief of any mourning heart has been healed by time, do not seek to revive it.

273 460–5. Plato, in order to account for our knowledge of general conceptions and abstract ideas, supposes that these have a real exist-

ence in another world from which our spirits come at birth. Of these general forms (or "ideas," as Plato calls them) the actual things of this world are imperfect representations, which, however, serve to awaken in the soul of man a 'reminiscence' of the perfect types which it knew before birth. To this theory of Plato, Shelley was attracted by his intense dissatisfaction with all earthly things and by his love of the mysterious. In the stanza before us he supposes that the spirit of man at death enters into the world of 'ideas,' and there contemplates the perfect types of which the various concrete manifestations in this world give partial and unsatisfactory representations. When Shelley beheld anything beautiful, notwithstanding the pleasure it afforded, there was a sense of imperfection, a yearning for more complete satisfaction. He longed for a world "where music and moonlight and feeling are one." This perfect type, or 'idea,' is like the white light which combines in one impression the effects of all the colored lights.

273 466–8. Rome's azure sky, ruins, statues, music, words, — each of these may give some impression of that beauty in which all things work and move, but the perfection of absolute beauty cannot be expressed by these; we must pass from this unsatisfactory world of shows into the world of reality beyond death, if we would enjoy beauty in its entirety.

273 469–477. Here and elsewhere Shelley yearns for death as opening the way to the world of the ideal (cf. *Alastor*, 211–222, and Introduction, p. lxii).

273 480–1. Cf. these lines with the idea in Wordsworth's *Ode on Intimations of Immortality*, that birth shuts off the spirit from the full presence of the divine.

274 487–495. The poet, rapt above all earthly things, feels the influence of the Spirit of which he has been speaking.

274 494. Cf. the motto on the title-page of this poem. Like Hesperus, the star of Adonais has sunk on this earth only to rise again ; cf. also *In Memoriam*, cxxi.

SONNET: POLITICAL GREATNESS.

In the Harvard MS. entitled *Sonnet to the Republic of Benevento*.

274 8. obscene : foul, ugly ; cf. *Adonais*, l. 245.

274 9–10. If men allow themselves to be controlled by force or custom, they are utterly unmanly. Cf. the concluding lines of this sonnet with *Prometheus*, III, iv, 193 ff.

THE AZIOLA.

Published in *The Keepsake* for 1829 with the text as here printed.
Aziola : Italian name for a species of owl.
275 4. In Mrs. Shelley's collected editions "the" is introduced
before stars.
275 9. **or :** "and" in Mrs. Shelley's collected editions.
275 19. The reading in the text is that of the poem as published in
The Keepsake. Mrs. Shelley's collected editions read *they* for "them. '
" Mr. Garnett suggests that *them* should be inserted after *unlike,*—a
very tempting emendation, for which I should be glad to find authority "
(Forman's note).

A LAMENT.

First published in *Posthumous Poems*, 1824.
275 3. Trembling as I look back upon what I have passed through,
as the climber trembles when he gazes upon the precipices which he has
surmounted.
276 8. Mr. Rossetti inserts *autumn* after "summer" in this line,—
to the ordinary mind a somewhat plausible suggestion as completing
both sense and metre ; yet Mr. Swinburne says : "If there is one verse
in Shelley or in English of more divine and sovereign sweetness than
any other, it is that in the ' Lament ' — ' Fresh spring, and summer, and
winter hoar.' The music of this line taken with the context — the
melodious effect of its exquisite inequality — I should have thought
was a thing to thrill the veins and draw tears to the eyes of all men
whose ears are not closed against all harmony by some denser and less
removable obstruction than shut out the song of the Sirens from the
hearing of the crew of Ulysses. Yet in this edition the word 'autumn'
is actually foisted in after the word 'summer.' Upon this incredible
outrage I really dare not trust myself to comment. . . . A thousand
years of purgatorial fire would be insufficient expiation for the criminal
on whose deaf and desperate head must rest the original guilt of defac-
ing the text of Shelley with this damnable corruption."

REMEMBRANCE.

Mr. Rossetti states that this song was sent to Mrs. Williams with the following: "Dear Jane, if this melancholy old song suits any of your tunes, or any that humour of the moment may dictate, you are welcome to it. Do not say it is mine to any one, even if you think so; indeed, it is from the torn leaf of a book out of date. How are you to-day, and how is Williams? Tell him that I dreamed of nothing but sailing and fishing up coral. Your ever affectionate, P. B. S."

There are at least three versions of this poem, doubtless representing various stages of the poet's work, *viz.*: as printed in the *Posthumous Poems*, as contained in a MS. belonging to Trelawny, as existing in Shelley's handwriting on a fly leaf in a copy of *Adonais* which belonged to Lord Houghton. The latter is followed in our text.

276 2–3. In Trelawny's version these two lines were transposed.

276 5–7. Houghton MS. The other versions read:

> As the earth when leaves are dead,
> As the night when sleep is sped,
> As the heart when joy is fled.

276 8. The Trelawny version has *alone, alone.*

276 10. Houghton MS. The other authorities have *her* for "his."

276 13. The Trelawny version has *to-day* for "each day."

277 24. The Trelawny version has *Sadder flowers find for me.*

Pansies: referring to the significance of the flower; the name is derived from French *pensée*, thought; cf. *Hamlet*, IV, 5: "There's pansies, that's for thoughts."

BRIDAL SONG.

This song is here printed as it appeared in *Posthumous Poems*. Medwin, in his *Life of Shelley*, gives another version written as a chorus for a drama by Edward Williams, and a third version is furnished by Williams's MS. of his play. These two versions, which differ in their form from the poem printed in the text, may be found in the complete editions.

SONG FROM "HELLAS."

Hellas is a lyrical drama inspired by the proclamation of Greek independence in 1821, and written towards the close of that year. It
describes, by anticipation, the fall of the Turkish Empire and the triumph
of Greece.

This extract begins at l. 34 of the drama, and in the original the first
and third portions are assigned to Semi-chorus I, the second to Semi-
chorus II.

CHORUS FROM "HELLAS."

The extract contains ll. 1031–49 of the drama.

This *Chorus*, as well as in the *Final Chorus* which follows, anticipates
the universal "Golden Age" upon earth, of which the Greek revolution
is but a prelude.

FINAL CHORUS FROM "HELLAS."

"The final chorus is indistinct and obscure, as the events of the
living drama whose arrival it foretells. Prophecies of wars and rumors
of wars, etc., may be safely made by poet or prophet in any age, but to
anticipate, however darkly, a period of regeneration and happiness is a
more hazardous exercise of the faculty which bards possess or feign.
It will remind the reader 'magno *nec* proximus intervallo' of Isaiah and
Virgil, whose ardent spirits, overleaping the actual reign of evil which
we endure and bewail, already saw the possible and perhaps approaching state of society in which 'the lion shall lie down with the lamb'
and 'omnis feret omnia tellus.' Let these great names be my authority
and excuse" (Shelley's note). The reference in the case of Virgil is, of
course, to the famous "Pollio" eclogue, imitated by Pope in his *Messiah*.

281 1. **The world's great age:** the *annus magnus* of the ancients,
at the end of which the sun, moon, and planets return to their original
relative position (see Plato, *Timæus*, 39; Cicero, *De Nat. Deorum*, 2,
20). With the astronomical conception was connected the idea that
the history of the world would recommence and repeat itself.

281 9. **Peneus:** a river in Thessaly.

281 10. **Tempe:** the beautiful valley through which the Peneus flows.

281 12. **Cyclads**: the Cyclades, a group of islands in the Ægean.

281 13. **Argo**: the vessel in which Jason sailed in search of the Golden Fleece.

282 18. **Calypso**: the nymph of the island of Ogygia, with whom Ulysses would not remain, though she promised him the gift of immortality.

282 19–24. In the previous stanzas the poet has been imagining various events which according to Greek tradition happened in earlier ages as repeating themselves when the "great age begins anew"; but, the story of Troy coming to his mind, he recoils at the thought that the horrors of war and of crime should be renewed, even although he admits that death will not be abolished (see *Prometheus*, III, iii, 105 ff.).

282 21. **Laian.** Laius, king of Thebes, learned from the oracle that he was destined to perish at the hands of his son, who should also wed his own mother, Jocasta. To avoid such horrors, this son, Œdipus, was exposed immediately after birth; was found, however, by a shepherd, and ultimately adopted by the king of Corinth. Œdipus, on arriving at maturity, learned at Delphi the fate that was in store for him, and, ignorant of his true parentage, thought to shun it by leaving Corinth. He turned his steps to Thebes, met his true father, and slew him in a scuffle. Meanwhile Thebes was afflicted by the presence of a monster, the Sphinx, who, sitting by the roadside, proposed a riddle to each passer-by, and, on his failing to solve it, slew him. In their distress, the Thebans promised the kingdom and the hand of Queen Jocasta to him who should rid them of this plague. Œdipus solved the riddle and received the reward. The gods visited these unwitting crimes with a series of dire calamities, which afforded a favorite source of material to the Greek tragedians.

282 31–33. "Saturn and Love were among the deities of a real or imaginary state of innocence and happiness. *All those who fell*, or the Gods of Greece, Asia, and Egypt; the *One who rose*, or Jesus Christ, at whose appearance the idols of the Pagan World were amerced of their worship; and *the many unsubdued*, or the monstrous objects of the idolatry of China, India, the Antarctic islands, and the native tribes of America, certainly have reigned over the understandings of men, in conjunction or in succession, during periods in which all we know of evil has been in a state of portentous, and, until the revival of learning and arts, perpetually increasing activity" (Shelley's note).

282 37–42. According to the idea connected with "the world's great age," the whole of history repeats itself, so that not only the 'Golden Age' returns, but this must be followed by ages of degradation and

evil. Hence the cry of the poetic seer. The stanza is also character-istic of Shelley's temperament. His periods of intense hopefulness and exaltation were liable to be followed by moods of depression. He seemed often to feel the unreality and unattainableness of those dreams of regeneration in which at other times he fondly indulged.

TO EDWARD WILLIAMS.

This poem, in the MS. which Trelawny possessed, is accompanied by the following note: "My dear Williams, — Looking over the port-folio in which my friend used to keep his verses, and in which those I sent you the other day were found, I have lit upon these; which, as they are too dismal for *me* to keep, I send you. If any of the stanzas should please you, you may read them to Jane, but to no one else. And yet, on second thoughts, I had rather you would not. Yours ever affectionately, P. B. S."

The occasion of the lines, as we gather from the poem itself, was some jealousy of Mrs. Williams on the part of Mary, which put a check to the freedom of intercourse between the two families. According to Trelawny, Mary was prone to jealousy. With the feeling expressed in the poem we may compare the following extract from one of Shelley's letters to Mrs. Gisborne, dated June 18, 1822 (quoted in Dowden's *Life*, Vol. II, p. 472): "As to me, Italy is more and more delightful to me. . . . I only feel the want of those who can feel, and understand me. Whether from proximity and the continuity of domestic inter-course, Mary does not. The necessity of concealing from her thoughts that would pain her, necessitates this, perhaps. It is the curse of Tan-talus that a person possessing such excellent powers and so pure a mind as hers, should not excite the sympathy indispensable to their application to domestic life."

283 1. Byron named Shelley 'the Snake'; "his bright eyes, slim figure, and noiseless movements strengthening, if they did not suggest, the comparison" (Trelawny's *Records*, p. 85).

284 41–43. Cf. *Alastor*, ll. 280 ff.

284 43. **When:** *whence* is the reading of Mrs. Shelley's first edition, but *when* of her second and of the Trelawny MS.

SONG ("A widow bird sat mourning for her love").

This song was printed as it stands in the text in the *Posthumous Poems*. Mr. Rossetti discovered the same poem in a fragmentary scene of Shelley's incomplete drama, *Charles the First*, where it is put into the mouth of Archy, the Court Fool, with the following introductory stanza prefixed:

> Heighho! the lark and the owl!
> One flies the morning, and one lulls the night:—
> Only the nightingale, poor fond soul,
> Sings like the fool through darkness and light.

THE MAGNETIC LADY TO HER PATIENT.

"The Magnetic Lady" is doubtless Mrs. Williams; a copy of the poem in Shelley's writing among the Trelawny MS. is headed, "For Jane and Williams only to see." According to Medwin, Shelley was hypnotized by Mrs. Williams, by Mrs. Shelley, and by Medwin himself to relieve him from paroxysms of pain to which he was subject. In one of these trances he gave the answer to Medwin recorded in the forty-second line of this poem.

285 11. **he:** Williams.

286 42. The reading in the text is that of the Trelawny MS. As given by Mrs. Shelley and by Medwin in his *Memoir of Shelley*, the line reads:

> 'T would kill me what would cure my pain.

LINES ("When the lamp is shattered").

This poem as here printed follows Mrs. Shelley's text; there is an autograph copy among the Trelawny MS. which has *notes* for "tones" in l. 6, *in* for "through" in l. 14, and *chose* for "choose" in l. 23.

287 17-24. The weaker heart is the more faithful, and retains its love, though love has turned to pain because the loved one has grown cold.

287 25. **Its:** the weaker heart's.

thee: Love.

TO JANE — THE INVITATION.

" A part of this and a part of the next poem were published by Mrs. Shelley in the *Posthumous Poems* (1824) as one composition, under the title of *The Pine Forest of the Cascine near Pisa*, and this arrangement was followed in the first edition of 1839; but in the second edition of that year the poem was divided into two as in the text, and given in substantial accordance with the autograph in Mr. Trelawny's hands " (Forman's note). There are considerable variations between the earlier and later forms, for which the reader is referred to the collected editions.

289 43–45.   There is confusion between " thy " and " your."

290 58.   **The daisy-star,** etc. : cf. *The Question*, l. 11 and note.

TO JANE — THE RECOLLECTION.

290 6.   **fled :** so in the earlier edition and the later collected editions ; but the second edition of 1839 and the Trelawny MS. have *dead*.

291 24.   This line reads in the earlier version : *With stems like serpents interlaced ;* with this text, the "as rude " of the previous line might be interpreted either *as rude as giants* or *as rude as storms.* It might seem as if Shelley, on revising the poem, had mended the halting metre without noting that the change involved an inappropriate comparison : "serpents interlaced " can scarcely be called " rude."

291 42.   **white** stands in the Trelawny MS. and in the earlier version ; but in the second edition of 1839 *wide* is found. " White " is evidently the better reading ; the mountains were on the horizon, and the *width* of the mountain waste would not be apparent.

292 52.   After this line in the earlier version stood :

> Were not the crocuses that grew
> Under the ilex tree,
> As beautiful for scent and hue
> As ever fed the bee ?

292 53–80.   Note Shelley's delight in the reflections in the water ; the reflection, with its softened outlines and mysterious suggestiveness, is a sort of idealization of the real scene.

WITH A GUITAR TO JANE.

" The strong light streamed through an opening of the trees. One of the pines, undermined by the water, had fallen into it. Under its lee, and nearly hidden, sat the Poet, gazing on the dark mirror beneath, so lost in his bardish revery that he did not hear my approach. . . . The day I found Shelley in the pine-forest he was writing verses on a guitar. I picked up a fragment but could not make out the first two lines. . . . It was a frightful scrawl; words smeared over with his finger, and one upon the other, over and over in tiers, and all run together 'in most admired disorder'" (Trelawny, *Records*, I, pp. 103, 107).

Shelley's identification of himself with Shakespeare's infinitely poetical and spritelike Ariel, now imprisoned in a body, is a very happy and suggestive fancy.

294 23–24. See note on *Prometheus*, II, iv, 91.

———

LINES WRITTEN IN THE BAY OF LERICI.

The Bay of Lerici is a portion of the Bay of Spezzia, upon which Casa Magni, where Shelley was residing at the time of his death, was situated.

SELECT BIBLIOGRAPHY.

———•·———

TEXT. — The best critical edition of Shelley's complete works is that by H. B. Forman in eight volumes (four of poetry and four of prose), London, 1880. Mr. Forman has also published a popular edition of the poetical works, without notes, in Bell's *Aldine Series*, five volumes. A useful and excellent critical edition of the poetical works is that of Prof. G. E. Woodberry in four volumes, Boston and New York, 1892. Mr. W. M. Rossetti's edition, London, 1881, contains in three volumes a revised text, notes, and memoir. The most convenient edition of the complete poetical works for the ordinary reader is that by Professor Dowden in one volume.

The chief sources for the text are (1) the various existing MSS. in the poet's handwriting or in that of his wife ; the bulk of these are among the family papers at Boscombe Manor, but there is also a valuable collection at Harvard ; (2) the various volumes printed in Shelley's lifetime (several of these have been reprinted in the *Shelley Society's Publications*), and for some of the shorter poems, the pages of the *Examiner*, *Keepsake*, and other periodicals to which the poet occasionally contributed ; (3) Mrs. Shelley's editions of her husband's works, *viz.*, *Posthumous Poems*, 1824, and her editions of the collected poetical works, two of which appeared in 1839, and a third in 1841. *Relics of Shelley*, edited by Dr. Garnett, London, 1862, affords poetical matter which had not hitherto been printed.

For an account of these various earlier publications of Shelley's works, *The Shelley Library, an Essay in Bibliography*, by H. B. Forman (*Shelley Society's Publications*) should be consulted.

BIOGRAPHY. — The most comprehensive and authoritative life of Shelley is that by Professor Dowden in two volumes, London, 1886. Among the shorter biographies may be mentioned those by W. M. Rossetti (*Shelley Society's Publications*), by J. A. Symonds (*English Men of Letters Series*), and by Wm. Sharp (*Great Writers Series*). J. Cordy Jeaffreson's *The Real Shelley*, in two volumes, presents the view of the *Advocatus Diaboli;* it is one-sided and digressive, but acute and, as a corrective, sometimes useful.

Among the more important original sources generally accessible, besides Shelley's own letters, etc., are the notes in Mrs. Shelley's editions, the life by Shelley's friend Hogg (which does not cover his later years), an account of the last months of the poet's life by Trelawny in his *Records of Shelley, Byron, and the Author* (these accounts by Hogg and Trelawny based on personal knowledge are specially vivid and interesting), and the *Memorials of Shelley* in Peacock's collected works.

MISCELLANEOUS. — Among the numerous critical essays may be mentioned those by Stopford A. Brooke (being his introduction to his *Poems of Shelley*), Walter Bagehot (*Literary Studies*), R. H. Hutton (*Literary Essays*), W. H. Myers (*Ward's English Poets*), Professor Baynes (*Edinburgh Review*, Vol. CXXXIII), Leslie Stephen (*Hours in a Library*).

The *Shelley Society's Publications* include *A Shelley Concordance* by F. S. Ellis, a *Shelley Primer* by H. S. Salt, an essay on the *Prometheus* by W. M. Rossetti, and various other essays, notes, etc., on matters pertaining to Shelley. A volume of selections from his letters edited by Dr. Garnett is in the *Parchment Library;* from his essays and letters, in the *Camelot Classics. A Study of Shelley* by J. Todhunter gives an extended examination of his works. Annotated editions of the *Prometheus* by Miss Vida D. Scudder; of the *Adonais* by W. M. Rossetti (*Clarendon Press*), and by Professor Hales (*Longer English Poems*) ; of the *Alastor*, with translation into French prose, by Al. Beljame (Hachette, Paris); of the *Essay on Poetry* by Professor Cook. For sources and parallel passages, Dr. Richard

Ackermann's *Quellen, Vorbilder, Stoffe zu Shelley's Poetischen Werken* (*viz.*, *Alastor*, *Epipsychidion*, *Adonais*, *Hellas*), Erlangen and Leipzig, 1890, and the same author's article on the *Prometheus* in *Englische Studien*, Band XVI, may be consulted. A bibliography is appended to *Shelley* in the *Great Writers Series*.

INDEX OF FIRST LINES.